DARKNESS AVENGED

"Are you always so confident in your ability to please a woman?"

His lips shifted to the base of her neck, his hands skimming down the curve of her waist.

"Confident in *us*," he corrected her, his fangs scraping over her tender skin. "Don't pretend you don't feel the explosive chemistry between us. It's . . . magic. There's no other word."

"It's been . . . a long time," she admitted, unsure why she needed him to know.

"Then let me take care of you," he whispered against her skin, his hands trailing around her waist.

He kissed a path up the tender curve of her throat, nuzzling below her ear. The air was filled with cherry-scented steam and raw male desire, wrapping them in a mist of privacy.

As if they were in their own world, she hazily acknowledged, her hands lifting to steady herself against the black tiles of the shower.

"This is dangerous," she muttered.

"Yes," he instantly agreed, giving the lobe of her ear a nip before he was stroking his lips downward. "But inevitable . . ."

Books by Alexandra Ivy

WHEN DARKNESS COMES

EMBRACE THE DARKNESS

DARKNESS EVERLASTING

DARKNESS REVEALED

DARKNESS UNLEASHED

BEYOND THE DARKNESS

DEVOURED BY DARKNESS

BOUND BY DARKNESS

FEAR THE DARKNESS

DARKNESS AVENGED

MY LORD VAMPIRE

MY LORD ETERNITY

MY LORD IMMORTALITY

PREDATORY
(with Nina Bangs, Dianne Duvall, and Hannah Jayne)

And don't miss these Guardians of Eternity novellas

TAKEN BY DARKNESS in YOURS FOR ETERNITY

DARKNESS ETERNAL in SUPERNATURAL

WHERE DARKNESS LIVES in
THE REAL WEREWIVES OF VAMPIRE COUNTY

Published by Kensington Publishing Corporation

DARKNESS AVENGED

ALEXANDRA IVY

ZEBRA BOOKS
KENSINGTON PUBLISHING CORP.
http://www.kensingtonbooks.com

ZEBRA BOOKS are published by

Kensington Publishing Corp.
119 West 40th Street
New York, NY 10018

All Kensington titles, imprints and distributed lines are available at special quantity discounts for bulk purchases for sales promotion, premiums, fund-raising, educational or institutional use.

Special book excerpts or customized printings can also be created to fit specific needs. For details, write or phone the office of the Kensington Special Sales Manager: Kensington Publishing Corp., 119 West 40th Street, New York, NY 10018. Attn. Special Sales Department. Phone: 1-800-221-2647.

Zebra and the Z logo Reg. U.S. Pat. & TM Off.

ISBN-13: 978-1-4201-1138-5
ISBN-10: 1-4201-1138-8

First Printing: June 2013

eISBN-13: 978-1-4201-3354-7
eISBN-10: 1-4201-3354-3

First Electronic Edition: June 2013

10 9 8 7 6 5 4 3 2 1

Printed in the United States of America

Prologue

The Legend of the Veil

The myths surrounding the creation of the Veil were a dime a dozen, and worth even less.

Some said it was the work of angels who had become lost in the mists of time.

Others said that it was a rip in space made during the big bang.

The current favorite was that Nefri, an ancient vampire with a mystical medallion, created the Veil to provide a little slice of paradise for her clan, the Immortal Ones. According to this particular rumor, it was whispered that on the other side there was no hunger, no bloodlust, and no passion. Only an endless peace.

It was a myth that Nefri, as well as the Oracles that sat on the Commission (rulers of the demon world) were happy to encourage.

The truth of the Veil was far less romantic.

It was nothing more or less than a prison.

A creation of the Oracles to contain an ancient mistake that could destroy them all . . .

Chapter 1

Viper's Vampire Club
On the banks of the Mississippi River south of Chicago

The music throbbed with a heavy, death metal bass that would have toppled the nearby buildings if the demon club hadn't been wrapped in spells of protection. The imp magic not only made the large building appear like an abandoned warehouse to the local humans of the small Midwest town, but it captured any sound.

A damned good thing since the blasting music wasn't the only noise that would freak out the mortal neighbors.

Granted, the first floor looked normal enough. The vast lobby was decorated in a neoclassical style with floors made of polished wood and walls painted a pale green with silver engravings. Even the ceiling was covered with some fancy-assed painting of Apollo on his chariot dashing through the clouds.

Upstairs was the same. The private apartments were elegantly appointed and designed with comfort in mind for those guests willing to pay the exorbitant fees for a few hours of privacy.

But beyond the heavy double doors that led to the lower levels, all pretense of civilization came to an end.

Down in the darkness the demons were encouraged to come out and play with wild abandon.

And no one, absolutely no one, could play as rough and wild and downright nasty as demons.

Standing in the shadows, Santiago, a tall exquisitely handsome vampire with long raven hair, dark eyes, and distinctly Spanish features allowed his gaze to skim over his domain.

The circular room was the size of a large auditorium and made of black marble with a series of tiers that terraced downward. On each tier were a number of steel tables and stools that were bolted to the marble. Narrow staircases led to a pit built in the middle of the lowest floor and filled with sand.

The overhead chandeliers spilled small pools of light near the tables, while keeping enough darkness for those guests who preferred to remain concealed.

Not that there was a need for secrecy in the club.

The crowd was made up of vamps, Weres, and fairies, along with several trolls, an orc, and the rare Sylvermysts (the dark fey who'd recently revealed their presence in the world). They came to fight in the pit for a chance at fleeting glory. Or to indulge in the pleasures his various hosts and hostesses offered, whether it was feeding or sex.

None of them were known for their modesty. Especially when they were in the mood to celebrate.

Santiago grimaced, his frigid power lashing through the air to send several young Weres scurrying across the crowded room.

He understood their jubilation.

It wasn't everyday that an evil deity was destroyed, the hordes of hell turned away, and Armageddon adverted.

But after a month of enduring the endless happy, happy, joy, joy, his own mood was tilting toward homicidal. Well, perhaps it was more than just tilting, he grimly conceded as a tableful of trolls broke into a violent brawl, knocking each other over the railing and onto the Weres seated below.

The domino effect was instantaneous. With infuriated growls the Weres shifted, tearing into the trolls. At the same time the nearby Sylvermysts leaped into the growing fight, the herb scent of their blood swiftly filling the air.

Santiago's massive fangs ached with the need to join in the melee. Perhaps a good old-fashioned beat-down would ease his choking frustration.

Unfortunately, his clan chief, Viper, had trusted him to manage the popular club. Which meant no extracurricular bloodbaths. No matter what the temptation.

Buzz kill.

Watching his well-trained bouncers move to put an end to the fight, Santiago turned his head as the smell of blood was replaced by the rich aroma of plums.

His lips curled as the violence choking the air was abruptly replaced by a heated lust.

Understandable.

Tonya could make a man drool at a hundred paces.

Strikingly beautiful with pale skin and slanted emerald eyes, the imp could also claim perfect curves and a stunning mane of red hair. But Santiago hadn't chosen her as his most trusted assistant because of her outrageous sex appeal.

Like all imps, she possessed a talent for business and the ability to create powerful illusions. She could also hex objects, although Santiago made sure that particular talent was only used on the humans who patronized the tea shop next door. Most demons were immune to fey magic, but Tonya had royal blood and her powers were far more addictive than most.

His loyal customers would never return if they suspected he allowed them to be enthralled by the beautiful imp.

Wearing a silver dress that was designed to tempt rather

than cover, she came to a halt at his side, a smile curving her lush lips even as her shrewd gaze monitored the hosts and hostesses that strolled through the room offering their services.

"A nice crowd," she murmured.

Santiago grimaced. Unlike his assistant, he was wearing plain black jeans and a dark T-shirt that clung to his wide chest. And, of course, he'd accessorized the casual attire with a massive sword strapped to his back and a handgun holstered at his hip.

Never let it be said he went to a party underdressed.

"'Nice' isn't a word I'd associate with this mob."

Tonya glanced toward the tribe of Sylvermysts who were reluctantly returning to their table. The warriors possessed the striking features of all fey with long hair in various shades of gold to chestnut. But their eyes blazed with a strange metallic sheen.

"Oh, I don't know," she purred. "There's one or two I'd consider edible."

"Your definition of edible is appallingly indiscriminate."

She turned her head to study him with an all-too-knowing gaze. "Yeah well, at least I haven't been neutered."

Santiago curled his hands into tight fists, fury jolting through him. Oh no, she didn't just go there. "Careful, Tonya."

"When was the last time you got laid?"

The air temperature dropped by several degrees.

"We're so not going to discuss this," he snarled, his voice pitched low enough it wouldn't carry. Despite the earsplitting music, there were demons present who could hear a freaking pin drop a mile away. "Especially not in front of an audience."

Foolishly ignoring his don't-fuck-with-me vibes, Tonya planted her hands on her full hips. "I've tried to discuss it in private, but you keep shutting me down."

"Because it's none of your damned business."

"It is when your foul mood begins affecting the club."

His fangs throbbed. "Don't press me."

"If I don't, who will?" The female refused to back down, the words she had clearly longed to fling at him for days at last bursting past her lips. "You prowl through the halls snapping at everyone who is stupid enough to cross your path. I've had six waitresses and two bouncers quit in the past month."

His jaw hardened with a stubborn refusal to admit she was right. If he did . . .

Well, that would mean he'd have to admit he *had* been neutered.

Not only sexually, although that was god-awful enough to admit. After all, he was a vampire. His appetite for sex was supposed to be insatiable.

But his general lust for life . . .

Suddenly his enjoyment of pursuing beautiful women and spending time with his clan brothers was replaced by a gnawing frustration. And his pride in running a club that was infamous throughout the demon world was replaced by an itch that he couldn't scratch.

It was something he was trying to ignore under the theory that it was like a bad hangover—something you suffered through and forgot as soon as the next party came along.

"Hire more," he growled.

Her eyes narrowed. "Easy for you to say."

"Hey, you know where the door—"

"I'm not done," she interrupted him.

His dark brows pulled together in a warning scowl. "Imp, you're pissing on my last nerve."

"And that's my point." She pointed a finger toward the belligerent crowd that continued to eyeball one another with the threat of violence. "This mood of yours is not only infecting the employees, but the patrons as well. Every night we're a breath away from a riot."

He snorted, folding his arms over his wide chest. "I run a

demon club that caters to blood, sex, and violence. What do you expect? Line dancing, gin fizzes, and karaoke?"

"The atmosphere is always aggressive, but in the past few weeks it's been explosive. We've had more fights lately than we've had in the past two years."

"Haven't you heard the news? We're celebrating the defeat of the Dark Lord," he tried to bluster. "A new beginning . . . blah, blah, blah."

Like a dog with a bone, Tonya refused to let it go. "Does that look like celebrating?" Once again she stabbed her finger toward the seething crowd. "Your frustration is contaminating everyone."

Santiago couldn't argue. The club wasn't Disneyland, but it wasn't usually a bloodbath.

At least not unless you were stupid enough to join in the cage matches.

"So what are you suggesting?"

"You have two options." Tonya offered a tight smile. "Go kill something, or fuck it. Hell, do both."

He snorted. "Are you offering?"

"I would if I thought it would do any good," she admitted bluntly. "As it is . . ." Her words trailed away as she gave a lift of her hand, gesturing toward a distant corner.

"What?"

"I have something more suitable to your current taste in females."

Santiago wasn't sure what he expected. Maybe twin imps. He'd always had a weakness for matched sets. *Twinning* . . .

Or maybe a Harpy in heat.

Nothing was more certain to distract a man than a week of incessant, no-holds-barred, balls-aching sex.

Instead a female vampire stepped from the shadows.

"Mierda," he hissed in shock.

Not because the woman was stunning. That was a given. All vampire females were drop-dead gorgeous.

But this one had an eerie familiarity with her long black hair and dark eyes, which contrasted so sharply with her pale skin.

Nefri.

No, not Nefri, a voice whispered in the back of his mind. Her face was more angular and the approaching female was lacking the regal aloofness that shrouded the real Nefri.

Not to mention a lack of kick-ass power that would have all of them reeling beneath the impact of her presence.

But she was close enough to make his gut twist into painful knots.

"Will she do?" Tonya murmured.

"Get rid of her," he commanded, his voice thick.

Tonya frowned in confusion. "What?"

"Get rid of her. Now!"

Spinning on his heel, he headed toward the stairs leading out of the lower levels.

He had to get out.

"Santiago," Tonya called behind him. "Goddammit."

The crowd parted beneath the force of his icy power, most of them scrambling out of his way with a gratifying haste as he climbed the stairs and entered the lobby.

Not that he noticed.

He was way too busy convincing himself that his retreat was nothing more than anger at Tonya's interference.

As if he needed the fey prying into his sex life. She was supposed to be his assistant, not his pimp. If he wanted a damned female he could get one himself. Hell, he could get a dozen.

And not one of them would be some pitiful substitute for the aggravating, infuriating, impossible female who had simply abandoned him to return behind the Veil. . . .

"Trouble in paradise, *mi amigo?*"

It was a testament to just how distracted he was that he

was nearly across the marble floor of the lobby and he hadn't noticed the vampire standing near the door to his office.

Dios.

If he could miss the current Anasso (the ultimate King of All Vampires), then his head was truly up his ass.

Styx was a six-foot-five Aztec warrior dressed in black leather with a sword strapped to his back big enough to carve through a full-blooded troll. And of course, there was his massive power that pulsed through the air like sonic waves.

It would be easier, and certainly less dangerous, to overlook an erupting volcano.

"Perfect," he muttered, regarding his unexpected guest's bronzed face. His visage had been carved on lean, arrogant lines emphasized by his dark hair, which was pulled into a tight braid that fell nearly to the back of his knees. He didn't look like he was there to party. Which meant he wanted something from Santiago. Never a good thing. "Could this night get any better?" he muttered.

Styx arched a dark brow. "Do you want to talk about it?"

Share the fact he was no better than a eunuch with his Anasso? He'd rather be gutted.

And, speaking as someone who actually had been gutted, that was saying something.

"I most emphatically do not," he rasped, shoving open the door to his office and leading his companion inside.

"Thank the gods." Styx crossed the slate gray carpet, perching on the corner of Santiago's heavy walnut desk. "When I took the gig of Anasso I didn't know I had to become the Vampire Whisperer. I just wanted to poke things with my big sword."

Santiago veered past the wooden shelves that held the sort of high-tech surveillance equipment that only Homeland Security was supposed to know about, unlocking the door of the sidebar that was set beneath the French Impressionist paintings hung on the paneled walls.

"I hope you didn't come here to poke anything with your sword," he said, pulling out a bottle of Comisario tequila.

"Actually, I need your help."

"Again?" Santiago poured two healthy shots of the expensive liquor. The last time Styx had said those words the Dark Lord had been threatening to destroy the world and he'd been teamed up with Nefri in an attempt to find the missing prophet. "I thought we'd gone beyond the sky-is-falling to yippee ki yay, everyone back to their neutral corners so we could pretend that we didn't nearly become dog food for the hordes of hell?"

Styx hadn't become king just because he was baddest of all bad-asses. He was also frighteningly perceptive. Narrowing his eyes, he studied Santiago's bitter expression with a disturbing intensity.

"Does this have something to do with Nefri and her return to her clan?"

Nope. Not discussing it.

Santiago jerkily moved to shove one of the glasses into Styx's hand. "Here."

Briefly distracted, the ancient vampire took a sip of the potent spirit, a faint smile curving his lips. "From Viper's cellars?"

"Of course."

Styx's smile widened. Despite being predatory alphas, Styx and Viper, the clan chief of Chicago, had become trusted friends. It was almost as shocking as the fact that vampires and Weres had become allies. At least temporarily.

Which only proved the point that doomsday truly did make for strange bedfellows.

"Does he know you're enjoying his private stash?"

"What he doesn't know . . ." Santiago lifted his glass in a mocking toast before draining the tequila in one swallow. *"Salud."*

"You know," Styx murmured, setting aside his glass, "maybe I should try my hand at *Dr. Phil*."

Santiago poured himself another shot. "You said you needed my help."

"That was the plan, but you're in a dangerous mood, *amigo*. The kind of mood that gets good vampires dead."

"I'm fine." Santiago drained the tequila, savoring the exquisite burn. "Tell me what you want from me."

There was a long pause before the king at last reached to pull out a dagger that had been sheathed at his hip. "Do you recognize this?"

"Dios." Santiago dropped his glass as he stared in shock at the ornamental silver blade that was shaped like a leaf with a leather pommel inset with tiny rubies. "A *pugio*," he breathed.

"Do you recognize it?"

His short burst of humorless laughter filled the room. Hell yeah, he recognized it. He should. It belonged to his sire, Gaius, who had once been a Roman general.

Centuries ago he'd watched in awe as Gaius had displayed the proper method of killing his prey with the dagger. What a fool he'd been.

Of course, he wasn't entirely to blame. Like all foundlings, Santiago had awoken as a vampire without memory of his past and only a primitive instinct to survive. But unlike others, he hadn't been left to fend for himself. Oh no. Gaius had been there. Treating him like a son and training him to become his most trusted warrior.

But all that came to an end the night their clan was attacked. Santiago had been away from the lair, but he knew that Gaius had been forced to watch his beloved mate, Dara, burned at the stake. And lost in his grief, Gaius had retreated behind the Veil where he sought the peace it supposedly offered.

Of course, it had all been a load of horseshit.

Gaius had allowed himself to be swayed by the promise of the Dark Lord to return Dara, and he'd gone behind the Veil to betray them all.

And as for Santiago . . .

He'd been left behind to endure hell.

Realizing that Styx was studying him with an all too knowing gaze, Santiago slammed the door on his little walk down memory lane.

"Gaius," he said, his voice flat.

"That's what I suspected."

"Where was it found?" Santiago frowned as the Anasso hesitated. "Styx?"

Styx tossed the dagger on the desk. "A witch by the name of Sally brought it to me," he at last revealed. "She claimed that she worked for Gaius."

"We know he had a witch who helped him along with the curs." Santiago nodded his head toward the *pugio*. "And that would seem to confirm she's speaking the truth. Gaius would never leave it lying around." He returned his gaze to Styx. "What did she want?"

"She said she had been using Gaius's lair in Louisiana to stay hidden in case she was being hunted for her worship of the Dark Lord."

"More likely she knew that Gaius was dead and decided to help herself to his possessions."

Again there was that odd hesitation and Santiago felt a chill of premonition inch down his spine.

Something was going on.

Something he wasn't going to like.

"If that was the case, then she was in for a disappointment," Styx said, his expression guarded.

"Disappointment?"

"She says that a week ago she returned to the lair to discover Gaius was there."

"No." Santiago clenched his hands. This was supposed to

be over, dammit. The Dark Lord was dead and so was the sire he'd once considered his father. "I don't believe it."

Something that might have been sympathy flashed through Styx's eyes. "I didn't either, but Viper was convinced she was speaking the truth. At least, the truth as far as she knows it. It could be that she's being used as a pawn."

Santiago hissed. His clan chief possessed a talent for reading the souls of humans. If he said she was telling the truth then . . . *dios*.

"I witnessed him coming through the rift with the Dark Lord, but how the hell did he survive the battle?"

"Actually, he only survived in part."

Santiago struggled against the sensation he was standing on quicksand. "What the hell does that mean?"

"This Sally said that Gaius was acting strange."

"He's been acting strange for centuries," Santiago muttered. "The treacherous bastard."

"She said that he looked filthy and confused," Styx continued, his watchful gaze never wavering from Santiago's bitter expression. "And she was certain he didn't recognize her."

Santiago frowned, more baffled by the claim that Gaius had been filthy than his supposed confusion. His sire had always been meticulous. And Santiago's brief glimpse of Gaius's lair beyond the Veil had only emphasized the elder vampire's OCD.

"Was he injured?"

"According to the witch, he looked like he was under a compulsion."

"Impossible. Gaius is far too powerful to have his mind controlled."

"It depends on who is doing the controlling," Styx pointed out. "Sally also said that he was obviously trying to protect something or someone he had hidden in the house."

With a low curse Santiago shifted his gaze to make sure the door was closed. No need to cause a panic.

"The Dark Lord?"

"No." Styx gave a firm shake of his head. "The Oracles are certain the Dark Lord is well and truly dead."

Santiago's stab of relief was offset by Styx's grim expression. The Dark Lord might be dead, but Styx clearly was afraid something was controlling Gaius.

"You've spoken to the Oracles?"

Styx grimaced. "Unfortunately. Since my first thought was like yours, that he'd managed to salvage some small part of the Dark Lord, I naturally went to the Commission with my fears."

"And?"

The room suddenly filled with a power that made the lights flicker and the computer monitors shut down.

"And they politely told me to mind my own business."

He gave a sharp laugh. How many times had Styx been told to mind his own business? Santiago was going with the number zero.

"How many did you kill?"

"None." Styx's crushing power continued to throb through the room. "My temper is . . ."

"Cataclysmic?" Santiago helpfully offered.

"Healthy," Styx corrected. "But, I'm not suicidal."

That was true enough. The King of Vampires might approach diplomacy like a bull in a china shop, but he was too shrewd to confront the Commission head-on.

No. He wouldn't challenge the Oracles, but then again, Santiago didn't believe for a second he was going to sit back and meekly obey their command.

Obey and *Styx* shouldn't be used in the same sentence.

"If this is none of your business, why did you come to me?" he demanded.

"Because Gaius is one of mine, no matter what he's

done," Styx said, his face as hard as granite. "And if he's being controlled by something or someone, I want to know what the hell is going on."

"What about the Oracles?"

"What they don't know . . ." Styx tossed Santiago's words back in his face.

Santiago narrowed his eyes. It was one thing to sneak a bottle of tequila from Viper's cellars and another to piss off the Oracles.

"And you chose me because . . . ?"

"You're the only one capable of tracking Gaius."

Santiago shook his head. "The bastard did something to mask his scent along with our previous bonding. I don't have any better chance of finding him than you do."

Styx's smile sent a chill down Santiago's spine. "I have full faith you'll find some way to hunt him down. And, of course, do it without drawing unnecessary attention."

Great.

Not only was he being sent on a wild goose chase, but he was in danger of attracting the lethal anger of the Oracles.

Just what he didn't need.

With his hands on his hips, Santiago glared at his companion. "So you're not willing to risk the wrath of the Commission, but you're willing to throw *me* under the bus?"

"Don't be an ass." Styx allowed his power to slam into Santiago, making him grunt in pain. "If you don't want to do this, then don't. I thought you would be eager for the opportunity to be reunited with your sire."

Santiago held up a hand in apology. *Mierda*. He truly was on the edge of sanity to deliberately goad the King of Vampires.

"You're right, I'm sorry," he said. And it was true. Styx *was* right. He'd waited centuries for the opportunity to confront his sire. Now he'd been given a second chance. Why wasn't he leaping at the opportunity? "It's—" He broke off with a shake of his head.

"Yes?"

"Nothing." He pulled out his cell phone, concentrating on what needed to be accomplished before he could head out. "I need to contact Tonya to warn her she'll be in charge of the club."

"Of course."

"Where's the witch?"

"She's at my lair in Chicago. Roke is keeping an eye on her in case this turns out to be a clever trick."

Santiago sent his companion a startled glance. Roke, the clan chief from Nevada, was in an even fouler mood than Santiago since Styx had refused his return to his clan after Cassandra had revealed that she'd seen Roke in one of her visions.

"The poor witch," he muttered. "That's not a punishment I would wish on anyone."

Styx shrugged. "He was the only one available."

Santiago froze. "Is there something going on that I should know about?"

A strange expression tightened Styx's lean features. Was it . . . embarrassment?

"Darcy insists that I devote my Ravens to trying to locate that damned gargoyle."

Ah. Santiago struggled to hide his sudden smile. The Ravens were Styx's private guards. The biggest, meanest vampires around. The fact he was being forced to use them to locate a three-foot gargoyle who'd been a pain in Styx's ass for the past year must be driving him nuts.

"Levet is still missing?" he murmured. The tiny gargoyle had astonishingly played a major part in destroying the Dark Lord, but shortly after the battle he'd disappeared into thin air. Quite literally.

"You find that amusing?" Styx growled.

"Actually I find it a refreshing reminder of why I'm happy to be a bachelor."

Styx's annoyance melted away as a disturbing smile touched his mouth. "Who are you trying to convince?"

Santiago frowned. "Convince of what?"

"That you're happy?" the older vampire clarified. "From all reports you've been storming around here, making life miserable for everyone since Nefri returned to her clan behind the Veil. That doesn't sound like a man who is content with his bachelor existence."

Damn Tonya and her big imp mouth. Shoving his phone back into his pocket, Santiago held out an impatient hand. "Do you have directions to Gaius's lair?"

"Here." Handing over a folded piece of paper, Styx suddenly grabbed Santiago's wrist, his eyes glittering with warning. "For now all I want is information. Is that clear?"

"Crystal."

"The Oracles won't be happy if they find out you're trespassing in their playground," Styx warned. "Stay below the radar, *amigo,* and be careful."

Santiago gave a slow nod. "Always."

Chapter 2

Nefri made her return to the mortal world on a high bluff overlooking the Mississippi River.

She shivered, wrapping her long cape tight around her tall, slender body. Not from the cold, although the October night held a chill that had been absent during her last visit to this side of the Veil. But instead from the onslaught of sensations.

It was all so . . . overwhelming.

The scent of damp earth and the thick moss that edged the banks of the nearby river. The screech of an owl and the rustle of dead leaves. The feel of her long black hair stirring in the breeze.

And, of course, the more intimate sensations.

Fear. Hunger.

Passion.

Standing perfectly still, Nefri smoothed her pale, oval face to an unreadable mask, a serene smile curving her lips and her ebony eyes revealing none of her inner turmoil.

Her considerable strength could overcome most dangers in

this world, but the Commission was made up of the most powerful demons. They could eradicate her with a mere thought.

It was always like walking a tightrope when she was forced to meet with them. A tightrope that might snap at any second and plunge her to her death.

At last prepared, Nefri stepped through the entrance of the caves that had been hidden behind a spell of illusion and moved to the center of the large chamber. On cue a Zalez demon appeared.

Just for a second there was the impression of a tall gaunt body with an overlarge head and tilted, almond-shaped eyes. Then the creature shifted into its human form, a Viking warrior with short, spiky blond hair and eyes the stormy blue of the Baltic Sea. His magnificent body was bronzed and fit for a god, which wasn't surprising considering he'd been worshipped by more than one primitive society. At the moment that magnificent form was covered only by a pair of faded denims that hung low on his hips.

Nefri gave a small dip of her head, fiercely leashing her female reaction to the sexual pheromones released by the demon.

Zalez demons were part incubus and capable of becoming whatever form their companion most desired. Nefri had no desire to reveal her deepest fantasy.

Not after she'd devoted the past month to pretending those fantasies didn't exist.

"Recise," she murmured.

"Ah, Nefri, so good of you to come." His voice stroked over her like warm velvet, his smile charming despite the fact they both knew she hadn't had a choice.

An invitation from the Commission was an imperial command that only the most idiotic demon would ignore.

"Your messenger insisted that it was important," she said.

Recise gave a slow blink. "The Oracles do not interfere in matters of the world unless it is of the utmost importance."

Not boasting. Just simple arrogance.

"Yes, of course."

"This way."

Moving with a fluid grace, Recise led Nefri through the darkness, the pulse of his sexual energy easing as if realizing Nefri wasn't in the mood to play.

They moved in silence through the tunnels that angled deep into the earth. The air was cool but surprisingly without the dampness that she expected, although she could hear the splash of a waterfall not far away.

More distantly she could catch the sound of muffled conversations, the languages as diverse as the creatures who made up the Commission. Like the United Nations, only with lethal demons who were happier killing things than negotiating.

Nefri hid her grimace as her companion came to a halt at the entrance to a large cavern.

"The Oracle is waiting for you in the back chamber."

"Thank you."

She waited until the Zalez continued down the tunnel before stepping into the cavern and allowing her senses to flow outward. It wasn't that she expected a trap. If the Oracles wanted her dead, she'd be dead.

But the Oracles had a varied sense of moral values. She didn't want to walk in on demons having a public orgy, or sacrificing an innocent to their particular gods.

It wasn't until she caught the scent of brimstone that she moved forward. She was familiar with this particular Oracle.

Crossing the smooth stone floor, she ignored the barren surroundings that were hardly suitable for the most powerful creatures on earth.

Each of the Oracles had their own private, and usually lavish lairs, but during the battle against the Dark Lord they'd gathered together in these caves. The fact that they remained wasn't particularly reassuring.

Reaching the back of the cave, Nefri caught sight of the tiny demon who was staring into a shallow pool of water, her three-foot body covered by a long white gown.

At a glance it would be easy to mistake her for a human child, with her heart-shaped face and silver hair that was in a long braid nearly brushing the ground. But a closer look revealed the strange oblong eyes that were a solid black. Eyes that were filled with an ancient knowledge.

Oh, and then there were the sharp, pointed teeth.

And the barely leashed power that could shatter cities.

"Siljar?" she murmured when the female continued to gaze into the water, studying some image she'd scryed.

With a wave of her hand, Siljar dismissed the image and heaved a heavy sigh. "Children today," she complained as she turned her attention toward Nefri.

"I can return another time if you're busy."

"No, this is important." Siljar pointed a finger toward the lone wooden chair. "Sit."

Nefri obeyed without hesitation, perching on the edge of the chair and folding her hands in her lap.

"Does this have anything to do with the Dark Lord?"

Siljar shook her head. "No, that chapter is closed."

"Thank heavens," Nefri said in genuine relief.

Siljar held up a small hand. "Do not be overly hasty."

Nefri's serene expression never faltered. It rarely did. She'd had centuries of practice in hiding her emotions. To the point that many assumed she no longer possessed them.

Inside, however, a ball of dread was forming in the pit of her stomach. If new trouble was brewing there was no reason to specifically seek her assistance, unless . . .

"This has something to do with the Veil, doesn't it?"

Siljar gave a slow dip of her head. "It has more to do with what the Veil was created to contain."

The ball in Nefri's stomach doubled in size. It had been nearly four centuries ago that she'd approached the Commission asking for sanctuary and been given the medallion that allowed her to lead her clan beyond the Veil.

So far as the world was concerned her only interest was creating a new home for those vampires who sought absolute peace.

Only she and the Oracles knew the truth.

Or actually, only the Oracles knew the truth, she wryly conceded.

She had a few, bare-bones facts and dire warnings. And she'd been fine with that. The less she knew, the easier it was for her to pretend that the paradise she'd created wasn't built on a cesspit.

"I don't understand," she said.

Siljar paced to the ceramic pitcher set on a flat slab of rock. Pouring herself a glass of some golden liquid that smelled remarkably like Hennessy, she tossed it back like a seasoned drunk.

"It is suspected that Gaius came through the rift with the Dark Lord."

"I heard rumors that he'd been seen during the battle, but no one could say with any certainty what happened to him," Nefri said. "I assumed he was killed."

"No, he was recently seen in the lair he used during his stay in this world."

Nefri's lips tightened. No one blamed her for Gaius's betrayal. Well, no one but the aggravating Santiago. He, of course, assumed she was to blame for every evil in the world. The annoying ass.

But she couldn't help but regret the fact that she hadn't

suspected there was more to Gaius's desire to become a part of her clan beyond his pretense of grieving for his dead mate.

"Do you believe he intends to cause trouble?" she asked.

"Not the vampire."

Nefri blinked. "Is this a puzzle?"

"A puzzle with too many pieces."

By all the gods, why couldn't Oracles just say what they wanted without all the mumbo jumbo?

"Why are you troubled by Gaius?" Her tone was carefully bland. "Without the power of the Dark Lord he should be easy enough to defeat."

"Because of this." Setting her empty glass on the flat stone, Siljar picked up a folded newspaper and handed it to Nefri.

She read the top of the front page. A small town newspaper from Louisiana? She continued to skim down to the lead headline.

"'An outbreak of violence in southern Louisiana'?" she quoted out loud before lifting her head to meet Siljar's piercing scrutiny. "I assume this is somehow relevant?"

"That is where Gaius is hidden."

Nefri remained confused. "You think he's responsible for the violence?"

"I am not entirely certain." There was a long pause, as if Siljar was holding a silent debate with herself. Then the tiny demon squared her shoulders. "This must stay between us."

Oh, those words were never good. Even worse, Siljar waved a hand to put up an invisible barrier so her words couldn't be overheard despite the fact they were sitting in the most highly secure spot in the entire universe.

"As you wish."

"I have sensed the presence of an old enemy," Siljar confessed, her expression troubled. "It is very faint, but I . . . fear."

"An old enemy?"

"The one the Veil was created to keep from this world."

Nefri rose to her feet before she even knew she was moving. "But how is that possible?" she demanded in shock.

"It is my suspicion that when the Dark Lord was destroyed it left Gaius stripped bare of all his defenses. He was dangerously vulnerable."

"Did he attempt to travel beyond the Veil?"

"No, but he still possesses the medallion."

It'd been an unpleasant shock to everyone when it was discovered that Gaius had a medallion similar to her own. And that he'd intended to use it to break the Dark Lord out of his prison.

"Forgive me, but I still don't understand."

Siljar lowered her gaze to the heavy gold medallion that hung around Nefri's neck. Scrolled with ancient spells, the medallion shimmered with a glow that had nothing to do with the torches set in the corners of the cavern.

"The ancient amulets were forged at the same time the Veil was created." Siljar folded her hands in front of her, giving the impression of a very small history professor. "Long before you were asked to lead your people through the barrier."

Nefri stiffened in surprise. "But . . ."

"Yes?"

"Gaius claimed his amulet was made by the Dark Lord," she explained.

Siljar snorted. "Pompous douche."

Nefri blinked. *Pompous douche?* Those weren't words she expected to hear from a mighty Oracle.

"The Dark Lord?" she asked, cautiously.

"Of course." Siljar peeled back her lips to reveal the razor sharp teeth. "The nasty creature was very skillful in destroying things, but he had no talent for creation."

Yes, that made sense. The Dark Lord had been worshipped as a god, but never as a creator. Something she should have realized herself, she acknowledged with a pang of annoyance.

"Then how did he get it?"

"He stole it during the time we were finishing the Veil."

Nefri's brows lifted at the reluctant confession. Stealing from the Oracles seemed . . . suicidal. "How was that possible?"

Siljar shrugged. "We were distracted. Constructing the Veil took all our combined efforts and still we nearly failed. In fact . . ."

"In fact?"

Siljar gave a sharp shake of her head. "Nothing."

Nefri knew damned well it wasn't "nothing." But she also knew that "nothing" could force Siljar to share if she didn't want to.

"Why didn't the Dark Lord keep it?" she instead demanded.

"The prophecy of his banishment had already been spoken," Siljar said. "I think he hoped he would be able to reach the medallion from his prison and use it to bring an end to the dimensions between worlds. So he imbued it with his essence and hid it beyond the Veil."

Ah. It would, of course, be the perfect hiding place. Unfortunately for the Dark Lord, it was also the most difficult to penetrate.

"So when he couldn't reach it, he instead manipulated Gaius into stealing it for him."

"Yes. And when the Dark Lord was destroyed the medallion was left empty, ready to be filled by another power."

Another power.

The power that was never spoken of.

The power that scared even the Oracles.

"What can I do?"

"The simplest solution would be to question Gaius ourselves."

Nefri held up the newspaper. "You know where he is. Why don't you just go get him?"

Siljar shrugged. "That's why you were called."

Nefri frowned. "You requested I leave my people so I

could travel to Louisiana and ask Gaius if his medallion has been hijacked by a strange spirit?"

"The Commission is . . . occupied with other matters at the moment." Siljar tilted her head, looking like an inquisitive bird. "If you hurry you should be able to tend to this task within a few nights."

Just . . . perfect.

Nefri hid her stab of annoyance. She didn't want to be in this world. Not when she was still raw and unsettled from her last visit.

But she wasn't idiotic enough to be fooled by Siljar's polite pretense. This wasn't a request.

"So you just want me to question him?"

"No. He must be brought to us. We will do the questioning."

Nefri nodded. At least she didn't have to kill him. It was always difficult when she had to deal death to one of her clansmen.

"I will do my best."

Siljar suddenly widened her eyes in a poor attempt at innocence and said, "Oh, perhaps I should warn you."

Nefri stilled, her predator instincts on full alert. "What?"

"The vampires know that Gaius survived."

"And?"

"I told Styx to keep his meddling nose out of Commission business."

She hid her hands behind her back so Siljar couldn't see she was clenching them in frustration.

"Which, of course, was the perfect guarantee to make sure he meddles," she murmured softly.

"Naturally."

Nefri didn't miss the hint of satisfaction in her companion's voice. "What is it that you're not telling me?"

"In good time."

"Siljar."

Intent on discovering what disaster she was being forced

to walk into, Nefri nearly lost her legendary calm when two small shapes abruptly appeared directly beside her.

Good . . . lord. There'd been no shift in air pressure that would warn of an opening portal, or a prickle of heat that usually went along with magic.

Just two creatures stepping out of thin air.

Taking an instinctive step back, Nefri assessed the danger of the intruders. One was obviously related to Siljar. Actually, she was nearly a replica with the same heart-shaped face and large black eyes. Only her hair was blond rather than silver and her eyes lacked the solemn wisdom of the Oracle.

Her companion, on the other hand, who was barely three feet tall, was obviously a gargoyle despite the fact he had large, gossamer wings that shimmered in shades of crimson and blue with gold veins. His features were suitably gargoyle-ish with gray eyes and a pair of stunted horns.

This had to be the infamous Levet, she silently acknowledged.

The gargoyle who'd been vital in destroying the Dark Lord while she'd been unconscious. Although at the moment he looked more like a petulant child, with his wings drooping and his tail twitching while the younger version of Siljar shook a finger in his face.

"I told you that it's too soon for you to leave your bed," she chastised, clearly continuing a long-standing argument. "Mother, would you tell him?"

The Oracle heaved the sort of sigh that could only come from a mother. "Yannah, how many times have I warned you not to interrupt when I have company?"

So, this was Siljar's daughter, Nefri realized, her unease shifting to a wry amusement.

Yannah turned her head to glower at her mother, but her finger remained pointed in Levet's face. "He won't listen to me."

"Well, dear, he is a male," Siljar soothed. "They rarely listen to good sense. It has something to do with their unbalanced hormones."

The gargoyle's long tail snapped at the insult. "Hey, I am standing right here."

Siljar sent him a confused glance. "Yes, I know. You are not invisible."

Levet sniffed. "I am also not *un bébé*."

Yannah turned back, her hands planted on her hips. "You were nearly killed."

"And now I am well." Levet lifted his hands. *"Voilà."*

"You're still weak."

"Weak?" The gargoyle went rigid, manly outrage tightening his ugly features. "I have the strength of a . . . of a . . . very large and very dangerous demon. And my magic is *formidable*." He lifted his hands. "Shall I demonstrate?"

"No!" Siljar and Yannah cried in unison.

"Fine, then stop saying that I am weak," Levet muttered.

Belatedly accepting that the tiny gargoyle possessed the same bullheaded temperament as every other male, Yannah allowed her lower lip to quiver. "Why don't you just admit the truth?"

Levet narrowed his eyes, clearly sensing he was about to be outmaneuvered. "What truth?"

"You're simply trying to get away from me."

He hunched a shoulder. "Absurd."

"It's not absurd. You're just—"

Siljar rolled her eyes as she stepped forward. "Children, please."

"You're bored with me," Yannah continued, ignoring her mother.

"Bored?" Levet's wings quivered. "Are you natty?"

"Nutty," Yannah gritted. "It's nutty."

Levet waved a hand. "I chased you from Russia to London to the pits of hell."

"And once I allowed you to catch me, the thrill was gone. Admit it."

"I—"

A sharp burst of power flooded the room, threatening a pain that made them all freeze in wariness.

"Enough," Siljar snapped. "Yannah, you will find Recise and resume your training."

"But . . ." Yannah swallowed her words as she met her mother's smoldering gaze, belatedly realizing that Siljar had reached the end of her patience. "I'm going." She turned to glare at Levet. "We will continue this conversation later."

"Mon dieu," the gargoyle breathed.

Siljar waited for Yannah to stomp from the cavern before turning her attention to Levet.

"And you."

"Moi?"

"You will accompany my guest on her mission."

Levet glanced toward Nefri, his expression melting to offer her a smile of pure male appreciation. "But of course."

"I must warn you that there is a potential for great danger," Siljar said.

"Bah." Levet tilted his chin to a proud angle. "Danger is my maiden name."

"I believe you mean 'middle,'" Siljar corrected him.

"It is all the same." The gargoyle waddled over to stand directly in front of Nefri, bending at the waist in an old-school bow. "My lady."

"Nefri," she insisted, finding herself charmed by the tiny demon. Why did Styx and Santiago spend so much time complaining about the creature?

"It will be my greatest pleasure to assist you in your quest," he assured her. "I did, after all, save the world from a certain apocalypse only weeks ago." He abruptly scowled, glancing toward the Oracle. "Wait."

Siljar lifted her brows. "Yes?"

"There isn't going to be another apocalypse, is there?"

"No."

"Dieu merci."

"Well, at least not if we can prevent it," Siljar corrected herself.

Levet tossed his hands in the air. "Why me?"

Chapter 3

Louisiana wetlands

Santiago wasn't the only predator to prowl through the cypress trees that were painted silver in the moonlight. Alligators, rattlesnakes, and occasional cougars hunted through the swamp along with the far more dangerous water sprites, who could lure a man to his doom, and a rare Dalini serpent, a demon who could transform from serpent form to look human. Always born male, they had to mate with mortal females.

Santiago was, however, the most lethal.

Moving with a grace that was impressive considering the spongy ground and thick undergrowth, Santiago slowly circled the isolated swamp, coming to an abrupt halt as a sensation he hadn't felt in centuries flared to life.

Dios.

It was his bond to Gaius.

Not all sires allowed a "child" to form a physical attachment. In the good old days, most vampires rarely stuck around to find out if their creation actually survived the process of transformation, let alone continued to feed their offspring to give them the best possible chance for survival.

Gaius had gone a step further by taking Santiago into his clan and into his lair.

A true son.

The blood connection had given Santiago the ability to sense his sire. Or, if he was far away, to sense his general direction.

Santiago had assumed the bond had been destroyed when he traveled beyond the Veil. After all, he hadn't felt his sire for centuries, not even when he returned to this world. Now he could only wonder if the Dark Lord had somehow kept the older vampire from being discovered.

Holding perfectly still, Santiago allowed his powers to spread toward the distant house, built on brick stilts and painted white.

Large with two stories, it had black shutters and a screened-in porch that wrapped around the side. The roof had recently been replaced, but the nearby chicken coop looked like a stiff breeze might blow it over.

The structure was effectively hidden by the large trees draped in Spanish moss that surrounded it and was set far enough from the path leading to the nearby small town to avoid unwanted interest.

A perfect lair for a vampire seeking solitude.

Confident that nothing was creeping through the shadows beyond the native wildlife, Santiago focused his powers on the house.

It took only a second for a jolt of recognition to blaze through him.

Gaius wasn't there, but something else was.

Something powerful enough to make the very air sizzle.

So much for being the most lethal predator around, he conceded, his hands clenched as he was slammed by a combination of shock and dark, unwelcomed arousal. The Oracles had sent in the big guns.

Nefri.

No vampire beyond Styx had that kind of juice.

Certainly no other vampire could make him hard by her mere scent.

Jasmine.

Enticing, elusive, dangerous.

And his own personal kryptonite.

His spine stiffened as he moved forward, silently sliding through the front gate and up the wide staircase.

Not this time.

During their last encounter Nefri had managed to lead him by the nose and then dumped him like a bad habit.

Tonight she was going to discover that he wasn't her lap dog.

In fact, he might just be her worst nightmare.

Entering the house, he glanced around the front room, which was filled with padded bamboo furniture. A frown touched his brow as he realized that the sofa and chairs had been shoved aside so a large circle could be scraped into the wooden floorboards.

The witch's work, no doubt.

Not that he gave a damn at the moment. His senses were filled with a beguiling jasmine scent that filtered deep into places that he'd forgotten existed. *Mierda*. His entire body was resonating with awareness. As if Nefri had infected him with a brutal craving that only she could satisfy.

He should turn and walk away, a voice whispered in the back of his mind. A call to Styx for a replacement and he would be returning to his club to find a woman who could make him forget he'd ever met a female named Nefri.

But of course he didn't.

His infamous talent for remaining in command no matter what the situation had been destroyed the moment he'd realized that Nefri was within his grasp. Now he stalked forward, following the trail of his prey into the back kitchen.

Distantly he was aware of peeling linoleum, the ancient human appliances, and a small wooden table. But it was the female vampire standing in the center of the room that commanded his attention.

Regal.

There was no other word for Nefri's tall graceful beauty. Even surrounded by shabby white-painted cabinets and drenched in fluorescent light, she looked like a queen with her hair falling to her waist like a river of liquid ebony. Her face was a perfect, pale oval with features carved by the hands of angels and eyes dark and deep enough for a man to drown in.

Her lips . . . *dios*. How many fantasies had been devoted to imagining those cherry red lips wrapped around his cock? The same cock that was already standing at painful attention.

"Well, well. Look what the cat dragged in," he drawled, moving to lean against the tiled countertop, his gaze narrowing as he took in the faded jeans that clung to her long, slender legs and the jade cashmere sweater that allowed him to appreciate the full curve of her breasts.

The last time she'd left the Veil she'd draped herself in long robes that only hinted at the feminine flawlessness beneath.

Now he felt as if he'd just been punched in the gut.

Trying to pretend a nonchalance he was far from feeling, Santiago folded his arms over his chest and met her piercing gaze.

"Santiago," she murmured, taking a brief inventory of his own jeans, gray hoodie, and big-ass sword strapped to his back, her aloof composure rousing his most primitive instincts.

She wouldn't look so cold and untouchable once he had her tumbled into his bed, he silently swore. She would be warm and willing and wild enough to sate his hunger.

He wouldn't accept anything less.

He smiled, not bothering to hide his raw desire. Hell, she already thought he was a barbarian. No need to disappoint her.

"I thought you had scurried back behind the Veil."

"Scurried?" A slow lift of her brow. "I returned to my home."

"Without so much as a good-bye?"

"My people needed me."

Bull. Shit.

"For what?"

She shrugged. "It was difficult for us to accept that we could have a traitor living among us and not have suspected the truth."

Now that he believed her. Immortal Ones were arrogant enough to assume that they couldn't be deceived. Their pride must have taken quite a beating for them to accept they'd harbored the traitor.

Still, he knew it was more than concern for her clan that had made her disappear without warning.

"And you were running away?"

A cool smile of disdain. "Running away from what?"

He was lunging forward before he even realized he was moving, grasping her by the shoulders, swooping down his head.

"This," he muttered as he kissed her with all the frustration that had plagued him over the past month.

For a shocking minute Nefri went rigid beneath his hands, and Santiago felt a cold shard of fear pierce his heart. He couldn't be wrong. Beneath all her ice, this female burned with an awareness that was as fierce as his.

Then, as his kiss gentled with a gut-aching need to taste her response, he felt a revealing quiver. It was faint, but unmistakable as she swayed toward him, her lips softening in invitation.

Sí.

Relief combined with a dark, intoxicating need threaded

through Santiago. The scent of jasmine teased at his nose, the cool silk of her lips as potent as the finest aphrodisiac.

But before he could wrap her slender body in his arms and quench the lust that had raged through him for weeks, Nefri was lifting her hands and pushing them against his chest.

Grudgingly Santiago lifted his head to study her pale face with a brooding gaze. "Don't expect an apology," he muttered.

The dark eyes flashed with an indefinable emotion before they were once again calm pools of ebony. "You are . . ."

"What?"

"Uncivilized."

His hands trailed up her arms, luxuriating in the soft caress of cashmere beneath his fingers. He was a tactile vampire who took intense pleasure in touching and being touched. It had been far too long since he'd indulged his senses.

All his senses.

"Why?" he demanded, not even randomly offended by her accusation. "Because I haven't been neutered like those so-called Immortal Ones?"

"My clansmen aren't neutered," she denied, a faint accent threaded through her low, enticing voice. Like many ancient vampires she deliberately cultivated the current slang, but often slipped into a more formal speech pattern when she was distracted. "In fact, they happen to be extremely intelligent, thoughtful, articulate. . . ."

"Eunuchs."

Her lips thinned. "I may have left this world a few centuries ago, but I'm fairly certain that men are no longer allowed to maul women whenever they feel the impulse."

His soft chuckle filled the room. "Oh, I haven't even started my mauling," he assured her. He wasn't stupid. This female had the power to crush him into little squishy bits if she was truly offended by his behavior. "This is only a small taste of my pre-maul."

"Savage."

He placed a kiss on the tip of her proud, aquiline nose. "And loving every minute of it."

"That's enough." This time she pressed against his chest with enough force to assure Santiago she wasn't teasing.

Reluctantly he dropped his hands and took a step back. "Not nearly, but it will have to wait for a more appropriate time and place."

She tilted her chin, looking untouched. Only the faint tremble of her fingers as she adjusted the heavy gold medallion around her neck assured Santiago he hadn't imagined her reaction to his kiss.

"You actually have the word 'appropriate' in your vocabulary?"

Aggravated by her calm while he was being seared alive with hunger, Santiago planted his fists on his hips. "What are you doing here?"

Unfazed by the abrupt question, she met his gaze squarely. "I could ask the same of you."

"I'm Gaius's only living child," he said without missing a beat. "By rights I can claim his property after his death." He ran an intimate glance up and down the stately length of her body. "In fact, by law anything or anyone attached to that property is mine."

She ignored his insinuation, regarding him with a cool disbelief. "So you're just here to inspect your latest acquisition?"

"If I leave it empty too long who knows what nefarious creature might decide to poach on my territory?"

"I see. Then I'll leave you to your"—a bland smile—"inspection."

His hand shot out with blurring speed, grasping her arm as she attempted to move past him.

"Not so quick, *cara*."

The heavy pressure of her power filled the cramped space, his long hair stirring in the sudden breeze.

"You should release me," she warned, oh so softly.

He loosened his grip, but his fingers remained on her arm. She wasn't disappearing on him. Not again. "You haven't answered my questions."

"Nor do I intend to."

He studied her pale, exquisite features. "Such a perfect ice queen," he murmured, his gaze lowering to the lush fullness of her lips. Those weren't the lips of an ice princess. They spoke to him of hot Spanish nights and decadent pleasure. "Did the Oracles send you?"

It was only because he was touching her that he felt her stiffen at his question.

"Only a fool discusses Commission business."

No shit. Unfortunately, Styx had tossed him straight into the lion's den. He needed to know why the Oracles were interested in Gaius. And what they were trying to hide from the vampires.

"You're here looking for Gaius, aren't you?"

"Why would I?" Frost coated her words. "I was told that Gaius died during the battle against the Dark Lord."

His short laugh held an edge of bitterness. "Yeah, a lot of us were told that."

Just for a second he thought he could glimpse something flash through her dark eyes. Sympathy? He shook his head. Not freaking likely.

The female was in pure ice mode.

"And since you're here to claim your inheritance, it would be a wasted effort to search for him."

"Half truths and evasion, Nefri?" He leaned forward, drawing deeply of her jasmine scent. "That isn't your usual style."

"You know nothing about me."

A smile curved his lips as he felt her faint tremor. Not fear. Nefri was a woman who was beyond fear of anything. Or anyone.

No, it wasn't fear. But need.

"I know more than you ever wanted me to," his voice lowered, his fingers stroking up the back of her arm to her shoulder. "Which is why you bolted behind the safety of your Veil."

Her extravagantly long lashes lowered to hide her eyes, but it was too late.

They both knew she was vulnerable to his touch, even if she would rather have her tongue cut out than to admit the truth.

"I have to go," she jerked from his grasp, her steps measured as she headed toward the door.

Santiago let her take several steps, keeping his hands at his side. He had an ace up his sleeve.

"He was here, but he left," he said softly. "One, maybe two nights ago."

Nefri froze, her back held ramrod straight, before she slowly forced herself to turn and meet his mocking gaze. "Gaius?"

"Who else?"

The dark eyes narrowed and Santiago knew she was weighing her desire to keep walking against her mysterious duty to the Oracles.

In the end there really was no choice.

For either of them.

"How do you know?" She at last forced the question past her stiff lips.

"He's my sire."

She studied him a long moment. "You couldn't sense him before."

"No," he instantly agreed. Did she think he was lying? "There was something blocking our bond."

"And now?"

He shrugged. "It didn't kick in until I reached this lair, but now I can feel him, although it's still muted."

Her dark brows drew together. "Why?"

Santiago moved to stand directly before her, obsessed by the need to keep her close.

"Since I'm 100 percent certain you know a hell of a lot more about what's going on," he drawled, "why don't you explain it to me?"

She took a deliberate step backward. "I have no information."

Step forward. "Nefri."

"What?"

"Can you sense him?"

Her slender fingers lifted to touch the medallion, her jaw tightening. "No."

He reached out to capture her fingers, which still clutched the medallion like a lifeline, his knuckles resting against the soft curve of her breast. "Can you catch his scent?"

"No."

"Then you need me."

"Your lack of manners is only exceeded by your complete arrogance."

A wicked smile curved his lips at her icy rebuttal. "Oh no, *cara,* the rules of the game have changed."

She tensed. One predator sensing another. Not that she was going to concede defeat. Not without a fight. Good. Strong women were so damned sexy.

"What game?"

"The last time you called the shots, this time—" His words broke off as he caught the unmistakable scent of granite approaching the back steps.

No. Oh no. Fate couldn't be that cruel.

But it seemed it was.

Even as he turned, the door leading to the bog of a backyard was being shoved open and a tiny gargoyle waddled into the kitchen.

"Did something die in here?" the creature muttered, his

ridiculous wings twitching. "I smell"—he came to a halt, regarding Santiago with a sour smile—"vampire."

"*Santa madre.*" Santiago turned back to glare at his beautiful companion. "Have you gone completely *loco?*"

Yes, Nefri silently answered the question.

In this moment she was fairly confident that she was at least skirting the edges of becoming *loco*. And had been since the moment she realized which vampire Styx had sent to spy on her.

What was it with this man? Granted, he was gorgeous. Breathtaking, mouthwatering, do-me-right-now gorgeous.

And powerful enough to challenge her despite the fact he wasn't a clan chief.

And edible. Even when he was being stubborn and so aggravatingly arrogant she wanted to slug him in the nose, he made her think of running her hands over those hard muscles and tasting his warm Spanish blood.

But she'd met thousands of gorgeous, powerful, even sexy men over the past centuries and none of them had made her react like a . . . She swallowed a low growl. Why not admit it? She was reacting like a Harpy in heat.

And worse, he was all too aware of her vulnerability.

That knowledge only reinforced the need to get rid of him as soon as possible. As if ticking off the Oracles wasn't reason enough.

At least her inner turmoil wasn't visible as she met Santiago's searing black gaze. "Excuse me?" she asked in the cool tones she knew set his fangs on edge.

He pointed a finger toward Levet. "Why are you traveling with that pest?"

She narrowed her gaze. "Please do not insult my companion."

"*Oui,* do not insult her companion," Levet muttered,

moving to stand at her side with an offended sniff. "In case you missed the mammogram, I'm a hero."

Santiago scowled. "Mammogram?"

"Memo," Nefri corrected him. "Missed the memo."

The exasperated male gave a shake of his head. "Are you being punished?"

"I didn't think so." She allowed her gaze to flick over his lean, muscular form, shown to perfection in his tight jeans. "Until now."

Santiago muttered a curse. "There's no need for him to be here."

"That's not your call." She nodded toward the nearby doorway. "If you'll excuse us, I need to speak with Levet in private."

It couldn't be that easy.

"No."

"I wasn't asking for your permission."

"He can't follow Gaius's trail."

Her lips thinned as she realized he'd so easily read her mind, but with a grim hold on her composure she turned her attention to the gargoyle as he stuck his tongue toward Santiago.

"For your information, I am a superb tracker."

"Can you find him?" she asked softly.

"Given time," Levet assured her, then with obvious embarrassment, wrinkled his ugly little snout. "Well, perhaps it will be more difficult than usual. The vampire somehow managed to have his . . . essence stripped. There's no scent to follow."

"There, you see," Santiago mocked.

She turned back with a lift of her brow. "See what?"

"You need me."

Oh . . . damn. She did.

Even the Oracles would agree there was nothing more vital than finding Gaius. And more importantly, what was currently controlling him.

Of course, she had to be sure that he could actually produce results before she agreed to anything.

"How do I know this is not a trick?" she demanded.

He scowled, as if offended by her question. "Why would I want to trick you?"

"Your male pride was obviously wounded by my return to my people without first gaining your approval."

His lips curled back to expose his fangs. Like all males, he didn't want to admit he might be unreasonable. "I'll admit your disappearance annoyed me, but not because of my pride." He deliberately paused. "It was the coward's choice."

A dangerous silence filled the kitchen, broken only by Levet's gasp of shock.

"I . . . umm . . . I think I will go investigate the upstairs," the tiny gargoyle muttered, his tail twitching as he hurried out of the kitchen.

Nefri and Santiago ignored his abrupt departure, both busy glaring at one another.

At last, Nefri found her voice. "Did you just call me a coward?"

Santiago didn't so much as flinch at the lethal edge in her voice. Something she might have admired if she hadn't been so infuriated.

"I said you made a coward's choice," he corrected her.

"Did you ever consider for one minute that my decision to leave had nothing to do with you?"

"No."

"That I have duties that are more important than appeasing your ego?" she grimly continued.

"You—" Santiago bit off his words, hissing as the sharp stench of rotting flesh filled the air.

"Sacrebleu," Levet called from above them. "You will want to see this."

Santiago rolled his eyes heavenward. "Damn that gargoyle."

Chapter 4

The vast mansion on the north side of Chicago looked more like a palace than a lair for one of the most powerful and feared vampires in the world.

There were acres of marble floors, sweeping staircases, and lofted ceilings that were painted with museum-grade artwork. The hallways were lined with fluted columns and shallow alcoves that held Grecian statues. The furnishings were straight out of Versailles and there was enough gilding to make a sensible demon shudder in horror.

The lower dungeons, however, were straight out of the Pentagon's wet dreams.

Dug deep beneath the mansion, the spiderweb of cement corridors led to a variety of cells. Some lined with lead, others with steel, and still others with silver. And all of them heavily hexed to prevent even a spark of magic.

Which was a true pain in the ass for Sally Grace.

Standing in the center of the cell, the powerful witch considered all the bad decisions that had led to this particular moment. There were a number of them.

The decision to run instead of trying to kill her crazy-ass mother.

The decision to give in to the Dark Lord's promises of power in return for becoming his servant.

The decision to help the vampire Gaius and his idiot cur partners in their attempts to capture the prophet and her Were protector.

All bad.

But nothing topped her latest.

Why the hell had she ever thought it would be a good idea to approach the King of Vampires?

Only a month ago she would have laughed at anyone who suggested she would be seeking out the Anasso. She was, after all, determined to lay low now the Dark Lord was dead and forget she knew anything about demons or witches or evil deities. In a few years she could change her name and start over. Only this time she intended to stay strictly among humans.

With that in mind she'd washed the black dye from her shoulder-length hair to reveal the deep red tresses streaked with gold that nature had intended for her. Her pale, almost fragile features were no longer marred with piercings or the black, goth makeup she'd used to disguise herself. In fact, her big brown eyes and full lips were devoid of cosmetics. Even her love for short skirts and barely there tops had been re-placed by jeans and sweatshirts.

Then she'd disappeared into Gaius's home in the Louisiana swamps. Why not? There were few places more isolated, and it wasn't as if the vampire would need the place. Not after he'd been killed in the battle with the Dark Lord.

Everything should have been perfect.

Only it wasn't perfect.

A week ago she'd returned to the house after a quick visit to the nearest grocery store to find that not only was

Gaius alive, but he'd become a mindless, feral animal who was obviously protecting something or someone in the house.

Terrified by the vampire's strange behavior, not to mention wanting him out of the house she'd claimed for herself, she'd retreated into the swamps and prepared a repulsion spell that should have worked on even the most powerful vampire.

She might hate her mother, but the bitch had trained her to brew some wicked black magic.

But once the spell was prepared and she'd crept back to the house to cast it during the power of the full moon, she'd discovered the house was being protected by a force that went beyond anything she'd felt before.

And that was saying something for a witch who'd been in the employ of an evil god.

Realizing there was something seriously weird going on, she had impulsively driven to this lair and demanded an audience with Styx. It was worth a try.

She wasn't sure what she'd expected, but it hadn't been for the powerful, lethally beautiful vampire to invite her into his private study where another vampire with long, silver hair and the face of a fallen angel had been standing in the corner. She'd somehow assumed she would be handed off to a flunky to deal with her concerns. But instead the two powerful demons had listened to her claims with a convincing display of interest.

Styx had murmured all the right words and even offered her a cup of her favorite tea. And she'd fallen for his faux sincerity hook, line, and sinker.

"Come into the parlor, said the spider to the fly. . . ."

Sipping her tea, she'd been in the middle of telling him precisely why Gaius had to be captured when she'd felt her tongue go thick and her eyes drift shut.

Drugged.

The coldhearted, treacherous jackasses.

She'd woken only a few minutes ago, her tongue coated in

fuzz and her magic muted by the hexes scrawled on the silver walls.

She did have her secret weapon, but it was a talent that only worked on humans, never demons. Or at least it hadn't until a few weeks ago when she'd accidentally used it on a hellhound who had strayed too close to the house.

She didn't know if her connection to the Dark Lord had muted her natural talents, or if she'd reached some critical age where it finally blossomed. More likely the hellhound had been weak and she'd been pumped up on adrenaline when it had suddenly appeared on her porch.

In any case, she'd have to be an idiot to try it on a vampire or even a pure-blooded Were.

If she failed and they realized what she'd tried to do . . . Well, being tossed in a cell would be the least of her worries.

Damn Styx and his leech squad. She hated this feeling of helplessness. She'd promised in the past that she would never again allow herself to be at the mercy of others.

Why else would she have agreed to worship the Dark Lord? Or partnered with Gaius?

Now she was back to the beginning.

Prey.

No. With a fierce effort she shook off the rising tide of panic. She wasn't prey. Never again.

Turning toward the camera hidden in the corner of the cell, she waved her arms. "Heeeellllooo. Can anyone hear me?" she screamed, knowing the vampire monitoring the cameras would be flinching at her shrill voice. Super hearing could be a bitch. "What's wrong with you freaks? I came here to help you." She stepped closer to the camera, her voice raising another painful octave. "I risked everything to just try to warn you about Gaius. And what do I get? A reward? An 'atta girl'? Hell, no. I get locked up like a rat in a cage. Thankless bastards."

A second later she heard the sound of a distant door

opening and closing, then the soft whisper of approaching footsteps. Instinctively she turned toward the bars of her cell, denying the urge to back into the distant corner as a cold, sharp-edged power filled the air.

Vampires thrived on fear. It was an aphrodisiac to the bloodsuckers. She wasn't going to give them the satisfaction.

The brave thought had barely passed through her mind when it tumbled into an abyss of shock at the sight of the male who stepped into view.

And despite being a dreaded leech, he was a male with a capital M.

Wearing jeans, a leather jacket over his T-shirt, and moccasin boots that reached his knees, he had the hard, lean body of a predator. His skin was bronzed and his dark hair brushed his broad shoulders. His features were lean with the high cheekbones of his Native American bloodlines and a proud nose. His brow was wide and his lips cut on sensual lines.

But it was his eyes that made her forget how to breathe.

They were . . . astonishing.

In the overhead light they glinted with a silver sheen, but they were so pale they appeared almost white, the shocking paleness emphasized by the rim of pure black that circled them.

She shivered, feeling as if he could see through every layer of defense she'd wrapped around her vulnerable heart.

Halting close to the bars of her cell, the stranger folded his arms over his chest and regarded her with a mocking smile. "Did you learn such language from your mother?"

The edge of disdain in his voice effectively squashed her unwelcome fascination. Jerk. What right did he have to look at her as if she were something he scraped off the bottom of his moccasin?

"My mother was too busy trying to kill me to teach me anything beyond how to run. Really, really fast," she mocked in return, moving forward to grasp the bars. As if her knees weren't trembling and her heart wasn't slamming against her ribs. "And, oh yeah, never to trust anyone. Something I was stupid enough to forget."

The astonishing eyes widened, as if she'd truly managed to surprise him.

"Your mother tried to kill you?"

She shrugged. Families. What'cha gonna do?

"Why was I drugged and thrown in the dungeons?" she demanded. "I came here in good faith."

"We have only your word on that." He planted his hands on his hips, his jacket shifting to reveal the dagger attached to his belt and the gun holstered at his side.

Holy crap. He had enough firepower to bring down a rabid troll. She didn't know whether to be flattered or horrified. In the end she was just pissed off.

"And a witch's word can't be trusted?" she snapped.

"You admitted you worshipped the Dark Lord," he said without apology. "That hardly encourages faith in your moral compass."

"Moral compass? Are you kidding me?" She gave a disbelieving shake of her head. "You're a vampire."

"So?"

"You're the last one who should be judging my morals."

A slow smile curved his lips and Sally's fingers tightened on the bars. If he'd been handsome when all haughty and disdainful, he was outrageously gorgeous when he smiled.

"Fair enough."

Concentrate, Sally. This beast is the enemy. No matter how beautiful a beast he might be.

"Then let me out," she challenged him.

"It's not my call."

"This is bullshit." She glared between the bars. "Complete and utter bullshit."

"Are you hungry?"

She blinked, taken off guard by the abrupt question. "What?"

"You've been out for forty-eight hours; do you need food?"

"Forty-eight hours?" she breathed in shock. Dammit. She'd thought she'd been out an hour, maybe two. "What did you give me?"

"A drug to make you sleep." He shrugged. "It's harmless to humans."

Fury raced through her at the risk the leeches had taken with her life. The drug might very well have been safe for humans, but she wasn't entirely human.

Not that she was going to admit as much. It was a secret she intended to take to her grave.

"Have you ever heard of allergic reactions?" she instead growled. "You could have killed me."

His bored expression revealed his supreme indifference to whether she lived or died.

Yeah. Über-jerk.

"Do you want food or not?"

She wanted to tell him to shove his offer up his ass. Thankfully she wasn't stubborn enough to cut off her nose to spite her face. She needed to keep up her energy if she was going to find a way out of the dungeons.

And fuel if she was going to risk using her secret mojo.

"I'm starving."

"I suppose you nibble lettuce like most females?"

"A double bacon cheeseburger with loaded potato skins and a chocolate shake," she ordered. "Oh, and one of those deep-fried apple pies."

He snorted. "Is that all?"

"You can throw in a few Buffalo wings with blue cheese dipping sauce."

His gaze briefly lowered to her tiny frame, which barely weighed a hundred pounds soaking wet. For a fleeting second his gaze lingered and his eyes flared, as if he'd just been hit by an unpleasant sensation. Then, with an obvious effort, he was shaking off his strange reaction.

"Your funeral," he muttered.

Sally rolled her eyes. "I hang around with deranged curs and megalomaniac vampires, not to mention evil deities; I doubt it's cholesterol that's going to put me in my grave."

Again that glorious indifference to her expected life span. "It will be at least half an hour. The chef here only cooks vegetarian, so they'll have to order out."

"Vegetarian?" She blinked, wondering if it was some sort of inside joke. "I thought the Anasso's mate was a pure-blooded Were?"

"She is."

"And she . . ." Sally gave a shake of her head. "Never mind. I've clearly stumbled into a madhouse."

"That about sums it up," he said, so low that she barely caught the words.

She frowned. "If that's how you feel, then why are you here?"

"Because my king commands it."

Hmmm. A stewing mutiny?

"And you're always an obedient little soldier?"

Easily seeing through her attempt at "divide and conquer," the vampire turned to leave. "I'll return with the food."

"Wait."

He muttered a low curse, glancing over his shoulder. "What now?"

"How long am I going to be held a prisoner?"

"That's up to Styx."

"You can't just leave me trapped down here."

"Watch me."

He walked away, exposing the most delectable butt she'd ever seen encased in denims. She swallowed a groan at the desire that flared through her, pretending she was leaning her head through the bars to yell at the bastard and not to admire his fine backside.

"You're a cold-blooded and heartless bastard, leech."

"Roke."

She frowned as his disembodied voice floated through the air. "What?"

"My name is Roke, not leech."

Roke walked away despite the annoying urge to turn around and release Sally Grace from the barren cell.

Dammit, what was wrong with him?

Okay, the female was pretty. Astonishingly pretty. He'd known that from the moment he'd caught sight of her in the dungeon's monitor. So what? Weren't there thousands of women who were far more beautiful? Certainly they were all more charming.

The spiteful little witch had the tongue of a shrew and the temperament of a rattlesnake.

Then why did he have to force his feet to carry him out of the dungeons?

It had to be because she managed to look so pale and young and defenseless, he grimly reassured himself, grimacing as he entered the marble hallway. There was a part of him that was an instinctive protector of the weak. Perhaps it was natural to be bothered by the sight of such a small, fragile creature locked in the cells that were a level beneath the original dungeons and devised for only the most dangerous of Styx's enemies.

A nice explanation.

Unfortunately it didn't explain why he'd been so fascinated by the warm scent of peaches that seemed to cling to her skin. Soap? Perfume?

Or the jolt of arousal that had slammed into him when he'd allowed his gaze to trail down to her slender body, which was curved in all the right places.

He growled low in his throat. He didn't want to be aroused

by the female. Not only because she was a witch. Vampires hated magic and magic users. All magic users. Or even because she'd been a toady for the Dark Lord.

Roke was male enough to understand that his cock didn't give a shit about the race, religion, species, or moral integrity of a potential lover. It responded to primitive needs that were disconnected from his brain.

But he'd learned long ago that only a fool gave in to his passions. Especially when it involved an unworthy female.

These days he was very selective about the women he took to his bed. He wanted a female he could respect and who understood his duty to his clan. One he could depend on not to make demands.

"And I thought I had piss-poor people skills," a deep voice drawled.

"You do," Roke retorted, watching the massive Aztec step through an open door to block his path.

The Anasso was casually dressed in jeans and a black T-shirt, his hair pulled into a long braid, but there was nothing casual in the heavy, pulsing power that filled the air.

Roke clenched his hands. He was too alpha not to react to the unspoken challenge in the air, although he was wise enough to keep his instincts tightly leashed.

Styx narrowed his dark eyes. "Is this mood because I asked you to keep an eye on our prisoner, or because she's a witch?"

"I'm not a nanny," he growled, not about to admit the arousal that continued to plague him.

Styx's lips twitched. "Thank the gods."

"I'm glad one of us finds this amusing."

"You're stuck here for now," the king pointed out. "You can snap and snarl like a rabid hellhound or you can accept your fate with a little grace."

Grace?

Roke hadn't wanted to come to Chicago in the first place,

but the Anasso had insisted they needed his rare talent for reading prophecies. Then, just when he was preparing to return to his clan in Nevada, the prophet, Cassandra, had claimed to have seen him in one of her visions.

Now he was stuck in this godforsaken palace of marble and gilt, so bored out of his mind that he was beginning to imagine he could be attracted to a pint-sized witch.

"Just because that damned prophet—"

"Careful, Roke," Styx interrupted, his power edged with pinpricks of warning. "That 'damned prophet' is part of my family."

Cassandra was the sister to Styx's mate, Darcy. Both pure-blooded Weres, but well-deserving of respect.

"I, like everyone, revere the prophet. But, just because she saw me in one of her visions, the gods only know how long ago, doesn't mean I have to be trapped in Chicago," he clarified.

"Trapped?"

His fangs ached. He needed to bite something.

Or someone.

Perhaps a tiny female with hair the color of autumn, rich brown eyes, and the sweet scent of peaches . . .

No, dammit.

He turned to glare at the Mary Cassatt painting framed on the wall. Not that he could disguise his unease from Styx. The ancient vampire wasn't the Anasso just because he had the biggest sword.

"I need to be with my clan."

"Cassandra doesn't have random visions," Styx reminded him with a growing impatience. "It has to be important."

Roke shoved his hands into the front pockets of his jeans. "Your lair isn't the center of the universe. Something important could just as easily happen in Nevada."

There was a long pause and Roke could physically feel the weight of Styx's searching gaze.

"Roke, is there something going on I should know about?" he asked. "Some reason you're so eager to leave?"

"I've wanted to leave since the day I got here," he reminded his companion, there was enough truth in his words to divert the persistent vampire. "Besides, the prophet hasn't had another vision. Maybe whatever is supposed to happen is years away."

"Until we know what the danger is, I won't allow you to be without our protection."

"I've been taking care of myself for a very long time," he muttered.

"Now you have us."

"Lucky me."

Styx slammed a hand on his shoulder. "Damn straight."

Nefri ignored Santiago as she moved with blinding speed out of the kitchen and up the narrow stairs.

No, that was not entirely true.

Who could ignore a six-foot-plus male who was only a step behind her as she made her way down the narrow hall? Especially when he was nearly quivering with the need to pull her behind him and take the lead. A typical male with a big sword and bigger ego who always wanted to be in charge.

Or maybe he merely wanted to protect her, a renegade voice whispered in the back of her mind.

A voice that she easily crushed as the stench of rotting flesh became nearly overwhelming.

"Dios," Santiago muttered. "What has that gargoyle done?"

Levet abruptly stepped around a corner, his gray skin an ashen shade in the moonlight. "I did nothing beyond locate a room hidden behind a spell of illusion," he said, defending himself.

Santiago made a sound of disgust. "That's why we didn't catch the stench miles away."

Nefri muttered an ancient curse, infuriated by the knowledge she'd allowed Santiago's arrival to distract her. She'd been too long behind the Veil. The constant peace and sense of security had dulled her senses and made her sloppy. "I should have searched for illusions the moment I arrived," she chastised herself.

"Ah yes, I forgot that little talent," Santiago drawled, referring to her rare ability to break through lesser spells.

"I wish I had left the illusion in place." Levet shifted uneasily, his wings drooping. "I do not believe you want to see what has been done, *ma chérie.*"

Nefri was certain he was right. The smell alone was enough to make her stomach clench. And there was something else. Something as dark and ancient as time.

But she'd been sent by the Oracles for a reason. She couldn't turn her back on her duty.

"*Merci,* Levet, but I must know what's happened."

"A massacre," the tiny gargoyle breathed, reluctantly stepping aside as Nefri rounded the corner and moved toward the open door.

She'd barely reached the edge of the threshold when Santiago was angling to put his body between her and whatever was waiting inside, his sword drawn and his fangs exposed.

She rolled her eyes at his protective manner. She was one of the most powerful demons ever to walk the earth. The last thing she needed was a knight in shining armor. But even as the clan chief in her warned she needed to nip his Neanderthal behavior in the bud, another part was wryly accepting that Santiago was far too stubborn to be properly trained.

A knowledge that should have annoyed her, not sent a tiny thrill of excitement shooting through her heart.

The inane thought was swiftly forgotten as Santiago came to a sharp halt, his broad back tensing. "What the . . ." He made a sound of disgust. "*Cristo.* It looks like the set of *Saw.*"

She frowned in confusion. "What?"

"A horror flick."

Nefri shuddered. Her time behind the Veil meant that she wasn't always up to date with human entertainment, but she did know that the current trend in films included a lot of blood and violence.

Steeling her nerves, she forced herself to step past Santiago's large body and studied the carnage spread across the room.

Levet had been right.

It was bad.

Even by demon standards.

The victims were all human, some male and some female, although it was nearly impossible to tell in the hideous mix of body parts, some of which were still shackled to the walls while others were piled in the middle of the blood-soaked floor.

"Were they tortured?" she asked, pointing to the knives and even an ax that were nearly hidden beneath the gore.

Santiago returned his sword to its scabbard, his expression grim. "Worse."

"What could be worse?"

"They were forced to torture themselves trying to escape. The room reeks of . . ."

"Fear," she finished for him, the lingering terror in the room crawling over her skin like an insidious disease.

They fell silent as they considered the slaughter. With an effort, Nefri coldly stripped away the horror of what she was seeing to concentrate on basic facts.

There were five—no six—humans spread across the wooden floor. They were all young, perhaps in their early twenties, and what was left of their clothing suggested they hadn't been homeless. Local college students?

They'd been held in the room for at least a week and occasionally fed and watered if the amount of waste mixed in with the mess was any indication. They'd been physically fit. There was no other way they could have endured such punishment for such a length of time.

And all were mutilated beyond the point of recognition.

To have been able to keep so many suffering people hidden behind the illusion for such a length of time took more than the usual enchantment.

She took a step further into the room, allowing her senses to flow through the thick air. She should be able to pick up something. A scent. A lingering trace of power. A stray piece of DNA left behind.

But there was nothing.

Which spoke for itself.

"This isn't Gaius's doing," Santiago at last broke into the heavy silence. "At least not on his own."

"No," she softly agreed.

Strong, slender fingers closed around Nefri's upper arm and Santiago pulled her back into the hallway, turning her to meet his piercing gaze. "Nefri, this is no longer a game."

"I never said it was."

"Then tell me what the hell is going on."

She tilted her chin. "You know I can't discuss this."

"Are you freaking kidding me?" he hissed.

"No."

His raw power swirled through the air, reminding her that he wasn't one of her docile clansmen. Santiago was ruled by primitive passions and male impulses.

"Do you see that massacre?" he snapped, pointing toward the open door.

She met him glare for glare. "I can hardly miss it."

"And you still want to play politics?"

Her hands clenched at the unfair accusation. The *last* thing she wanted was to be caught in politics. Wasn't that the reason she'd retreated behind the Veil in the first place?

"If you want answers, then approach the Oracles and ask your questions," she informed him in icy tones, turning on her heel to walk away.

It was that or tossing him through the nearest window.

"Nefri." In the blink of an eye he was standing in front of her, blocking her path. "You're not leaving until you tell me the truth."

She lifted a warning hand, her fangs extended. "You're a typical alpha male, Santiago, but you're not stupid."

His eyes narrowed. "What's that supposed to mean?"

"I give orders, I don't take them."

Gaius's new lair in Wisconsin

Unlike Louisiana, northern Wisconsin was already in the grip of late autumn. The night air was edged with frost and the countryside filled with sugar maples that were in full glory, painting the dark sky in shades of gold and crimson.

Locating a remote cabin in the middle of a thick patch of woods, Gaius made swift work of the elderly couple, draining them dry before burying them deep in the rocky ground. Then, ensuring his beloved Dara was comfortable in the upstairs loft, he spent the remainder of the night covering the windows with heavy shutters and reinforcing the doors, belatedly thankful that his essence had been destroyed weeks ago by the witch. No one would be able to follow his trail.

Still it was only when he was certain that he'd made the place as safe as possible that he climbed the narrow stairs and crossed the wood-planked floor to the bed covered by a hand-stitched quilt.

His feet briefly faltered as the body in the center of the bed faded to a black mist, as if it were as insubstantial as a cloud. Then, the darkness coalesced into a slender female form that was covered in a short skirt and halter top he'd found in his previous lair.

A figment of his imagination, he assured himself, ignoring the fact that it wasn't the first time his mate had appeared less than . . . corporeal.

Continuing forward, he gazed down at the perfect oval of Dara's honey-tinted face framed by a curtain of straight, blue-black hair. She was so beautiful, he acknowledged with a pang of longing.

Exquisite.

A daughter of the desert.

Carefully, he perched on the edge of the bed, running a hand through his black hair he kept short and slicked back from his lean face, which had once been considered handsome with a wide brow and prominent nose. Although now it was covered with dirt and blood, making him look more like a savage than the proud Roman general he'd once been.

Even his black chinos and silk shirt that had once been pristine were wrinkled and torn and so filthy they were impossible to recognize.

He needed to remember something, he thought in confusion. Something important. But what?

Almost as if sensing his growing confusion, Dara lifted her lashes to reveal eyes as dark as the night sky. "Gaius."

He leaned forward, unconsciously careful not to touch her. "Yes, beloved?"

"I need to feed."

He frowned at the soft words. "Again?"

"I'm still weak."

Gaius shuddered. He was a vampire who had more than a passing acquaintance with violence. During his years with the Dark Lord he'd committed atrocities that would once have sickened him.

But Dara's uncharacteristic lust for feedings that were as depraved as they were bloody was more than disturbing. They were dangerous.

"Yes, but—"

"Is something troubling you, *habibi?*"

"The humans become annoyingly agitated when their families begin to disappear."

"So?"

"We just got settled here."

A pleading expression touched her beautiful face. "Do you want me to suffer?"

"No, of course not," he harshly denied. "What if I bring you a few demons? An imp or some fairies?"

"And draw the attention of the Oracles?" A strange heaviness filled the room. "Don't be stupid."

A warning fluttered at the edges of his mind. "The Oracles."

She slowly sat upright, her liquid gaze holding him with a gripping intensity. "I warned you, *habibi,* they will send me back if they learn I have escaped my grave."

Stark fear filled his heart at the mere thought of losing his mate. He'd mourned her for decades. He couldn't endure such loss again.

"I will protect you with my life," he swore.

A smile of satisfaction touched her lips. "Yes, you will."

Chapter 5

Louisiana wetlands

Santiago's seething frustration was briefly forgotten as he glared at the pale face that flushed with anger. Her quiet, aloof perfection was transformed into a vivid, blazing beauty that seared through him, changing him on some fundamental level.

The odd thought had barely time to form before Nefri was smoothly returning behind her frigid barriers, her emotions retreating to a place he couldn't reach.

Santiago's hands clenched, a snarl caught in his throat. He didn't know why her icy composure set his teeth on edge, but the sight of her rigid expression made him want to smash through her defenses. She could play the ice princess with everyone but him.

Never him.

Ignoring his power, which sizzled through the air and stirred the silken curtain of her ebony hair, she squared her shoulders, as if preparing herself for some unpleasant duty.

"Can you find Gaius?" she at last demanded.

He studied her with a brooding gaze. "He's moved far

enough away that I have only a general direction, but once I'm closer I won't have any trouble cornering the bastard."

"Then I will allow you to lead me to him."

His eyes narrowed. "You'll *allow* me?"

She gave a regal nod. "Yes."

So, not just an ice princess, but Queen-of-the-freaking-Universe.

"No."

She went predator-still at his blunt refusal. "I don't understand."

"Then let me make it easy." A humorless smile touched his lips. "N. O. No."

She frowned. "You just demanded that you be included in the search."

"I told you that the rules have changed."

"And I told you that you don't make the rules."

"And if you want my help you will not only plead nicely—"

"Never."

He ignored her interruption, reaching to run his fingers down the cool silk of her hair. "But you will tell me what you know."

He expected her to knock aside his hand; instead she turned smoothly away, offering him a view of her rigid back.

"Levet," she murmured.

With a smug twitch of his wings, the aggravating pest waddled forward. *"Oui, ma chérie?"*

"We're leaving."

Santiago was moving to block her path before his brain was fully engaged. "Don't be a fool, Nefri."

The gargoyle made a choked sound, stepping behind Nefri to avoid being damaged in the crossfire. Not so stupid as Santiago had assumed.

Nefri arched a dark brow, the temperature dropping by several chilling degrees. "Do you think because I'm a female I won't hurt you?"

His brain jerked back into gear, forcing him to halt and actually consider his words. "I think that you will do anything to prevent another massacre," he said, not hesitating to use her horror at the brutal slaughter to his advantage. There was no way she was leaving this house without him. Not because Styx had ordered him to discover what was going on with Gaius. Or because he had a score to settle with his sire. But because. That was it. Just because. "Even endure my distasteful company."

Levet sent Santiago a raspberry, but his expression was resigned as he glanced back at Nefri. *"Ma chérie."*

"Yes, I know, Levet," she said, her words coated in ice, her gaze never wavering from Santiago. "It appears we must be temporary allies."

"I—"

"Don't speak," she overrode his response. "That doesn't mean I will be treated with anything less than respect. Is that clear?"

He stepped back in her personal space. "The one thing you will always have, *cara,* is my respect," he said with a blunt sincerity she couldn't miss. Even when she was driving him nuts he respected everything about her. Her strength, her intelligence, and her obvious loyalty. "But you're not my clan chief and I will never take commands from you."

"Do you take commands from your own chief?" she demanded.

Santiago shrugged. "When I agree with them."

"I pity Viper."

"He's always been pleased with my service." His gaze skimmed down to her cherry lips. "You would be even more pleased if you would give me the opportunity to service you."

Something hot and wild flared through her midnight eyes before she was giving a sharp shake of her head and firmly skirting past his large form. "This will never work."

He muttered a curse as he once again moved to block her path. "Wait."

Her lips thinned. "For what?"

"A truce."

Her expression was predictably wary. "I beg your pardon?"

He held up his hands in a gesture of peace. "I will try my best not to be excessively annoying and you will treat me as a partner, not your minion."

"You will halt your crude innuendos?"

"No."

"Santiago . . ."

"I won't make promises I can't keep," he admitted, knowing his gnawing need to break through her ice wouldn't allow him to back off. "But I do swear that I'll do everything in my power to track down Gaius."

She considered his promise for a long minute. "And your demand that I reveal my private business with the Oracles?"

"Keep it private." He grimaced. "I have a horrible premonition I'm going to discover for myself why they've decided to meddle after standing on the sidelines during the battle against the Dark Lord."

"Someday that tongue of yours is going to get you in deep trouble," she smoothly warned.

He snorted. "I've been there, done that, and have the scars to prove it."

Her dark, piercing gaze studied the bitter twist to his lips. "Is there a reason you don't learn from your mistakes?"

"Survival in the pits means never giving ground, even when the result is a beating."

"The pits?" A shadow touched her face. "You were a Gladiator?"

His jaw tightened, the memory of the vampires who'd caged him like an animal and forced him to fight for his life every night searing through his mind. "Not by choice."

"I . . . see," she said softly, and Santiago had a terrible

sensation that she did. More than he wanted. "How long were you forced to fight?"

"Too long," he said in clipped tones, turning to move down the hallway. "Let's go."

Most females would have retreated in fear as the air thickened with his power. Nefri, of course, wasn't most females. Without seeming effort she was walking at his side, not bothering to hide her curiosity. "Do you ever talk about those days?"

"No."

"Because they're too painful?"

He turned to stab her with an annoyed glare. "Do you ever talk about the reason you retreated behind the Veil?"

Her pale features were suddenly wiped of all emotion. *"Touché."*

The dungeons of Styx's lair

Sally wasn't sure how much time had passed. An hour? Two?

Not that she was in any hurry for her irritating guard to return, she assured herself. He might have the finest butt in the Northern Hemisphere, and the sort of eyes that could make some idiotic women melt, but he was as cold as ice and as smugly superior as every other leech.

Still, she was becoming bored out of her mind stuck in this bleak cell. Not to mention she needed food to replenish her fading strength.

And, with any luck at all the poor schmuck who was stuck playing babysitter to the nasty witch would be a lesser demon.

One she could attempt to use her powers on.

Of course, her luck had been downright shitty over the past few years, so it really shouldn't have been a surprise when the door to the dungeon opened and she caught the distinctive scent of a powerful male vampire.

Cold steel and ruthless sensuality.

So much for a lesser demon.

Roke was as lethal as they came.

Crap.

She halted her pacing near the door of the cell, her heart missing a painful beat as he stepped into view. She told herself that it was fear. What female in her right mind wouldn't be terrified at the sight of a demon who could kill her between one breath and the next?

It certainly had nothing to do with the stark male beauty of his perfectly chiseled face, or the haunting mystery of his strange silver eyes.

No. Nothing at all.

And to make certain she wouldn't be so stupid as to forget the beautiful creature was anything but her enemy, Roke approached the door of her cell with a dark scowl. Clearly he'd pissed off Styx and was serving some sort of penance. With her as his punishment.

"Stand away from the door," he commanded, holding a tray in his hands filled with plates of hamburgers, fries, a chocolate shake, Buffalo wings, and deep-fried apple pie.

She planted her hands on her hips, telling herself she wasn't hurt by the vampire's barely concealed disdain. What the hell did she care? He was nothing but a . . . a member of the walking dead.

Okay, he was gorgeous and there was a bad boy vibe that some females might find fascinating, but right now she wanted nothing more than to kick him in the nuts.

"What do you think I'm going to do?" she mocked. "The hexes prevent me from using my magic. And in case you haven't noticed, I'm half your size."

His gaze slid down her slender curves, a muscle knotting in his jaw as he jerked his stare back to her face. Was he repulsed by her less than voluptuous shape?

Well, screw him.

"I never underestimate an enemy," he retorted. "Especially when they appear helpless."

"Enemy?" She offered a humorless smile. "I came here to help, in case you've forgotten, you ass. So exactly when did I become your enemy?"

"When you tried to unleash the Dark Lord and his minions," he retorted without hesitation.

She hunched a shoulder, wondering just how long she was going to have to pay for that unfortunate decision.

"I didn't have any choice," she muttered.

"You were forced?"

"It was the only way to survive—"

"An easy excuse," he interrupted her with cold disapproval. "But then I would expect nothing else of a witch."

"What's that supposed to mean?"

"Magic is a cheat against everything that is natural. An abomination."

"Hey, don't feel like you have to hold back," she rasped, acting as if she didn't give a damn what he thought of her. He wasn't the first, and he certainly wouldn't be the last to hate her for no good reason. "What do the feelings of a witch matter?"

Something flared in his silver eyes. Regret? Guilt?

Yeah, and pigs could fly.

Emphasizing his absolute "I don't give a shit" attitude, he made a sound of utter boredom. "Do you want to eat or not?"

Every fiber of her being wanted to tell him to shove the tray of food up his ass. Thankfully the empty growl of her stomach prevented her pride from overcoming common sense.

What was the point in starving herself? It wasn't as if anyone would give a damn. And the goddess knew it wouldn't get her out of this dungeon.

With slow, deliberate steps, Sally backed into a corner, her smile mocking. "Is this far enough, oh mighty leech?"

With a muttered curse, he used his powers to unlock the

cell door and stepped inside. "I should let you starve," he grumbled.

She wrapped her arms around her waist, shivering as the cool surge of his power filled the air. *Shiver in fear,* she grimly assured herself. *Not excitement.*

"When can I speak with the Anasso?"

He frowned at her abrupt question, placing the tray on the narrow bed that was her only furniture.

"Why?"

"Obviously to plead my case."

Straightening, Roke regarded her with an unreadable expression. "You'll remain here so long as he believes you might be a threat."

A threat? All she wanted was to disappear into a small cottage in the middle of nowhere. How could that be a threat to anyone?

"I'm assuming that means you haven't captured Gaius."

His eyes narrowed. "Do you know where he's gone?"

"Why would I know?"

"You were his accomplice."

"Hardly," she denied, her voice harsh as she recalled her short alliance with Gaius. "I was forced to help him search for the prophet. I barely knew the arrogant ass, and what I did know I didn't like."

Roke dismissed her explanation with a wave of his slender hand. "Did you travel with him to any other lairs?"

"No," she hissed between gritted teeth. "And before you ask, he never spoke of any. Our relationship wasn't based on trust."

He snorted. "Then what was it built on?"

"Mutual need and fear."

His jaw tightened, as if he didn't want to think she might not be the evil, unrepentant bitch he wanted to paint her.

"Eat."

Forcing herself to cross the cell, she perched on the edge

of the bed and picked up one of the cheeseburgers. She was a multitasker—could eat and glare at the bastard at the same time.

"Are you always so bossy?" she demanded between bites.

"Yes."

She rolled her eyes. "Give your mate my deepest sympathies."

"My mate is none of your concern," he snapped.

Thank the goddess, she told herself. Being stuck with this surly beast would be nothing short of hell.

Of course, a night or two exploring that chiseled body . . .

No. She was obviously delusional from hunger.

Working her way through the hamburger and the plate of fries, she did her best to ignore the grim-faced predator watching her every move with a brooding intensity. At last reaching for a Buffalo wing, she pointed it toward her silent companion. "Are you going to just stand there watching me?"

"Yes."

"Why? Do you think I can use a French fry to escape?" she asked in sickly sweet tones. "Or maybe the cook hid a file in my apple pie?"

"Styx believes you could help us locate Gaius."

She returned her attention to her plate, hiding her expression as she dipped her wing into the blue cheese dressing. "I've told you everything I know."

"You said Gaius was different when he returned to his lair. What did you mean?"

She shrugged. "I had a few errands to run and when I came back Gaius was just standing in the hallway like a zombie. For a minute I thought his carcass had been stuffed and left there as some kind of sick joke. But when I actually stepped into the hallway he reacted like a feral animal. It was creepy as hell."

Roke frowned. "Was his intent to kill you?"

"I wasn't stupid enough to remain around long enough to find out if he wanted me dead or just injured."

"And you claim he didn't recognize you?"

She ate her wing and reached for another. "He acted like he didn't. I suppose he could have been pretending, but I don't see the point."

"And you suspect he had someone with him?"

"Someone or something he was protecting."

"Why?"

She doggedly kept her head down, replenishing her energy as he put her through the Inquisition. The only thing missing were the whips and chains.

"Why what?" she said with a full mouth.

He shifted with impatience. "Why do you suspect that he was protecting something?"

She trembled at the memory of the malevolent energy that had surrounded the house, repulsing her spell and contaminating the very air with evil.

Not that she was going to confess her true reason for suspecting that Gaius had a new and very powerful ally.

Not when she would have to confess she'd used dark magic against a fellow vampire of Roke's.

She was in enough trouble as it was, thank you very much.

"He was behaving like a wild dog guarding his favorite bone," she at last hedged.

She felt his gaze boring into the top of her head like a laser.

"You're lying."

With an effort she tilted back her head to meet his fierce glare. "I am not."

There was enough truth in her words to make him hesitate. "At the very least you're not revealing everything you know," he at last accused her.

"You're a mind reader?"

"One way or another I'll discover the truth, little witch," he growled, turning on his heel to head out of the cell.

Briefly startled by his departure, Sally rose to her feet. Her strength was returning, but what good would it do her if she couldn't use it to escape?

She needed someone she could manipulate.

Someone who wasn't a powerful vampire who made her think of sweet, forbidden things.

"Does it have to be you?"

Halting, he glanced over his shoulder at her abrupt question. "Me?"

"Can I have a different guard?"

"Why?"

"I should think that was obvious."

"Indulge me."

Her chin tilted. "I don't like you."

His body went rigid, his eyes darkening with something that might have been outrage. "In case you didn't notice, you're in the dungeons," he snarled, his power nearly suffocating. "You're lucky the keys haven't been thrown away and your luscious little body left for the wolves. Literally."

What the hell was wrong with him? He acted as if she'd insulted him . . . Wait—did he just call her body luscious?

Dammit, Sally, concentrate.

Sucking in a deep breath, she refused to back down. "Even a condemned criminal gets a last request, Roke. And mine is that I don't have to see you again."

Chapter 6

Louisiana wetlands

Nefri allowed Santiago to lead her from the house, resolutely maintaining her air of detachment while deep inside she was an emotional mess.

That room . . .

It wasn't just the blood and guts.

She was an ancient vampire who'd witnessed just about every depravity that demons and humans could imagine. It was the lingering evil that seemed to cling to the air. Like an oil slick that polluted everything it touched. Dear lord. She wanted to stand beneath a shower and scrub herself from head to toe.

And just as confusing were the violent emotions the vampire walking at her side inspired. He was infuriating, illogical, stubborn, and so typically male that she wanted to scream. He was also wickedly charming, unexpectedly intelligent, and intensely loyal to his clan.

One minute she wanted to have him muzzled, and the next she wanted to wrap herself in his raw power and kiss him senseless.

Which terrified her.

Granted, it'd been a long time since she'd last taken a lover, but she knew that this extreme awareness of Santiago had nothing to do with sexual frustration. Or even a brief bout of lust.

She wished it was.

Lust she could easily satisfy. Either with Santiago or with one of her own clansmen.

But this restless craving that was spreading through her body wasn't going to be ended by a swift, discreet tumble. *Not that Santiago would ever be swift or discreet in bed*, a renegade voice whispered in the back of her mind. He would be fierce and dominant and outrageously demanding. No doubt he would leave a female feeling thoroughly ravaged . . . in the most gratifying way.

Her hands clenched as she banished the image of Santiago poised naked above her, his hips nestled between her parted thighs.

Had she gone mad?

There was something out there that terrified even the Oracles. Now was not the time to be reacting as if she were a silly foundling still at the mercy of her passions. With an effort she hid behind the cool composure that allowed her to pretend a control she was far from feeling.

"Where are we going?" she asked as Santiago headed up the narrow path. With the thick canopy of trees and creeping moss it looked more like a tunnel to some weird Land of the Lost than a main road to the nearest town.

Somewhere overhead Levet was hunting for his evening meal, but the thick foliage made it impossible to sense anything beyond a few feet.

At her side, Santiago pulled his sword from its scabbard, his eyes scanning the shadows. "I left my truck hidden outside town."

She rolled her eyes. Of course he would have a truck. A heavy bully of a vehicle with a too-powerful engine that wouldn't be stopped by a mere roadblock. Her lips thinned with annoyance at her unruly thoughts.

"After that."

He shrugged, his gaze continuing to search the thick line of trees that bordered the road.

"North."

"North? That's it?"

"That's all I got."

"Are you being deliberately vague?"

"No, I only have a faint sense of Gaius," he explained. "I told you, once I'm closer I'll be able to pinpoint his location."

She believed him, even if she didn't want to. The bond she'd formed with her own sire had been destroyed several centuries ago, but she did remember that she rarely had more than a vague impression of his direction.

But the thought of spending several nights with Santiago as they searched for Gaius was more disturbing than she wanted to admit.

"We could travel much faster if we use my medallion."

He hissed, shooting her a startled glance. "No fuc—" He bit off his crude response, but his expression remained resolute. "No way."

"Why not?" She lifted her fingers to touch the warm medallion that rested just above her unbeating heart. "It would be much quicker."

"I just regained my bond with Gaius. I'm not going to do anything to risk it."

She tilted her head to the side. "And that's the only reason?"

"You want me to admit that popping from one place to another freaks me out?" he growled, clearly still pissed at the last time she'd taken him mist-walking. "Fine. It freaks me out."

She resisted the urge to tease. Not because Santiago couldn't laugh at himself. His ready sense of humor was one of his more disarming traits. But because with this man it felt too much like flirting.

"Perhaps it's for the best."

His eyes darkened with suspicion. "Why do you say that?"

"The medallion that Gaius possesses is connected to mine." She allowed her fingers to drop from the metal that always felt alive. Even sentient. "I can't be certain he wouldn't sense me if I use it."

His pace slowed, as if he'd been struck by a sudden thought. "Have you used it since you returned to this world?"

"It's necessary to travel through the Veil, but I haven't called on its powers since I've been here. Why?"

"It seems more than a coincidence that Gaius would abandon his lair only a night or two before we arrived."

Ah. Smart vampire. Gaius might very well have sensed her approach if she'd used the medallion. Instead it had been Siljar who'd opened a portal a few miles from the house.

Which meant that she had no answer for why Gaius had abandoned his lair.

"There was a scent of humans in the area," she speculated aloud.

He nodded. "The witch?"

"Her scent was distinct and fading," Nefri said, making a mental note to tell the Oracles that there'd been something odd about the witch's scent. She was more than she seemed. "The humans were more recent," she told Santiago. "Within the past day."

Santiago accepted her claim without argument. He was one of the few men who didn't seem intimidated by her superior powers.

"How many?" he instead demanded.

"Impossible to say, but there were more than a dozen."

He considered the various possibilities. "A search party?"

"That was my thought. Such a large number of missing humans wouldn't go unnoticed."

"Typical," he growled. "If they'd just waited a few days we would have had Gaius cornered."

"Maybe," she hedged, unwilling to fool herself that it would be simple. The Oracles wouldn't have sent her if it was just a case of finding Gaius and asking him to come along nicely.

He turned to study her with a searching gaze. "I don't like the sound of that 'maybe.'"

"Gaius has obviously been altered," she hedged. "We don't know what new powers he might have."

"No," he abruptly denied. "Not altered."

Tread warily, Nefri. . . . "What do you mean?"

"The witch said he acted like he was under some sort of compulsion," he said, his tone accusing.

She bit back her words of annoyance. The witch was not only more than she seemed, but she was far too observant for her own good.

She needed to be watched. If only for her own safety.

"He's too powerful a vampire to be enthralled," she pointed out.

"Then you're saying the witch was lying?"

She shrugged. "I don't know."

"Is he alone?"

"Possibly not."

His flare of irritation swirled through the air, biting into her skin.

"Let me guess—you can't tell me anything about his companion," he rasped.

Her lips twisted into a wry smile. The buzz of insects fell silent and a dozen small animals scuttled away in sharp fear at Santiago's sour mood. How long had it been since she'd spent time with a man who was willing to stand up to her?

Too long, if the strange sensations sizzling through her veins were anything to go by.

It was one thing to feel a measure of admiration for

Santiago after centuries of being surrounded by sycophants who rarely dared to question her decisions, let alone treat her as if he were her equal. And quite another to shiver in sizzling arousal.

"I can't because I truly don't know," she informed her companion, her voice coated in an extra layer of ice. There was no way she was going to allow this man to sense her growing vulnerability. He was a predator who would pounce on the first hint of weakness. "I'm merely a servant of the Oracles, not their confidante."

Santiago growled, but before he could express his smoldering frustration, there was the rustle of leaves above them and the pungent scent of granite.

"Gargoyle," Santiago instead muttered, stepping back as Levet floated down on his fairy wings to land on the path between them.

The gargoyle stuck his tongue toward the male vampire. "I do have a name."

"I thought you were hunting," Nefri intruded into the male sniping.

Levet readily turned in her direction. "I was until I noticed the herd of people heading this way."

Santiago frowned. "At this hour?"

"It could be another search party," Nefri suggested.

"More like a lynch mob," Levet corrected, his tail twitching. "*Sacrebleu.* They were shouting and waving their guns like they were overdosed on steroids."

A lynch mob? Nefri deliberately avoided Santiago's sharp gaze, a bad feeling growing in the pit of her stomach at the gargoyle's warning. Not because there was a group of people out there looking for trouble. Humans took a peculiar delight in stirring their passions to a fever pitch. She had a terrible premonition that this was more than just an overabundance of testosterone.

"How far?" she asked.

Levet pointed up the path. "Five miles and headed this way."

"We'll cut through the swamp," Santiago announced, taking instant command. "Once we're clear of the town we can circle back and pick up my vehicle."

Nefri didn't protest. She didn't have any more desire than Santiago to run across a group of humans looking for blood, even if she was more accustomed to giving orders than taking them.

"Tromp through the bogs? Ewww." Levet wrinkled his snout. "I am no slimy lizard. I will join you on the other side."

Nefri reached out to lay a gentle hand on the gargoyle's shoulder. "Take care, Levet."

"Merci, ma chérie." He offered a low bow, a sparkle in his gray eyes. "You have my promise I will take the greatest care. And if you have need of me you only have to call my name."

She nodded. "I will."

With a flap of his wings, Levet was headed upward, dodging the overhanging branches with astonishing grace.

"Thank the gods," Santiago muttered. "That creature would try the patience of a saint."

"And you're no saint," she muttered, pointing out the obvious.

"Not even close." With a wicked grin he leaned forward and claimed her lips in a short, bone-melting kiss. Then, before she could slug him, he was turning to jog off the pathway, sliding his sword back into its sheath so he could pull out a large dagger and battle through the overgrown vegetation.

Nefri stoically followed in his wake, pretending that his lethal kiss hadn't inflamed the sensual hunger that was becoming more than a mere inconvenience. That her lips weren't tingling with an excitement that she felt to the tips of her toes.

Damn it all. Why this aggravating vampire?

And why now?

Shoving aside the questions that had no answers, Nefri focused her concentration on their shadowed surroundings. With every step away from the path, the ground became more treacherous, a scent of rotting vegetation seeping from the thick layer of moss and duckweed. And while they were moving away from the angry humans, there were just as many dangers in the swamps.

Actually, more.

Cougars and alligators lurked among the dense undergrowth as well as a dozen snakes that might not be able to kill a vampire, but could certainly make one ill for a short period of time. There were also a variety of demons who lived in the bayous, far away from the noisy mortals.

But it wasn't the lurking hazards that slowly wore on Nefri's nerves. Or the discomfort of wading into the water that came to her knees.

It was, instead, the strange sensations that crawled over her skin, that made a shiver inch down her spine.

"I don't like this," she at last said, breaking the thick silence.

"I can't say I'm overly fond of the swamps myself, but it's better than dealing with the rabid locals," Santiago countered, his dagger slicing through a layer of Spanish moss.

"It's not the swamp," she said, shivering. "Can't you feel it?"

He glanced over his shoulder. "Feel what?"

Another shiver. "It's as if there's a lingering echo of violence."

"Magic?"

"If it is, it has nothing to do with witches."

"You're right, this is far more primal," he agreed with a grimace, his head tilted back as he tested the fading tang of aggression. "*Mierda.* It's no wonder the humans are roaming the countryside with torches and pitchforks."

She smiled wryly. "Very . . . atmospheric."

Santiago turned to battle a path through the stubborn vegetation. "Stay close," he commanded.

Santiago wasn't easily spooked. He'd been beaten, carved up like a Thanksgiving turkey, tortured, and taken to the edge of death more times than he could count.

What was left to be afraid of?

Well . . . besides the exquisitely beautiful woman walking behind him. Any man in his right mind would be terrified by a female who tied him into knots even as she left him hard and aching with desire.

But the prickles of violence that hung in the air like a bad memory were as unnerving as hell.

And the fact that they were being followed by at least six glowing orbs that were dancing ever closer didn't ease his tension.

They had reached the middle of the swamp when the orbs shifted to block their path.

"Santiago," Nefri warned, moving to stand at his side.

"They've been trailing us since we entered the swamp," he said, squashing the urge to shove her behind him. She was not a female who needed protection, and she wouldn't thank him for undermining her authority. Especially not with these particular demons. "The question is, why?"

On cue the glowing orbs began to pulse and expand, taking on physical forms.

Holding the dagger in a loose grip, he resisted the urge to pull out his sword. No point in ratcheting up the tension until he was certain the demons intended a fight. Besides, his fangs and claws were far more lethal than any blade, no matter how sharp it might be.

There was a surge of electricity, and then the glowing

lights faded to reveal the six female Harpies standing in front of them.

They were gorgeous, of course. With long black hair and gray eyes that swirled with the power of thunderclouds, their naked bodies were leanly muscled with large wings on their backs. Always formidable warriors, they used their beauty to distract their enemies before striking them down with the fire-balls they could conjure from thin air.

They were also crafty as hell, easily trapping unwary males in hidden snares to hold them captive during their mating season. Not that the males usually protested, he wryly conceded. A Harpy in heat was most men's idea of a sexual fantasy. Endless days of aggressive sex with no commitment. And if some men took exception to being treated as a mere stud, the majority found their imprisonment nothing short of paradise.

Santiago, however, wasn't thinking about sex as the warriors studied him with their stormy gray eyes. Instead he watched them with a wary frown.

"We follow you because you trespass in our territory, vampire," the tallest of the Harpies said, her voice stirring the thick air.

Nefri took a half step forward, offering a regal bow. "It was not our intention to disturb your nest."

Continuing to glare in Santiago's direction, the Harpy appeared unimpressed. "The foul air has disturbed us, sister," the Harpy said.

"Hey, not my fault," Santiago muttered.

The closest Harpy held out her hand, a sudden ball of fire dancing just above her palm. "Be quiet, male," she snarled.

"He speaks the truth," Nefri smoothly interjected.

"We will decide who speaks the truth," the taller Harpy informed them, pointing a finger in their direction. "Take them."

Santiago reached for his sword, only to be halted when Nefri laid a restraining hand on his forearm. "No, Santiago.

There's no need to fight," she said softly. "I'm certain we can reason with our companions."

His gaze never wavered from the females, who looked eager for an opportunity to singe him with their fireballs. "They don't seem to be in the mood to reason," he growled.

"Which is why we shouldn't provoke them."

It was the violent urge to shake her hand off and launch himself at the Harpies that made him hesitate. He could be impulsive, but never in battle. He'd learned long ago the best war was the one never fought.

It had to be the effects of the lingering spell, or whatever the hell was contaminating the air, he grimly acknowledged. Which meant one wrong move and this entire encounter could descend into a bloody massacre that none of them wanted.

"Fine." With an effort he forced himself to tuck away his dagger, and lifted his hands in surrender. "But don't blame me if this goes to hell."

The lead Harpy gestured toward the Harpy at her side. "Charis, take the male to our guest rooms."

"No," he snapped, stepping back. "I'm not leaving."

The Harpy narrowed her stormy eyes. "It wasn't a request."

"Santiago." With a cool brush of her fingers over his cheek, Nefri managed to capture his full attention. "It will be fine. I promise."

"Dios," he muttered, knowing he'd been undone by a mere touch. This female was going to be the death of him.

Keeping his gaze on Nefri's pale, perfect face, Santiago allowed the female Harpy to grab his arm, her wing stroking over his back with an unwelcome intimacy.

"This way, my pretty leech."

Chapter 7

Only centuries of training allowed Nefri to disguise her flare of fury as Charis tugged Santiago through a curtain of clinging vines and disappeared from sight. How dare the young Harpy attach herself to Santiago like a barnacle. And the way she was rubbing her wings over him . . . it was indecent.

Santiago wasn't here to become her sex toy.

In fact . . .

With an effort, Nefri squashed the image of grabbing the lovely Charis by her dark hair and shaking her until her teeth rattled. Instead she calmly allowed herself to be led through the brackish water and thick undergrowth, she was only briefly startled when they stepped through a thin barrier of magic to enter a vast parkland that had cement dykes to hold back the swamp and perfectly manicured gardens that bloomed beneath the fading moonlight. In the center, a large wooden structure was suspended off the ground by a dozen sturdy trees and built on several different levels that disappeared among the thick branches.

It was large enough to house at least three dozen Harpies, with room for the communal nursery that traditionally consumed the top floor.

Acutely aware she was being watched by guards hidden

among the leaves, Nefri kept her head held high and her pace steady as she was led past the flowering bignonias and pure white lilies. They left the gardens through a high archway and entered a narrow foyer that was lined with panels of glossy oak carved with elaborate designs.

A spiral staircase stood in the middle of the room and three of her companions peeled off to jog up the steep steps, while the remaining two escorted her down the hall to a room at the back of the building.

Halting at the door to stand guard, the two indicated for Nefri to enter.

As if she had a choice?

Refusing to reveal any hint of weakness, she stepped over the threshold and took a quick inventory of her surroundings. It was a large room with an open-beamed ceiling and fur rugs thrown on the wood-planked floor. She didn't look too closely at the fur, knowing it was more likely the pelt of a demon than an animal. Harpies made very bad enemies.

There were a number of priceless tapestries hung on the walls and the furniture was finely crafted and covered in a pale blue satin.

An elegant room that spoke of authority and yet with enough womanly touches to make it comfortable.

As a female ruler, Nefri appreciated the subtle statement, even as the warrior in her took in the sword leaning in a far corner and the silver letter opener on the desk near the stone fireplace. She also noticed a faint scent of gunpowder that warned there was a gun hidden somewhere nearby.

At last her attention turned toward the female standing in the center of the floor. She was tall with the long, black hair of most Harpies. There were a few silver strands threaded through the darkness, which indicated she was several centuries old, and a hard-fought wisdom in the gray eyes. At the moment she was wearing a plain white gown that was slit down the back to allow room for her wings and wide gold bracelets around her wrists that indicated she was the leader of this particular nest.

"Matron," she murmured with a respectful bow of her head. Unlike most men, Nefri understood that good manners were often more persuasive than any amount of bluster and intimidation.

"Vampire," the woman responded, the low voice rumbling through the room like thunder.

"Please, call me Nefri."

The woman nodded. "And I'm Solaris, Matron of this nest."

"I am honored to meet you."

"We shall see." The storm gray eyes held a warning as she waved her hand toward the built-in bar. "I have refreshments. Or I can call for one of my sisters. There are a few who enjoy donating their blood to vampires."

"No, thank you." Nefri's smile remained, but the sudden realization that Santiago might even now be at the throat of some willing Harpy jolted through her, exposing a raw emotion she hadn't felt in centuries. Was that . . . jealousy? Good lord, she was losing her mind. "Where is my companion?"

The Harpy regarded her with a piercing intelligence. "He's your property?"

Nefri paused to consider her answer. In Harpy society males were treated as possessions that were meant to be shared with the entire nest.

"He is under my protection," she at last said. "And unavailable."

"A pity." A mysterious smile curved the woman's lips. "We have several younglings about to enter their first mating heat."

Nefri's expression never altered, but she couldn't control the frigid burst of power that made the overhead chandelier sway and at least one crystal vase shatter.

"A vampire can't breed."

Solaris arched a brow. "I'm aware of your reproduction

deficiencies, which is why I encourage the young ones to choose a vampire for their first lover. They can have all the pleasure of mating without the concern of pregnancy. Most aren't ready yet for motherhood."

Oh no. Hell no.

Two more vases shattered.

"As I said, Santiago isn't available."

The Matron ignored the destruction of her expensive collection, her own power a steady pulse that could unleash a deadly barrage of fire.

"It's not nice to be so selfish," she chided Nefri. "Such a beautiful creature should be enjoyed by all."

Don't overreact, Nefri, she silently warned herself, *the woman is only trying to provoke you.*

"For now I have need of his skills."

"Will you return him when you're done with his"—deliberate pause—"skills?"

"No."

"Ah." Solaris gave an abrupt laugh. "Be careful, my sister. That one will not be easily trained."

Trained? Santiago was a barbarian.

Not that his primitive passions didn't have a certain appeal, she grudgingly conceded. In fact, she was beginning to think that a few hours of raw, untamed sex might just be what she needed to bring an end to her annoying fascination with the male vampire.

With a silent curse, she shoved Santiago to the back of her mind. Soon enough she would have to deal with her disturbing reaction to him. One way or another. But for now she needed to focus on the most immediate danger.

And the Matron was a danger, despite her gracious manner. One wrong answer and Nefri would go from being a guest to a prisoner.

Or a pile of ash.

Something she intended to avoid.

"Perhaps we should discuss the reason you've had me brought to your nest," she suggested.

"Straight to the point?" Solaris shrugged. "Very well. I want to know why the vampires have declared war on us."

Nefri was on instant, full alert. War? Was this a trick?

"I assure you the vampires have no desire for war with anyone, least of all the Harpies," she cautiously addressed her companion.

Solaris allowed her power to thicken the air in the room. As if Nefri needed a reminder that she was more than a match for a vampire, even one as ancient as Nefri.

"Then why are they attempting to poison our lands?"

"I'm afraid I don't understand."

With a smooth step, Solaris crossed to pour herself a glass of some milky white liquid. Nectar? Taking a sip, she turned back to study Nefri with a hard gaze.

"Peace had finally settled among my people with the death of the Dark Lord."

"It has been a blessing for all of us," Nefri agreed.

"A blessing as well as an opportunity for the more powerful demons to flex their muscles." The gray eyes turned dark with the threat of a looming storm. "It wouldn't be the first time vampires enslaved those too weak to fight back."

Nefri wasn't stupid enough to deny the charge. The vampires had once been little better than savages who'd wielded their superiority to use and abuse the less fortunate. Even if they were fellow vampires.

"That's the past," she pointed out, meeting the accusing glare with a calm composure. "The new Anasso is eager to build alliances, not to make enemies."

"And yet he sent a vampire to the border of our lands who has been spreading his infection."

Damn. Nefri had harbored a small measure of hope that the local demons hadn't been aware of Gaius. Or whoever (or whatever) had caused the bloodbath in his lair.

Fooling humans was simple. Demons wouldn't be nearly so easy.

"You're referring to Gaius?"

"I didn't ask his name. He was medium height with dark hair and a prominent nose. And a most"—the female shuddered—"pungent aroma."

Nefri hesitated. The Oracles had wanted this mess cleaned up as swiftly and quietly as possible, but with every passing minute it was obvious the danger was snowballing at a terrifying rate.

This was no time for diversions or discreet lies.

She not only needed whatever information the Harpies could offer, but she had to make sure they were safe. Her duty to the Commission would never be more important than the lives of innocents.

Of course, she'd been a diplomat for centuries. A small amount of truth was often preferable to a full disclosure.

"The vampire you refer to is a traitor to his people and a servant of the Dark Lord," she admitted. "I traveled here to make sure he faces punishment for his crimes."

Solaris emptied her glass before setting it aside. "A convenient claim."

"I can only give you my word."

"And what of his strange abilities?" the Harpy demanded, her voice thickening with a dangerous power. "Do you want me to believe they come from his worship of the Dark Lord?"

"I'm not sure what strange abilities you're referring to."

Solaris's wings gave an impatient flap. "His ability to infect others with his bite."

Nefri frowned, not having to pretend her confusion. She expected claims of brutal killings or missing younglings. Not . . . infections.

"I don't fully understand. What do you mean by infecting others?"

The Harpy studied her with a piercing gaze, perhaps

seeking some sign that Nefri was lying. Then, with a powerful stride she was headed toward a door hidden behind one of the tapestries. "Come with me."

Nefri followed behind Solaris, startled to discover herself being led through a steel-lined corridor that opened into a large room filled with a number of high-tech computers and surveillance equipment.

"I had no idea that Harpies built such elaborate nests," she murmured as Solaris paused before a heavy door, using a key card to trip the lock.

The last Harpy nest that Nefri had entered had been little more than a few walls and a thatch roof.

"We've had to keep up with technology, although there are still matriarchies who prefer to live in a more primitive environment," she said, leading Nefri down another corridor, this one lined with doors.

A glance through one open door was enough to reveal they'd reached the prisons.

"Is Santiago being held in these cells?" she demanded, uncertain why Solaris had brought her here.

Solaris glanced over her shoulder. "Of course not. For now he's a guest and being offered our finest hospitality." A taunting smile touched her lips. "Happy?"

Well aware that Harpy hospitality included food, drink, and sex with a willing female, Nefri was forced to swallow a low growl. "Not particularly," she muttered.

"Here."

Coming to a halt at a door being guarded by an older Harpy with a hard face and the air of a seasoned warrior, Solaris gestured toward the small window set in the steel door.

With a frown Nefri moved forward, studying the gaunt human male who was pacing the cell with short, jerky steps. He looked young, perhaps twenty, dressed in filthy jeans and a Polo shirt that was torn and covered in blood. His hair was matted with dirt and his face shredded by claw marks that Nefri suspected were self-inflicted.

A pathetic creature, but what did it have to do with her? She returned her attention to the female at her side. "Is he mad?"

"If that was all that was wrong with him, I would have killed him the minute he stumbled close to our nest." Solaris glanced toward the silent guard. "Open the window."

With a grimace the warrior leaned sideways and slid the pane of glass open a few inches. Immediately a choking cloud of . . . aggression—the only word that came to her mind— filled the air.

Nefri shuddered, her fangs fully extended and aching for blood. "Good lord," she rasped.

Solaris hissed as her muscles tensed and her eyes swirled with the power of an approaching hurricane. "He was in our territory for less than one day and he triggered a dozen fights that broke out among various demons, including two of my Harpies, and caused an entire pack of hellhounds to turn on one another," she said between clenched teeth, as vulnerable to the evil in the air as Nefri. "Four of them are dead."

Nefri took an instinctive step back. She was close to snapping. "Is he the only one?"

"The only one who has survived. We found several corpses that had been drained and two others that looked as if they'd fought to the death."

"Please." Nefri clenched her hands, her mind clouding with a bloodlust that she hadn't felt in centuries. "Close the window."

Solaris nodded toward the guard, who hurriedly slammed the glass shut. For a minute there was a heavy silence as each of them struggled to leash the violence that bubbled through their veins.

At last, giving a low curse, Solaris turned to stab Nefri

with a frustrated glare. "Are you prepared to confess what is going on?"

Nefri gave a slow shake of her head, feeling a stab of betrayal. What had the Commission done?

This . . . spirit . . . or whatever the hell it was, had been locked behind the Veil for endless centuries and never once had the Oracles warned her that it could be a danger to her people, let alone turn them into savage zombies.

And now she was learning that Gaius's bite might actually be infecting humans. . . .

Holy hell.

"I don't know. Truly," she told her companion, her expression troubled. "I've never heard of a vampire's bite causing this reaction in a human."

"But you knew something was wrong?" the Harpy pressed.

"Yes, but I had no idea Gaius was causing such damage," she carefully hedged before turning the conversation away from what brought her to Louisiana. "I felt the lingering consequences of the infection as we were traveling through the swamp. Is it fading?"

Solaris's lips thinned, but she allowed herself to be diverted. "Yes. Once the human was locked away the hostility began to lessen. Hopefully it will be completely gone by tomorrow."

The words didn't ease the tight knot of dread in the pit of her stomach, but it did give her hope that if they moved with enough speed they could contain the worst of the plague.

"What do you intend to do with him?" she asked, nodding toward the cell.

"Study him for now," Solaris said with a shrug. "He'll be dead in a day or two."

Nefri was caught off guard by the blunt announcement. "Dead? He's not ill. At least not physically."

"No, but he refuses to eat and he continues to damage

himself no matter how often we sedate him. He won't survive for long."

Lord, what a mess.

Nefri pressed a hand to her temple, suddenly aware of her heavy weariness. Dawn was approaching at a rapid rate and she needed to rest and feed to regain her strength.

"I must speak with the Anasso," she said, more to herself than the Harpies who eyed her with open suspicion. "He has to be warned."

"First, will you tell me what is happening?"

"The only thing I can tell you is that I will do my best to track down Gaius and put an end to his contamination," she promised.

Solaris arched a brow. "And if I decide I wish to keep an insurance policy until I can be certain the vampires clean up their mess?"

Nefri met the stormy gaze without flinching. She was an ancient clan chief who had faced down the most powerful demons. She didn't allow herself to be intimidated.

Not by anyone.

"Then I would have to confess that it wasn't Styx who sent me to capture Gaius."

Solaris froze. "Then who?"

"The Commission."

Santiago should have been happy as a freaking lark.

After being escorted into the Harpy nest, he'd found himself ensconced in a luxurious set of rooms. The large living room had an Oriental flavor with black and gold furnishings and jade figurines set on low lacquer tables. The connecting bedroom shared the Oriental theme, the king-size bed canopied in gold silk and the poofy chaise lounges covered in black satin.

Even the lavatory was matching in the dramatic color

scheme, although he had no idea why women insisted on such elegance in a mere bathroom. Give him a shower and a bar of soap and he was satisfied.

Not that he didn't spend several painful minutes imagining Nefri soaking in the marble tub that was deep enough to drown in and surrounded by a dozen different oils, soaps, and shampoos.

Oh, the things he could do to that female in that tub . . . her raven hair floating on the water and her lips parted in astonished pleasure as he knelt between her thighs.

It was the scent of female Harpy that pulled him out of his fantasies and back into the living room to discover Charis had returned, a smile of invitation on her beautiful face and her lean body still naked.

"Hello, gorgeous," she purred, leaning against the edge of a sofa so her pale wings could contrast with the dark material and the arch in her back could emphasize her full breasts.

Never let it be said a Harpy didn't know how to flaunt her assets.

"Have you come to release me?" he demanded.

She pouted, giving a toss of her dark curls. "Don't you like our little nest?"

Santiago swallowed his impatience. The female looked harmless, but one misspoken word and he'd find himself being roasted by a barrage of fireballs.

"I'm always delighted to be in the company of beautiful women."

She licked her lips. "How beautiful?"

"As beautiful as a freshly bloomed orchid."

"Would you like to touch?"

His lips twisted. The female couldn't know how much her simple question troubled him. She was tender, exquisite, and oozing with sexual invitation. Only a eunuch wouldn't want to toss her on the sofa and give in to temptation.

But his body remained stubbornly indifferent to the pleasures the woman had on offer, his fangs refusing to lengthen, and his cock unimpressed. Instead, he was wracked by a compulsive need to find Nefri and make sure she hadn't been hurt.

"Unfortunately, I don't have time to enjoy the delights of Harpy hospitality."

"Why not? Your female is busy with the Matron." Abruptly straightening, Charis strolled toward him, running a finger down the line of her throat. "And I brought you dinner."

His short burst of laughter held no humor. "It looks delicious, of course, and I can't express how desperately I wish I wanted a sip or two."

She halted, her brow furrowing in confusion. "Aren't you hungry?"

"My appetite seems to have become extremely selective," he said dryly.

The gray eyes flashed with anger, but Harpies had rigid rules of protocol and Charis had been well trained. "Very well," she conceded defeat. "If you would prefer another female, that can be arranged."

"I would prefer to return to my companion."

"Why? You're not mated."

He shivered at the mere thought. This . . . obsession with her was bad enough. How much worse would it be if they were actually mated?

Mierda.

Aware that the Harpy was waiting for his response, he managed a thin smile. "I've pledged to protect her."

"She's in no immediate danger," Charis said, her expression petulant. "And she won't be leaving until we're satisfied she isn't responsible for the nasty humans invading our lands."

Santiago's irritation was replaced by a sharp curiosity. This had to be the reason they'd been forced to the Harpy nest. "Nasty humans?"

Charis wrinkled her nose. "They carry violence with them, infecting the entire area with their madness."

Hmmm. He folded his arms over his chest. "Why do you think Nefri or I might be involved?"

"The Matron hasn't shared her suspicions with the younger warriors, but the humans were bitten by two fangs. Most of us assumed it was a vampire who infected them." She sent him a questioning gaze. "What else could it be?"

Gaius. It had to be.

He could feel it in his very bones.

"Yes, what else," he muttered.

"Can we play now?"

Santiago barely noticed as Charis moved close enough to tug the leather band from his hair, allowing it to spill down his back. He was far more interested in the scent of jasmine and feminine power that sliced through him like a bolt of lightning.

Suddenly the hunger that Charis hadn't been able to stir was charging through him at full throttle, hardening and lengthening his body in all the right places.

Hiding a smile of anticipation, he covertly watched as Nefri strolled into the room, her body stiffening at the sight of the young Harpy running her fingers through his hair.

"Maybe later," he murmured softly, gently dislodging her fingers and pushing her away. "Can we have some privacy, Charis?"

With yet another toss of her head, Charis headed toward the door, pausing to send a flirtatious smile over her shoulder. "I'll be in the common rooms if you change your mind."

Waiting until the Harpy had disappeared down the hallway, Nefri offered Santiago a smile frigid enough to give him frostbite. "Please don't let me interrupt."

His lips twitched, his eyes running a slow survey down her

rigid body. Even with her jeans covered in swamp muck and her hair tangled, she appeared as regally beautiful as always.

Perhaps it wasn't so shocking that no other woman could satisfy him. None could possibly compare to this magnificent female.

"Jealous, *querida?*" he taunted, moving to stand directly in front of her.

"Tired," she corrected him, clearly hoping that he didn't notice the way her dark eyes dilated with arousal. "The Matron has kindly extended an invitation for us to remain within her nest until nightfall."

He was instantly distracted. "Invitation or command?"

"We're not prisoners if that's what you're asking, but dawn is less than an hour away." She gave a dismissive lift of one shoulder. "It seemed preferable to remain here than to risk being caught without a suitable place to rest."

His eyes narrowed. "And you've come to discuss your decisions with your partner?"

"If you prefer to leave I won't stop you."

Yeah, like that was ever going to happen. Not until he had fulfilled his promise to Styx, and more importantly, not until he had this aggravating female well and truly out of his system.

"What I want is an explanation for why the Harpies believe the vampires are infecting the humans."

Her jaw clenched at his smooth attack, but astonishingly she didn't try to pretend she didn't know what he was talking about. In fact, she met his gaze squarely. "Not vampires," she said. "Gaius."

"So it's true?"

"Yes. I witnessed the human. He's . . ." Her words broke off with a grimace.

"He's what?"

She took a few seconds to answer, her composure a brittle

facade that was clearly about to shatter. Santiago resisted the urge to tug her into his arms and offer her comfort. Not only was she more likely to slug him as thank him for his efforts, but he needed to know just what the hell was going on.

"He carries violence with him like a plague," she at last admitted.

"Did you know this was possible?"

"No," she denied, her sincerity unmistakable. "But we must warn Styx. He'll need to send his Ravens to track down any infected humans and contain them."

He made a sound of disbelief. People accused him of being arrogant? He was an amateur compared to Nefri.

"You expect the Anasso to send his personal guard to clean up a mess that the Oracles specifically told him was none of his business?"

"Yes."

He gave a rueful shake of his head. There was no point in arguing. Styx would agree that the humans had to be halted before they could cause chaos.

"And what do you intend to do?"

She shrugged. "Find Gaius."

"And his companion?"

Her expression gave nothing away. "If he has one."

Santiago gave a low hiss. Not just at her refusal to admit exactly what they were facing, but at the growing fear that they were all stumbling in the dark.

Including the Commission.

"I don't like this."

She gave a weary shake of her head, stepping around him without warning to move toward the back of the room. "Neither do I."

With a swift motion he was blocking her path, ignoring the burst of her icy annoyance that crawled over his bare skin, just a breath from true pain.

"Where are you going?" he demanded.

"I intend to have a shower and then rest for a few hours."

His earlier fantasies of Nefri in the black and gold bathroom consumed his thoughts, instantly making him as hard as a rock.

"Here?"

"This is the only guest room available." Her head was held at a proud angle, but she couldn't disguise her reaction to his blatant arousal. "We'll have to share."

"Share?" He chuckled in wicked anticipation.

Chapter 8

Nefri sniffed at her companion's male pleasure, pretending as if she hadn't been the one to insist that she share a room with Santiago.

Why give him the satisfaction of knowing she couldn't bear the thought of him in another woman's arms while she spent the day alone and aching with unfulfilled desire?

Besides, she hadn't actually lied.

These were the only guest rooms, although Solaris had offered to have one of the numerous bedrooms belonging to the Harpies cleared for her use. It was ridiculous to put the younglings out of their own beds.

Right?

Turning her head, she avoided the dark promise smoldering in his eyes.

"Can you contact Styx or would you prefer that I speak with him?" she asked, her tone brisk.

He reached to smooth a strand of hair behind her ear, his fingers lingering against her cheek. "I'll take care of it."

She shivered beneath his soft caress, a tingling excitement racing through her blood. Oh . . . heavens. It had been so long. So insanely long.

And now the desire that she'd kept locked away for more

years than she could remember threatened to turn into an avalanche.

Too fast, a voice whispered in the back of her mind. *This is all going too fast.*

"Then if you don't mind, I'll use the shower first," she said in a sudden rush. "Once I'm done you can have the bedroom and I'll use the couch."

His grin widened as he stepped back and waved a hand toward the connecting door. "It's all yours, *cara.*"

Jackass.

She swept regally out of the room and crossed directly to enter the large bathroom.

He'd sensed her growing desire. Just as he sensed the flare of panic at allowing herself to be consumed by the unfamiliar sensations.

And he found it . . . amusing.

Amusing.

She closed the door with emphasis (it wasn't a slam, dammit) and stripped off her nasty clothes, dropping them into the laundry chute.

Why? Of all the endless males in the world, why was it Santiago who set her on fire?

He was stubborn and arrogant and maddeningly impulsive and . . . so deliciously gorgeous and unapologetically male she didn't have a chance in hell of resisting, she grudgingly admitted, stepping into the shower and turning on the water.

In the distance she could hear the muffled sound of Santiago's voice as he spoke on his cell phone, relaying what he'd learned to the Anasso.

Styx would no doubt be aggravated by her refusal to confess all that she knew, but he would do his duty. It's what a leader did, no matter what their personal feelings.

Stepping beneath the flow of warm water, Nefri thankfully washed away the clinging stench of the swamp, shampooing her long hair before reaching for the soap. Just as her fingers closed around the bottle, the door to the shower was pulled open and a naked Santiago stepped into the large stall.

"Let me," he murmured, easily removing the bottle from her hand.

"I'm not finished," Nefri hissed in shock, her gaze lowering against her will to take in Santiago's hard, perfectly chiseled body.

Okay, maybe it wasn't entirely against her will, she admitted with a jolt of excitement.

He was . . . magnificent.

Like an exquisite work of art.

The water poured over his bronzed skin, plastering the long raven hair to the smooth muscles of his chest and glistening on the lean beauty of his face.

How was she supposed to resist the temptation to run her fingers, and then her lips, down that sleek male form?

Easily scenting her sharp burst of arousal, he squeezed a dollop of soap into his palm and smiled with a sinful promise. "Good, then I can wash your back," he offered.

She struggled to think clearly. "I can wash my own back."

"You were the one who said we had to share."

"These rooms, not the shower."

His lips twitched. "Conservation is always a good thing, isn't it?"

She allowed her gaze to be snared by the dark hunger that smoldered in his eyes. A stupid mistake. Suddenly she understood what it must feel like to drown. The choking heat, the sluggish lack of coordination, the quivering sense something momentous was about to happen.

And worse, she couldn't find the intelligence to care.

"Santiago . . ."

"Turn around, *cara,*" he prompted, his voice thick.

This is dangerous, she told herself. She should shove him away. It wasn't as if she were some helpless female who didn't have the strength to take care of herself.

But for the first time since becoming clan chief, she felt like a woman.

A woman with needs.

A woman who ached for a man's touch.

No, she abruptly corrected herself, not just a man's touch.

Santiago's touch.

Only his.

Banishing the voice that warned she was about to make a decision that would alter her life forever, Nefri slowly turned, offering him her back.

Why shouldn't she indulge her needs just this once?

Every other clan chief managed to have a robust sex life and function as a leader. Being a control freak didn't mean she had to take a vow of chastity.

Did it?

"Ah, the mark of *Cú Chulainn*," he murmured, referring to the tattoo of a dragon that flowed down her back. It revealed that she had gone through the battles of Durotriges to earn the title of master. Clan chief. "Very sexy."

"Sexy?" She frowned. Most vampires found the mark a source of intimidation, not arousal.

"Relax, Nefri," Santiago murmured, his lips tracing the outline of the tattoo even as his clever fingers began to soap her back. "I promise this is going to be magic."

"Magic?" She closed her eyes, forcing her rigid muscles to ease. "Are you always so confident in your ability to please a woman?"

His lips shifted to the base of her neck, his hands skimming down the curve of her waist.

"Confident in *us*," he corrected her, his fangs scraping over her tender skin. "Don't pretend you don't feel the explosive chemistry between us. It's . . . magic. There's no other word."

She made a choked sound, her head tilting to the side in an unspoken invitation.

It was magic.

Enchantment at its most primitive level.

"It's been . . . a long time," she admitted, unsure why she needed him to know.

"Then let me take care of you," he whispered against her skin, his hands trailing around her waist before gliding up to cup the fullness of her breasts. "Tonight you don't have to be in charge."

Easy enough for him to say, she wryly conceded. Her need to be in control was a fundamental part of who—

The thought, in fact all thoughts, were shattered as his thumbs brushed over her straining nipples, sending an electric current of sensation jolting through her.

Oh lord. Yes. Her toes curled. If this was how he took care of a woman, then she was all for handing him control.

He kissed a path up the tender curve of her throat, nuzzling below her ear while his fingers continued to torment the sensitive tips of her nipples. The air was filled with cherry-scented steam and raw male desire, wrapping them in a mist of privacy.

As if they were in their own world, she hazily acknowledged, her hands lifting to steady herself against the black tiles of the shower.

"This is dangerous," she muttered.

"Yes," he instantly agreed, giving the lobe of her ear a nip before he was stroking his lips downward. "But inevitable."

Perhaps it was, she silently agreed, her back arching as his mouth continued its downward path, following the line of her spine. His touch was cool, but it seemed to brand her skin with fire, making her shudder in pleasure.

Astonishingly he went to his knees, his hands sliding down her hips before he was firmly tugging her legs apart. Unable to resist temptation, she turned her head to glance over her shoulder, a strange emotion piercing her heart at the sight of the male kneeling behind her, his power barely leashed as he tilted back his head to meet her startled gaze.

He looked like a pagan god with his stark male beauty, emphasized by the water that shimmered on his bronzed skin.

Holding her gaze, he leaned forward, using his lips and fangs along the lower curve of her back as he continued to inch her legs further apart.

A soft moan was torn from her lips. There was something unbearably intimate in watching him pleasure her. As if his touch was reaching someplace deep inside her.

Nibbling down the curve of her hip, he made a sound deep in his throat as he at last reached the smooth skin of her inner thigh.

"Deliciosa," he murmured. "You taste of sweet jasmine."

It was the sensation of his lips moving against her most responsive flesh that made her eyes slide shut in sinful pleasure. She hissed, her knees going weak. This was so good. Exactly what she'd been craving.

Then, while she was still adjusting to the light caress, his clever tongue was sliding through her tender cleft and the tingles of anticipation became a tidal wave of bliss.

"Santiago," she groaned, her forehead pressed against the slick tiles.

"I'm here, *cara,*" he reassured her, his hands holding her hips steady as he continued his exquisite assault. "Let yourself go."

Let yourself go . . .

Such simple words, but for a woman who maintained a rigid clamp on her every emotion, they were as difficult as telling her to walk into the sunlight.

Not that Santiago was giving her any option, she acknowledged with a shaken sigh. Prepared for his touch to be as hard and demanding as he was, she was caught off guard when the stroke of his tongue was a soft, seeking exploration. She quivered, her fingers digging into the tile.

Holy hell. This was . . . indecent. And so wickedly wonderful she couldn't remember why she thought this would be a bad idea.

His tongue found the tiny bundle of nerves and her head tilted back as his steady licks sent a blaze of arousal through her body.

"Yes," she muttered. "Don't stop."

"Not a force in this world would make me stop," he growled.

Thank the gods. Her fangs lengthened and her entire body bowed as his soft strokes quickened, his hands firmly holding her in place.

Distantly she was aware of the warm cascade of water and the feel of Santiago's power stirring the thick air. And if she tried hard enough she could sense each and every Harpy as they moved through the large building. But at the moment her only interest was in the acute pleasure that was rapidly spiraling toward an explosion she wasn't sure she was going to survive.

And she didn't give a damn.

She moaned softly, hanging on the cusp. She needed . . .

He shifted his head just a fraction, changing the pressure of his tongue. Yes. That was it. The small movement was enough to send her hurtling over the edge, and with a cry of sheer pleasure she crushed the tiles beneath her hands.

Her entire body shook at the force of her climax, leaving her feeling oddly dazed.

Which was the only reason she allowed Santiago to scoop her in his arms and carry her out of the bathroom, she assured herself.

No matter how great the sex, she would never, ever be one of those females who liked being treated like a fragile flower.

Ignoring the water that dripped from their bodies, Santiago

crossed to the large bed, lowering her into the middle of the mattress with a powerful ease.

"You look like a mermaid," he murmured, his eyes dark with a smoldering hunger as they swept down her naked body. "Although I've never seen one so beautiful."

She snorted. "Mermaids are a myth."

He moved onto the mattress to kneel next to her, his full arousal standing at attention. Her hands itched to grasp that proud length, exploring it from its broad head to the base.

"Most people assume that the Immortal Ones are a myth," he reminded her with a taunting smile. "Especially their mysterious leader, Nefri."

It was true that her people had remained in peaceful isolation for centuries, and that their occasional visits to this world had been done in secret, but . . .

But what?

She was finding it increasingly difficult to think as he leaned over her, his hands planted on the mattress next to her shoulders and his shaft pressing against her hip.

She might have just enjoyed a mind-blowing orgasm, but clearly her body wasn't opposed to round two.

Or three.

"I'm no myth," she at last managed to mutter.

"No?" A lethal smile curved his lips. "Maybe I should discover for myself."

Always a man of action, he leaned down and allowed his mouth to skim over the curve of her breast.

She trembled at the teasing caress, needing more. Much more.

"Santiago," she pleaded softly.

"Yes, *querida*."

Closing his lips over the tip of her nipple, he used his tongue to tease her sated body back into full arousal. Without hesitation she lifted her arms, shoving her fingers into the tempting silk of his hair.

She'd wanted to do this since the moment she caught sight of this gorgeous vampire, she realized with a faint stab of surprise. To loosen the long strands of his raven hair and allow it to slide through her fingers.

"You're so beautiful."

The revealing words slipped past her lips before she could stop them, but instead of the smug smile she expected, Santiago lifted his head to regard her with a fierce need that stripped away any pretense that this was just lust.

She didn't know what was happening between the two of them, but one night of madness wasn't going to satisfy it.

"I need you to find me beautiful, *querida,*" he rasped. "I need you to hunger for me with the same insanity that plagues me."

Not giving her a chance to respond, he shifted to cover her with the cool weight of his body, his head swooping down to claim her lips in a searing kiss.

An exquisite shudder shook her body. Insanity summed it up nicely.

But sometimes a woman had to toss aside logic and let the magic consume her.

As if sensing her reckless thoughts, Santiago growled low in his throat, his hands molding the soft curve of her breast as he spread frantic kisses over her face.

"Jasmine and midnight silk," he muttered, his tongue outlining her lips. "You were sent here for me to devour."

Nefri might have protested if his hand hadn't trailed down to stroke between her thighs with experienced ease.

She moaned as his finger slid into her tight flesh, her back arching in growing pleasure. It didn't seem possible that she could need him again so soon, but as his finger dipped in and out of her, she found her hands tightening in his hair.

"If you're going to devour me, then do it," she rasped.

His lips brushed over her cheek, then down the line of her jaw. "Patience, *cara.*" He scraped his fangs down the length of her throat. "All good things"—he nibbled down her collarbone—"in time." He covered the aching tip of her breast.

She hissed. Her patience was legendary. She'd spent over a century cataloguing every plant that could grow beyond the Veil where the sunlight never pierced the thick mists. But how the hell was she supposed to be patient when her entire body was on fire?

She didn't *want* to be patient. She just wanted to once again feel that glorious release that hovered just out of reach.

Fisting her fingers in his thick hair, she lifted her hips and wrapped her legs around his waist. "The time is now," she informed him.

Pulling back, he regarded her with a rueful smile. "Always so bossy."

She deliberately rubbed herself against the straining length of his erection. "If you wanted submissive you should have went with Charis."

His eyes darkened, his fangs long and lethal in the dim lamplight. "What I want is you." Holding her gaze, he shifted until the tip of his cock pressed against her entrance. "Only you."

"Then take me."

"Sí."

With a low hiss, Santiago tilted his hips forward, sliding into her with a slow, relentless thrust.

Lowering her hands, Nefri clutched at Santiago's shoulders, moaning in approval at the delicious sense of fullness. In this moment they were joined as deeply as it was possible for two people to be joined.

As lovers . . .

Her mind instantly shied from the implied relationship.

"Nefri," he whispered close to her ear. "Is something wrong?"

"Nothing," she muttered, burying her face in the curve of his neck to absorb the rich male scent of him. "Nothing at all."

"Then hang on, *querida.*"

The words had barely left his lips when he was pulling out and thrusting forward with enough force to bang the bed against the wall. Her eyes squeezed shut. Santiago's tenderness had been a delightful surprise, but this was . . .

This was the raw, aching sex her body had longed for. This was perfection.

Meeting him thrust for thrust, Nefri scored her nails down his back, digging them into the firm muscles of his butt. He made a choked sound of pleasure, his lips finding hers in a kiss that demanded utter surrender.

"*Dios,* I've waited so long."

She nipped at his lips, her fangs careful not to break his skin.

Vampires mated by exchanging blood. Not that she thought they were . . . or could . . . or ever would. . . .

Never. The mere thought was ridiculous.

But, no use taking unnecessary risks, right?

Shoving aside the unwelcome distraction, she instead concentrated on Santiago as he stroked deeper, faster, taking her ever closer.

He felt so good as he moved inside her, his hands slipping beneath her hips as he gave a last surge and sent them both skyrocketing to paradise.

She gave a muted cry, her flare of power intertwining with Santiago's to fill the room with a shimmer of brilliant colors, as if a rainbow had exploded.

"Good . . . lord," she whispered in shock.

Styx's lair in Chicago

It was the steady pulse of power that led Roke from the privacy of his rooms to the large library just past nightfall.

There was only one thing that could create the nuclear level energy. Which meant he wasn't surprised when he stepped into the long room that was lined by ceiling-high bookshelves to discover Styx's Ravens gathered.

A mocking smile curved his lips as he leaned against the doorjamb and surveyed the collection of massive vampires who were draped on the delicate Louis XIV chairs and sofas. They looked like oversized G.I. Joe action figures stuck in a miniature dollhouse.

"A powwow and you didn't invite me?" Roke drawled as the vampires turned to regard him with varying degrees of impatience to downright irritation. He hadn't made any effort to win friends and influence people since being forced to remain in Chicago. "I'm crushed."

As if sensing that Roke was frustrated enough to pick a fight just to have a reason to hit someone, Styx crossed the room with long strides and stood directly in front of him, blocking his path. "Santiago called just before dawn," he said.

Ah. Roke had heard the stirrings as he'd lain down to rest for the day, but it had been too late to seek out the cause.

"It must have been a helluva call for you to summon the A-team from their gargoyle duty." He sent a taunting glance toward the larger-than-usual vampire with a long blond braid and fierce blue eyes. Jagr had recently become the official leader of the Ravens. "Is the world coming to an end?"

The vampire stepped forward, looking every inch the Visigoth warrior he'd once been. "No, but your end can be easily arranged, Tonto," he growled.

Roke snorted. "Don't you have a village to plunder, Goth-boy?"

Styx allowed his power to slice through the air with an icy edge. The surrounding vampires flinched in pain.

Clearly the Anasso was in a mood.

"Jagr, I'll leave it to you to arrange the patrols. Make sure no one goes alone," he commanded, his dark gaze never wavering from Roke. "You, come with me."

Not giving Roke an option, Styx grabbed him by the

upper arm and led him down the marble hallway. They halted on the landing of the wide staircase.

Roke pulled free of his companion's grasp, studying Styx's tense features. "Is Santiago in trouble?" he abruptly demanded.

The older vampire grimaced. "Santiago spends his life skirting on the edge of trouble."

"Perhaps I should have asked if he was in more trouble than usual."

"No, his call was concerning Gaius."

"What about him?"

"It seems the bastard has acquired a nasty new talent."

That didn't sound good.

"Should I ask?"

"Santiago claims that his former sire is capable of infecting humans with his bite."

"Infecting them with what?"

"Violence."

Roke frowned. Was this some sort of joke? "I don't understand."

"I don't either, but I'm sending out scouts to make sure we prevent any unwelcome surprises," Styx muttered.

"Perfect." Roke pounced on the excuse to escape the lair. "Sign me up."

"Not you." Styx swiftly shut him down. "I need you to stay here."

Roke barely swallowed his growl of annoyance. "Why?"

"I'm leaving in a few minutes to try and gain an audience with the Oracles."

"And?" Roke prompted.

Styx shrugged, his expression guarded. "And I need you to protect the lair."

Roke was getting a bad feeling about this.

A very bad feeling.

"And?"

"And to keep an eye on our guest."

Shit, he knew it.

"The witch?" he ground out.

"Unless you've added to our collection in the dungeons?"

"Why would I?" He planted his hands on his hips, glaring at the older vampire. "I don't want to take care of the one we've got."

"It's only until we've discovered what the hell is going on with Gaius."

"Easy for you to say."

"Easy?" Styx met him glare for glare. "Would you rather go speak with the Oracles?"

Oh . . . hell, no.

Not that he was about to admit as much to the towering Aztec in front of him. "You know what I want," he instead snapped.

Styx paused, studying Roke with a piercing intelligence. "Is there something going on with this witch I should know about?"

Roke clenched his hands. What was there to know about? That he'd spent the daylight hours plagued by the thought of warm ivory skin and glorious autumn hair that smelled of peaches? That he'd had to force his feet to carry him to the library rather than heading down to the dungeons?

"Not a damned thing," he snarled.

Styx lifted a brow, but he was smart enough to keep his opinion to himself. "Good, then I want you to question her again," he said. "See if she knows anything about the supposed infection that Gaius is spreading."

Roke was shaking his head before Styx was done. "Get someone else. She won't talk to me."

Styx leaned forward, the air taking on a distinct chill of irritation. "Then make her talk."

"Torture?"

"Oh, for Christ's sake. I don't torture helpless females locked in my dungeons." Styx shook his head, the tiny turquoise amulets threaded through his long braid tinkling at the movement. "I meant charm. You do remember how to seduce a young, beautiful woman, don't you?"

A combustible heat scalded through his lower body, assuring Roke that he remembered in exquisite detail how to seduce a beautiful woman, even if it had been far too long since he'd felt like indulging in it.

Until now.

Dangerous.

"She's not a woman, she's a witch," he muttered.

"Christ. Fine," Styx snapped in exasperation. "I'll send Spike to—"

"No," Roke interrupted before he could halt the harsh words. There was no way Spike was getting anywhere close to Sally. The younger vampire would have her flat on her back and his fangs deep in her throat before she knew what was happening. And that was . . . unacceptable. Why? That was a question he didn't intend to answer. "I'll take care of the witch."

Chapter 9

Harpy house in Louisiana

Santiago woke with every expectation of finding Nefri in his arms.

Why wouldn't he?

They'd come together in an earth-shattering explosion of pleasure. More than once. The sort of pleasure that made lovers want to linger in bed and explore one another for hours. Days. Perhaps centuries.

Instead Nefri was not only out of bed, but she'd showered and changed into a pair of clean jeans and a pale blue sweater that she must have gotten from the Harpies. More telling, she was putting off vibes that warned she wasn't in a hurry to leap back into bed.

With a grimace, Santiago headed into the shower, not surprised to discover a pair of jeans and sweatshirt waiting for him on the counter.

If Nefri didn't need him to track down Gaius she would no doubt have escaped while he was sleeping. As it was, she was doing everything in her power to make sure he understood that last night (or rather early this morning) was a mistake.

One she didn't intend to repeat.

Not that he was about to be tossed into the pile of Nefri's bad decisions, he grimly decided, stepping beneath the hot water.

She'd been with him all the way.

Hell, she'd nearly shredded his back during their last delectable tango.

A shudder raced through his body at the vivid memory of Nefri spread beneath him, her eyes dark with a passion that threatened to drown them both.

Oh no.

This wasn't over.

Not by a long shot.

Swiftly washing his hair and skimming the soap over his body, he exited the shower and dried off. Then, taking time to pull on the jeans and black sweatshirt, he braided his hair, and headed out of the bathroom.

The bedroom was empty. No surprise there. But the tidal wave of her power assured him she hadn't gone far.

He stepped into the living room, his brows lifting at the sight of Nefri seated cross-legged in the middle of the floor, her eyes closed and her hands folded in her lap as her hair floated on the faint breeze stirred by her powers.

At his entrance, her lashes lifted to reveal eyes that were carefully devoid of emotion.

"Meditation?" he drawled, trying to keep his temper in check. Not easy when she was studying him like he was a virus that had to be endured for the greater good.

"It clears my mind," she said, smoothly rising to her feet.

He snorted, not fooled for a second. A vampire didn't use that amount of power to find their inner self.

"And you were hoping to contact the Oracles?"

Her eyes narrowed. "If only you were as clever as you think you are."

He slowly paced to stand mere inches from her. "I'm not only as clever as I think I am, but I'm even better looking."

She stepped back before she could hide her revealing retreat. Then, squaring her shoulders, she forced herself to meet his wicked grin. "Did you convince Styx to send out his Ravens?"

His gaze lowered to the lush red lips, a ready heat spreading through his body. Oh, the havoc those lips could wreak.

"Once I assured him the gargoyle was no longer missing."

"Styx was concerned about Levet?" she asked in bewilderment.

"Not Styx. Darcy," he corrected her. "Like me, the Anasso couldn't care less if the aggravating pest stayed absent."

"Ah." The cool composure slammed back into place. "I've already had word that he's waiting for us just north of here." She waved her hand toward the glass of blood that was set on the low table. "You should eat so we can join him."

He crossed to lift the glass to his lips, draining it in one long swallow.

It held the rich flavor of Harpy, but it wasn't the jasmine-scented blood he longed for. Still, it replenished his strength. Anything else would obviously have to wait.

Replacing the empty glass on the table, he turned back to study his companion. "Aren't you going to join me?"

She shrugged. "I need very little sustenance."

Hmmm. Interesting. Santiago had heard rumors that there were those behind the Veil who abstained completely from blood. Just another way to make themselves superior to their more savage brethren, he wryly assumed.

"Because of your age or because of your time behind the Veil?"

She arched a brow. "It's hardly polite to discuss a woman's age."

"Why are you so secretive?"

"I'm not."

"Then answer the question. Do you feed?"

Something that was almost an emotion flared through her

eyes before it was ruthlessly squashed. "Not when I'm with my clan."

"So it's true that the Veil steals all hunger?"

Her jaw clenched. He knew she hated being questioned almost as much as she hated revealing anything about the mysteries beyond the Veil. Thankfully she'd learned that he was just as stubborn as she was.

"It diminishes the more primitive needs," she admitted in clipped tones.

"And passions?"

"For most."

He grimaced. Endless nights without desire or hunger or pleasure?

"Why the hell would anyone choose to live there?"

"There are those of us who have interests beyond physical satisfaction," she informed him with an edge of censure.

Ah. A challenge. He returned his attention to the temptation of her lips as he moved to stand close enough to be wrapped in her jasmine scent. "There's a lot to be said for physical satisfaction," he reminded her in a husky voice.

She stiffened, but held her ground. "And even more to be said for the powers that come from abstinence."

"What powers?" he swiftly pounced.

She abruptly turned away, heading toward the door. "If you're finished we should go."

He moved to stand in her path. "What powers?"

A burst of frigid energy lashed against him, just a small taste of her displeasure.

Damn. Why was that so sexy?

"I've told you before that the talents of vampires are as varied behind the Veil as they are in this world."

He pretended that he didn't notice the tightness of her features that warned he was wearing on her last nerve. Unless he pushed the issue he would never truly discover the woman beneath the clan chief.

And he wanted that.

With a brutal need that was more than a little frightening.

"I know there's shape-shifting and mist-walking."

"Yes."

"And the ability to pass as human?" he asked, referring to the rumors that there were vampires who could feign breathing, a heartbeat, and even warm their skin.

"For a rare few."

"Day-walkers?"

"Even fewer."

"Dios." He didn't bother to hide his surprise. He hadn't truly believed it was possible. "Can you walk in the daylight?"

"Long ago I could endure the sun for very limited periods of time."

"Why not now?"

"Because my visits have become more frequent to this world," she said, her composure a brittle shell. "It steals my abilities."

"Why have they been more frequent?"

"There was an . . . incident two centuries ago that I had to handle and more recently I devoted my attention to searching for the prophet." Her dark gaze shifted toward the door, her profile rigid. "I had hoped that once the Dark Lord was defeated I would be allowed to return to my studies."

Santiago scowled, disgruntled by her regret. It appeared painfully genuine. Was this a warning that her place was firmly behind the Veil?

And if it was, how could he argue?

She was a clan chief. A leader who was treated almost with godlike reverence by her people.

What was there for her on this side? Him? Big freaking deal.

The knowledge made him . . . irritable.

"Return to your studies or to forget me?" he growled.

She turned back to meet his smoldering glare. "What?"

"Admit the truth. You wanted to flee behind your Veil and pretend you hadn't lusted after a mere savage," he clarified.

With a cool glare she moved around his stiff form, her head held high. "We're wasting time."

"Sí," he hissed, not sure if he was more annoyed with her or himself for caring that she was eager to leave him behind. "We clearly have better things to be doing."

"Santiago?"

"Let's go."

Gaius's lair in Wisconsin

Gaius returned from searching the thick woods for any sign of intruders to discover Dara standing on the bottom of the stairs. With her hand on the wood banister and her dark hair floating on an invisible breeze, she appeared to be more a specter than a flesh and blood woman.

A part of him longed to rush across the narrow space to wrap her fragile form in the protection of his arms. A greater part, however, kept him standing frozen in the doorway.

"What are you doing out of bed, beloved?" he asked softly.

A pout marred her perfect face. "My dinner is dead."

He frowned. "Already?"

"You only brought me three and one escaped."

Escaped. It took long minutes for the word to sink through his sluggish brain. Then he was clenching his hands in weary frustration.

Dio.

This was how it started in Louisiana. One and then two survivors escaping to stir the locals into a panic. He couldn't allow it to happen again.

"Which one?"

"The male."

"I must track him down."

Dara lifted a slender shoulder. "Why bother?"

"Because he could lead the humans to us," he said, barely able to contain his rising irritation. The last thing he desired was spending the rest of the night trailing the stupid human.

He wanted . . . what? A few hours of peace, he abruptly realized. A chance to relax and enjoy the return of his mate without the constant need to tend to her hungers.

"No one would believe him," she sought to assure him, floating forward.

"It's too dangerous," he insisted.

"No, *habibi*." Her voice was surprisingly commanding, the dark eyes holding his gaze with a hypnotic power. "Allow him to return to the village. He will seed our garden."

"Seed our garden?" he parroted.

With a slender wave of her hand, Dara pushed open the nearest windows, a coy smile curving her lips.

"Can't you feel it, Gaius?" She shivered with delight at the strange sense of lust that pulsed in the air. "Our time has arrived."

Chapter 10

Roke headed down the stairs as Styx returned to his waiting Ravens.

"Charming," he muttered as he reached the lower floor. "I'd like to shove a charming fist right into his smug face."

It wasn't that he was arrogant enough to assume that the Anasso was deliberately trying to piss him off. It was obvious that Styx had his hands full with this latest threat. Still, he wasn't pleased to be back on witch duty.

He was supposed to be devoting this night to scrubbing away every thought of Sally Grace. Not giving his overactive libido even more reason to plague his day with erotic dreams.

Muttering a string of curses, Roke was only vaguely aware of his surroundings. Which explained why he'd nearly missed the male fairy who was hurrying down the hallway with a tray of food, along with a rose and several leather-bound books.

Roke came to a sharp halt, knowing beyond a doubt the overly pretty demon was rushing to be with Sally. Who else would put that smile of anticipation on the narrow face that was surrounded by a tumble of golden hair? Or the eagerness shimmering in the hazel eyes?

Although there were any number of lovely, not to mention lethal, females scattered around the mansion, most of them were mated. And not even a fairy was stupid enough to try and come between a vampire and his mate.

Or even a pure-blooded Were for that matter.

Besides, Roke recognized that vaguely bewildered expression beneath the enchantment.

That was a Sally Grace specialty.

"You," he called out.

The fairy came to a reluctant halt, eyeing Roke with impatience. "Me?"

"Is that tray for the witch?"

"I—"

"Is it or not?"

"Yes," the man grudgingly admitted.

"Give it to me." Roke held out his hands. Then, when the fairy just stood there staring at him like an idiot, he snapped his fingers. "Well?"

"There's no need to bother yourself," the man said, stubbornly holding on to the tray. "I'm sure you have better things to be doing."

Roke leaned forward, his power making the plates rattle. "That wasn't a suggestion, fairy."

"But—"

"Give. Me. The. Tray." As expected the fairy hastily shoved the tray into Roke's hands, tumbling over the rose and jostling the stack of books. Roke frowned. "What the hell is with the books?"

The fairy hunched a shoulder, his expression petulant. "I promised that I would bring her something to read. She's bored."

Bored? An image of how he could keep the pretty little witch entertained seared through his mind before he managed to slam shut the door on the treacherous temptation.

"This isn't the damned Ritz."

"I don't mind." A hint of eagerness returned to the narrow face. "In fact I'm happy to—"

"I mind," Roke snapped, infuriated by the man's obvious obsession with Sally. "You're not to return to the dungeons, is that clear?"

The fairy had the nerve to hesitate, almost as if he was actually considering defying Roke's command. Suicidal fey. Then, after a long moment, he gave a grudging nod. "It's clear."

Whirling on his heel, Roke headed toward the nearby stairs that led to the lower level. "Freaking fairies," he muttered, ignoring the startled glances from the vampires watching the surveillance equipment lining the entrance to the lower dungeons. Waiting for the younger vampire with short, brown hair and dark eyes to jump up and open the heavy steel door, Roke swept past them and headed down the corridor between the cells.

His knee-high moccasins that were laced over his black jeans made no sound as he ghosted forward. But something must have alerted Sally that she was no longer alone. He was barely halfway down the corridor when he heard her push herself off the cot and cross to the bars of her cell.

"Lysander?" she called softly, the sweet scent of peaches filling the air.

Roke's fingers tightened on the tray. Oh . . . hell. What was it about that maddening scent?

Annoyed as much by his instant, painful arousal as by the sound of another man's name on her lips, Roke took the last few steps to arrive at her cell. "No, not Lysander," he said, watching her expectant expression harden with a flare of obvious frustration.

"You," she breathed, shoving back her tangled curls that glowed with the rich colors of autumn beneath the overhead lights.

The sort of hair a man wanted brushing against his naked skin.

"Your pet fairy has resigned his babysitting duties."

"Resigned or was fired?"

"Take your pick."

Her hands clenched, her chin tilted to a militant angle. "Why? I thought we agreed you wouldn't return."

Roke ignored her accusation. He wanted answers on what was going on between her and the fairy. "What did you do to that poor man?"

She stilled, as if she were caught off guard by his question. "I don't know what you mean."

"He was foaming at the mouth to get down here. I thought I was going to have to wrestle him for the honor of bringing your dinner tray."

"So?" She licked her lips, her expression suddenly guarded. "He happens to be a gentleman. Unlike you."

Roke studied her pale face. What was she trying to hide? "How many times has he been down here?"

"Only once." She stepped away from the bars, her arms wrapping around her slender waist. "He came down to ask what I wanted for dinner."

"And in that short time you managed to bewitch him?"

"Don't be ridiculous," she denied with more force than was necessary. "I can't use my magic in this cell."

Was she joking?

His gaze made a reluctant trip over her small form, which was perfectly curved to entice a man's appetite. It didn't matter if he was vampire or fey.

"There's more than one kind of magic a female can use to bewitch a male, as you well know," he growled.

There was the slightest flicker of her lashes before her guarded expression was being replaced by a mocking smile. "Tell me, Roke, do you hate all women, or is it just me?"

Roke muttered a curse, abruptly recalling Styx's words: *You do remember how to seduce a young, beautiful woman, don't you . . . ?*

Dammit. He was supposed to be charming the female, not pissing her off.

Shifting the tray, he waved a hand in front of the cell door, using his powers to turn the lock. As it swung open he stepped through and closed it behind him with his foot.

Entering the cell, he moved to set the tray on the narrow cot before straightening to meet her frustrated glare.

Okay, time to be charming.

Forcing his muscles to unclench, he strolled forward. "Maybe you could change my opinion," he murmured, his gaze lowering to the sensual curve of her lips.

Sally blinked, clearly baffled by his abrupt change. "I don't care enough to make the effort," she at last retorted. "I prefer Lysander's company."

Roke battled back his surge of anger. "Forget the fairy," he warned in soft tones. "He's obviously too susceptible to be an adequate guard."

"Why?" she demanded. "Because he didn't beat me?"

He hissed, dangerously disturbed by the thought of any man daring to raise a hand to this female. "No one would dare mar that perfect skin," he rasped, moving close enough that he could run his fingers down the bare skin of her neck.

She shivered, her eyes widening. "What are you doing?"

Fan-fucking-tastic question.

"Sit," he muttered, lowering his hands to grasp her arms so he could steer her to the bed. Only when she was perched on the edge of the mattress did he release his hold. "Eat while it's hot."

Rolling her eyes, she reached for a ham sandwich and took a savage bite.

"Have you thought about taking meds for those manic mood swings of yours?" she muttered.

Mood swings? He gave a short, humorless laugh. If she truly understood his current mood she'd be hitting him upside the head with the tray.

"You have to admit you haven't been Miss Sunshine yourself," he countered.

"At least I have a reason for being so surly." She polished off the sandwich and reached for another. "You? Not so much."

With a brooding gaze he watched her work her way through the food. How the hell did such a tiny female consume so much? Weren't humans always concerned with calories and fat content and all that crap?

Not that there was anything wrong with her slender curves, he silently conceded. They were . . . mouthwatering.

Polishing off the plate of French fries, she lifted her head to meet his unwavering gaze with a frown. "Okay, you're freaking me out," she snapped. "What do you want?"

"What makes you think I want anything?"

"You're looking at me like I was a bug you're getting ready to squish."

"A bug?" His lips twisted into a wry smile. "You truly are an innocent if you think that's why I'm staring."

She surged to her feet, clearly sensing his smoldering tension if not the reason behind it. "Just answer the question."

He studied her pale face. He logically understood what he was supposed to do.

Charm her.

Seduce her.

Lure her into revealing what she was hiding.

So, what was the problem?

He might not be as insatiable as most vampires when it came to sex, but he was more than capable of seducing a female.

More than capable.

A teasing smile, a soft confession that he'd been staring at her because she was exquisite. He would gently tuck a strand of satin hair behind her ear and apologize for his rough manners. Perhaps even lead her over to the bed and press one of the ripe strawberries between her lips before urging her back onto the mattress and—

There.

That was the problem.

He couldn't make a game out of seducing her. Not when the mere thought of running his hands over that pale, peach-scented skin was enough to send him up in flames.

Shit. If he wanted the truth, he was going to have to find a less perilous means of acquiring it.

Folding his arms over his chest, he met her wary gaze with a determined expression. If he couldn't finesse her, he'd out-stubborn her.

"Tell me what you know about Gaius."

Predictably she heaved a sigh of resignation. "For god's sake, how many times do we have to go through this?"

"Until I'm convinced you're telling me everything you know."

She threw her hands in the air. "I already have."

"Has he always been able to infect humans with his bite?" Roke closely watched the shock that rippled over her pretty face.

"What did you say?"

He frowned. Her astonishment seemed genuine enough. Of course, she might have prepared herself for the question.

"You heard me."

"He infects humans?" She gave a shake of her head. "I've never heard of a vampire being able to do that."

"Because it's not natural."

"I . . ." She gave another shake of her head. "What does he infect them with? A disease?"

He stepped close enough to tower over her, trying to intimidate her at the same time he was futilely pretending her warmth wasn't seeping into his skin and heating his blood. "You would know better than I."

Waving away his accusation, Sally jerkily turned to pace

the small cell, chewing her bottom lip. "Why haven't you caught him?"

Roke grimaced. She wasn't acting. There was no mistaking the fear that was spiking the air. She didn't know about Gaius's newest trick.

Of course, he was still certain she was hiding something from him.

What better opportunity to discover just what it was?

"A little nervous, are you, witch?" he murmured. "Afraid that Gaius might suspect you came to Styx to tattle on him? Maybe wondering if he'll come hunting for you?"

He'd expected her to be worried by his soft words. That's why he'd chosen them, after all. But he didn't expect her to freak out.

"Do you think he will?" she breathed, the pulse at the base of her throat fluttering in terror. Then, with a panicked sob, she was darting toward the cell door, grasping the bars as if she could pull them apart. "Dammit, you have to let me out of here."

"Calm down," he commanded, taken off guard by her violent response. "Even if he did manage to track you here, there's no way he could get past Styx's security."

"Is that a joke?" She tried to shake the locked door. "He already got past Styx's supposed security."

Roke grimaced. It was true. At least in part. "Fine. Then there's no way he'll get past me."

"Like you would give a shit if he decided to have a little witch snack," she hissed. "You would probably cheer him on."

"He's not going to get you. You're—" He swallowed the word "mine," which had ridiculously formed on the tip of his tongue.

Holy hell, he was obviously losing his mind. This female was a pain in the ass who would make a man miserable even if she weren't a witch. He felt nothing but sympathy for the schmuck who would be stuck with her.

Didn't he?

She glanced over her shoulder. "I'm what?"

With a low growl Roke moved forward, grasping her by her upper arms and shifting her away from the door. "I'll come back for the tray later."

"Are you kidding me?" She desperately grasped his T-shirt, her eyes wide with horror. "You can't keep me locked up. I'm a sitting duck."

He glanced down at her pale face, his hands unconsciously skimming down her arms to lightly encircle her wrists.

Why was she suddenly so frightened of Gaius?

"Think, Sally," he urged in stern tones. "Where would you go where you'd be any safer?"

"I won't stay trapped here," she snarled. "I won't."

Roke parted his lips, but before he could demand to know just what was making her act like a crazed woman, he felt a sudden heat explode inside him, scorching through his veins with an incandescent force.

Oh . . . hell.

He'd known the witch was going to be trouble.

He'd known it on a cellular level.

And now she was killing him.

Nothing else could explain the sensation of his body being shattered into a thousand pieces as a light as fierce as the midday sun burst in the center of his being, transforming him even as it catapulted him toward the eternal sleep.

Magic.

A sweet, drugging magic that allowed him to smile with delight as a tidal wave of darkness crashed over him.

Sally watched in astonishment as Roke dropped to the floor with enough force to make his head bounce against the cement.

"Crap on toast, what have I done?" She fell to her knees at his side, her hand reaching to lightly touch his face.

It had been sheer panic that had released her secret magic. Certainly she hadn't deliberately tried to enchant this vampire, not when she was convinced that he was too strong to be swayed by her meager powers.

That was why she was so angry that he'd replaced the fairy. She'd had high hopes of swaying Lysander into setting her free.

But the fear of being trapped here while Gaius, and whatever strange creature was controlling him, came hunting for her, had tipped her over some mysterious edge.

She wouldn't become a helpless victim.

Not again.

Now, she was not only trapped in a cell, but Roke was going to be furious when he came around.

And worse, she'd revealed that she was more than just a human witch.

Dammit.

Her karma was clearly in need of a good cleansing.

Almost on cue, Roke's thick fringe of lashes lifted to reveal the astonishing eyes that were even more pale than usual, the black rim a startling contrast.

"What the . . ." His angry words cut off as he caught sight of Sally bending over him, his expression melting from confused fury to blind adoration. "Sally?"

Oh lord.

Was it possible?

Had she actually managed to enchant the mighty vampire?

The thought she had succeeded was almost as terrifying as having failed.

"How do you feel?" she cautiously inquired.

"Good." A slow smile curved his lips. "No."

She tried to swallow past the lump in her throat. Even consumed by fear, she was nearly blinded by his stark male beauty. The lean, bronzed face with the high cheekbones and chiseled lips. The wide brow and proud nose. The dark hair that held the sheen of silk in the overhead light.

He looked too perfect to be real.

At last realizing that she was gawking at him like an idiot, she forced herself to clear her throat. "No, you don't feel good?" she managed to rasp.

"I feel captivated." Without warning his hands lifted to frame her face, his eyes darkening with an unmistakable hunger. "Come here, my little witch."

Before she could react, Sally found herself being tugged downward. Instinctively her lips parted to protest, but the words were lost as Roke claimed her mouth in a kiss of unrelenting possession.

Holy shit.

As their lips met, her heart came to a shuddering halt. *It was like being hit with lightning*, she fuzzily acknowledged, forgetting to breathe as the shocking pleasure sizzled through her.

His tongue traced the line of her lower lip, his fingers plunging into her hair as he angled her head to the side.

"Roke," she muttered, shivering as his mouth shifted to allow his fangs to scrape along the slender curve of her neck.

"I've wanted to taste you from the moment I caught sight of you," he growled, his lips tormenting the pulse at the base of her neck, which was racing out of control. "This skin . . . as fine as ivory. And your scent of peaches." His fingers tightened in her hair. "It's driving me mad."

They were both mad, Sally accepted as she sighed in approval. Or maybe the spell she'd woven around him had somehow caught her in its web.

In this moment, she didn't care. She was completely lost in the blissful sensations. How had she ever called this man cold-blooded? His touch was igniting sparks of heat that threatened to consume her.

It was only the press of his fangs against her flesh that jerked her back to her senses.

"Oh . . . my god . . . no. Wait," she hissed, pressing her hands against his chest. "No biting."

"Why not?" he asked softly, his tongue running a path up her throat. "I hunger to taste you."

Tantalizing pleasure swept through her. "Mmm, yes . . . I mean no." With a sharp push, she was breaking free of his hypnotizing touch, sitting back on her heels as she pressed a hand to her throat. "I . . ."

"You?"

"I need my strength," she said, more to remind herself than to halt Roke. For god's sake, she was supposed to be escaping from this prison, not drowning in a sensual hunger for the man holding her captive.

Roke folded his hands beneath his head, regarding her with a sinful smile. "I like the sound of that."

She licked her lips, which still tingled from his skillful kiss. "I mean, I need my strength so we can escape."

"Escape?" He slowly sat upright, running a hungry glance down her body. "The only place we're going is to my private rooms. The faster the better."

He reached for her, but this time Sally was prepared. Scrambling to her feet, she retreated until her back hit the far wall.

Concentrate, Sally, she warned herself. *Concentrate or die.*

"Roke, please, you must listen to me."

Regret rippled over his lean face as he rose to his feet, roughly shoving back the thick strands of his hair. "Forgive me, my sweet. I'm not usually so lacking in control." He shook his head, his expression bemused. "You have bewitched me."

"Yeah, I got that," she breathed, guilt piercing her heart.

This proud warrior was going to hate her when he came to his senses and discovered what she'd done. She didn't doubt that he would rather die than feel emotions for a skanky witch.

Of course, he already hated her, she reminded herself. So what did it matter?

Pretending that it didn't, she made herself hold her ground as he cautiously approached, as if she were a wild animal he didn't want to startle. Then, cupping her face in a tender hand, he rubbed a thumb over her cheek.

"We can take this as slow as you need," he promised. "Just so long as we're together."

It was a spell. The warmth in his eyes. The gentleness of his touch. She knew that better than anyone. So why did it feel so real?

Crap. She thrust away the ridiculous thought, forcing herself to concentrate on the only thing that mattered.

Getting the hell out of this cell.

"Yes, but we both know that Styx won't allow that," she reminded him. "He thinks I'm the enemy."

"No," he denied. "Not the enemy."

"Then why am I being held in this cell?"

A muscle clenched in his jaw. "I will speak with him. . . ."

"No, please, Roke." She lifted her hands to clutch at his shoulders, her expression openly pleading. "We have to leave here."

He frowned as her magical compulsion clashed with his loyalty to his Anasso. "Leave?"

"It's the only way we can be together."

Several tense minutes passed before he at last gave a grudging nod of his head. "Yes."

She released a shaky sigh of relief. "Can you get us out of the dungeons?"

He frowned. "That's no problem, but we'll never be able to leave the lair without alerting Styx's guards."

"Once we're away from this cell I'll be able to use my magic," she assured him.

There was another pause, then abruptly taking hold of her hand, he pulled her toward the cell door.

"Stay close."

Chapter 11

North of the Louisiana wetlands

Nefri hid a grimace as they skirted past the small town. The violence that had tainted the air was slowly fading and the residents were gratefully settling in for a peaceful night.

Unfortunately, the promise of serenity did nothing to end the cold prickles of displeasure that radiated from her companion.

Santiago was in a crappy mood and he wanted to make sure he shared the misery.

Not that she was blameless, she ruefully acknowledged.

She'd been so intent on scurrying back behind her defensive walls that she'd totally forgotten the potency of male pride.

Santiago wouldn't consider the idea that her rigid composure might be her way of coping with the overwhelming night of passion. Or that she might not be comfortable with the realization that she'd made herself vulnerable to him in a way she hadn't for centuries.

Of course not.

He was used to females who fawned and fluttered over him. The kind of women who stroked his ego with assurances that he was a magnificent lover and no doubt begged for the opportunity to remain in his bed.

That knowledge did nothing for her own mood and it was a relief when there was a flutter of wings and Levet floated down from a nearby tree branch.

"At last," the tiny gargoyle complained. "I had begun to fear that you had forgotten me."

"I couldn't be so lucky," Santiago snarled, stepping past Levet to head toward the truck nearly hidden by the thick brush.

Levet sniffed, moving to walk at Nefri's side. "What crawled up his ear?"

"My ass, gargoyle," Santiago corrected, tugging open the door of the vehicle, which looked as if it should be headed for the junkyard. ASAP. "It's 'what crawled up my ass.'"

"Ew." Levet wrinkled his snout. "I do not wish to know anything concerning your nether regions."

Santiago narrowed his eyes, his beautiful features tight with irritation. "Just get in and shut up."

Nefri reached to pat the gargoyle on the head, her gaze never wavering from the cranky male. "Ignore him."

Levet gave a flick of his tail. "He's rather large to ignore."

A humorless smile curved Santiago's lips. "Nefri can give you lessons. She's made an art form of ignoring what she doesn't want to have to deal with." He waited until she reached the truck, his finger lifting to stroke down her cheek. "Haven't you, *cara?*"

She refused to flinch from his glare. Maybe she had been too swift to protect herself from the emotions Santiago threatened to expose. And clearly she could have been more sensitive to his male ego.

But now was hardly the time to be bickering.

"Are we going or not?" she demanded in cool tones.

"Oh, we're going."

"Yes, well." Levet cleared his throat. "Perhaps I should—"

"Don't even think about it," Santiago snapped, grabbing the gargoyle by one horn and tossing him into the truck.

"Mon dieu," Levet squeaked as he landed on the leather seat.

Rolling her eyes, Nefri rounded the back of the truck to slide into the passenger side, in a cowardly way pleased to have the gargoyle between her and Santiago.

Not that she believed he would ever try to harm her. Santiago was by nature a protector and no matter how she might infuriate him, he would never strike out. Besides, she had enough power to protect herself from any enemy.

No, she simply didn't want to spend the next few hours rehashing her impulsive decision to share Santiago's bed only to panic when she awoke in his arms.

It would mean exposing her scars from a past she simply wanted to forget.

With a low curse, Santiago climbed behind the steering wheel and used his powers to start the engine. Then, with a last glare at Nefri, he shoved the truck into gear and sent them jolting down the narrow road.

Once they reached the highway, Santiago pressed the accelerator to the floorboard, urging the truck into breakneck speed.

Thankful for her immortality, Nefri watched the landscape flash by, catching only blurred glimpses of tangled wetlands that eventually gave way to small farms, with the occasional town huddled in the soft glow of streetlights.

They had traveled nearly an hour in uncomfortable silence when Nefri's brooding thoughts were interrupted by the strange sensations that suddenly filled the air.

"Santiago."

Even as his name fell from her lips, Santiago was slowing the truck and turning onto a service road. "I feel it," he muttered, his gaze trained on the trees that lined the recently plowed fields.

"What?" Levet stood on the seat, his expression troubled. "What is going on?"

Nefri shivered, rolling down her window to test the chill breeze.

There was the same pulse of emotion that surrounded Gaius's lair. An unnatural coercion that could easily manipulate the feelings of both human and demon.

But this wasn't violence that brushed over her skin and tugged at her emotions.

This was . . . fear.

A drenching, unrelenting fear.

"It's not the same," she muttered.

"No," Santiago agreed, turning the truck onto an even smaller path, downshifting as they were forced to dodge fallen tree trunks and potholes large enough to swallow them whole. "But it's close enough we have to track it down."

"Yes," she agreed, clenching her teeth as he cut through an overgrown meadow to halt near an abandoned schoolhouse.

They crawled out of the truck, all three of them studying the three-story brick building with a rusting tin roof. The cement steps were crumbling and most of the windows had been smashed, while the double front doors hung at drunken angles.

The surrounding playground had long ago conceded defeat to the encroaching weeds, although someone had cut a path around the swing set and metal slide. No doubt the same someone who'd built the smoldering bonfire and brought the keg of beer.

Allowing her powers to flow through the thick air, Nefri swiftly sensed the human hiding in the building. She lifted one finger and Santiago nodded.

"I'll circle around and come in from the rear," he said, pulling loose the sword he kept strapped to his back.

She instinctively reached to touch his arm, an uninvited concern clenching her heart. "Whoever is inside is close to breaking," she murmured, able to feel the human's rising hysteria. "Be careful."

With a cocky smile Santiago melted into the darkness, moving with the fluid speed of a trained warrior. Nefri shook her head in annoyance. Why was she worried about him? Not only was he more than capable of taking care of himself, but she'd already decided that she was going to consider him as nothing more than a necessary tool to achieve her goals.

Hadn't she?

Refusing to admit that she was finding the task of cutting her connection to the aggravating male more difficult than it should be, Nefri turned to glance down at the gargoyle at her side. "Levet, could you keep watch?" she asked. "This might be a trap."

"Oui." Levet studied the surrounding trees before glancing back to the schoolhouse. "I'll be on the roof. It should give me the best vantage point."

"Contact me if anything approaches."

"Oui."

Confident that nothing could sneak past the gargoyle, Nefri crossed the playground to climb the stairs and enter the building.

She paused in the small vestibule. Ahead of her a set of stairs led to the upper floors, the stones worn in the middle by the thousands of small feet that had climbed them over the years. To the side of the stairs, a narrow hall led to the inner classrooms, which reeked of rotting wood and mold.

And fear.

Bone-deep, soul-crushing fear.

With a shiver, she moved down the hallway, following the overwhelming sensations.

"Santiago?"

"I found her," he said, his voice low and soothing.

Nefri stepped into the dark room, her gaze skimming the

overturned desks and decaying books that were scattered upon the warped planks of the floor.

Weaving her way through the debris, she found Santiago seated beneath a cracked chalkboard, a young human female shivering in his lap.

"Oh." Nefri studied the girl, who appeared no more than sixteen in human years. She was nearly naked with only a tiny thong to cover her thin body. Her long blond hair was tangled and her face coated with dust and tears. But, it was the unmistakable wounds on her neck that caught Nefri's attention. The girl had been bitten by a vampire. "The poor creature," she murmured.

Santiago glanced up as she approached. "Can you watch her?"

"Why?"

"I need to make sure there are no hidden surprises."

"I should do that," she countered. "You remain with the girl."

His brows snapped together. "Nefri."

"I won't take any risks, I promise." She interrupted the inevitable argument, knowing this wasn't about who had the most power, but his primitive need to protect her. "Only I can break through illusions. Besides, the human has attached herself to you. She's likely to panic if you leave her now."

His jaw tightened, but he gave a reluctant nod. "You're right," he admitted. "I'll try to question the female."

She lowered her gaze to the girl, who was clinging to Santiago like a barnacle, her soft whimpers muffled against his chest.

"Can you reach her? She appears . . . broken."

He ran a gentle hand over the girl's hair. "You have your talents and I have mine."

Nefri didn't doubt him for a minute.

For all of Santiago's swagger, there was something unquestionably comforting about his presence. *A safe harbor a woman could depend on . . .*

She took an abrupt step backward as the dangerous words whispered through her heart. "I won't be long," she muttered, turning to hurry from the room.

Speaking the words of power that would break any lingering illusions, Nefri moved through the remaining classrooms before heading upstairs. She concentrated on the gaping holes in the floors as well as the steel lockers that threatened to topple above the unwary. Anything to avoid examining her unruly emotions.

Santiago was right about one thing.

She'd become a master at sticking her head in the sand.

The ultimate ostrich.

It took only a few minutes to make her way through the upper rooms, but slipping out a broken window, she stood on the fire escape and motioned toward the gargoyle, who was on the highest peak of the sharply angled roof. "Anything?" she asked.

"Non." Levet's wings fluttered, shimmering in colors of blue and crimson and gold in the chilled moonlight. "Nothing is stirring, not even a mouse."

She paused at his odd words before giving a slow nod. He wasn't exaggerating. The surrounding countryside should be alive with nocturnal animals foraging for food and the predators that hunted them.

Instead an echoing silence spoke of a complete lack of wildlife.

There wasn't even the buzz of an insect.

The spreading fear had affected even the most basic of animal forms.

"There's a girl inside we must question," she at last said. "Can you remain on guard?"

Despite the gargoyle's unease, he gave a ready nod, his courage astonishing for such a small creature. *"Oui.* You can depend upon me."

Without conscious thought she reached to brush a light

hand over the tip of his wing. It was only when she was climbing back through the window that she realized how natural it felt to make physical contact.

Something she hadn't allowed herself for centuries.

Obviously being in this world was altering more than just her powers.

Affection, desire, concern . . .

What was next?

Love?

With a shake of her head, Nefri made her way back to the lower floor. How often did she have to warn herself that now was not the time to be distracted by such foolishness?

In fact, *never* seemed like a good time.

Smoothing her expression into a calm mask, she entered the classroom and crossed to where Santiago remained seated on the floor with the human cradled in his lap. "The building is clear," she assured him.

"This is Melinda." He lifted his head to send her a speaking glance as the girl trembled in his arms. Nefri halted, belatedly realizing her presence was adding to the girl's distress. "Sssh, *mija,*" Santiago murmured, running a comforting hand over her tangled hair. "No one is going to hurt you."

Nefri slowly bent down to sit on the floor. Towering over the child wasn't going to help. "Does she know what happened to her?"

"We were just getting to that, weren't we, Melinda?" His attention returned to the female, who gave a violent shake of her head.

"I don't want to talk about it."

"I know it was horrible for you," he sympathized in soothing tones.

"It was worse than horrible."

"Let's return to the beginning," Santiago urged. "Can you do that for me?"

Melinda shuddered, but clearly as susceptible as every other female to Santiago's potent charm, she sucked in a deep breath. "I'll try."

"Good girl. How long have you been here?"

Her brow wrinkled in genuine confusion. "I'm not sure. A day, maybe two. Does it matter?"

"No. Everything's fine." He tilted back her chin, studying her pale, tearstained face. "Why were you at this place?"

Nefri watched the girl struggle to swallow, the sound of her pounding heart thundering through the room.

"It was a party. A birthday party for Brian," she at last managed to rasp. "We always come here because the police never drive out this far."

"How many?"

"We started with a couple dozen or so, but once the keg ran dry a lot of people began returning to town." Her bottom lip stuck out, reminding Nefri of just how young she truly was. Barely more than a baby. "There was some stupid dance at the high school."

"But you stayed?" Santiago asked.

"Yes." She gave a slow nod. "I've waited forever for Robert to notice me and he . . ."

"Go on," Santiago urged.

The girl burrowed her face in Santiago's shoulder. "It's embarrassing."

"You can tell me," Santiago said, threading his words with a trace of compulsion.

Nefri lifted her brows at his delicate touch. It was rare for a vampire to be able to influence a human without seizing complete control of their minds and destroying their free will. At the same time he was able to soothe her hysterics despite the fear that continued to pulse in the air.

Amazing.

With a tentative motion, Melinda pulled her head back to

meet Santiago's dark gaze. "There were six of us left and we started kissing and stuff," she admitted in a husky voice.

"And?" he prodded.

"Santiago," Nefri softly protested.

He lifted a silencing hand, his gaze never straying from the humiliated girl. "Melinda, tell me."

She hunched a defensive shoulder. "I think someone must have spiked our drinks because one minute I was making out with Robert and the next we were all on the ground . . ." Her head dropped, a blush staining her pale cheeks. "You know . . . together."

"And that's something you don't usually enjoy?" Santiago asked.

"Of course not." She tilted back her head. "I'm not a slut no matter what Vicky Spearman might say."

"So you just couldn't stop yourself?"

"No. We were all out of control."

Santiago shot Nefri a glance and she gave a slow nod. The girl was incapable of lying under Santiago's compulsion, which meant that she was truly horrified by her participation in group sex.

Lust . . .

As powerful an emotion as violence and fear.

Santiago shifted his gaze back to Melinda. "Then what happened?"

She trembled. "The air was suddenly freezing and when I opened my eyes I realized there was a stranger standing over us."

"Describe him."

"Not super tall, thin with dark hair." She licked her lips, her heartbeat quickening. "Weird eyes."

"Weird?"

"It was like he was looking at us, but he wasn't really seeing us," the girl explained. "I thought at first he must be some crazy crackhead who wanted to be closer to the fire."

"Was he alone?"

"Yes."

Nefri leaned forward. Gaius was alone? Surely the girl had to be mistaken. "You're certain?"

Melinda never allowed her gaze to stray from Santiago. "I didn't see anyone else, I swear."

"I believe you," Santiago assured her. "What did the stranger do?"

She paused, as if struggling to remember. "At first he just stood there, but then Brian jumped up and tried to take a swing at him." She made a sound of distress. "The man laughed and grabbed Brian by the throat and . . ."

"Ssh. You're safe, *mija*." Santiago's voice eased the rising panic, as soft and beguiling as dark velvet. "Go on."

"He bit him." Melinda lifted a hand to her own neck, touching the wounds that still leaked a trickle of blood. "Like he was an animal or something."

"What did you do?"

"I wanted to run, but I was so freaked out I couldn't move. None of us could."

Had Gaius been able to shift the humans' emotions from lust to fear? Or had the mysterious spirit been hidden nearby?

"Did the stranger hurt your friends?" Santiago continued.

"Yes." Melinda bit her lower lip, tears filling her eyes. "I think . . . I think they're dead."

"And what did he do to you?"

"All I remember is being lifted off my feet and a pain." She pulled her fingers away from the wound, frowning as she noticed the blood staining her skin. "I woke up alone here."

Chapter 12

Santiago brushed the tears from the girl's cheeks, accepting that she'd revealed everything she knew of her encounter with Gaius.

"Melinda, I need to speak with my"—he glanced up to meet Nefri's steady gaze—"companion."

"No." The girl dug her fingers into his chest, her eyes wide with terror. "Please don't leave me alone."

"We'll be just outside the door," he promised, genuine sympathy stabbing his heart.

The girl might physically recover, but mentally . . .

Just one more reason to track down Gaius and gut him like a pig.

"He'll come back and get me if I'm left alone," Melinda sobbed.

"He's long gone, *mija*." He ran his hand down her cheek, using his powers to try and comfort her. "I promise you."

Beyond even his talents, Melinda quivered in fear. "Take me with you."

"Melinda. Melinda, look at me." Cupping her chin, he forced her to meet his gaze. "I want you to relax."

She blinked, struggling against the compulsion in his voice. "Please . . . I . . ."

"You're tired."

Her face went slack. "Tired."

"You need to sleep."

"I'm so scared."

"Close your eyes, Melinda." His voice hardened to a direct command. "You're safe."

"Yes." Her lashes lowered.

"Now sleep, *mija,*" he whispered next to her ear. "Sleep."

Waiting until her body was limp and her breathing was steady, Santiago laid her on the floor. Then, grabbing the sword he'd set aside when he'd found the girl hiding in the corner, he rose to his feet.

With a nod of his head toward the door, he led Nefri out of the classroom into the narrow hall.

"Talented, indeed," Nefri murmured. "How long will she be out?"

"Long enough," he said, annoyed by his flare of pleasure at her words of admiration. Dammit, he was still sulking. "I'll call Styx to have the local clan chief take her to a safe house until one of the Ravens can collect her."

She arched a dark brow. "The Oracles might want to have the first right to question her."

"I'll let Styx and the Commission hash out jurisdiction." He slid the sword into the scabbard angled across his back. "I have no interest in politics."

Some elusive emotion flickered through her eyes.

Relief?

But why?

Because he had no political ambition?

Yeah, right.

"I'll ask Levet to keep watch on her until the clan chief arrives," she offered before glancing around the rapidly decaying building. "Not that anyone would willingly come here. Even the animals have fled."

"Yes. Fear." He grimaced at the thick emotion that poured

off poor Melinda and filled the air. "It's as potent as the violence was in the swamps. And no doubt as potent as the lust that swayed Melinda and her friends into their first orgy. Do you see a pattern?"

"Emotions," she readily admitted.

Of course she would have connected the dots, he wryly acknowledged.

Her intelligence was as lethal as her powers.

"Strong, primitive emotions." He narrowed his gaze. "Why?"

"I don't know."

"Mierda." He rammed his hand into the pocket of his jeans, pulling out his cell phone. "Why do I bother?"

"Santiago." Her fingers landed lightly on his arm. "Wait."

"What is it now?" he growled, not giving a damn how rude he sounded. She'd slammed the door in his face for the last time. She wanted all business between them? Fine. They would be all business.

"I'll tell you what I do know," she said softly.

He froze, frowning at her with open suspicion. "Why?"

She blinked, clearly having expected him to jump for joy at her grudging offer. "I beg your pardon?"

"Why are you suddenly willing to share?"

She hesitated, then, stepping back, she wrapped her arms around her waist in an oddly protective gesture.

As if she was feeling . . . vulnerable.

"Because you were right."

He was right?

Was the sky falling?

"I need you to say that again," he said slowly.

"You were right," she repeated. "It's not fair to ask you to assist me in hunting Gaius without fully understanding the danger."

Hmmm. He wasn't sure he trusted her abrupt change of

heart, but he'd never been a vampire to look a gift epiphany in the mouth. "I'm listening."

"I'm sure you've heard rumors about the creation of the Veil?"

Santiago snorted at the ridiculous question. Like every vampire, he'd heard the fairy tales surrounding the Veil.

"The one where it's a rift in time and space that sucked you and your people through?" he asked. "Or the one where you ascended godlike to a higher plane of existence?"

She grimaced. "The Commission circulated a dozen different stories after they created the Veil."

So the Oracles had been responsible for the wild tales. Interesting. "Why?"

"So no one would guess their true purpose."

"And that was?"

"To trap a creature on the other side."

Santiago took a minute to consider her startling confession. Of all the stories that had circulated over the centuries, he'd never heard even a whisper that the Veil was some sort of cosmic prison.

"What creature?"

"I'm not entirely sure."

He snorted. Did she think he was stupid?

"How can you not know?"

She paused—not like she was going to refuse to answer, but as if she was carefully considering her words. "From what I was told, it's more a spirit than an actual creature."

He frowned. Spirit was a broad term. It could mean anything from a genuine ghost to a hundred different species that had no corporeal form in this dimension.

"So what made this spirit so dangerous that they would cage it behind a magical curtain?"

"They didn't share that information with me."

He studied her pale, perfect face. He couldn't sense a lie,

but that didn't mean anything. This female was a master at disguising her true emotions.

"You agreed to live in the same prison as a spirit that was so dangerous the Oracles had to create a rip in space to protect the world from it and you didn't even ask what it could do to you?" he drawled in disbelief.

She shrugged, her gaze steady and her expression unreadable. "The spirit had been in hibernation for centuries and most assumed that it would never awaken," she said. "I was merely there to be an early warning if it began to stir."

"How were you supposed to know it was"—he deliberately paused—"stirring?"

She shrugged. "The Oracles claimed that the peace my people sought would be disturbed."

"That's it?"

"Yes."

So, the Oracles create a rift to protect the world from some mysterious evil. Then, instead of letting sleeping evil spirits rest in solitude, they eventually sent Nefri and her clan to the other side.

There was something missing. Hell, there was a whole lot missing.

"Why you?" he abruptly demanded.

Nefri clenched her hands. Was this vampire never satisfied?

She'd revealed far more than she should have. Certainly enough to get her in trouble with the Commission.

Never a good thing.

But was he satisfied?

No.

He had to poke and prod and—

"Nefri," he repeated, his expression predictably stubborn.

She absently toyed with a lock of hair that had fallen on

her cheek and sternly reminded herself that Santiago was risking his life to assist her in finding Gaius.

He deserved the truth.

The *whole* truth.

"The Commission was aware that I sought asylum for myself and my clan."

He stepped forward, gently brushing her fingers aside so he could tuck the lock of hair behind her ear. "Asylum from what?"

Her lashes lowered to hide her eyes. "It's a long and boring story."

"It might be long, but I seriously doubt that it's boring," he said dryly. "Tell me."

A tiny shiver of pleasure raced through her body. "As you've so kindly pointed out, I'm ancient even by vampire standards."

"You can't make me believe you're sensitive about your age, *cara*," he protested, his fingers tracing the line of her cheek before moving to outline her lips. "Not when the years have given you the regal beauty of a queen and the powers of a goddess."

She pulled away from his touch. How could she concentrate when his lightest caress was sending distracting jolts of arousal through her body?

"Very pretty, but not entirely accurate."

A knowing smile curved his lips at her revealing retreat.

Aggravating vampire.

"No?"

"My powers haven't come with age," she corrected him. "They were a part of me from the night I was made into a vampire."

His smile disappeared as his eyes darkened with astonishment.

Not surprising.

Most vampires gained their powers in a slow evolution

over their foundling years. Some gained more than others, but it was a fairly predictable progression.

She, on the other hand, had been blessed with a profound excess of power from the night she'd been "turned."

At least she was told she'd been blessed.

It had felt more like a curse.

"Dios," he murmured. "That must have been a shock to your sire. Always assuming he stayed around."

It had happened so long ago Nefri barely recalled awakening alone and naked on the banks of the Euphrates River. She had a vague memory of roaming alone and disoriented, unable to recall her former life, before a man had appeared in the cave where she was hiding and carried her away.

At the time she'd been relieved to have someone explain what and who she was. But that relief hadn't lasted long.

"He returned for me once he realized I could be of use."

Santiago's features hardened. "I can imagine."

"Yes, I'm fairly certain you can," she said softly, struck by a sudden revelation that he was one of the few who truly could understand.

Was that why she felt so drawn to him? Because they shared similar scars from their past?

Well, that and the fact that he was insanely gorgeous, sexy, powerful, and fiercely loyal.

"Nefri?" he prompted, frowning in confusion.

"I wasn't placed in the pits," she said, turning to glance down the shadowed hallway. More to hide her expression than to make sure they were alone. Although the fear swirling through the air was muted as Melinda remained in a deep sleep, it was still potent enough to prevent any unwelcome trespassers. "But I was trained to become a weapon for my clan chief."

"You defended the clan?" he easily guessed.

She nodded. "When we were being attacked, but more often I was used in our battles to conquer other clans."

Santiago muttered in sympathy as he cupped her face in his hands, gently urging her head back to meet his searching gaze. In that moment, Nefri's earlier speculations of why she found this man so fascinating were instantly dismissed.

Yes, he was gorgeous and sexy and loyal. And yes, they both had suffered.

But it was his swift empathy that truly touched her heart.

What other vampire would so easily understand that far from taking pride in her battle prowess, she was horrified by what she'd done?

"You were forced to kill?"

Disjointed memories of bloody battles and mangled corpses flared through her mind, making her wince. "More times than I can count."

His fingers skimmed down her throat, his touch offering a blessed comfort. "It's no wonder you're so desperate for peace."

She knew she should push away his hand. His ability to offer her a sense of safety was as dangerously alluring as his potent sensuality.

Instead, she leaned into his lingering touch.

Foolish.

So very foolish.

"That wasn't even the worst," she said, the ancient pain a dull throb that never truly went away.

He scowled. "You don't have to go on."

"No, please." She stiffened her spine. She knew herself all too well. If he allowed her to scurry behind her defensive walls, then she'd never crawl back out. "Let me finish."

He gave a slow dip of his head. "Okay."

"The fighting was something I learned to endure, simply because I had no choice."

"Survival can be a bitch," he said. He, of course, understood exactly what she meant.

"Yes."

His thumb rubbed the sensitive hollow just below her ear. "What was your breaking point?"

"When my chief started hiring me out as a weapon for other clans."

"He pimped you out?" He made a sound of disgust, although it hadn't been unusual in the past for the chiefs to use their people for profit, whether it was as soldiers, whores, or just for sport.

"I was always available to the highest bidder," she said. "No matter what they wanted me to do."

He shook his head, his thumb stroking the line of her tightly clenched jaw. "It wasn't your fault, *cara*," he murmured. "You were at the mercy of a man consumed by greed and ambition."

"It didn't matter if it was my fault or not. The outcome was the same."

Accepting he wasn't going to be able to convince her that she was blameless, he studied her with a brooding gaze. "What did you do?"

"I bided my time and when I felt prepared I entered the battles of Durotriges to become a clan chief." She didn't have to say that she'd nearly died during her trials, or that she'd been forever altered by staring death in the face over and over. Only a small percentage of vampires went into the battles and came out the other side. It was accepted that they would gain a greater appreciation for life. Their own and others. Which made them particularly suited to becoming a clan chief. "I wasn't ever going to be a weapon for anyone again."

"And never out of control again, eh, *querida?*"

She nodded. Being stronger than every creature around her had taught her the danger of giving in to her emotions.

"When I become angry or frightened the people around me end up dead." She shivered. "Sometimes a lot of people."

The dark gaze swept over her upturned face. "And so you created a clan dedicated to peace?"

"Yes." She smiled wryly. It had seemed so simple. She knew there had to be like-minded vampires who wanted to build an oasis of peace. The only rub was finding someplace where they could be safe from the demons who would take their desire for tranquility as a sign of weakness. They had to be protected. "And I went to the Commission to discover if there was a place where we could be separated from the violence of this world."

"That's when they sent you beyond the Veil?"

She lifted her hand, her fingers brushing over the golden medallion that remained warm to the touch no matter what the temperature. "With the assistance of this."

Without warning Santiago's low growl trickled through the hallway, his dark eyes flashing with fury.

"*Dios,* the bastards knowingly put you in danger."

She shrugged. "They didn't lie to me. I went beyond the Veil knowing the creature was there."

"Only because you were so anxious to keep your people safe," he snapped. "And they used that desperation to lure you into taking care of their problem."

"The Commission rarely does anything out of the goodness of their hearts," she reminded him. "Besides, the past no longer matters."

Chapter 13

Santiago's power trembled with the need to explode. He wasn't entirely sure why he was so pissed off.

As Nefri said, the Commission wasn't a collection of do-gooders. They were ruthless leaders who would readily sacrifice an entire clan of vampires if they thought it necessary to protect the world.

But the thought that Nefri had been forced to choose between keeping her people safe and living on top of a potential time bomb . . . yeah, it pissed him off.

"The hell it doesn't matter," he muttered, lowering his head to capture her lips in a kiss of seething frustration. "But we can finish this discussion later." As he pulled back, he met her puzzled gaze. "What?"

"I thought you were angry with me."

"I have a habit of being an ass when I don't get my way," he readily admitted. He was hot tempered, but he was always willing to confess when he was in the wrong. He'd known there was a reason why she struggled so hard to keep him at a distance, but his pride had been pricked by her cold dismissal. Now he offered a rueful grin. "You'll get used to me."

"Will I?"

He swooped back down to steal another kiss. "Mmmm."

Her hands lifted to lie against his chest and for one tantalizing moment Nefri allowed her lips to part, conceding to the scorching heat that blazed between them.

Then all too soon her hands were pressing him away. "Santiago."

He nipped at her chin in punishment. "Is this important?"

She shivered in pleasure. "You need to call Styx so we can continue our search for Gaius."

His tongue traced the full line of her lower lip. "Soon."

"Santiago." She gave a tiny moan before shoving hard enough to break his clinging grip. "We don't have time for this."

He shut his eyes, shuddering at his swift arousal. *Mierda.* What was it about this female that made him behave like a damned Were in heat?

"Unfortunately, you're right," he conceded in thick tones, opening his eyes to meet her wary gaze. "But I still have a few questions."

"Very well."

"How did the spirit escape?"

"Siljar claimed that when the Dark Lord was destroyed it left a void in Gaius's medallion that the spirit used to enter this world."

He took a minute to consider her words, at the same time sending out his power to make sure that Melinda remained in her deep sleep. The last thing they needed was the girl waking up in a panic.

"As good an explanation as any, I suppose."

"They sent me to discover if it was the right explanation." Nefri shrugged. "Is that all?"

He snorted. All? *Dios.* He had a thousand questions. Unfortunately they would have to wait. Instead, he forced himself to concentrate on the most pressing problems.

"I would be a lot happier if I knew precisely what this creature is capable of," he growled.

"You know as much as I do."

"Which is what?" He gave a frustrated shake of his head. He'd fought more enemies than he could count over the years, but while many had been immortal, they'd at least been creatures he could make bleed. This . . . thing was something he didn't know how to fight. It made him twitchy. "It's obvious the spirit is capable of stirring emotions."

Nefri slowly shook her head. "Actually, it seems more likely that Gaius is the cause of the overwhelming emotions," she said. "Or at least his bite is."

True.

Which only made the crazy situation . . . crazier.

"So this creature infects vampires?"

She lifted her hands in a gesture of genuine bafflement. "It's impossible to say until we manage to find them."

"Dammit." He pulled out his phone. "You warn the gargoyle he'll need to stay while I call Styx."

"And you claim that I'm bossy?"

He frowned. "Do you have a better suggestion?"

"No," she denied, her expression one of cool challenge. "I just wished to point out that people in glass houses shouldn't—"

With a quick motion that caught her off guard, he wrapped an arm around her waist and yanked her against his body. "Shouldn't do this?" He leaned down to press his lips to the tender curve of her neck. "Or this?" He nibbled down to the edge of her sweater, savoring the intoxicating scent of jasmine. "Or maybe this?" His tongue traced a throbbing vein back up her throat.

"Enough," she protested, her voice unsteady as her cheeks flushed with arousal.

"Not nearly," he muttered, but with a stab of regret, he released her.

The spirit had to be found before it could ignite the humans into mass genocide.

But once it had been destroyed, along with Gaius, then . . .

Then he was going to lock this woman in his private rooms and throw away the key.

Styx's lair in Chicago

Sally was as miserable as a witch could be.

Roke had done his part. With the natural command of a clan chief he'd managed to convince the guards that Styx wanted to see her in his study. Then, avoiding the plethora of demons, servants, and video cameras, he'd halted only long enough to slip on a leather motorcycle jacket he'd left just outside the dungeon doors, before leading her to a forgotten pantry near the kitchens.

It wasn't until then that she had discovered that her magic refused to work.

She told herself it had to be some sort of dampening spell despite the lack of hex markings. If Styx had it in the dungeons, why wouldn't he have it in the rest of the house? It made perfect sense.

But, deep inside she feared the interference wasn't going to go away even when they were beyond the lair.

She'd never tried to use witch magic when she was using her natural talents.

Crap, crap, crap.

Absently rubbing the sleeve of her sweatshirt where it covered her inner forearm, she once again struggled to conjure a spell of illusion. It should be easy. It was a spell she'd performed a thousand times.

But there was nothing. Nada. Jack-squat.

Her magic was MIA.

And it was driving her crazy.

Almost as crazy as her arm. Why the hell was it itchy?

"How much longer is this going to take?"

With a tiny jolt, she realized that Roke had shifted to stand directly before her, his expression one of tender concern.

"I don't know," she muttered, ignoring her stupid stab of guilt. This vampire had held her prisoner, she reminded herself for the hundredth time. Why shouldn't she do everything in her power to escape? Her sudden inability to conjure a simple spell of illusion had nothing to do with karma. "My magic . . ."

His eyes shimmered with a startlingly pale light in the darkness. "What is it?"

"It's still muted." She dropped her head, afraid the lie might be written on her face. "There must be something dampening my powers."

"Well, Styx is nothing if not thorough." He thankfully accepted her explanation, brushing a hand down her back in unspoken sympathy. "But, we can't stay here."

She bit her lip, afraid of leaving the pantry without her magic protecting them. "What are we going to do?"

"We have to get out of here before the guards realize that you aren't meeting with the Anasso."

"Yeah, I got that, but—" Her words broke off as her companion turned toward the shelves of canned food, holding out his hands as he walked from one end of the pantry to another. "Roke?"

"Sssh," he replied, distracted.

She watched in baffled silence as he continued his pacing, his head tilted to the side so his raven hair brushed his shoulder. He looked like he was searching for something. But what?

French sliced green beans?

"Okay, you're starting to weird me out," she said, at last breaking the thick silence.

He chuckled, halting to shove aside the cans. "Have faith, my love."

My love. She grimaced. Man, but he was going to be sooooo pissed when her spell wore off.

And it would wear off. Even now she could feel her strength fading. In a half hour, maybe less, she would be completely drained and then . . .

She was thankfully distracted as Roke gave a sudden shove on the shelf and a section of the back wall parted with a low groan.

"A hidden door," she breathed in shock. "How did you know?"

"I have a talent for sensing structural anomalies." He offered a wicked smile. "Are you impressed?"

She briefly forgot how to breathe. God almighty, he was beautiful. Unreasonably, indecently beautiful, with an ability to make her knees go weak at the most inconvenient times.

"We should go."

"Be careful," he warned, pulling the narrow door wide before stepping into the darkness. "You won't be able to see once the door closes."

Hesitantly she followed him into the dusty shadows, grimacing at the choking darkness. Although she could see better than humans, she couldn't match a vampire's night vision.

"There's no lights?" she complained, wiping away a cobweb that stuck to her hair.

"No, I would guess that these tunnels were intended for an emergency escape."

He moved with fluid speed, indifferent to the steep decline of the passageway and the unevenness of the dirt floor.

"Great." She stumbled over an unseen rock.

"Hold on to me." He reached a hand back to capture her fingers in a tight grip. "I'll keep you safe."

Sally forgot the unnerving darkness and the suspicion that

the neglected passageway was filled with creepy crawlies as their hands connected with a shock of raw excitement.

She bit back a small gasp. Blessed goddess. How could such a casual touch make her entire body clench with pleasure?

Roke was the one who was supposed to be under the sway of a binding spell, not her.

Unfortunately, her body didn't care.

It was ready and eager to respond.

Trying her best to concentrate on anything but the awareness tingling in the pit of her stomach, Sally counted each downward step. They were at least six feet below ground, she judged when the path at last evened out and curved in a northern direction.

They continued on for nearly an hour before Roke at last slowed his steps and came to a halt.

Sally breathed a sigh of relief. Despite her grinding urgency to get away from Styx's lair, she was increasingly drained by the energy necessary to keep Roke bound by her spell.

Any minute he was going to slip her leash and then . . .

She shivered. It didn't bear thinking about.

"Is something wrong?" she asked, discreetly removing her hand from his grasp to lean against the dirt wall of the tunnel.

"This is the end of the tunnel," Roke said, tilting back his head to study the narrow opening directly over him. "There's an empty building above us."

She pressed a hand to the stitch in her side. "You're sure it's empty?"

"Yes."

"Thank god," she muttered. "How far are we from the house?"

He paused, glancing back down the tunnel. "A few miles."

"I suppose it will have to do."

Gritting her teeth, she forced herself to straighten from the wall. She'd barely taken a step forward, however, when Roke was standing directly in front of her, his hands rubbing up and down her arms.

"Let me go first; I want to make sure it's safe," he said.

Her heart skipped a beat as she met the pale silver gaze. There were the yummy flutters in the pit of her stomach at his touch, but more than that, there was a sense of . . . rightness.

As if she knew his touch from another time, another place.

"No," she said, the curt rejection as much for her ridiculous thoughts as his offer.

Jeez. Talk about Stockholm syndrome. Next she would be fantasizing she was his mate.

Almost as if sensing her stupid thoughts, he leaned down to brush his lips over her furrowed brow. "I won't be long, I promise."

"Roke." She grasped the lapels of his leather coat. "Please listen to me."

His lips skimmed down the length of his nose before nibbling at the edge of her mouth. "Later, my love."

Her fingers tightened on his jacket, wanting to jerk him even closer so he could kiss her properly. Heck, they were alone in the dark and for the moment they seemed safe enough. Why not enjoy a quick . . .

Wait.

What was she thinking?

"No," she rasped. "I have to talk to you now."

He lifted his head, but he remained close enough so that she could see the flash of his fully extended fangs even in the thick shadows. It should have reminded her that he was a lethal predator. Instead all she could think about was the fact he was obviously as aroused as she was.

"What is it?" he asked, the rough edge in his voice sending a shiver of anticipation down her spine.

Oh, she needed to get away from this man.

Before she did something truly stupid.

"I want you to return to the house."

He stilled, his expression almost impossible to read in the darkness. "Did you leave something behind?"

She made a sound of self-disgust. "My sanity."

"Sally?" He gently slid a hand beneath her hair to massage her nape. "Tell me what's going on."

Like she knew?

For a panicked minute her mind refused to work. She had to get rid of him so she could release her fading binding spell and hopefully have enough juice left to activate her hidden amulet. That should disguise her presence long enough to escape the area.

But how?

"We can't outrun Styx's guards, not while my magic is on the fritz," she finally managed to blurt out.

"Once we're out of the tunnels your magic will return."

"Maybe or maybe not." She shuddered as his hand continued to soothe her tense muscles. "I need you to distract them long enough for me to escape."

"Without me?" His brows drew together. "Never."

"Once I'm far enough away I'll contact you and you can join me."

"No."

"Roke," she protested his stubborn refusal to obey.

Obviously her spell was rapidly losing its grip on him. And worse, she was growing weaker with every passing second.

"I won't leave you," he said grimly. "It's too dangerous."

"I'll be fine."

"Yes, because I'll be with you."

Suddenly it was all too much. "Damn," she groaned, sliding down until her butt hit the dirt floor. "I'm too tired to fight."

Roke squatted in front of her, his expression concerned. "Rest here. I'll make sure the path is clear."

"Roke . . ."

"Close your eyes, little witch," he murmured, brushing a finger over her chilled cheek. "I'll keep you safe."

If only that were true, she thought with a twinge of wistful longing.

If only this man did want to keep her safe.

Not because of some spell, but because he thought she was worth saving.

"You're so stupid, Sally," she whispered as he pressed his hands against the floor and with one impressive shove was launching himself up and through the opening above. "Stupid and downright pathetic. You're going to end up dead in this tunnel and no one is going to give a damn."

It took Roke less than five minutes to scout through the empty house. It was obviously one of Styx's numerous safe houses that were used only in emergencies.

As he had told Sally, the Anasso was nothing if not thorough.

Sally.

Roke came to a halt in the middle of the never-used kitchen. What the hell? With a sharp shake of his head he felt the urgent, driving need to rescue the beautiful witch from his brothers slowly fade.

Like a fog was being lifted from his mind.

He clenched his hands at his side, his fangs lengthening.

He vividly remembered going to the dungeons with a dinner tray. He'd entered the cell and tried to convince Sally to confess the truth of Gaius's strange new talents.

And then . . .

And then he'd been overwhelmed by a potent desire to do whatever was necessary to protect the woman who was his sole reason for living.

Goddammit.

The bitch had hit him with a spell.

There could be no other explanation.

Why else would he have suddenly been filled with an unshakable conviction she was his? Not just a pretty female he desired. But his. On a most primitive level.

Hell, even now he could . . . feel her. As if their very souls were entwined.

And worse, she had forced him to sacrifice everything, even loyalty to his people, to keep her safe.

Of all things, that was the one act he could never, ever forgive or forget.

He'd taken a vow when he became clan chief that he would always put his people first. How could he offer them anything less? The previous chief had nearly destroyed them all by his obsession with a female who'd demanded he pamper her every whim.

Now he'd been forced to follow in the footsteps of the man he'd hated.

She was going to pay for that.

With a roar that shattered the nearby window, he returned to the back bedroom where the trapdoor was hidden in the closet. Dropping into the lower tunnel, he landed lightly on the balls of his feet and stormed toward the female who was deeply asleep, curled on her side on the floor.

He was so angry the walls trembled from the force of his temper and the air was frigid enough to form ice crystals. But, as he squatted down to grab Sally and shake her awake, he hesitated.

Christ, she looked so tiny. And exhausted. The fragile features were more pale than usual, with bruised shadows beneath the thick crescents of her lowered lashes. Her autumn hair was splayed over the dirt, and her lips slightly parted, as if inviting a prince to kiss her awake.

Unfortunately for her, he was no prince, Roke bleakly reminded himself. And he'd returned to discover just what nasty spell she'd cast on him, not because of worry that she had pushed herself too hard.

Dammit.

Her magic had to be screwing with his head.

Not to mention his renegade body, he conceded, abruptly shifting his fingers to her shoulder rather than brushing over her cheek as they started to do.

"Sally." He gave her a small shake. "Wake up."

Her brow furrowed as she struggled to lift her lashes, the rich brown eyes dazed as she tried to focus on him.

"Roke?" She blinked in confusion. "I can't . . . tired . . ."

He leaned down so he could grasp her shoulders, pulling her into a sitting position with far greater care than she deserved. "Wake up," he commanded, not for the first time irritated that it was impossible to enthrall a witch. It would have saved them all one hell of a lot of trouble.

She groaned, her head tilting back to smack against the wall of the tunnel. "What?" she demanded in thick tones. "What's happened?"

"That's what you're about to explain, little witch," he snarled. "Just what the hell did you do to me?"

"Do?"

His threatening growl echoed through the tunnel. "Don't even try to deny you put a spell on me."

"Oh." He could hear her heartbeat quicken, her muscles clenching beneath his fingers. "I didn't."

He ignored her ridiculous denial. "Is it black magic?"

"No." Her words remained slurred with exhaustion. "I swear."

"Like I would take your word."

"How could I?" She licked her lips and Roke swallowed a choked curse. Was it deliberate? Did she know the small provocation sent a jolt of hunger through his body? "The dungeons are hexed to prevent magic."

"You obviously found a way to get around Styx's protection." His lips twisted. "Unless you expect me to believe I took one look at you and tumbled head over heels in love?"

She flinched at his cruel mockery, but the foolish female didn't back down. "It wasn't a spell. It was . . ."

"I'm listening."

There was a long pause before she heaved a weary sigh. "My natural powers."

"Natural?" he scoffed. "Humans have no powers."

Her lashes lowered, hiding her eyes. "Then the logical answer is that I'm not entirely human," she murmured.

His brows snapped together. It *was* the logical answer. The hexes would have prevented any spell cast by a witch. Even the most powerful witch.

But how could he have missed the fact that she was a mongrel?

Did the fact she was a witch conceal her demon blood?

"What are you?"

Her eyes remained closed as she shook her head. "I don't know."

His fingers dug into her shoulders. "Tell me."

"I . . . can't."

With a tiny sound of distress her head flopped forward and Roke sensed her consciousness slip away.

"Shit." He glared down at the top of her head. Now what?

The sensible thing to do would be to return her to the dungeons and let Styx deal with her.

Once he revealed that he was susceptible to the female's powers (yeah, and wouldn't that be a fun and jolly confession?) the Anasso would be careful to assign a new guard to keep watch on her.

But even as the thought crossed through his mind, he was shoving it aside. Not just because he didn't want to share his spectacular failure with Styx. But because he could still feel the damned woman lodged deep inside him.

When she woke, she was going to remove whatever curse she'd put on him.

Then . . .

Then he was returning to Nevada and Styx could shove the prophet's vague warning up his ass.

Chapter 14

The middle of nowhere, Louisiana

Nefri returned from her search of the countryside to join Santiago at his vehicle.

While the male vampire had been burying the bodies of Melinda's drinking companions to prevent any lingering infection, Nefri had left Levet keeping watch over the sleeping girl while she'd scouted for any signs of Gaius.

She couldn't shake the sensation that she was missing something.

Something that might very well be the difference between success and failure.

But no matter how hard she tried to pinpoint her source of unease, it slipped away as swiftly as a mist fairy.

Stepping around the bed of the truck, the nagging sensation was abruptly forgotten at the sight of Santiago leaning against the driver's side door.

What was it about this vampire that sent a shock of excitement through her just by catching sight of him?

She was an ancient clan chief who'd assumed she had seen and done everything possible.

But this . . .

It made her feel as if she were a giddy foundling who had yet to gain command of her hungers.

The logical part of her understood the sensations he aroused were dangerous. Not only to her hard-earned control, but to the part of her that was still very much a woman.

But a larger part of her accepted that there was no way to fight what was happening between her and this gorgeous, sexy vampire. There seemed no choice but to allow their relationship to develop to an inevitable conclusion.

Whatever that conclusion might be.

Almost on cue, Santiago turned to send her one of those smiles she felt to the tips of her toes.

"Anything?" he demanded.

With an effort, Nefri returned her mind to Gaius and his odd behavior. It was certainly more pressing than her girlish reaction to a charming male.

"The emotions were far more contained than those near Gaius's lair," she said, moving to stand near Santiago while her gaze returned to the schoolhouse.

"I assume he just stopped by for a quick snack," Santiago said. "No doubt the longer he stays in one spot the further his infections spread."

"Yes."

"You don't sound convinced."

She shifted her gaze to meet his frown. "I agree with your logic."

"But?"

"But I don't understand his need for any snack, quick or otherwise."

He considered her words. "Because he didn't feed while he was with your clan?"

"No, since his return to this world he's clearly indulged his most primitive hungers, but he's a very old vampire. He shouldn't have to feed so often." Nefri grimaced. The Harpies had claimed they'd found corpses disposed of in the swamps, not to mention the crazed human male they were holding captive. "Especially not after he seemingly gorged before leaving his lair."

"Unless he's still recovering from injuries," Santiago suggested. "We don't know how badly he was hurt during the battle with the Dark Lord."

"It's possible."

The dark eyes narrowed. "What are you thinking?"

"I'm wondering if the spirit is somehow draining Gaius," she said slowly.

Santiago straightened from the truck, taking time to mull over her suggestion. "You mean feeding off him?"

She shrugged. "It's just a theory."

"It makes as much sense as anything else."

Not the most comforting assurance considering nothing about Gaius or the spirit made sense.

"Can you feel Gaius?"

He closed his eyes, concentrating on his connection to his sire. "I know he's north of us."

"Are we gaining on him?"

"We are," he said after a beat. He opened his eyes. "It feels like he's settled in one place."

Yet another anomaly. She shook her head in frustration "Odd, isn't it?"

"What?"

"He doesn't expect to be followed."

"He always was arrogant."

"But not stupid."

Santiago easily followed her train of thought. "You suspect Gaius is setting an ambush?"

"It's rather convenient that your connection to him returned just in time to follow his trail," she pointed out.

He scowled, clearly already having considered the possibility he was being played by the vampire he'd once considered his father. "True."

"It could be a coincidence. Or . . ."

"Or an elaborate trap," he finished for her.

"Yes."

He turned to pull open the door of the truck. "There's only one way to find out."

Nefri crawled into the cab, scooting across the leather seat. She wasn't nearly so eager to confront Gaius. Not until she had more information on the spirit that she feared was far more powerful than she'd first suspected.

But how?

The Commission had revealed all they intended to. It would be a waste of time to try and question them. And it wasn't as if there was a textbook lying around that explained mysterious spirits.

At least . . .

Not in this world.

She turned to study Santiago's profile as he put the truck in gear and headed back toward the highway. "Can we reach Gaius tonight?"

"No." He shot her a curious glance. "Even if he stays where he is it would take too many hours to reach him."

"Then I would request we make a small detour."

"Request?" He grinned. "Where's my commanding Nefri?"

She sniffed. "You called me bossy, remember?"

"So we're partners?"

She gave a slow nod, wondering if he truly understood how difficult it was for her to concede to his demands.

It wasn't about accepting someone could be her equal. She wasn't that vain.

It was allowing herself to be vulnerable.

Something easier said than done.

"Partners," she murmured.

"I like the sound of that." His grin widened. "Even if it was like pulling teeth."

She rolled her eyes. "You're very . . . persistent."

"I'm a stubborn, impulsive bastard who too often allows

his heart to rule his head," he admitted, his smile fading as he held her gaze. "But, I would die for those I consider mine."

Warmth flared through her heart. "I know."

He turned his attention back to the field they were cutting through, slowing as they neared the narrow road. "Which direction?"

"North," she said, hoping she wasn't taking them on a wild goose chase. "For now."

"Wait." He shot her a suspicious glance. "You aren't taking me to the Oracles, are you?"

She arched a brow. "Not unless you wanted to drop in for a visit."

"I'd rather poke out my eye."

A feeling shared by most of the demon world, she wryly acknowledged. Including herself on occasion.

"No, we're not going to the Oracles," she assured him. "I have an acquaintance who might be of assistance."

His suspicion remained. Smart vampire.

"What kind of acquaintance?"

"I think I should wait and let you see for yourself," she murmured, struck by a sudden thought. "Oh, we need to find a ring or a necklace. Preferably made of diamonds. The larger the better."

His suspicion transformed to confusion. "Not that I mind buying you all the bling your heart might desire, *querida,* but I'm not sure there are any stores open."

"Has that ever stopped you?" she asked dryly.

His soft chuckle brushed over her skin with sinful pleasure. "Never."

Northern Arkansas

Santiago had used up most of the swear words he'd learned during his considerably long life as he crawled through yet another mud-filled sinkhole that at last led to a hidden meadow.

An acquaintance, Nefri had claimed. Why hadn't he demanded more details? Like whether or not the creature lived in the Ozark Mountains in an area so remote not even a damned billy goat could find it?

Of course, he should have known something was up when she'd demanded to be taken to the clan chief of Arkansas rather than a jewelry store to acquire a diamond the size of an ostrich egg. At the time, however, he was distracted by the clan chief's eagerness to impress Nefri with his generosity. Hell, Santiago didn't doubt the bedazzled vampire would have given his entire fortune if Nefri had requested it.

Now he wondered what kind of acquaintance demanded a priceless jewel and lived in the middle of nowhere.

Indifferent to his strange litany, Nefri led him out of the sinkhole and straight across the meadow, the clinging mud flaking off her jeans and sweater to leave her looking as fresh as a fucking daisy.

Even her long hair was perfect, shimmering like a river of ebony beneath the fading stars.

It was no wonder that the Arkansas clan chief had turned over a million-dollar diamond without batting a lash.

"If you're lost you can just admit it," he muttered as she at last came to a halt in front of a dead tree that somehow managed to stay upright in the center of the meadow. "I swear I won't tell anyone."

Her gaze remained locked on the tree. "I'm not lost."

"Then you're punishing me?"

Her lips twitched. "If and when I decide to punish you, Santiago, you will know."

"Comforting."

"Mmm."

"Where are we going?"

"Here."

He glanced around the empty meadow. Did she expect someone to be taking a late night stroll in this isolated area? "You made me ruin my boots to meet a tree?"

"Hush," she murmured, leaning down to place the diamond in a small hollow beneath a gnarly root.

"Now what?"

She turned to offer a mysterious smile. *The ice-princess at her most seductive.*

"Now we wait."

He stepped forward, trailing his fingers through the cool silk of her hair. This was a woman made for night. As distantly remote and beautiful as the moon.

Unless she was wrapped in his arms.

Then she was a shimmering, passionate creature who burned as hot as the sun.

"I'm not very good at waiting," he informed her.

"No?" She arched a brow. "You shock me."

His fingers stroked down the line of her throat, relishing the feel of her smooth skin. "I have a way we could pass the time."

"You're covered in mud," she chided, but he didn't miss the tiny spark of heat deep in her eyes.

He leaned down to brush his lips along the curve of her ear. "There's a creek just over the hill," he told her, his superior hearing able to catch the sound of shallow water as it danced over rocks. It was all too easy to imagine stripping off Nefri's clothes so she could play mermaid. "You could wash me."

She shivered, the rich scent of her arousal lacing the breeze. "Maybe later."

He nipped the lobe of her ear, careful not to draw blood. His possessive fascination with the female was enough to deal with at the moment.

He wasn't going to take the risk of mating her.

Not when she might disappear back behind the Veil.

He'd been abandoned by his sire and then again by this female just a few weeks ago. He wasn't ready to take the risk again.

Instead he concentrated on the delectable taste of her jasmine-scented skin. "You promise?"

"We'll see," she teased, her voice a husky invitation.

He muttered low words of need as his lips stroked down the line of her jaw. His hands gripped her waist, but before he could yank her hard against his stirring body, a warning prickle brushed over his skin.

On instant alert, Santiago stepped back far enough to pull his sword free. The air felt charged with electricity, as if lightning was about to strike.

Not a vampire's favorite sensation.

Being flammable had a few downsides.

When lightning didn't strike him down, he began to lower his sword, his puzzled gaze searching the meadow. There was something near.

Something powerful.

With his senses on full alert, he didn't miss the strange fog that began to form around the diamond. Still, he wasn't prepared for the massive jewel to abruptly disappear at the same time the tree split in half.

"Meirda," he muttered, staring at the black hole that hovered in the space between the two halves of the tree. "What's that?"

"A doorway." Nefri sent him a warning glance as she moved forward. "Stay close."

Reluctantly he fell into step behind her. "We're not about to tumble into some weird version of Wonderland, are we?"

She gave a soft snort. "Weird version?"

"Okay, the first version was pretty weird," he conceded, his knuckles white as he gripped the hilt of his sword.

Like any self-respecting vampire, he detested magic. And there was no mistaking that the black hole was made by magic, not nature. But, gritting his teeth, he forced his feet to carry him forward.

Hadn't he been the one to insist on joining Nefri? He couldn't back down now.

Shivering as they moved through the darkness, Santiago nearly stumbled over his own feet as they stepped into what looked like a throne room in a grand palace.

Startled, his gaze skimmed over the long, highly glossed floor of inlaid wood that was framed by ivory walls inset with arched mirrors. Above his head the coved ceiling displayed an exquisite mural of Aladdin and his lamp that came to life in the blaze of light from the massive chandelier.

At the far end of the room was a gilded throne with crimson velvet padding that was set on a high dais. On each side of the dais were a matching set of ivory and gold double doors.

"Where are we?" he asked in confusion.

Nefri continued toward the throne, her air of nobility only emphasized by her elegant surroundings. *Regal,* a voice whispered in the back of his mind.

"It's a small fold in dimensions," she murmured softly.

"A fold?" He followed several steps behind Nefri, giving himself room for a full swing of his sword if they were attacked. "I've never heard of it."

She slowed her steps, perhaps considering how best to explain the strange phenomenon. "You know that Laylah found the babies hidden in what she called a 'bubble'?"

"I've heard the stories."

She waved a slender hand. "This is basically the same, only on a larger scale."

He frowned as he glanced around the room, realizing the opening had closed behind them.

Trapped.

A very elegant sally port.

He shuddered, far from happy by the knowledge he had no easy exit.

"So are we in another dimension?"

She again considered her words. "We're in a sliver of space where our worlds intersect with one another."

Santiago grimaced. He hadn't considered the possibilities that dimensions overlapped one another. Hell, he hadn't spent any time thinking about other dimensions at all. He was a warrior, not a philosopher. But now that he considered Nefri's explanation, it made sense.

"How did you know it was here?"

She came to a halt a few steps from the empty throne, her hand absently stroking the medallion hung around her neck. It was a gesture that revealed she was more nervous than she wanted to admit.

"I devoted a number of years to studying obscure histories and forgotten languages," she said, her tone distracted. "In one I discovered the rumors of a . . ."

He shifted back to study his companion's perfect profile. "A what?"

"It's difficult to translate, but I suppose the nearest description would be hall of records." She shrugged, her explanation smooth. Too smooth. She was hiding something from him. "Or a library, if you prefer."

"I crawled through the muck to come to a library?"

She turned to meet his chiding gaze. "Where else do you go when you need information?"

"Google?"

She shook her head. "Google doesn't have the answers we need."

He pointed a sword toward the mirrored walls that were

markedly devoid of books. As far as he could see, it looked more like a room Paris Hilton would choose, not a scholar.

There was something she wasn't telling him.

"And this place does?"

"The actual texts are protected by a very special guardian. We must wait for an invitation to go further."

"Perfect." He rolled his tight shoulders. He wanted out of the strange fold in space; it felt too much like a trap. "I'm still curious about how you found this place. Did one of your texts have a map?"

"Something like that."

Hmmm. What the hell was she hiding?

A familiar warning flared through his blood, distracting him from the suspicion that he should have asked a lot more questions before entering Wonderland.

"You do know that dawn is only an hour away?"

"We'll be safe here."

"You're sure?"

"Trust me."

About to remind her that she'd given up the right to trust when she'd disappeared on him without a word, he caught a faint scent wafting beneath the doors.

Tilting back his head, Santiago tested the air, his predatory senses on full alert. "Do you smell that?"

Nefri gave a calm nod. "Yes."

"What is it?"

"Dragon."

"Mierda." Santiago's eyes widened in shock. "Do you have a death-wish?"

Chapter 15

Nefri was an ancient vampire of immeasurable strength and a clan chief who'd led her people for centuries with a combination of compassion and a shrewd intelligence.

Among many, she was considered almost a god.

But she was also a woman. And she wasn't above taking pleasure in the sight of Santiago's stunned disbelief. He was always so damned arrogantly confident.

Not that she blamed him for his reaction. Dragons would make any demon run in the opposite direction.

Even the mighty vampires.

Not only were dragons capable of destroying their enemies by breathing fires that reached nuclear-level status, but they possessed magic as old and powerful as the universe.

The only good thing was that the rare, reclusive creatures had little interest in the mortal world, and often disappeared for several millennia at a time.

"There's no need to get excited," she murmured.

He stared at her as if she was demented. A legitimate hypothesis, she wryly accepted, shivering as icy prickles teased over her skin.

Any female would have to be insane to be more distracted by a sexy vampire who was arousing her with nothing more than the brush of his power, than the approaching dragon who could roast her with an accidental burp.

"You bring me to a dragon's hoard and you tell me not to get excited?"

"You will never find a larger collection of ancient texts," she explained.

"Yeah, guarded by a lethal, bat-crazy lizard who can charbroil us with a yawn."

Nefri stilled, abruptly puzzled by Santiago's reaction. "I'm surprised."

"That I let myself be led to certain death?" he muttered. "Yeah, me too."

"No, that you so easily accepted my explanation." She studied his unreasonably beautiful face. "Most demons no longer believe in dragons."

"During my years in the pits I was locked in the catacombs with a number of interesting demons, including a clan chief." His smile was without humor. "It's amazing what a person will reveal when they face death on a nightly basis."

Nefri gave a slow nod. Clan chiefs were strongly discouraged from discussing the trials they endured, even with each other. No doubt in an attempt to add mystery to the process of becoming a chief.

But there were always exceptions. Including Nefri, who didn't hesitate to question chiefs on their own experiences.

"Ah, he revealed the secrets of the battles of Durotriges."

"Only small bits and pieces." Santiago gave a lift of his shoulder. "He claimed he fought a dragon."

"It's my hypothesis that the creature was a half-breed. Which meant . . ." She waved a hand to indicate their elegant surroundings.

"That there must be a full breed around somewhere," he easily followed her implication.

"One who could enter this world," she said. "At least, that was the hypothesis."

"Your hypotheses tend to have an uncanny habit of being proven right."

She wrinkled her nose. During her battle with the strange lizardlike creature with leathery wings who'd nearly barbecued her during her last trial, she'd become convinced there had to be some truth to the ancient rumors of dragons. Unfortunately, the folklore of the beast had become so twisted over the centuries it was almost impossible to discover what was truth and what was myth.

"This one was more difficult than others to prove one way or another. There's very little information on dragons."

"What about other clan chiefs?" he demanded. "Surely they must have investigated the truth of dragons if they had to fight them?"

"From the few chiefs who would discuss their trials, I learned that the battles are never the same for any of us." That was an understatement. The trials were so wildly different for each combatant that Nefri had wondered if they actually were sent to different places. Then, she'd become convinced they all went to the same *place* only at different *times*. She couldn't prove her theory, of course, but the idea that the battlegrounds floated in a different space-time continuum was the only thing that made sense.

"I have only heard of one other clan chief who claimed dragons existed. Unfortunately he disappeared before I could discover if his belief came from Durotriges or from some other source."

"Perhaps he was my unfortunate roommate."

"It's possible."

"So what did you do?"

"I searched through the ancient texts," she said. "Then after I learned all that was written about the mysterious creatures, I used my medallion to search for a doorway. It took several centuries, but eventually I discovered this place."

"So you did."

The low voice filled the air as the double doors to the right of the throne flew open to reveal the creature of myth and legend.

Surprisingly, Baine's human form wasn't as large as might be expected for a monster who could supposedly transform into a flying lizard with a forty-foot wingspan and an elongated body that weighed in at over a ton. In the past, the Lu demon had often been mistaken for a dragon since it shared the same scaled head with its long snout and mouthful of razor teeth; not to mention they were impossible to kill without magic. But the Lu was half the size of the mythical dragons and they couldn't shape-shift.

This particular dragon had chosen a leanly muscular human male body with a narrow face that had delicate, Asian features. His straight black hair fell just short of his shoulders and he was wearing nothing more than a pair of loose *dojo* pants that allowed a dizzying view of the numerous tattoos that glowed with a metallic shimmer beneath the light of the chandelier. More unnerving, the strange symbols changed colors as they crawled over his pale, perfect skin.

Almost as if they were alive.

It was beautiful, hypnotizing. And so distracting that it was all too easy to forget just how lethal this creature truly was.

At least until you looked into the almond-shaped eyes burning with an amber fire that spoke of vast, primordial magic.

Enough magic to scorch the world.

"Por dios," Santiago growled, and Nefri instinctively stepped between him and the advancing dragon.

Two alpha males in the same room was always a pain in the neck.

Folding her hands at her waist, Nefri offered a respectful bow. "Baine."

"Nefri."

"Thank you for accepting my humble offering."

The dragon held up his slender fingers to reveal the large diamond that shimmered with a white fire. "You know I can never resist pretty baubles. And I was . . . intrigued." A hint of a smile curved his lips as he tucked the diamond into the pocket of his loose pants. "You are one of the few demons brave enough to enter the lair of a dragon."

Santiago shifted to stand at her side, his expression tight as he braced himself against the heavy throb of Baine's power. It was like the constant beat of a bass drum, pulsing through the air with enough force to make the floor tremble beneath his feet.

"Brave isn't the word I would use," the male vampire pointedly chastised.

The scorching gaze turned toward Santiago, and Nefri tensed. For now Baine was enjoying his role as beneficent host, but dragons were rumored to be fickle and vain with a quicksilver temper.

Who knew when he might decide he was no longer amused?

"And you are?" he demanded of Santiago.

"This is—" Nefri cut off her words as Baine gave a sharp wave of his hand.

"I'll hear it from the male."

Nefri bit her lip. Naturally, Santiago couldn't offer a bow, or even lower his eyes as Baine slowly circled his rigid body. Instead he tilted his chin and subtly tightened his grip on his sword.

Stubborn vampire.

"I'm Santiago," he said, his voice clear and steady.

Baine came to a halt directly in front of him, the amber eyes smoldering with an inner fire. "You don't fear me?"

"Of course I do." Santiago shrugged. "I'm not an idiot."

The dragon's tattoos continued to swirl over his body in a dazzling display. "You disguise it better than most," Baine murmured.

"I've had a lot of practice."

"Yes." Baine sucked in a deep breath, as if savoring their scents. "Such a violent world you live in."

Santiago took a wise step backward at the hungry edge in the dragon's voice. "It keeps me on my toes."

"Mmmm." The dragon's smile widened. In anticipation? Difficult to say. "I miss it."

"The violence?" Santiago asked.

"The violence. The blood." Baine moved with lightning speed to stand nose to nose with Santiago. "The crunch of vampire bones in my teeth."

Nefri took a swift step forward, laying a restraining hand on the dragon's arm. Almost instantly she yanked it back, her fingers tingling with pain from the heat generated by his skin.

Good lord, it was like touching an open flame.

"Baine," she murmured in urgent tones.

There was a tense beat as the two alphas met stare for stare, then with a throaty chuckle Baine at last turned to meet her concerned gaze.

"I can't play with your toy?"

"I've come to seek your assistance."

Baine shrugged, thankfully stepping away from the bristling male vampire.

Santiago was one goad away from doing something truly stupid.

"I am always delighted to be of service to a beautiful female, but I no longer interest myself in your world," Baine informed her.

"It's actually your knowledge of the past I seek."

The dragon paused, inwardly debating her request. At the same time Nefri discreetly moved close enough to make it impossible for Santiago to take an impulsive swing of his sword. He might be more annoying than any vampire had a right to be, but she wasn't going to let him die.

Eventually, Baine gave a languid wave of his hand. "You may continue."

"I need information on a spirit who can infect a vampire."

Baine tilted his head, eyeing her with a sudden curiosity. Which, of course, was better than hunger.

Just slightly.

"I've never heard of such a spirit."

"Perhaps a book in your collection . . . ?"

"If the information was available in my library I would know." He deliberately stroked a finger over the swirling tattoos on his stomach. "Dragons have very long memories."

Nefri bit her bottom lip. Well that was . . . disappointing. "I see."

"Tell me more of this spirit."

She grimaced. Siljar wouldn't be pleased to know that Nefri had shared the details of the MIA spirit with Santiago, let alone a dragon, but what choice did she have?

The closer they came to locating Gaius, the more she realized they needed information. She wasn't going to blindly attempt to capture a spirit that terrified the Oracles enough to have it locked away.

Not when . . .

She grimaced again. Why not admit it? Not when Santiago might be harmed.

Thrusting aside the vulnerable thought, she met the fiery dragon gaze. "It was contained by the Oracles by a rift in space."

"When?"

Santiago moved to stand directly behind her shoulder at Baine's sharp tone, but he was smart enough to keep the sword at his side.

"I don't have an exact date," she admitted. "But it was when the world was still young."

"The Veil," Baine murmured.

"Yes."

An odd purring filled the air. Not the cute purring of a kitten, but the lethal vibration of an irritated dragon.

"I should have suspected the idiots were hiding something."

"No love lost for the Commission?" Santiago demanded.

A tiny wisp of smoke curled from one nostril, revealing the dragon's opinion of the ultimate leaders of demon kind.

"They have tried to pass themselves off as impartial judges who rule the demon world with no thought beyond justice." He made a sound of disgust. "When the truth is much less noble."

"Definitely no love lost," Santiago muttered.

Nefri studied Baine's finely carved features, sensing his dislike of the Oracles was more personal than irritation with their positions of authority.

"You weren't aware of why they created the Veil?" she asked.

"No." Another wisp of smoke. "Tell me more of the creature."

She felt the light skim of Santiago's fingers down the curve of her spine. As if she needed the silent warning to be careful. The very air was heating with Baine's rising temper.

"Unfortunately I know little more than it was dangerous enough to prompt the Oracles to bar it from the mortal world," she carefully confessed. "And that it's currently traveling with a vampire named Gaius."

"And you believe the vampire is infected?"

"Gaius seems capable of spreading intense emotions among the humans with his bite. Fear, violence, lust . . ." She shook her head in frustration. Until she understood how and why he was infecting humans, she couldn't risk coming into contact with him. "We don't know if it's a deliberate act or a symptom of his own sickness."

The amber eyes widened, as if her words had startled the dragon. Rather amazing considering the beast was rumored to be older than the world and possessed the knowledge of thousands of species.

Then, without warning, a mysterious smile was curling his lips. "Intense emotion?"

"Is something funny?" Santiago growled.

Turning with a sinuous motion, Baine paced across the narrow room, his chuckle sending a rash of unease over Nefri's skin.

"It really is the perfect irony," he murmured.

"Do you know this spirit?" Nefri asked.

"Perhaps."

"Are you going to share?" Santiago snapped.

Nefri elbowed him with enough force to make him wince in pain.

"Santiago," she muttered.

Baine slowly turned back. "I must consider what I'm prepared to reveal."

"Thank you." Nefri dipped her head in respect. "We would appreciate any information you can share."

"Ever the diplomat, eh, beautiful Nefri?" Baine drawled.

Nefri shot a chiding glance toward the vampire still scowling at her side. "It's necessary when surrounded by impetuous males who love to flex their muscles."

Baine sent a mocking glance toward Santiago, at the same time waving a slender hand toward the double doors on the opposite side of the throne. With a faint squeak one door swung slowly inward, as if it hadn't been opened in centuries.

"The hallway leads to a private suite," Baine told her. "We will speak again when I've made my decision."

"Of course."

Grabbing her companion by the arm, she led him toward the door before he could demand the dragon tell them what he knew.

There was nothing they could say or do to force Baine to speak. Not even the Hope Diamond could sway him.

For now they would have to wait until he decided they were worthy of his secrets.

And pray that it didn't take until the next millennium.

Chapter 16

Santiago allowed Nefri to lead him down the long, shadowed hallway. Not that he was happy about it.

A dragon. A freaking dragon.

Like it wasn't bad enough to be chasing a mysterious spirit and his crazy-ass sire who could infect humans. Now he was trapped in the lair of a dragon.

"You have a habit of collecting dangerous friends, *cara*," he growled, his wary gaze trying to focus on the paneled walls that seemed to waver in and out of focus. As if they were walking through the strange corridors between dimensions.

Nefri had the nerve to send him a puzzled frown. "Dangerous?"

He snorted. "Dragons, Oracles . . ."

"Baine is hardly a friend," she interrupted him.

"And the Oracles?"

She grimaced. "I'm nothing more than a lowly servant for the Commission."

This proud, beautiful woman a servant?

Yeah, and stars were mere specks in the sky.

Santiago lifted a hand to brush his fingers down the cool silk of her hair. "You may have been forced to do things against your will, *querida,* but you have never been a servant. Not to anyone."

"A fine distinction," she murmured, although there was a hint of appreciation in the dark, velvet eyes as she halted at a door that abruptly appeared from the shadows. Pausing for a brief second, she reached for the knob and pushed the thick wood door open and stepped over the threshold. Then, with a startled sound, she came to a sudden halt. "Good . . . lord."

Without thought, Santiago had his sword lifted and was moving past Nefri to confront whatever had caused her astonishment.

What he found was . . . nothing.

At least, nothing beyond a circular room with a domed ceiling that was decorated with paintings of tiny cupids at play. Inlaid with narrow bands of gold, the floor was made of marble that was polished until it glowed beneath a Venetian chandelier.

The walls were the same marble, but veined with a pale green that matched the velvet upholstery on the chaise lounge near a built-in armoire, as well as the comforter on the large, canopy bed set in the center of the room.

A little too pretentious for his taste, but he would have bet his last dollar it was perfectly suited to Nefri.

"What is it?" he rasped, stepping further into the room, his gaze searching for a hidden enemy.

She moved to stand at his side, her expression wary. "This is an exact replica of my private rooms."

Santiago hissed, his mind instantly consumed with the image of the handsome, lethal predator prowling through Nefri's most intimate territory. "Baine's been in your bedroom?"

Her brows lifted at his snarled question, the temperature dropping by several degrees. "That's your concern? Whether or not Baine's been in my bedroom?"

He wasn't stupid. He knew there was something wrong

with his logic. But beyond being a warrior or a vampire, he was a man. And men didn't think clearly when they were obsessed with a particular woman. "Yes."

She rolled her eyes. "No, Santiago, I didn't entertain a dragon in my bedroom."

"Then how is this possible?" he demanded, his gaze taking in each detail of the classically graceful room.

Again he was struck by just how suited it was to Nefri's regal yet understated beauty. It was all too easy to imagine her lying on the bed, her hair spread like a river of ebony across the green velvet cover.

"I don't know, but it's uncanny." Nefri moved to run a hand over a Chinese vase that stood as tall as Santiago.

Compelled by his own need to make sure his eyes weren't deceiving him, Santiago stepped forward to grasp the wooden post of the bed. He could feel the sanded grains beneath his fingers, just as he could catch the scent of polish.

"Are you sure this sliver of another dimension doesn't overlap the Veil?"

She shook her head. "No, this is an illusion."

"A damned real illusion."

She crossed to pull open the armoire, revealing several long robes that she preferred to wear when she was among her clansmen. "Yes."

Santiago narrowed his eyes. "That doesn't explain how the dragon knew what your bedroom looked like. Or what you wear when you're home alone."

She closed the door of the armoire with a controlled bang, turning to meet his suspicious gaze. "Either he took the image from my thoughts or somehow I'm manipulating the illusion to reflect my preferences."

"Your preference, but not mine?"

"And your point?"

Point? He didn't have a point, dammit. "It just seems odd."

"I'm not going to waste my energy trying to convince you

that Baine is not and never has been my lover." A cold blast of power rattled the silver candelabra. "Quite frankly my past is none of your business."

A wave of possessive satisfaction flared through him at the fierce sincerity in her sharp reprimand. A satisfaction that was swiftly followed by the knowledge he was behaving like an ass.

Again.

With an effort, he reengaged his brain. "I know that," he admitted with a grimace.

"Then why are you pouting?"

"Because the thought of any other man touching you makes me want to punch something," he said. "Really, really hard."

She blinked at his blunt confession. "That makes no sense."

He moved with fluid speed to stand directly before her, his hand reaching to cup her cheek. Beneath his fingers her skin was cool, but the feel of the satin smoothness sent licks of flame through his body.

"It's not supposed to."

Her gaze lowered to his lengthening fangs. "Santiago."

He stroked his thumb over her lower lip. "I need a shower."

"Don't let me stop you."

He smiled at her stiff tone. She could glare daggers if she wanted, but he could already catch the sweet musk of her arousal.

"You don't expect me to wash my own back, do you?"

"I'm annoyed with you."

His thumb tugged at her lower lip, allowing him to view the tips of her fully extended fangs.

The thought of them sinking into his flesh was enough to make him so hard it was painful. *Dios*. He needed to be inside this woman.

Now!

"Can you be annoyed with me in the shower?" he demanded thickly.

She nipped his thumb, her eyes darkening with the same hunger that thundered through him. "You're impossible."

"Agreed." Santiago lowered his head, touching their lips together in the lightest of caresses. "Jasmine silk," he murmured as he caught her lower lip between his teeth. "It's no wonder I can't think straight. You have me completely befuddled."

"You blame me?" Her lips moved against his as she spoke.

He gently outlined her mouth with his tongue. "I'm not complaining. I like it very, very much."

"Santiago . . ."

Her hands lifted as if she was going to put a swift end to his seduction and Santiago gave a low groan. *Dios*. He could feel her need. He could feel it tugging at things hidden deep in his soul.

But she was so determined to remain isolated behind her barriers that even accepting his desire became a battle.

Braced for her rejection, he wasn't prepared when her hands instead slid beneath his sweatshirt to trace over the tense muscles of his chest.

He clenched his jaw in delicious agony. Her touch was little more than a brush of her fingers, but it was enough to send a white-hot jolt of pleasure through his body.

"Nefri," he whispered, his kiss deepening with blatant greed.

A tiny voice might warn this was a hollow victory, but his body was eager to accept whatever she was willing to offer.

Trust, loyalty.

Genuine emotion?

He had never wanted or needed those things from a lover before. So why now?

Impatiently ripping off his shirt, Santiago wound his fingers through the satin softness of her hair and pressed impatient kisses over her upturned face. He wanted to taste every inch of her slender body. To wrap himself in her jasmine scent until they were both drowning in satisfaction.

"Nefri, I need to have you naked," he muttered. "I want to feel your skin against mine."

"This is madness," she muttered as he peeled the sweater over her head and tossed it onto the floor.

He regarded her with a wry smile, his hand cupping her full breasts and his thumb gently teasing a nipple into a tight bud.

No bra. He liked it.

A lot.

"Madness perhaps, but I no longer care," Santiago muttered as he lowered his head to close his lips around the tip of her nipple.

Nefri made a soft sound of surrender as she dug her nails into his shoulders, her body instinctively arching in silent invitation.

Santiago didn't hesitate. Tormenting her sensitive flesh with his tongue, he skimmed his hands down the curve of her waist. She tasted of cool power and sweet woman. An intoxicating combination, he decided as he easily dealt with the zip of her jeans and slid them down her hips.

With a last lingering taste of her nipple, he trailed his lips down the curve of her breast. Then, with a fluid grace he lowered himself to his knees, allowing the tips of his fangs to lightly caress the skin over her taut belly. She shivered, her fingers roughly tugging his hair out of its braid as he pulled her jeans downward, surprised to discover the tiny wisp of lacy . . . what were those under-thingies called?

Panties. Yes, his fogged mind acknowledged. That was it. Panties.

Hmmm. Tasty.

Reaching down he yanked off her shoes so he could get rid of the jeans. Tossing them aside, he paused to simply appreciate her exquisite beauty.

The bit of lace only served to wet his appetite. Like a bow on a much anticipated gift.

And it was a gift.

The most precious gift.

Grasping her hips, he leaned forward to nibble along the edge of the panties. He smiled as she yanked at his hair, her soft groan sweet music to his ears.

"Good lord," she muttered.

Tilting back his head, he met Nefri's smoldering black gaze, her features tight with a stark desire.

"I need you," he husked.

"I . . . yes."

He swallowed a chuckle at her rare loss for words and instead lowered his head to slice through the tiny string of her panties with a razor-sharp fang. Barely waiting for the bit of lace to hit the floor, he was tugging her legs further apart to nuzzle a path down her inner leg.

Slowly he explored the curve of her knee, the muscle of her calf, and the delicate joint of her ankle. At last reaching the tips of her toes, he moved to reverse the same service up the other leg.

"Santiago, are you deliberately trying to torture me?" she demanded in thick tones.

"I've promised myself I'm going to taste every inch of you," he said, recalling every restless day he'd lain awake, haunted by the memory of this woman.

Unaware of his dark thoughts, Nefri shifted restlessly beneath his lingering touch. "Enough . . . please."

He smiled as he at last sought out the tender flesh that begged for his touch. "Your wish is my command."

His tongue parted her, searching for the spot that made her hips jerk forward, and her toes curl.

"Santiago," she groaned.

He laughed. "More?"

He spread her even further as he teased the tiny nub hidden in the soft folds. Her fingers stroked restlessly through his hair, the scent of jasmine filling his senses.

His erection threatened to self-combust at the drugging

scent, but with ruthless determination he concentrated on Nefri's tiny shivers. He wanted the taste of her orgasm on his tongue.

Only then would he seek his own pleasure.

Sliding his hands upward, he teased at the hardened peaks of her breasts while his tongue began a steady stroke that had her groaning in quickening anticipation.

"Don't stop . . ." she commanded, her voice unsteady as her head tilted back in mindless need.

Stop?

Hell, a tribe of rabid trolls couldn't make him stop.

Sensing her muscles clenching in anticipation, he gave her one long, last stroke that sent her screaming over the edge.

Holding her hips in a ruthless grip, he coaxed her to yet another climax before he was rising upward and swiftly carrying her toward the bed.

Tumbling her into the center of the mattress, he followed her downward and positioned himself above her while she was still trembling with her release. Thrusting deep, he claimed her lips in a kiss of sheer possession.

His eyes closed and a moan was wrenched from his throat.

This was sheer paradise.

The slender female body that fit beneath him with absolute perfection. The feel of her slender hands as they swept down his back to grasp his hips. And the potent pulse of her outrageous power.

This was a woman like no other.

Rare.

Exceptional.

And . . . his.

With a slow movement he pulled out to his very tip before thrusting back into her silken body. *Dios,* but he was lost.

Completely and utterly ruined for any other woman.

Burying his face in the curve of her neck, Santiago pistoned his hips over and over, keeping his pace steady as she wrapped her legs around his waist. Her nails bit into his skin as she met him thrust for thrust, heightening his pleasure.

The climax was building and he lifted his head to press tiny kisses over her face.

"Nefri, I can't wait," he rasped.

"Good," she muttered, cupping his face in her hands as he plunged within her.

He managed to hold on until he could feel her ripples of satisfaction clenching him, then with a last groan, he lost himself in the fierce orgasm that ripped away all pretense and left him with the unshakable knowledge his life would never be the same.

Just north of Chicago

Sally woke with a throbbing head and a nasty premonition that she was ass-deep in trouble.

Like a coward she kept her eyes squeezed shut and tried to will herself back to sleep. If something bad was coming, why be conscious for it?

Unfortunately, she was sprawled on a hard cement floor that was giving her a cramp in the neck. And since whatever might be lurking in the dark didn't seem to be in a hurry to kill her, she grudgingly forced her heavy lids to lift.

She grimaced. On the up side, the large unoccupied room was thankfully empty of a ravaging horde. On the down side, it was coated in a thick layer of dust that now covered her from head to toe.

Stifling a sneeze, she managed to rise to her feet, pressing a hand to her aching temple.

Where the hell was she?

And more importantly, how did she get there?

Her gaze skimmed over the brick walls and the windows

that had been boarded over. The floor was cement and the lofted ceiling lined with steel beams.

A warehouse? A closed factory?

Taking a hesitant step forward, she desperately tried to remember what had happened. She'd been traveling through the tunnel with Roke, right? And then they'd come to the end of the tunnel even as her powers were running on empty.

What then? Vaguely she recalled Roke leaving to search the building overhead.

Had he abandoned her? Or had something happened to him? Was he hurt?

Or worse . . . ?

Before the disturbing thoughts could fully form, she was shaking her aching head. No. He'd come back. Yes. That was right. He'd come back and . . .

Her heart slammed painfully against her breastbone. Oh, crap.

He'd come back ready to murder her.

So had he succeeded? Was this her version of hell? An eternity alone in an empty, dusty warehouse?

It could be worse, she decided, heading toward the steel door across the barren room. She could be stuck with an arrogant bully of a vampire who had gone from loathing to downright hatred.

Almost as if the thought of Roke stirred some primitive connection to him, Sally came to a slow halt.

She sensed him. Not just physically, although she would swear she could feel the icy prickles of his power brushing over her skin.

But somewhere deep inside her.

Her mouth went dry as she glanced around the shadowed room. "Hello?" Her voice echoed eerily through the darkness, bouncing off the walls. "Is anyone there?"

There was the faintest swish of sound before a dark shape

was falling from the rafters. She instinctively leaped backward as the shadow revealed itself as Roke.

Holy crap.

Had he been hanging up there like a bat?

With a chilling smile, he folded his arms over his chest. He was still wearing the black jeans and leather jacket from earlier, but his dark hair lay as smooth as polished silk framing his stark, disgustingly handsome face.

"Going somewhere, witch?" he mocked, the pale eyes glowing white in the dim light.

"Roke," she breathed.

"Yes, Roke." His power bit into her skin like tiny shards of ice. "Your devoted love-slave."

She winced, rubbing her hands over her arms. "I'm sorry."

"Not yet, but I promise you're going to be."

She believed him. The threat of violence was a tangible force. She shivered, hoping he would at least make her death quick.

"I . . . it wasn't my fault."

He curled back his lips to reveal a set of fangs that looked massive to Sally.

And deadly.

And . . . painful. Really, really painful.

"Tell me exactly what you did to me," he snarled.

"I don't know."

He stepped forward, leaning down until they were nose to nose. "Try again."

"Stop." She stumbled back, her heart racing with a fear that threatened to consume her. "I can't think when you're looming over me like some avenging angel."

"Angel?" He gave a derisive snort. "That's a first."

She held up a pleading hand. "Just back off and I'll tell whatever you want to know."

"Fine." With a glare he took a deliberate step backward, his expression carved in granite. "Talk fast."

She cleared the lump from her throat, struggling to think through the panic clouding her mind. "Unless it was a part of my nightmare, you already know I'm not entirely human," she managed to rasp.

"You refused to tell me what blood runs in your veins."

"Because I truly don't know."

The pale, unnerving eyes narrowed. "Convenient."

"Convenient. Yeah, real convenient." Her short burst of laughter echoed eerily through the room. "My mother was a witch, and before you ask, yes, she practiced black magic," she bitterly admitted. She'd devoted a lot of energy to burying the memories of her mother. The last thing she wanted was to dig them up and relive them. "She was, in fact, everything that people fear most in witches. She was vain, selfish, and willing to sacrifice everything for power."

"A black witch." He shuddered in disgust.

"Yes," she hissed, absently rubbing her inner arm. The dang thing still itched. "I knew you would be suitably horrified."

"And your father?"

"A mystery."

He growled in warning. "Sally."

"I'm not done," she snapped, her terror not enough to halt her burst of anger. Did the damned vampire want her story or not?

"Then finish," he commanded in icy tones.

Why hadn't she slugged him in the nose when she had him in her power?

"After decades of making enemies my mother decided she needed to expand her power base," she said through clenched teeth. "Or at least that's what she always claimed."

"Didn't she have a coven?"

"She did, but she could never really trust that they wouldn't stage a coup d'état." Sally grimaced. Her mother had been as paranoid as she was power hungry. No doubt because everyone hated her guts. "She wanted a partner of absolute, unquestioning loyalty."

"A daughter."

"Give the vampire a gold star," she muttered.

There was another flash of fang. "This isn't the time to be a smart-ass."

It wasn't. Unfortunately, the more nervous she became the more mouthy she tended to be.

"Yes, a daughter," she forced herself to answer in reasonable tones. No sense antagonizing the already infuriated vampire. "Or more specifically, me."

"And she chose a demon to impregnate her?"

"Good god, no." She shook her head. "My mother had a pathological hatred of demons."

He frowned, almost as if he were offended by her confession. "Why?"

"Maybe because demons spend a great deal of time trying to kill witches," she pointed out.

He shrugged aside her accusation. Typical. Vampires were allowed to go around killing willy-nilly, but they weren't so happy when they were the prey.

"Then how did a demon end up in her bed?"

"From what I could discover my mother performed a secret fertility rite that would not only make sure she would become pregnant, but would lead her to the best candidate to be the"—she felt a ridiculous blush stain her cheeks—"donor."

His brows lifted. "And it led her to a demon?"

"So it would seem." She shrugged. "And beyond just being a demon, it had to be skillful enough to hide the fact it wasn't human from a very powerful witch. Not an easy task."

He studied her for several seconds. "Didn't your mother try to track him down after she discovered the truth?"

With an abrupt motion she turned away from his piercing

gaze. Her raw sense of betrayal was something she wasn't willing to share.

Certainly not with a vampire who wanted her dead.

"It took several years before she actually learned the truth."

"She didn't realize when you were born?"

"I was one of those half-breeds who didn't start showing my demon blood until I hit puberty." She hunched a shoulder, her stomach cramping at the agonizing memory. "Needless to say, my sweet sixteenth birthday is one I'll never forget."

"What happened?" His voice sounded odd. Tense.

"It doesn't matter."

"It does if it helps me determine what sort of demon you are."

God almighty. He truly was a masochist.

"You want the gory details?" She whirled back to glare at his carefully blank face. "Okay. I was assisting my mother with a spell that demanded a blood sacrifice, so I sliced open my palm. I'd done it a hundred times, but this time . . ."

"It healed."

"Yep, just like magic." Her lips twisted. She could still re-member every detail of that moment. The smell of smoke from the candles protecting their circle. The sound of her blood dripping on the wood floor. The hiss of horror from the woman who'd raised her as the wound had slowly sealed shut. "Only it wasn't magic. It was a death sentence."

"What do you mean?"

"I was still wondering why the heck my hand was healing when my mother hit me with a spell that was intended to evis-cerate me on the spot. It was only because she'd drilled me on how to block the most vicious spells that I managed to escape." She blinked back the tears that threatened. She didn't cry for that terrified girl who'd fled the cottage that night. Not anymore. "Ironic, isn't it?"

"Ironic?" Something dangerous smoldered in the depths of his pale eyes. "It's a damned mess."

Chapter 17

Roke glared at the female who continued to screw with his emotions.

Why else would he be feeling pity for her? What did he care if her psycho mother had tried to kill her? Or that she didn't know what sort of demon had fathered her?

He didn't.

It was nothing more than an effect of the spell.

Well, that wasn't entirely true, he was forced to concede. For the moment the demon blood running through her veins was very much his concern.

Damn it all.

"What other powers do you have?" he growled.

"Besides healing, I can see better in the dark, although not as good as you. And I'm stronger than most women." She shoved her fingers through her tangled hair, her expression one of self-derision. "Oh, and I think I might be aging slower, unless I just have really good genes."

He frowned, trying to ignore just how vulnerable she looked with her pale face covered with dust and the purple shadows beneath her eyes.

This female was his enemy.

Period.

"And you can compel others to your will?" he snarled.

She flinched. "Not exactly."

"Then explain *exactly* what it is you do."

She heaved a frustrated sigh. "Over the past few years I discovered I can, on a rare occasion—a very rare occasion," she emphasized, "I can influence someone."

"Influence?"

She nervously licked her lips, the tiny gesture sending a jarring bolt of desire through him.

Christ, he had to get rid of the spell.

"Okay, I'll admit that it seems to be increasing in potency, but I swear I didn't think for a minute that it would actually work on a vampire." She shivered, rubbing her arm as if it bothered her. "I was just so desperate I had to try something."

"Desperate?" He shrugged off her lame excuse. "That's ridiculous. Why would you be desperate?"

"Are you kidding me?" She gave a shake of her head. "I was locked in a dungeon with the threat that a demented vampire who I narced on might track me down at any second."

The tiny pang he felt was not guilt.

It was . . . contempt.

If she was so terrified of Gaius, then she shouldn't have joined his demented band of misfits.

Even if she had been abandoned—no, nearly killed—by her mother and left on her own to figure out the shocking changes going through her body?

He gave a disgruntled wave of his hand. He couldn't trust his thinking. Not when he was under the influence of her spell.

"We'll finish this conversation once we've returned to Styx's lair."

She backed away, shaking her head even as she dug her fingernails into the sleeve of her sweatshirt, scratching at her inner arm. "No way."

"Don't press me, little witch." His brows snapped together

as his frustrated glare shifted to where she rubbed at her arm. It was distracting. "What's wrong?"

"My arm itches."

"Why?"

She sucked in an angry breath. "Probably because I'm allergic to ill-mannered jerks who get their jollies from intimidating helpless women," she said. "It's that or you gave me cooties."

"Fine." He leaned forward, his blood heating as the enticing scent of peaches teased at his senses. Damn witch. "You want to see the last of me?"

"Yes."

"Then take off this goddamn spell."

She actually pretended to be puzzled. "What?"

"I'm not in the mood, Sally." He grabbed her by the shoulders, his grasp tight, but oddly careful not to bruise. "Take it off or I promise you that you'll be very, very sorry."

She futilely tried to pull away. "The spell was broken the moment I passed out."

"I don't believe you."

"It's only a temporary enchantment," she protested. "It was fading when we reached the end of the tunnel. By the time I fell asleep it was completely gone."

"No—you're lying. You're trying to use me in some nefarious plot."

"Nefarious?" she muttered. "Really?"

He lifted her off her feet, glaring straight into her wide eyes. "You bitch . . ."

"Chill," she rasped, her dark eyes flashing with irritation. "And watch what you call me."

Such stubborn courage.

Such exquisite beauty.

With a growl, he abruptly dropped her back to her feet, taking a step away from her sweet temptation. "What I call you should be the least of your concern."

She stumbled before regaining her balance, tossing back her brilliant autumn hair as she glared at him in frustration. "What do you want from me? My promise? No freaking problem." She drew an X on her sweatshirt, directly over her heart. He clenched his hands as the gesture emphasized the soft curve of her breasts. "I cross my heart and hope to die that the spell is gone." Her hand dropped. "If it was still active don't you think I would be making you lead me away from here, not freezing my ass off in this nasty . . ." She glanced around the warehouse where he'd brought her before the sun rose hours ago. "Where are we anyway?"

He stiffened, grimly allowing the humiliating memories of fleeing through the tunnels to escape with this female to rise to his mind.

At the time he would have done anything to keep her safe. Anything.

And then he'd climbed out of the tunnel and the driving compulsion had been gone. Just as if a spell had suddenly been broken.

He shook his head. No. This had to be a trick.

What could be more clever than to release him from the greater compulsion so he would presume the spell was gone, while all along keeping him tied to her by far more subtle means?

A Manchurian candidate ready to be triggered when she felt the urge.

"That's impossible."

She shivered as his power wrapped around her in icy warning. "It's the truth," she protested.

"No."

"Dammit, why are you so convinced I'm lying?"

"Because I can still feel you."

"I . . ." Her words trailed away, her already pale face becoming downright ashen.

The sight wasn't reassuring. "No smart-ass denial?"

"The spell is gone." She hunched her shoulders, rubbing at her arm. "It has to be a—"

"A what?"

"Just a lingering side effect," she said. "Yeah. A lingering side effect. That has to be it."

She didn't believe her excuse.

He knew because he could actually feel her growing agitation.

As if it were his own.

"Sally."

She scrambled back as he reached to grasp her shoulders, her breath coming in short, painful pants.

"Look, I don't know, okay? I told you I haven't had much practice at being a demon." She gave a sudden cry, yanking up the sleeve of her sweatshirt. "Dammit. Why is my arm itching?" There was a startled silence before Sally released a strangled moan. "Oh . . . shit."

"Now what?" he growled, wondering if she was trying to distract him.

"I think I have a disease."

She turned her arm to reveal the intricate red scrolling that crawled the length of her inner forearm. The marking wasn't a disease. Or a reaction to his cooties. Or even the result of a drunken trip to the local tattoo parlor.

This mark was beneath the pale skin and only one thing could cause it.

A mating.

Swearing in several languages, Roke ripped off his leather jacket to glare down at the matching tattoo that marred his own arm.

The demon in him howled in disbelief.

"God . . . dammit."

Sally glanced at him in confusion. "Am I dying?"

"Only if I decide to kill you."

"That's not funny." She tried to meet him glare for glare but she couldn't hide her growing fear.

And for some stupid reason that pissed him off more than the mark of bonding on his arm.

"Nothing about this FUBAR situation is funny," he roared, moving with lightning speed to slam his hand into the brick wall.

His knuckles split open beneath the impact and the bricks crumbled to dust. Ignoring the blood dripping onto the cement floor, he slammed his hand into the bricks again, allowing the pain to hold back the blinding fury that threatened to consume him.

"Stop," Sally cried from behind him. "You might be immortal, but I'm not so sure I am."

Belatedly realizing his temper tantrum was sending a shower of dust and plaster from the ceiling, Roke turned to glare at his companion. "Do you know what you've done?"

She jerkily brushed the dust from her hair. "I haven't done . . ." She seemed to forget what she was going to say as her gaze shifted over his shoulder. "What's that?"

He turned back, startled to discover the large hole he'd punched into the wall had revealed the top of an old-fashioned steel strongbox complete with a combination lock.

"A safe of some sort," he said with a shrug.

What did he care? He'd discovered this forgotten warehouse during his first week in Chicago. It was not only isolated from most humans, but it was far enough from Styx's lair that he could enjoy his nightly meditation without fear of interruption.

He'd never given much thought to who had owned it before it was abandoned.

"There's something strange about it." She moved to stand at his side, her brow furrowed. "I think we should open it."

"We have much bigger things to worry about than some forgotten treasure."

"I'm not interested in treasure," she snapped. "There's something wrong with the aura around it."

"Aura?" With a roll of his eyes, Roke reached to rip the top off the safe, ignoring the ear-splitting screech of metal as it was wrenched apart. The sooner he was done with Sally's latest attempt to distract him, the sooner they could deal with the catastrophe she'd created. Peering into the safe, he made a sound of impatience. "It's empty. Are you happy . . . ?" He frowned, blinking as there was a strange shimmer, like the sheen of a soap bubble before it burst to reveal something at the very bottom. "No, wait. There's a book."

Reaching into the safe, Roke was caught off guard when Sally grabbed his arm in a frantic grip.

"No. Don't touch it."

He sent her a wary glance. "Why?"

"There's a spell wrapped around it." She shivered. "A very nasty spell."

"Can you get rid of it?"

"Not without time to prepare a counterspell." She turned to meet his narrowed stare. "Don't look at me like that."

"Like what?"

"Like you're certain I must be lying." She folded her arms over her chest, her expression militant. "You don't believe me, go ahead and touch it."

Yeah, right. As if magic hadn't screwed up his life enough. He wasn't about to be turned into a newt. Or worse.

Of course. If he was a newt, then he wouldn't have to worry about whether or not he'd been trapped with this female for the next eternity.

With a shake of his head, Roke returned to pull on his leather jacket before grabbing Sally around the waist and, with one smooth motion, tossing her over his shoulder.

"This night could truly not get any worse," he muttered, heading toward the door.

"Hey, what do you think you're doing?" she protested, slamming her hands against his back.

His arms wrapped around her thighs, keeping her from kicking him.

"If you hope to survive the night, little witch, you'll keep your mouth shut until I tell you to speak."

There was another flurry of fists to his back, hard enough to crack a rib.

"Bastard."

The woods of Wisconsin

Gaius stood hidden in the trees that circled the honky-tonk joint. The wooden structure with a brick chimney that belched smoke toward the star-speckled sky was barely adequate to contain the large crowd of humans that gyrated to the blaring country music. Not that they seemed to notice as they chugged their beer and laughed with increasing frequency.

They were young and arrogant and confident that they were impervious to harm.

Fools.

Not one of them sensed that death hovered just out of sight.

Gaius's fangs lengthened, the scent of fresh blood overcoming even the stench of brats and sauerkraut. His stomach rumbled. Tasty.

Somewhere in the back of his mind he knew he shouldn't be hungry. Hadn't he fed the night before last? Or was it last night?

Time was starting to run together. Something that should have troubled him. Just as his filthy, tangled hair and blood-stained clothing should have troubled him.

Ah well.

With a shake of his head, he moved forward, wincing as the shouts of drunken revelry turned to shrieks of terror.

His pace remained steady. They wouldn't run. They never ran. At least not anymore.

It was a shame, really.

What was the point of being a predator if you couldn't chase your prey?

Of course, if he were to be completely honest, he wasn't certain that he had the energy to play the role of hunter. Since Dara's return he hadn't been able to rest. Not just because he had to be on guard to protect her, but fulfilling her constant needs was draining.

Perhaps that explained his incessant hunger. . . .

Climbing the wooden steps, Gaius entered the building and paused to savor the overwhelming emotions that filled the air. In the far corner the twenty humans cowered together in frozen terror, some crying softly while others gave panicked little moans. None, however, made a move to attack him.

Passing by the long, waist-high bar, he reached over to grab the bartender, who had been trying to ram his three-hundred-pound body beneath a shelf. With a strength that revealed his was anything but human, he hauled the struggling man over the bar and with one smooth strike had his teeth buried in the thick neck.

The man screamed, struggling to pull a large knife from its sheath at his waist. Gaius easily knocked the weapon from his hand as he sucked the blood from the bartender's body, his burning hunger barely assuaged.

Dropping the corpse, he turned his attention toward the huddled mass, pointing his finger toward a slender, dark-haired female.

A tender bud of female temptation.

With a crook of his finger he had her on her feet and walking toward him. Her eyes were blank of emotion beneath his compulsion, but she readily went to her knees and reached for his belt buckle.

Dara wouldn't mind. She was too ill to satisfy his needs.

And as long as he remembered to take four or five of the shivering mortals back to satisfy her strange cravings, she would be happy enough.

The female wrapped her lips around his aching cock and Gaius allowed the nagging sense of . . . wrongness . . . to melt away.

Chapter 18

The Ozark Mountains

Nefri perched on the edge of the bed with Santiago seated directly behind her, his legs bracketing hers as he ran a brush through the thick strands of her damp hair.

It was the sort of casually intimate moment that most lovers shared.

Except for her.

She never indulged in love play. It made her feel exposed. Even more exposed than the actual act of sex. After all, sex was a primitive need that could be shared between complete strangers.

This . . . this was true intimacy. It took a level of faith she was never comfortable offering.

Until tonight.

After hours of pleasure, she'd fallen asleep wrapped in Santiago's arms, only to awaken to his wicked kisses stirring the hunger she had thought sated for the next century.

It wasn't until she could sense the sun setting that they'd at last made it to the long overdue shower.

Now they were forced to wait for Baine to either reveal his secrets or tell them to go.

Something that should be making Santiago nuts. He wasn't a patient sort of vampire (understatement of the century). He should be snorting and fuming and threatening to castrate Baine for forcing him to sit around and wait for the dragon's decision.

Instead he calmly ran the brush through her hair, his prolonged silence as uncharacteristic as his lack of irritation.

"You seem . . ." She searched for a word that wouldn't rub against his pride. Men were so sensitive. "Pensive."

She felt him shrug. "I'm a pensive kind of guy."

She made a sound of disbelief. "You're the least pensive man I know."

"I'm not sure if I've been insulted or not."

"No. I like your ability to listen to your instincts." She shifted so she could study his guarded expression. He was dressed in a gray sweatshirt and jeans that had magically appeared in the armoire along with jeans and a lovely peach cashmere sweater for her. His hair had already been brushed and braided, emphasizing the sharp angles and planes of his achingly handsome face. "And your heart."

"Like, hmmm?" He smiled with decadent promise, the tips of his fangs visible. "How much do you like me?"

A shiver inched down her spine. Her instant reaction was downright indecent.

"Well enough."

The dark eyes smoldered with a rising heat. "I think I can make you like me better than well enough." His head dipped downward, nuzzling at the sensitive spot at the base of her throat.

Her hands lifted to press at his shoulders. She had to stop him now or she'd be lost. "Santiago?"

"Yes?"

"What were you thinking about?"

The tip of one fang scraped down the line of her collarbone. "You want to discuss it now?"

Of course she didn't. She wanted to close her eyes and drown in the melting heat. But if she allowed herself to be distracted, she knew she'd never discover what was troubling him. "Yes."

He reluctantly pulled back, regarding her with a brooding gaze. "Why did you leave last time without even saying good-bye?"

Nefri froze. Oh . . . lord. That wasn't what she'd been expecting. If she had, she certainly wouldn't have pressed him.

Now she turned to stare blindly at the hand-carved dressing table that had been a gift from a grateful Persian king. Or at least the illusion of her table. Anything to avoid his unwavering gaze.

"Because I was afraid if I saw you again I wouldn't have the courage to leave," she said, her voice so low only a vampire could have picked up her words.

"And that would have been a bad thing?"

"My people needed their clan chief."

"And what about what I needed, *cara?*"

She clenched her hands. Okay, she hadn't told him the full truth.

A part of her had fled because it was safer to scurry back behind the Veil and forget about the vampire that made her feel as vulnerable as a foundling.

But, she truly had needed to return to her people.

They'd been deeply disturbed to realize that Gaius was a traitor who had taken advantage of their secluded clan to acquire the skills to assist the Dark Lord in ripping apart the barriers between worlds.

"What do you want from me?" she demanded.

"Everything."

She frowned. Did he expect her to turn her back on her people? To walk away from her responsibilities?

The mere thought should have been infuriating, but she found herself actually considering the possibility.

Could she leave her people to return to this world? Could she give up her leadership to be with the man who had reminded her that there was more to life than just duty?

"I . . ."

She didn't know what she was going to say, and in the end it didn't matter as the bedroom abruptly melted around them.

"What the hell?" Leaping to his feet, Santiago caught her as the bed disappeared.

The air around them shimmered, before becoming a long hallway with a set of double doors at the far end.

"It seems that Baine has reached his decision," she said.

Santiago grasped her by the shoulders, turning her to meet his resolute expression. "This conversation is postponed, not finished."

She resisted the urge to roll her eyes. Like she doubted for a second the stubborn vampire would press until he had the answer he wanted?

"I know." She gently pulled out of his grasp. "But later. We shouldn't keep Baine waiting."

He grimaced, but he fell into step beside her, his hand automatically reaching to unsheathe the sword that he'd strapped to his back.

Nefri held her tongue until they reached the end of the paneled hall. Then, laying her hand on his arm, she halted him from opening the door. "Santiago."

He glanced at her with a lifted brow. "I thought you didn't want to keep the dragon waiting?"

She chose her words with care. "Baine might be one of the oldest, most powerful creatures in several universes, but in some ways he can be almost childish. If you offend him he might very well refuse to share what he knows."

His lips twitched at her careful diplomacy. "I promise to be on my very bestest behavior. Is that what you want to hear?"

"I was hoping you would let me deal with the dragon." She met his deliberately blank expression. "Just . . ." She bit off her words and gave a resigned shake of her head. The vampire would do exactly what he wanted to do. "Oh, never mind," she muttered, reaching to shove the door open. "So stubborn."

"Stones in glass houses, Nefri," he whispered into her ear as she stepped past him.

Ignoring his taunt, Nefri entered the throne room, not surprised to find the dragon indolently sprawled on the large throne. He was again dressed in nothing more than a loose pair of *dojo* pants, his shimmering tattoos crawling over his skin and his eyes burning with an amber fire.

"Baine." She came to a halt and performed a respectful bow. "Thank you for speaking with us again."

The amber gaze shifted to Santiago, who stood protectively at her side, his sword in hand.

"I would prefer not to; I certainly have more intriguing matters to claim my attention," he murmured, his attention turning back to Nefri. "Unfortunately, I have a debt to pay."

"A debt?" Santiago asked.

Baine shrugged. "A beautiful vampire once saved my life. I will attempt to return the favor."

Nefri shook her head as Santiago slid a questioning glance in her direction. She'd never heard rumors of a vampire rescuing a dragon, although she didn't doubt it would prove to be a fascinating story.

For now, however, she was far more interested in Baine's implication that the vampires needed to be saved.

"Are we in that much danger?"

"Yes."

Nefri shivered at the blunt agreement. "From the spirit?"

"It's more than just a spirit. It's a—" Baine halted, seeming to consider his words. "A creator."

Beside her, Santiago stiffened. "A god?"

"That depends on your definition of god." Baine absently touched a tattoo that resembled an ancient Sanskrit mark that briefly appeared on his neck. Nefri suspected that Baine had been considered a god by more than one cult over the centuries. "It's no longer worshipped, or even remembered by most, but it did spawn several species of demons."

Nefri's growing concern only intensified. It hadn't occurred to her that the spirit had family in the world.

"Demons that still exist?" she asked.

"Of course," Baine assured her. "You're familiar with Lamsung demons?"

"Soul-suckers," Santiago said in disgust.

The Lamsung had been forced into a hell dimension centuries before. Few demons were willing to risk their souls to a creature that could drain them for dinner. It was claimed that the Sylvermysts possessed rare swords that were made with the heart of a Lamsung demon and capable of giving them strength through the enemies they slayed.

"Descriptive," Baine mocked.

Nefri ignored Santiago's prickle of power that crawled over her skin. She didn't have time for a male pissing match.

"Is that what this spirit does?" she demanded. "Steal the souls of his victims?"

"No." Baine shook his head. "The feeding of souls is unique to the Lamsung, just as the spirit's other children have their own special dietary habits."

"What other children?" Santiago growled.

Baine smiled. "Can't you guess?"

The truth hit Nefri with blinding force. What other creature lived off the life force of their victims?

"Vampires?"

The dragon's smile widened. "Vampires."

Santiago wasn't a philosophical vampire.

Oh, he was intelligent and well read, and a cunning warrior.

But he'd never understood the need to brood and ponder on matters that had no straightforward answer.

He preferred action to reaction.

This, however, was enough to make any man hesitate.

"So you're saying this . . . thing is the creator of vampires?" he demanded.

Baine gave a wave of his hand. "That's my assumption."

Santiago's low growl rumbled in his throat. This dragon would be greatly improved by a good ass-kicking. A damned shame he'd promised Nefri to be on his best behavior.

"Assumption?" he snapped.

"Santiago." Nefri sent him one of those glances that held a combination of exasperation and warning before turning back to the dragon. "As you can imagine, this has been a shock."

Baine lifted a brow. "Don't you know anything of your history?"

"There's very little written on the origins of vampires. And the oral history . . ." Nefri gave a lift of her hands. "Well, I don't have to tell you, we're an arrogant species. It's not surprising that most believe we were sent to this world by superior beings to become the ultimate rulers."

"And it never occurred to you that you might be a mutation from a more primitive demon?" Baine demanded.

Nefri shook her head. "My studies have been slanted toward the mystical rather than the scientific. I've never researched evolution."

The burning amber gaze shifted to Santiago. "And you?"

He shrugged. "I like the 'ultimate rulers' theory."

Baine snorted, a hint of smoke curling from one nostril. "Predictable."

Nefri ignored their little interchange, her expression hinting that she wasn't nearly so calm as she was trying to pretend.

"Will you share what you know?"

"My knowledge is fragmented and far too much relies on stories I've heard secondhand," the dragon admitted. "I never encountered the actual spirit in person. Thank my own very mysterious gods."

Santiago instinctively tightened his hand on his sword. Knowing that the all-powerful dragon was afraid of the spirit wasn't particularly heartening. "Why?"

"It's claimed that the spirit is capable of feeding off any demon, no matter how strong they might be."

"It feeds off demons?" Santiago rasped.

"Demons or humans." Baine shrugged. "It doesn't seem to be particular."

Well, this just got better and better.

Grimacing, Santiago tried to shove aside the growing list of reasons why he should return to Styx and tell him to appoint another vampire to hunt down Gaius.

The spirit was an enemy. He needed to approach it as he would any other enemy. Which meant gaining as much intel as he could.

"You said that its spawn had their own means of feeding," he said. "Which I assume means it doesn't drink blood or suck souls."

Baine smiled, the amber eyes smoldering with fire. "No."

"Then what the . . ." Santiago stilled, cursing himself for being so dense. It all made perfect, horrible sense now. *"Mierda."*

Nefri sent him a puzzled glance. "What is it?"

"Emotion," he rasped. "It feeds off emotion."

Her eyes widened, easily able to make the same connection that he had. "Of course."

"So, not all brawn," Baine drawled.

Santiago narrowed his gaze. "I have my moments."

"If this creature feeds off emotion, it makes sense that it would inspire fear and lust and violence among humans," Nefri murmured, speaking her thoughts out loud.

"And demons," Baine reminded her.

"Yes, and demons." Her brow furrowed. "But why use Gaius to spread the emotions? Does it need a conduit?"

Baine tapped a finger on the arm of his throne. "Are you certain it's Gaius that's creating the emotions?"

Nefri gave a hesitant nod. "As certain as we can be at this point."

"This spirit," Santiago abruptly interrupted, "is it able to take corporeal form?"

Baine shook his head. "Like vampires it's symbiant."

Santiago scowled. "What's that supposed to mean?"

"It must take possession of a body that belongs to another."

Santiago glanced toward Nefri. They'd been chasing what they thought were two demons. Was it possible that it was just one and he was being possessed by the spirit?

"Gaius?"

She chewed her bottom lip. "You said that the witch claimed he was protecting someone."

"She never did see the 'someone,'" he pointed out.

"True," she agreed, although her expression remained troubled.

Santiago didn't blame her. Right now they could do no more than make wild suppositions that didn't do them a damned bit of good.

He turned back to the dragon. "The most important question is how do we kill it?"

"Are you sure that's what you want?" The amber flames in Baine's eyes became oddly hypnotizing. "It is, after all, your ultimate sire."

Santiago shook off the dragon's intrusion into his mind. The bastard was no doubt hoping to enjoy a full-blown spiritual crisis. Unfortunately for him, Santiago was a warrior, not a monk.

"What will happen if it's left free?"

A mocking smile touched Baine's mouth. "Strong emotions

have inevitable conclusions. It begins with murder and rape and the always favorite pillaging. Eventually it will disintegrate into war, genocide, and famine."

He felt Nefri grow rigid at the stark warning and he instinctively rubbed a comforting hand down her back.

Not that he had much comfort to offer.

Dammit, hadn't they just prevented the end of the world? Now they had to face war and genocide and famine?

Where was the justice in that?

"You didn't answer the question," he reminded the dragon, in no mood to be diplomatic. He snorted. Who was he kidding? He was *never* in the mood to be diplomatic. But after the past few weeks he was even more impatient than usual. "How do we kill it?"

Baine's tattoos swirled in warning, although his voice remained soft. "I don't know."

So the mighty dragon knew everything but the information they most needed.

Predictable.

"Great."

Baine leaned forward. "But I do find it intriguing that the Commission chose to imprison the spirit rather than destroying it, don't you?"

Santiago paused. He'd rather have his tongue cut out than admit it, but the oversized lizard had a point.

Why hadn't the Oracles killed the creature? Because they were demon conservationists who didn't believe in killing off the potential last of a species? Yeah, right. More likely it was because they didn't know how to get rid of the thing.

So instead they sent Nefri to do their dirty work, not giving a shit that she might die in the process.

Fury raced through him at the same time Baine rose from his throne, his surge of power making the earth shake beneath their feet.

Instinctively, Santiago shoved Nefri behind him, his sword raised. "Do we have a problem, dragon?" he growled.

"Your companion is searching for you," Baine growled, his tattoos darkening. "And he's not alone."

Santiago frowned. "What companion?"

Nefri elbowed him in the side. "Levet."

He rolled his eyes. He wouldn't call the miniature pest a companion. More like an unwelcome boil on his ass.

"Our"—his lips twisted as he forced out the word—"*companion* can wait. I still have questions."

Baine shook his head. "I have paid my debt." He shifted his attention to the silent Nefri, the amber flames consuming his eyes. "My last word of warning, beautiful Nefri, is not to hesitate. With every passing day the spirit grows more powerful."

"Wait . . ." Santiago stepped forward, but even as he moved, the throne room was dissolving around him.

Dammit.

He held on to Nefri as Baine offered a last mocking wave and the throne room faded to be replaced by the rolling meadow and large tree that was no longer split in two.

Barely managing to keep his balance at the abrupt change from a polished wood floor to muddy, uneven ground, Santiago's seething frustration became pure male outrage at the stench of granite and . . . was that brimstone?

"There you are," a French-accented voice proclaimed. "*Mon dieu.* I thought you'd been stolen by leprechauns."

"Leprechauns," a female voice taunted. "Everyone knows there are no leprechauns."

Spinning on his heel, Santiago discovered the stunted gargoyle standing a few feet away, accompanied by a tiny female demon with black, oblong-shaped eyes and razor sharp teeth.

Gods almighty, the gargoyle had a friend?

Okay, maybe not a friend, he hastily revised his opinion as the two glared at one another.

"It was a metaphor," Levet informed his companion, his wings quivering with anger.

The female gave a toss of her long braid, her hands smoothing down the long, white robe that covered her diminutive body. "It was idiotic," she muttered.

"Dios." Santiago turned to discover Nefri regarding the tiny couple with a faint smile. "Shoot me now."

Chapter 19

Styx's lair in Chicago

Sally didn't know why she was caught off guard when Roke carried her directly to Styx's dungeon.

Did she think making him her temporary love-slave would soften his hatred for her? Or hey, maybe he would be grateful she'd made him betray his people and help her escape?

Yeah, he should be thrilled-to-freaking-death with her.

Still, as he entered the house by the hidden tunnel and headed directly to the dungeon, she was overwhelmed by a sudden avalanche of panic.

What did he intend to do to her? He'd been furious in the warehouse. How did she know he didn't intend to kill her and leave her body for the scavengers?

And once she was back in the hexed cell, she would be utterly helpless.

Pounding his back with her fists, she futilely attempted to kick him in the one place vampires were as vulnerable as any other man.

"No," she shrieked. "I won't be locked up again."

His steps never faltered as he bypassed the curious guards. "I didn't ask for your opinion."

"Let me go." He ignored her, shoving open the door to the dungeon and heading down the narrow corridor that ran between the line of cells. "Roke, did you hear me?"

"I'm sure your screechings are audible to half of Chicago."

Sally bit her lip. Her hands ached from hitting the unyielding muscles of his back and with every step the cell grew nearer. Soon she would be locked away. Or worse.

Abruptly something inside her broke and to her utter humiliation she burst into tears.

"You . . . bastard."

Apparently as shocked as she was by her emotional meltdown, Roke slid her off his shoulder so she was standing directly in front of him.

"Sssh," he muttered, frowning as his thumbs brushed the tears from her cheeks. "I'm not going to hurt you."

She sniffed, telling herself that she wasn't comforted by his gentle touch.

He was a . . . a . . . cold-blooded leech.

"You already have," she muttered.

"Me?" He appeared ridiculously outraged by her accusation. "What have I done?"

Was he serious? She lifted her arm to reveal the strange rash on her inner arm.

"This, for one thing."

His jaw tightened, as if angered by her reminder of the crimson mark. "Don't blame me. That's entirely your fault." He lifted his own arm, pushing back the sleeve of his jacket to reveal a matching rash.

"I don't . . ." Her words faltered. Wait. How could he have the same exact rash as her? Was it some side effect from her powers? She hadn't heard of anything like it. All right, there was the brand between mated vampires that was supposed to be some sort of red tattoo, but it couldn't be that. Impossible. Abruptly she remembered his fury as he'd ripped off his jacket and her heart stuttered to a painful halt. "Oh crap. Is that . . ."

"A mating mark," he assured her in icy tones.

She shook her head, stumbling backward as her brain refused to accept what he was saying.

"How's that possible? I thought leeches had to exchange blood to become bonded." She unconsciously ran her fingers over the markings on her arm, as if she could rub them away. "Not to mention lack the homicidal urge to murder each other."

He curled back his lips to reveal his fully extended fangs. Yep. Definitely murder on his mind.

"Obviously your spell triggered the mating instinct."

She shivered. Mating instinct. It was primitive. Uncivilized.

And not at all a reason for her stomach to flutter as if she were . . .

Excited?

No. Way.

"I don't care how it happened," she said, an edge of panic in her voice. "Just get rid of it."

He lifted a dark brow, his pale eyes reflecting the overhead light. "And how would you suggest I do that?"

"I . . ." She licked her dry lips.

"Yes?"

She wrapped her arms around her body, which continued to shake with uncontrollable tremors. "How do vampires break the bond?"

"They don't." He held her wary gaze, his expression grim. "A mating is for eternity."

"But this isn't a real mating."

"Isn't it?"

She frowned. Was this some sort of trick? Did he think she'd intentionally tried to trap them together? "Of course not."

"You can't feel me deep inside you?" His voice thickened,

his fingers lightly touching the narrow valley between her breasts. "Here."

An erotic burst of heat speared through her at his touch. A heat that was nearly as shocking as the realization he was right.

She could feel him.

His burning frustration. His barely leashed fury.

His unwanted arousal.

She'd tried to tell herself that the sensations were just an echo of the spell that had bound them together.

That it would quickly fade.

But the words rang hollow.

He was . . . a part of her.

"Roke," she breathed, her heart skipping a beat as he turned smoothly toward the far door.

"Styx is coming."

His muttered words had barely left his lips when the door to the dungeon was flung open with enough force to make the hinges squeak in protest.

A bare second later the six-foot-five Aztec warrior entered the dungeons, bringing with him an icy tidal wave of power.

As far as entrances went, this one was a doozy, and Sally instinctively stepped backward, pressing herself against Roke, as if he were a safe harbor in the midst of a gathering hurricane.

"What the hell is going on?" the Anasso roared, the lights flickering in and out to create an unnerving strobe effect.

"Sally, look at me," Roke commanded in a low voice, grasping her chin to force her to meet his shimmering gaze.

She struggled to breath, suddenly so cold her teeth were chattering. "I'll take a wild stab and say he's pissed," she managed to mutter.

He leaned down until their noses were nearly touching, an oddly possessive expression tightening his lean features. "Not nearly as pissed as I'm going to be if you try to use your powers on him," he rasped. "In fact, you can consider that particular skill off-line for the foreseeable future."

Her fear remained. Full-scale. She was trapped between two angry vampires. There wasn't a witch alive who wouldn't be frightened out of her mind.

But she was female enough to be annoyed by his blatant command. "You're not the boss of me."

His thumb brushed her lower lip, his gaze searing a path over her stubborn expression. "Don't push this, witch."

"I . . ." She became lost in the compelling beauty of his eyes, her annoyance floundering as she felt his fierce tension. This wasn't just a male need to toss out orders. It . . . mattered to him. "Trust me, I never intend to use it again," she at last conceded.

"Good," he growled. "Because if you try to bond with another man, I'll . . ."

She scowled. "You'll what?"

Without warning he grabbed her face and kissed her with a raw yearning that she felt to the tips of her toes.

Holy shit.

"You're making me nuts," he muttered against her lips.

She clutched at his leather jacket, her knees stupidly weak. "The feeling is entirely mutual."

"Roke," a dark, frigid voice broke into their brief moment of madness. "Am I intruding?"

Releasing his hold on her, Roke turned to face his king, angling his body so she was half shielded behind him.

Sally blinked in surprise. He couldn't feel a need to protect her. Could he?

"I thought you went to speak with the Oracles?" Roke said to the towering vampire who was regarding him with a narrowed glare.

"They refused to see me." He folded his arms over his massive chest, testing the limits of endurance for the black T-shirt that was matched with a pair of black leather pants and heavy boots. "Which meant I wasn't in the mood to return to my lair and discover I've been harboring a traitor."

Sally went rigid at the accusation. "He's not a traitor," she blurted out before she could halt the words.

"No?" The King of Vampires turned his alarming attention in her direction. "My guards informed me that Roke took you from this cell against my strict orders, and then with the excuse he was taking you to meet with me, he assisted in your escape."

"Only because I forced him."

Styx stepped forward, emphasizing her distinct lack of stature. "You?"

"Yes." Her chin tilted even as her brain screamed to shut her mouth. Unfortunately, the two weren't currently connected. "I'm not completely helpless. And, as you see, he brought me back."

Styx studied her for a long, nerve-wracking minute. "Such a fierce defense of your captor," he at last murmured.

"I'm not defending him." She hunched a shoulder, well aware she sounded like an idiot. Crap. Could she blame it on the mating? Obviously it was destroying what few brain cells she had left. "I'm just . . . explaining."

"Styx." With a fluid movement, Roke was shifting to stand at Styx's side, as if he were trying to distract the large vampire from Sally. "I need to speak with you in private."

She frowned, pretending she didn't notice her treacherous flare of warmth at Roke's protective gesture. Instead she sent him a warning scowl.

She'd be damned if she'd be abandoned alone in this dungeon.

Not again.

"Hey, you're not leaving me here."

Styx started to offer a condescending smile at her sharp words only to freeze as his gaze caught sight of the markings on her inner arm. "Christ," he rasped. "Roke, what have you done?"

The Anasso reached to grab her arm, but without warning Roke was slamming into the larger vampire, pinning him to the bars of the nearest cell.

"Don't touch her," he growled.

A deathly silence filled the dungeon. A silence even more shocking after the unexpected flurry of violence.

Sally didn't dare breathe as the two powerful demons glared at one another. Then, curling back his lips to display his enormous fangs, Styx spoke in low, commanding tones.

"Release me, brother." Enough power filled the air to send Roke stumbling backward. "Now!"

Roke rammed his fingers through his hair, his jaw clenched so tight it was a wonder his teeth didn't crack under the strain.

"Dammit," Roke hissed.

Styx straightened, his warrior features carved from granite. "You're right, we do need to speak."

Sally sucked in an unsteady breath as the two men turned, clearly preparing to leave the dungeons without her.

"Roke, if you abandon me here I swear I won't help with the book."

Styx halted, sending her a puzzled frown. "What book?"

"Sally," Roke growled.

She slammed her hands onto her hips. It was no doubt suicidal to challenge two of the most powerful vampires she'd ever met, but the mere thought of being locked away overcame any claim to sanity.

"I mean it," she snapped.

The dark band around the pale, pale eyes narrowed, a sure sign of annoyance. "You aren't the only witch."

"Maybe not, but you'll never find another who has my power, or my familiarity with black magic," she reminded him. It wasn't bragging. The gods knew she hated her connection to black magic. It was the simple truth. "You need me."

For a second they glared at one another in silence, then realizing he was going to eventually need her help, he conceded defeat with all his usual grace.

"Shit," he growled, turning to stomp his way toward the dungeon door. "She's coming with us."

Peaches.

Roke clenched his teeth as they entered Styx's private study and the large vampire shut the door behind them.

He was furious with the female. Hell, furious didn't even cover it. She'd bespelled him, forced him to act against his will, mated him, and now blackmailed him to get out of the dungeons. But, that didn't keep him from placing a possessive hand on her shoulder as Styx moved past them to lean against a heavy desk that held a computer and several monitors.

And it didn't halt that maddening scent of peaches from making his fangs ache with a desire to sink them deep into her flesh and taste if her blood were as sweet as that tantalizing perfume.

Folding his arms over his chest, Styx studied Roke's tense expression before turning his attention to Sally.

"I should warn you, Ms. Grace, that this room has been hexed," he said, his low voice edged with warning. "Your magic won't work here."

Roke snorted. "Actually, you shouldn't be so certain, old friend." His gaze slid to the tiny witch at his side. "Ms. Grace is full of surprises."

"Yes, I suppose she is," the Anasso murmured. "Are you going to tell me how you two ended up mated?"

Roke watched in fascination as a blush crept beneath Sally's pale face and for the first time he considered the fact that despite her sharp tongue and foolish courage, she was extremely young.

Why did the thought make him feel like a letch? None of this catastrophe was his fault.

"Do you want the honors?" he growled.

Her blush deepened as she warily met Styx's unwavering gaze. "I'm part demon."

The ancient vampire hissed, obviously caught off guard by her confession. "What demon?"

Roke's lips twisted into a humorless smile. *Welcome to my world, bud.*

"I don't know." She held up a silencing hand as Styx's lips parted. "I truly don't know. But to make a long story short, over the last few years I've discovered an ability to . . . coerce people to obey me for short periods of time."

Roke made a sound of disgust. "Coerce?"

"Maybe it's more of an enchantment," she reluctantly conceded. "But I've only used it once or twice on humans. Until a few weeks ago it was never strong enough to influence demons, and then it was only a hellhound. I never dreamed it could affect a vampire. It was only because I was desperate I even tried."

Styx's gaze transferred to Roke. "And that's when you mated?"

"I didn't notice the bonding until the initial spell was broken." Roke's grip tightened on his companion's slender shoulder. "Or at least, when Sally claims it was broken."

With an impatient gesture, Sally lifted her arm, waving the crimson marking beneath his nose.

"You think that if there was a way to get rid of this I would hesitate for even a heartbeat?" she squawked. "The last thing I want is to be tied to a leech."

Roke stiffened as her accusation sent a stab of anger through his heart. As if he were . . . what? Upset by her fierce rejection of their bonding? She was only saying what was exactly on his mind, wasn't she?

Thankfully his ridiculous broodings were interrupted by Styx.

"You didn't exchange blood?"

Roke shook his head, refusing to acknowledge the ruthless

hunger that had plagued him since Sally had trapped him in her spell. "No."

"Strange." Styx pushed away from the desk, stepping toward Sally. "You have no idea what demon blood runs in your veins?"

"None."

"Your magic interferes with my senses. Perhaps your blood . . ." Styx's words were bitten off as Roke abruptly shoved Sally behind his rigid body, his lips peeled back to emphasize his fully exposed fangs. "Shit, Roke," the ancient vampire muttered.

"You're not tasting her blood," he snarled.

Styx scowled, the icy throb of his power warning Roke who was in charge.

"Unless we discover what kind of demon she is, we won't know how this happened." He allowed a strategic pause. "Or if it can be reversed."

Roke refused to back down. "No one takes her blood but me."

"Hey," Sally protested, kicking Roke on the back of his leg.

The two men ignored her.

"No way," Styx snapped. "For now we can hope this is the result of her demon powers. If you take her blood—"

"No one's taking my blood—are we clear on that?" Sally again intruded into their conversation, this time giving Roke a punch to the arm.

Styx arched a startled brow as he glanced toward the furious witch. "She's feisty for such a little thing."

"She's a pain in the ass," Roke muttered.

She growled. Not an animal growl. But an I'm-so-pissed-I-could-kill-you growl. "Someday I'm truly going to turn you into a newt," she threatened Roke.

Without warning Styx tilted back his head to laugh with genuine amusement. "I'd go for a cave troll if I were you," he informed the astonished Sally. "His vanity could use a few warts."

Roke glared at his king. Traitor. "I'm glad you can find humor in this."

Styx shrugged. "Imagine my reaction when I found myself mated to a pure-blooded Were."

An emotion he refused to identify darted through Roke at the thought of this powerful vampire with Darcy. There was no mistaking the fact that the two adored one another and had no embarrassment in displaying their love whenever they were together.

Not that he wanted that sort of mating, he hastily reassured himself. His heart and loyalty belonged to his clan.

"It's not the same," he said roughly.

"No, I don't suppose it is." With a grimace Styx reached to grasp Roke's shoulder. "Don't worry, my brother, we'll figure this out."

Roke avoided glancing at the woman who had turned his life upside down. "We damned well better," he muttered.

There was an awkward silence as Roke felt Sally take a deliberate step away, shaking off his clinging hand.

"Now tell me about this book," Styx commanded.

Resisting the urge to wrap his arm around the female and tuck her back against his side, Roke rigidly concentrated on Styx's abrupt change in conversation.

"It was hidden in a safe that was bricked over in an abandoned warehouse ten miles north of here."

Styx nodded, not bothering to ask how Roke had managed to knock through the bricks to expose the safe. "And why do we need a witch?"

"Because it's protected by black magic," Sally answered. "Deadly to anyone foolish enough to touch it."

Styx curled his lips in the typical vampire reaction to magic. "Can you get rid of it?"

Sally hesitated before giving a wary nod. "I think so, but

the magic was more potent than any I've tried to deal with before. It will take time and specific ingredients to prepare a counterspell with enough punch to break through."

Styx was speaking before Roke could protest. "Darcy will get what you need."

"Fine, but I'm not returning to the dungeons," she warned. "If you want my help, then you can't treat me like a prisoner."

The Anasso studied her with a narrowed gaze. "I have your word that you won't try to escape?"

She blinked in surprise. "You trust the word of a witch?"

"Do I have your word?" Styx repeated, his voice as hard as granite.

Sally shrugged, lifting her arm to reveal the mating mark. "I swear I'm not leaving until you get rid of this. Good enough?"

Styx gave a rueful nod. "Good enough. You'll find Darcy in the kitchen. Just tell her what you need."

Clearly thinking it had to be a trap, the tiny witch backed her way out of the door, never taking her gaze off the massive Aztec warrior.

Roke watched her wary departure with gritted teeth, telling himself to let her go. The more space between them the better.

But the instant she was out of sight, his good intentions shattered. With a muttered curse he was heading out of the room, catching his fleeing prey just as she was turning the corner.

"Sally."

Coming to a grudging halt, the witch turned to send him a sullen frown. "What do you want? I already gave my word I wouldn't escape."

"You don't have to," he said, grabbing her wrist to study the delicate tattoo with a brooding gaze. *Mate.* "There's nowhere in the world you could go where I wouldn't find you."

It took a minute for her to realize that their connection

meant he would always know where she was. Hell, he would know what she was feeling, and if he truly concentrated, he would know what she was doing.

The blush faded to a sickly white, her eyes velvet dark. "Then what do you want?"

Want? His fangs lengthened. What he wanted was to yank her into his arms and sink his aching fangs deep into her throat. His body wasn't conflicted. It accepted this woman was now his and it wanted to indulge in all the benefits of a mate.

But, Styx was right, as much as he hated to agree with the oversized mother hen.

Besides, he had a more pressing reason for charging after her.

"Is this spell dangerous?"

"It can be if I make a mistake in mixing the ingredients or when I cast the actual spell." She frowned, clearly baffled by his question. "But you don't have to worry, I'll create a protective circle before I begin. You won't be in any danger."

He took a step forward, standing close enough to be drenched in her peach-scented warmth. "And you?"

She licked her dry lips. "I don't understand."

"It's simple. Will you be at risk?"

"The caster is always at risk. Why?"

His thumb rubbed her inner wrist, lingering on the feel of her racing pulse as his gaze rested on her damp lips.

Oh . . . hell.

He was in trouble.

Ass-deep, never-be-the-same-again trouble.

"For better or worse you're my mate," he rasped.

"So . . ." Her eyes widened in sudden horror. "Oh. Do vampires die if something happens to their mates?"

He shuddered, unable to even imagine the devastating sense of loss.

"No, but I'll wish I was dead."

Chapter 20

Outside the dragon lair

Nefri ignored Santiago's bristling annoyance as she stepped toward the small female demon.

"Yannah. Did your mother send you?"

Yannah gave a sniff, waving her hand toward the scowling vampire and sulking gargoyle. "I'm not allowed to say in front of them."

"Ah." Nefri wisely hid her smile as she pointed toward the small copse of trees. "Perhaps we can step over here?"

Santiago made a strangled sound. "Nefri, we don't have time for this."

Yannah widened her black eyes, the heavy pressure of her magic beginning to swirl through the air. "I'm a messenger from the Commission," she announced. "Everyone has time for me."

Without warning Levet tossed his hands in the air. "There. You see? How is a man supposed to live with such a bossy creature?"

Nefri sent a warning glance toward Santiago, who had a sudden glint of amusement in his eyes. "Careful."

"Hey, I'm not saying a word," he said, an exaggerated expression of innocence on his handsome face.

"Good choice," she murmured, turning back to the female demon. "Shall we, Yannah?"

Together they moved over the uneven ground, not halting until they were far enough away to avoid being overheard by even a vampire.

"Why must men be so difficult?" Yannah abruptly burst out.

"I have come to the conclusion it's a genetic defect of males," Nefri consoled her companion. "That would explain why their numerous faults appear to include all species."

Yannah gave a slow nod. "That makes sense."

There was a moment of silence as they pondered the oddity of the male gender, and then Nefri was giving a shake of her head. "I believe you have a message for me."

"Oh. Yes." Yannah smoothed tiny hands down her white robe. "My mother says 'That which was lost is found again.'"

Nefri remained silent, waiting for the rest of the message. At least until she realized that Yannah was staring at her with an expectant expression.

"That's it?"

"Yes."

"But . . ." Nefri frowned. "I don't understand. What was lost?"

"How should I know?" Yannah gave an impatient wave of her hand. "I'm just the messenger."

Nefri was careful to keep her expression devoid of her stab of frustration. Yannah might appear to be a child, but she had enough power to destroy them all.

"Very well. Thank you, Yannah." She offered a small bow. "I will be sure to tell Siljar that you performed your task with honor."

"I must return." Yannah glanced toward the two men who stood in stiff silence. "You'll keep him safe?"

Nefri nodded, sensing Yannah's concern was genuine,

despite her enjoyment in nagging the small gargoyle. "I will do everything in my power to make certain he isn't harmed," she promised softly.

"Thank you."

With a last, longing glance at Levet, the small demon abruptly disappeared, leaving behind the scent of brimstone.

Nefri gave a faint shake of her head and slowly returned to her companions.

Why on earth had Siljar sent her daughter to share such a vague message? It wasn't as if she could actually use it to her advantage. Not when she didn't have a clue what it meant.

Instinctively moving to stand beside Santiago, Nefri was prepared for Levet's scowl as he realized she was alone.

"Where did Yannah go?"

"She had to return to the Commission," Nefri said in distracted tones.

"Hmmph. Typical," the gargoyle muttered, his wings drooping in the moonlight. "She comes here to pick a fight and then just disappears when she realizes I'm winning."

Ignoring the grouchy Levet, Santiago reached to tuck Nefri's hair behind her ear as he studied her with a worried gaze. "What did she say?"

"She said, 'That which was lost is found again.'"

Santiago was predictably unimpressed. "What was found?"

Nefri grimaced. "That was the message."

"The entire message?"

"Yes."

"Do you know what it means?"

Nefri shrugged. "I don't have a clue."

"Fantastic," Santiago growled. "So are we supposed to wait around for the Oracles?"

Nefri didn't hesitate. With every passing minute the danger to the world increased. "No. We need to find Gaius."

Santiago studied her with a searching gaze. "And then?"

"I'm not entirely sure," she admitted. Siljar had demanded that Gaius be captured, but Nefri wasn't going to sacrifice Santiago. If push came to shove she would kill her former clansman, and she would do it without hesitation. "But he has to be stopped."

Santiago nodded. "Yes."

Their gazes held as they silently shared their growing concern, then the moment was interrupted as Levet pressed his face against her leg to sniff her jeans.

"Why do you smell like dragon?"

With a low growl, Santiago leaned down to grab the gargoyle by his stunted horn, pulling him away from Nefri as if he was jealous of the tiny creature. "Does he have to come?" he demanded.

She gave a firm nod. "Yes."

Levet yanked free of Santiago's grasp, glaring at the male vampire. "What is the matter with you?"

Santiago scowled. "Do you have to ask?"

"Hey." Levet gave a sharp flap of his wings. "It is supposed to be farts before tarts."

"What the—" Santiago made a sound of disgust. "Oh, for god's sake, it's 'bros before hos.'"

"That is not very polite," Levet protested in shocked tones, his gaze moving to Nefri. "Forgive his crassness, *ma belle*."

"I do my best," she assured the gargoyle.

"I need to call Styx and update him," Santiago muttered, digging his phone out of his front pocket. "I'll meet you at the truck."

She sent him an overly innocent smile. "If you insist."

"Oh, I insist."

With a light touch on Levet's wing, she steered him toward the rugged path that eventually would lead to the truck parked in the foothills. As much as she enjoyed watching the tiny gargoyle drive Santiago nuts, she didn't want him pressing his luck.

Poking at an angry male vampire was never a good idea. "Come along, Levet."

They'd left the meadow and were traveling down the narrow path when Levet returned to his previous question. "You were with a dragon?"

"We were." She grimaced, wishing the powerful beast had offered more than vague warnings. "He revealed this spirit that we're tracking might be the creator of vampires."

The gray eyes widened in shock. "Truly?"

"Yes."

"That sounds . . ." Levet shuddered in horror. "*Sacrebleu,* I do not even have the words."

Nefri gave a slow nod. "My thoughts exactly."

Even driving like a bat out of hell (a rather appropriate metaphor for a vampire), Santiago was forced to accept that they weren't going to reach Gaius.

They could have ditched the truck and moved faster on foot, but expending that much energy would have meant facing the vampire and a potential god of vampires when they were at their weakest.

Santiago was impulsive, but he wasn't suicidal.

Seeming to come to the same conclusion, Nefri sent him a questioning glance over the head of the ridiculous gargoyle who was perched between them. "Can you sense him?"

"He's still north of us." Santiago grimaced. "Close, but too far to pinpoint before dawn."

She nodded. "We should find a place to rest for the day."

"*Oui.*" Levet abruptly seemed to come awake, bouncing up and down on the seat. "Finding caves is my specialty."

Santiago shuddered. Twelve hours stuck in a damp cave with this aggravating gargoyle? No way in hell.

Which was exactly why he'd chosen this particular route. Thank the gods.

"Actually Viper has a club not far from here."

Nefri blinked, as if surprised by his claim. "Another club?"

"He has a dozen or more." Santiago shrugged. "Some higher rent than others."

Her brows drew together, no doubt expecting the usual offering of blood, sex, and violence. "And this one?"

"The Summerset Club is one of the more elegant establishments." He sent her a wry grin. "Not one cage or orgy to be found."

He expected a responding smile; instead Nefri studied him with an oddly searching gaze.

"Does it bother you?"

"Orgies?" He gave a teasing waggle of his brows. Not that he'd ever been into public displays. And now . . . he couldn't imagine being intimate with any female but Nefri in public or private. "Not at all."

She refused to be distracted. "The fighting."

He knew what she meant. After spending centuries fighting for his life on a nightly basis, no one had been more shocked than he was when Viper suggested that he manage a club renowned for its cage matches.

But after spending time in the club, he finally realized it was exactly what he needed.

"Just the opposite," he admitted, slowing the truck to take the off-ramp. "It's cathartic."

She cast a brief glance around the cornfields before returning her attention to him. "I don't understand."

"I'm in control now," he explained. "That means only demons 100 percent willing can enter the cages, and those who try to force a fighter into the matches answer to me. I can also make sure that the opponents are evenly matched and that the battle is ended before irreparable damage can be done." He took another turn onto a gravel road. "There's also a strict policy against masos."

"Masos?" she asked.

It was Levet who answered with a wrinkle of his snout. "A demon who gets off on pain, *ma belle*."

She frowned. "Why do you care if they enjoy being hurt?"

He offered a wicked smile. "Pleasurable pain is an extra charge."

She stiffened in distaste. "Charming."

"To each his own," he murmured.

"I suppose."

Santiago slowed to a mere crawl, his senses on high alert. For most people this deserted path several miles south of Iowa City would have seemed like a road to nowhere, but he was well aware that there lurked a number of nasty surprises for those who dared to trespass.

The Summerset Club was one of Viper's more exclusive establishments and was guarded with better surveillance than Area 51.

Of course, he'd been a part of Viper's inner circle long enough that even the lowest ranking vampires would easily recognize him. He hoped that there wouldn't be any trouble passing through the hidden checkpoints.

He turned twice more before they arrived at the manicured parkland that surrounded the sprawling colonial building.

Painted white with black shutters, the central double door was flanked by high, arched windows and a wide porch with fluted columns. The roof was low-pitched with a balustrade that connected the two long wings to the central house.

Pulling the truck to a halt at the side drive, he shut off the engine. One of the flunkies would move it later.

"This is it."

They crawled out of the truck and headed toward the door. Or at least, Santiago and Nefri headed that way.

The ridiculous gargoyle hovered on the drive.

"Levet?" Nefri murmured.

"I should try to contact Yannah," the gargoyle said, his tone indicating that he wasn't overly eager to confront the female. "I will return at nightfall."

"No need to hurry back on my account," Santiago muttered.

Levet sniffed, pointing a claw toward Santiago. "You should take lessons in how to treat a hero."

"I'll show you how I—"

"Santiago." Nefri grabbed his arm, her attention remaining on the three-foot pest. "We'll see you at dusk."

Levet gave a dip of his head. *"Bon."* With a flap of his fairy wings, the creature was taking off, no doubt making the surrounding guards wonder if they were hallucinating.

Santiago gave a shake of his head. "Why do you encourage him?"

"He truly is a hero."

Yeah. And wasn't that a kick in the fangs?

"Don't remind me."

"Well, well, look what the cat dragged in," a smooth male voice with a distinct English accent drawled from the side door. "Did you slip Viper's leash?"

Santiago jerked around to glare at the tall, slender vampire with light brown hair that was cut short on the sides and layered on top to lay with glossy perfection. His face was chiseled with an austere beauty that Santiago considered arrogant but the females seemed to find enthralling. His eyes were so dark a blue they looked black from a distance and usually shimmered with a wicked amusement that disguised his razor-sharp intelligence.

As always, he presented the image of the ultimate gentleman. Elegant, perfectly polished. And attired in a black Armani tuxedo that cost more than Santiago had spent in the past century on his clothes.

With a roll of his eyes, Santiago climbed the steps to stand face to face with the vampire he'd known since his days in the pits.

He wasn't the only Gladiator who Styx had rescued.

"Gabriel. We need rooms."

"Of course." The vampire's gaze shifted over Santiago's shoulder, an expression of male appreciation settling on his face. "Is this your latest? Nice. Very nice."

"Watch it," Santiago snapped, plagued with a sudden desire to rip out those blue peepers. "This is clan chief Nefri."

The hint of sexual invitation was abruptly replaced with a bone-deep reverence as the older vampire performed a smooth bow. "My lady, forgive me."

"Please," Nefri murmured softly, moving to stand at Santiago's side, "call me Nefri."

"You've honored my humble establishment." Straightening, Gabriel waved a hand toward the open door. "Please follow me."

Chapter 21

Santiago didn't know why he was so discombobulated (who the hell would have thought he would use such a prissy-ass word, even in the privacy of his mind?). He'd known from the moment he'd crossed paths with Nefri that she was more than just a powerful clan chief.

It was impossible to miss the fact that she was far superior to others.

But his overriding bitterness at Gaius's defection behind the Veil had made him ignore his instinct to treat her as a rare treasure. Then, even worse, his male desire had kicked in. It'd insisted that he deny the knowledge that this female was far too good for a former Gladiator who was more comfortable among the dregs of society than royalty.

And she *was* royalty, even if she didn't carry the title of queen.

A fact hammered home with painful clarity as the vampires and a handful of fey crowded around her in speechless awe. Even among the most aristocratic members of society she was a VIP.

Hell, they barely gave her enough space to sip the blood that was brought to her in a Baccarat crystal glass on a silver tray. Oh, and then there'd been the scramble among females to assure Nefri they'd have fresh clothing sent from the most exclusive designers, clearly hoping to use this accidental meeting with the Great Nefri to inflate their own standing.

After a torturous hour of watching the crowd fawn over the always gracious Nefri, Gabriel at last led them down the stairs to the hidden tunnels beneath the building.

The club didn't encourage guests to linger during the daylight hours, but there were always spare rooms. Of course, unlike Santiago's humble establishment, these rooms were the size of most apartments and decorated in soothing shades of gray and silver.

Discreet, expensive, and sophisticated.

Escorting them into the sitting room with a low, velvet sofa and hand-carved coffee table, Gabriel placed a hand over his heart and offered a deep bow. "You're certain you have everything you need?"

"Absolutely," Nefri assured him with a warm smile. "This is lovely."

"Just hit the zero on the phone if you want room service," Gabriel said, the jaded vampire clearly dazzled by Nefri. "Anything."

"I will."

There was a long pause, as if Gabriel was having difficulty tearing himself away, then with a last dip of his head, he backed out of the room and closed the door.

A thick silence filled the air as Santiago moved to the wet bar that came complete with his favorite tequila.

Pouring a large shot, he downed it in one gulp. On the point of pouring another, he was halted when Nefri laid a gentle hand on his arm.

"Santiago?"

His fingers tightened on the glass before he was setting it aside and turning to meet her worried gaze. *"Sí?"*

"What's bothering you?"

He shrugged, wishing he'd managed a couple more shots before she'd interfered. He was feeling . . . raw. "Nothing."

Her brows snapped together. "You've barely said a word since we've arrived. And you have that"—she gave a wave of her hand—"that broody male thing going on."

He arched a brow. "Broody male thing?"

"You know what I mean." She searched his guarded expression. "Something is obviously bothering you."

"I told you . . . it's nothing."

Her eyes narrowed. "I thought it was a woman's prerogative to pretend she's not upset when she clearly is."

"Ouch," he muttered.

She moved a step closer, wrapping him in her sweet jasmine scent. "Please, tell me."

He grimaced. Dammit. He wasn't a "touchy feely" kind of vampire under the best of circumstances. Unless it was in bed. When his emotions were involved he became as articulate as a grunting orc.

"I sometimes forget," he eventually muttered.

"Forget what?"

"That you are who you are."

"Who I am?"

"You're Nefri," he said. "A creature of myth and legend."

She blinked in confusion. "Are you speaking in code?"

He reached up to yank the leather tie from his hair, ramming his fingers through the thick strands in an effort to relieve the tension throbbing in his head. It didn't help.

"Vampires all over this world would worship at your feet," he said, his voice rough. "Hell, you're treated like a queen by a dragon."

"That's ridiculous."

"No, it's the truth."

Her lips thinned, as if she was annoyed by his words. "Fine, let's say for argument's sake that you're right. What does that have to do with why you're treating me like I carry the plague?"

"You are . . ." He struggled for the words.

"What?"

"Way out of my league," he finally managed to say, expressing the fear that burned deep in his soul.

. Without warning Nefri was slapping a hand across his mouth, her eyes snapping with anger. "Don't you dare."

He grasped her wrist and gently tugged her fingers from his face. Now that he'd started, he intended to finish.

"We can't ignore the truth, *querida*."

"The truth is that I'm just a vampire with all the flaws and weaknesses of any other," she claimed, even as she stood there in a blaze of glorious beauty. "I've already told you that the Oracles spread rumors to disguise the truth of why they created the Veil."

He shook his head. Where was she going with this? "And?"

"And the rumors expanded to include me and my clan when we left this world."

"Your power is no rumor. And neither is your beauty," he countered. "Gabriel would have sliced open his throat if he thought it would please you."

Her lips twisted into a humorless smile. "Not me. His vision of who he thinks I am, or at least who I should be."

She wrapped her arms around her waist, a white fang nibbling on the fullness of her lower lip. He stifled a groan at the memory of those cherry lips skimming down his body. He was supposed to be concentrating on the reasons to keep this female at a distance, not dwelling on the devastating pleasure she'd given him.

"Perhaps it's my fault. Over the centuries it suited me to play the role of the aloof, mysterious clan chief. If people feared me, then it allowed my clan to live in peace away from our enemies."

He stilled, bothered by the sense that she was apologizing

for some sin she'd never committed. At least not as far as he was concerned. "You did what was necessary," he growled.

"I did more than was necessary."

"More?"

"I not only used my legendary reputation to keep my enemies at a distance, but everyone."

He hesitated. He'd been well aware of the distance she kept between herself and others. But he hadn't been certain if it had been on purpose or simply a defense mechanism.

"Why?"

She held his gaze, for the first time allowing him to truly see the ancient betrayal smoldering in her dark eyes. "Because then I could be absolutely certain no one would ever again use me as a tool for their own gain."

Before he could halt the need to touch her, Santiago reached to gently cup her face in his hands. "I understand, *cara*. I truly do."

She nodded. He was one of the few demons who actually could make the claim.

"I was satisfied with my choices until . . ."

"Until?"

"You."

He flinched at the blunt answer, not sure whether to sink to his knees in gratitude or shake some sense into her.

In the end he simply regarded her with a desperate hope. "What does that mean?"

"You reminded me that I'm more than a clan chief," she said in low, husky tones. "I'm a woman."

A groan escaped his lips as his gaze lowered to the slender curves that emphatically proclaimed her womanhood. "Yes, you are."

Her hands lifted to rest on his shoulders. "A very lonely woman who was too cowardly to risk sharing herself."

He muttered a curse. Just for a few minutes, he'd been determined to do the right thing. To stop his compulsive need to blast through her wary shields and instead return to his role of a protector. Nothing, after all, was more important than making sure they halted Gaius and the mysterious spirit before they could create even more havoc.

Now, his resolve faltered.

Because of the edge of vulnerability in her voice?

Or because he was a selfish bastard who urgently wanted to believe she needed him with the same intensity he needed her?

"Why me?" he murmured.

A hint of amusement drove the shadows from her eyes. "Are you seeking compliments?"

His thumb rubbed her lower lip. "I won't say no to any you want to offer."

"Hmmm." She pretended to consider her words. "For one thing, you're the only vampire I've met who is too stubborn to take 'no' for an answer."

"That's your compliment?" he complained. "I'm stubborn?"

Her smile widened, revealing a sexy hint of fang. "Your ego doesn't need for me to tell you that you're impossibly gorgeous and so sexy that females melt whenever you walk past them."

Desire roared through him, searing away his futile attempt at sanity. "That's better," he murmured. "Tell me more about how I make you melt."

Her smile faded, leaving behind an achingly somber expression. "I have no words that explain why it was you, Santiago. It's more than your courage and loyalty and the goodness in your heart that you try to hide." Her hands slid over his chest, the light caress sending lightning bolts of pleasure through his clenched body. "It is—and always will be—you."

The world came to a complete, perfect halt.

She captured the truth in those seven simple words.

It defined his very existence.

The knowledge exploded through him with a nuclear force. Bright and shiny and soul shattering.

"*Sí.* I was created to be yours, but . . ."

"Ssh." She pressed a finger to his lips, the tantalizing scent of her jasmine arousal spicing the air. "I don't want to talk anymore."

He shuddered, unable to resist temptation.

Not that he tried very hard.

"You do possess mystical powers," he rasped, sweeping her off her feet as he went in search of the bedroom. "You just read my mind."

Styx's lair in Chicago

Roke didn't think it was possible that the night, which was already in the crapper, could get any worse.

Tough to top being mated against his will.

But less than an hour after Sally headed to the kitchen to begin brewing her spell and Roke had gone to the gym to work off his seething frustration, he returned to Styx's study to discover the Anasso throwing his cell phone across the room.

It didn't take a genius to realize that the latest news wasn't good, but even forewarned Roke was caught with his mouth hanging open as Styx shared the latest update.

Santiago and Nefri had not only spent the day in the lair of a dragon (a dragon, for Christ's sake), but Santiago discovered that Gaius might be in the power of the ultimate vampire who was spreading violent emotions like a plague so he could feed.

Perfect.

Just perfect.

Folding his arms over his chest, he waited for Styx to

halt his pacing, impervious to the flickering electricity and shattering chandelier.

At least the house was still standing.

"Do you want me to join Santiago?" he at last demanded. "He's obviously going to need all the help he can get."

The towering Aztec gave a decisive shake of his head, the turquoise ornaments in his long braid glinting in the splintered light. "Not until we know more about this creature and its powers. I don't intend to turn my people into fodder for another crazed deity," he snarled, pausing to study Roke with an unnervingly piercing gaze. "And I doubt you could leave even if you wanted to."

"Don't be—" Roke snapped his lips together as his powers instinctively tested his bond with Sally, making sure that she was still near and unharmed. It was an unconscious reflex, but one that he did on a regular basis. Which proved Styx was right. "Shit."

Styx held his frustrated glare. "For now you need to concentrate on yourself."

Infuriated by the constant reminder that he was well and truly trapped, Roke slammed a door on his bond with Sally, momentarily succeeding in blunting his awareness of her.

It wouldn't last more than a few minutes. But it was a tiny win for his ravaged pride.

"I knew that witch was going to be trouble," he muttered, a bitterness edging his words. "Of course, all women are trouble in one way or another."

Styx blinked, as if startled by his vehemence. "You don't like women? Hell, I never considered the possibility."

Roke snorted. He wasn't offended. Immortality meant vampires who weren't mated often experimented with different genders, different species, and a wide variety of sexual appetites.

"I'm physically attracted to females," he corrected Styx.

"Good," Styx said. "Not that I give a damn one way

or another, but the female will be bound to you until we can find a way to break the mating. You don't need any additional"—he searched for a word to cover the hideous situation—"confusion."

"Confusion?" It was Roke's turn to pace from one end of the office to the other. "It's a fucking nightmare."

Styx grimaced. "We'll find a way to free you from the witch."

"And if you can't?"

"Easy, Roke," Styx murmured.

Abruptly Roke realized his anger was causing the floor to shake beneath their feet. Unlike some vampires, his own powers had little effect on electrical objects, but he could cause significant structural damage if he lost control.

With a grim effort, he leashed his powers. That didn't, however, ease his frustration, which threatened to combust at the least provocation.

"This is . . ."

"A nightmare," Styx murmured. "I got that."

Roke clenched his fists, his gaze trained on the glass cabinet that held Styx's priceless collection of ancient scrolls. "Did you know my previous clan chief?" he asked abruptly. He could sense Styx's confusion.

"Gunnar occasionally petitioned my master, but he tended to be a recluse when he visited. I doubt I exchanged half a dozen words with him," Styx at last admitted. "Why?"

Roke had to force the words past his stiff lips. Speaking about his former clan chief was always difficult. Even after all these years. "When Gunnar allowed me to join his clan he was a stable leader who demanded obedience, but treated us with a justice rarely found in those days."

"You were fortunate."

"I was," Roke agreed. Before the previous Anasso had taken control, vampires had been little better than savage beasts who brutalized one another as easily as they brutalized lesser demons. It was nothing less than a miracle to find a clan that respected one another. "Until Gunnar found his mate."

"Many clan chiefs are mated."

Roke curled his lip. "Not to a female who is so vain and needy that she demands constant attention."

"This mate was a vampire?" Styx demanded.

"Yes, but very weak," he explained, not bothering to disguise his disgust for the female who'd destroyed so much. "Her only true power was her beauty and she used it like a weapon to get her way. Gunnar went from being a strong, decisive leader of a clan no one would dare to attack, to a slave to his lusts who spent so much time pandering to his female we lost everything."

He sensed it as Styx moved to stand at his side. "Everything?"

He gave a restless shrug. "The mines that made our wealth were allowed to be overrun with humans and the majority of our land was taken by a rival vampire clan, along with our best warriors."

"What happened to Gunnar?"

Roke hesitated. The history of his clan wasn't a secret. But the ultimate fate of Gunnar was something that was never discussed.

Not by anyone.

"While I traveled to enter the battles of Durotriges he was killed when his lair was struck by lightning and burned to the ground." He reluctantly turned to meet Styx's unwavering gaze. "Or that was the story I was given."

Predictably the older vampire pounced on his suggestive words. "You don't believe it?"

"I made no secret of the fact that if I survived the battles I intended to challenge Gunnar to become the chief." He grimaced. "I fear . . ."

Styx laid a hand on his shoulder. "Roke?"

The memory of his beloved sire burned through his brain.

The female vampire had been a wisewoman before being turned, and while she had no memory of her past, she possessed an unshakable belief in mystic portents.

Including an omen that she'd read the night Roke was turned.

She'd claimed that it meant that Roke would one day be a great leader.

He'd always humored the ancient vampire, never suspecting she might take matters into her own hands.

At least not until Gunnar was dead.

"I suspect that someone made certain there wouldn't be any chance of me losing that challenge," he grudgingly admitted.

Thankfully Styx didn't press for answers Roke had no intention of giving. Instead he gave Roke's shoulder an understanding squeeze. "That's why you've been so anxious to return to your people," he said, his words a statement, not a question.

Roke nodded. "I swore when they made me their chief I would devote myself to protecting them. Instead I've abandoned them."

"You didn't abandon them," Styx interrupted him, his hawkish features unyielding. "I forced you to remain in Chicago."

"The result is the same. They're without their leader," Roke pointed out in sour tones, refusing to console himself with the knowledge he'd left them in perfectly capable hands. Kale might be dependable enough, but it was Roke's responsibility to be with his clan. "And now, for the true cherry topper, I'm mated to a witch who not only sold her soul to the Dark Lord, but who hates vampires."

Styx's fingers tightened to a painful grip. "Roke . . ."

He shrugged off the warning hand, on a sudden roll. "Hell, I couldn't possibly have been trapped with a worse mate if I tried."

The scent of peaches filled the air. No, not peaches . . .

scorched peaches. As if the scrumptious fruit had been tossed in a raging fire.

Shit.

Slowly turning, Roke met the furious glare of his mate, forced to hastily duck as she tossed a heavy crystal vase at his head.

"Right back at you," she hissed, tossing another vase. "Jackass."

Roke groaned. His only emotion should be relief that the female hadn't been able to use her magic. He would no doubt be missing a vital part of his male anatomy right now.

Instead, all he could feel was a fierce, searing need to gather the angry Sally in his arms and promise that she would never be hurt again.

Especially not by him.

Chapter 22

Gauis's lair in Wisconsin

Gaius struggled to shake off the clinging sense of lethargy that shrouded him in a thick blanket of unconsciousness.

He hated the sensation.

He hated it even more when he could sense a presence leaning over his helpless body.

With a threatening growl, he forced open his heavy lids, relieved to discover he'd taken the precaution of spending the day on a narrow cot in the cellar. The house might be sun-proof, but an enemy could always find a way to break through his shutters and expose him to the deadly rays.

Especially when he was so deeply asleep he couldn't detect an approaching trespasser.

Surging upward, he discovered Dara standing near the narrow door that was the only entrance to the cellar. She smiled as she slid an affectionate glance over his rumpled hair and naked body.

"*Habibi,* are you rested?" she asked in her soft voice.

He scrubbed a hand over his face, sensing that night had fallen while he'd been unconscious. "How long have I been asleep?"

"Since you returned last eve." Her smile widened. "You were always a lazy bug after you overindulged."

He grimaced. He'd done more than overindulge. He'd wallowed in a bloodlust that had been shocking even by his standards. And still he'd remained plagued by a gnawing hunger that refused to be appeased.

It was only the threat of dawn that had forced him to gather the few remaining mortals and return to his temporary lair.

"The humans?" he rasped, assuming something must be wrong for Dara to seek him out.

She shrugged. "They're safely locked in the attic."

"Then what's troubling you?"

Her beautiful eyes shimmered with a strange glow, as if they were being lit from within. "Something that should have remained hidden is now found," she whispered, the glow from her eyes filling the cellar with an eerie light.

He took an unconscious step backward. "That doesn't make any sense."

"It has to be one of the witches." Her brows pulled together, her tone absent.

"I thought we killed the last of them."

She pretended she didn't hear him. Or maybe she wasn't pretending. Gaius smiled wryly. It seemed the only time Dara truly acknowledged his presence was when she needed something.

"Or perhaps it's one of the Oracles." She gave a slow nod. "Yes, that is possible."

Gaius went rigid, an icy ball of dread forming in the pit of his stomach. "They're here?"

"Not yet. But I've felt them searching for me." Dara's eyes returned to liquid pools of darkness. "They know I'm here."

"Why?"

"Why what?"

"Why are they searching for you?"

"I've told you." She regarded him with a beseeching plea

that arrowed straight to his heart. "They don't like vampires returning from the grave. They will seek to banish me from this world."

With a reluctance that shamed him, Gaius moved forward to lightly brush a hand over her cheek. As always he was struck by the unpleasant sensation that his hand was passing through air.

"No. I won't let that happen," he swore. "Not again."

She moved back, dislodging his hand, but her smile was as warm as the long forgotten sun. "I knew I could depend on you, *habibi*."

Yes. He pressed a hand to his temple, trying to clear the weary fog from his mind. His mate depended on him. It was his duty to do whatever was necessary to protect her.

"We must hide," he murmured, shifting through the various possibilities. They had to lay low until the Commission lost interest. "We can return to our lair in Italy."

"Yes, eventually," she agreed. "But not yet."

Gaius frowned. "Dara, I don't have the strength to fight the Commission."

"You don't have to fight the entire Commission," she assured him. "Only their two emissaries."

He didn't bother asking how she could feel the approach of the Oracles, or how she seemed to mysteriously know that they'd sent two emissaries.

He wasn't sure he wanted the answers.

"Who did they send?" he instead demanded.

"The female clan chief."

Gaius hissed. There was more than one female clan chief, of course. But, there was only one whom the Oracles would send to try and capture him.

"Nefri." He clenched his hands, pretending the raw stab of guilt was anger. He wasn't going to admit that he'd abused Nefri's generous trust. What choice did he have? The Dark Lord had lured him with promises of Dara. Any vampire would betray their people for their beloved mate. "Damn her. How can she know I survived?"

"The Oracles, no doubt." Dara's features twisted with a bitter fury before her eyes grew distant, as if she were looking at something far away. "Now that is intriguing."

"What is?"

"Her companion." She slowly smiled. "This promises to be an interesting reunion."

Reunion?

Gaius began to shake his head in bafflement only to freeze as he was struck by the haunting memory of being ripped through the rift by the Dark Lord. At the time his only thought was to scurry away from the raging battle, but he was certain that he'd caught a glimpse of an unconscious Nefri being held in the arms of an all-too familiar vampire.

"Santiago," he said, his voice harsh.

"Yes." Dara's expression was . . . what? It almost appeared smug. "Our son."

"No." Gaius paced across the cramped space, hating the sick regret that flowed like acid through him at the thought of Santiago. "No longer."

"He will always be ours, Gaius."

"You don't know what I've done."

"Tell me."

He hunched a defensive shoulder. He didn't want to speak about his son. Of all the sacrifices he'd made, Santiago was the one that would always torment him.

Feeling the weight of Dara's stare, he at last muttered a low curse. "I betrayed him when I sold my soul to the Dark Lord and then I abandoned him and he became a slave to the blood pits," he forced out. "He'll never forgive me."

"He's angry and confused," she said softly.

He gave a sharp, bitter laugh. "He has every right to be."

"Perhaps." There was a misty brush against his naked

shoulder. Dara's touch? "But Nefri has used his emotions to manipulate him into becoming our enemy."

"I doubt it took much manipulation."

"You can't believe that. You know Santiago," she whispered directly into his ear. "No matter what you've done, if he's coerced into harming his sire he will be tortured by guilt. It will eventually destroy him."

Gaius tried to shut out her words.

The last time there was a whisper in his ear, the Dark Lord persuaded him to betray his son, his clan, and eventually the entire world.

He wouldn't be fooled again.

But then he turned his head to catch sight of the delicate, honey-tinted face and his logic sizzled beneath the burst of intense yearning.

Once he'd been happy.

Centuries ago he'd been a powerful clan chief with a devoted mate and a fiercely loyal son he was training to follow in his footsteps.

He wanted that back.

He wanted it with a hunger that destroyed any lingering threads of sanity.

"What can we do?" he at last rasped.

Dara smiled, pleased with his capitulation. "We must convince him that he's still our son and that all we want is to be a family again."

"A family."

"The three of us together," she continued, weaving her web of temptation. "Just imagine, *habibi*."

He frowned. "What if it's too late? I cut all ties with Santiago when I abandoned him."

"It's never too late," she assured him. "He's following our trail even as we speak."

He gave a slow nod. "Then, we can speak when he arrives. I can apologize and tell him how much I regret leaving him."

"Yes, yes, but first you must make him help us," Dara said impatiently, interrupting his fantasy of the long overdue reunion with Santiago.

"What do you mean?" he asked in confusion. "Help us with what?"

"I have something that needs to be retrieved and he's the only one who can get his hands on"—there was a faint hesitation—"it."

Gaius flinched. "We can't ask him to help as soon as he arrives."

"Why not? You said yourself that he's family."

"He'll assume that we just want to use him."

Dara studied him with an unblinking gaze. "I don't have time to wait. Unless you want to put me back in my grave, then we must *force* him to help."

Gaius shook his head. "I won't hurt him."

"Of course not," she swiftly agreed. "But we'll need leverage."

He paused. Once upon a time he'd been the master of strategy, the one who made the plans and was the driving force that made sure they were accomplished. Dara had always deferred to his stronger will, supporting him with her gentle belief he was always right.

Until that god-awful night when the neighboring vampire clan had come to seek vengeance.

Now . . . well, she'd obviously changed.

"What kind of leverage?" he found himself asking, accepting that for now Dara was in command.

"Let me consider." Her eyes grew distant again, as if she were seeing beyond the cellar. "Yes," she at last murmured.

"Dara?"

The dark gaze locked on him, sending a chill down his spine.

"You'll need your medallion."

Summerset House

Nefri glared at the piles of expensive boxes with fancy bows and silver tissue that were spread across the room. She felt her annoyance rising as each box was opened to reveal yet another slinky gown or scraps of lace that Santiago assured her were negligees. Clothing that ranged from the impractical to the ludicrous.

Standing across the room, Santiago pulled another box from the stack that had been delivered as soon as the sun had set.

Tossing off the lid, he pulled out a skirt that was barely long enough to cover her butt and sparkling with silver sequins. "What about this one?"

Her eyes narrowed at the amusement shimmering in his dark eyes. The male was taking an inordinate amount of pleasure in displaying one worthless garment after another.

"No," she ground out.

He reached for a tube of stretchy silk that she assumed was intended to be worn as a dress. "This one?"

She shoved her hands in the pockets of the robe she'd found in the bathroom. Santiago was wearing a matching robe, although he'd left it open to reveal the hard perfection of his bronzed body.

A body she now knew with a delectable intimacy.

A blissful shiver ran through her as her gaze slid over the lean, beautiful features that were framed by the hair that was left to fall in a smooth river of ebony over his shoulders and down his back.

His smile widened, revealing a hint of fang as the air became perfumed with her stirring arousal.

She gave an impatient click of her tongue. They'd just spent the past ten hours sating their seemingly endless desire. How could she possibly be hungry for more?

"I'm glad you're enjoying this," she muttered in a futile

effort to distract herself from the thought of tumbling him onto the nearby bed.

He flashed his fangs, dangling a minuscule thong from his index finger. "I'm enjoying the thought of you wearing this."

Damn the gorgeous, utterly sexy vampire. How was she supposed to concentrate?

Wrenching her mind away from tiny undies, half-naked males, and a bed that seemed to be calling her name, Nefri instead waved a disgusted hand toward the piles of discarded clothing. "What's the matter with the females?" she demanded. "None of these are sensible."

He glanced down at the thong. "Perhaps they assumed you would want to dress to please your man, not to be sensible."

She arched a brow. "Please my man?"

"Is that an unfamiliar phrase?"

With a concentrated burst of her power, she had the thong lying in tatters at Santiago's feet.

"It's a stupid phrase."

Santiago tilted back his head to laugh with rich enjoyment. Then, stepping over the piles of boxes, he prowled forward. He halted directly in front of her, reaching to tug a strand of her hair.

"You're just so easy, *cara*."

"Careful," she warned, even as her lips twitched.

He smoothed the strand of hair behind her ear, his touch gentle but possessive. Something that should have set her teeth on edge, not make her treacherous heart warm with pleasure.

"I'm sure the females were simply attempting to impress you with their exquisite taste and ability to offer the most expensive gowns," he assured her.

"Yes, I know." She wrinkled her nose, well aware she was overreacting. Unfortunately, the need to track down Gaius and whatever was controlling him was growing more urgent with every passing hour. It made her . . . tense. "And I appreciate their gifts, but I have no use for any of it."

He glanced toward a red leather bustier that had come complete with a whip. "Not even—"

"Santiago."

With a soft chuckle he bent down to press his lips to her forehead. "When will you learn you can depend on me?"

"Depend on you for what?"

"Everything," he assured her huskily before pulling back to regard her with a smug expression. "But in this particular case, I spoke with Gabriel last night and asked for him to find us suitable clothes to continue our journey." He reached to grab a plain bag from the end of the bed. "Ta da."

Reaching for the bag, Nefri pulled out several pairs of jeans, both male and female in various sizes, and two matching gray hoodies that would allow them to easily travel without attracting notice among the humans.

With a roll of her eyes, she tossed the clothes onto the mattress and stripped off her robe. "So all this was a waste of time?" She waved toward the clothes scattered across the floor.

His dark gaze made a slow, intimate survey of her slender curves. "Hardly a waste."

"You are impossible," she muttered, pulling on the jeans and the smaller hoodie before shoving her feet into the sneakers she'd been wearing when she arrived.

"Sí," he readily agreed, his smile filled with a lethal charm as he dressed. "But what would you do without me?"

She paused. Without him.

A hollow pain bloomed in the center of her very being. The sort of pain a vampire could die from.

"I don't intend to find out," she said, her voice so low she wasn't certain Santiago had heard her until he'd grabbed her by the shoulders and pulled her hard against his chest.

He gazed down at her pale face, his expression somber. "Nefri . . ."

Whatever he was about to say was interrupted by a sharp knock. For a minute, they stared at one another in silence, each unwilling to end the shockingly profound connection.

Then as there was another loud knock, Santiago was striding across the room, his curses filling the air. Yanking open the door, he glared at the handsome vampire who was attired in a gray tuxedo. "Dammit, Gabriel," he growled in obvious annoyance. "What do you want?"

Unfazed by Santiago's harsh tone, or the icy power that slammed through the air, Gabriel straightened the cuffs of his white, satin shirt. "There's a"—he paused, a wicked amusement in his dark blue eyes—"creature downstairs who says that he's your partner."

Santiago scowled. Partner? What the hell?

"Levet," Nefri murmured, coming to stand at his side.

Oh . . . hell. He'd forgotten the tiny gargoyle. Again. It had to be one of those Freudian things.

"A curious companion," Gabriel said, clearly enjoying the thought of Santiago stuck with such a ridiculous creature.

"Don't start," Santiago cautioned his host.

Gabriel smiled. "He claims to have vital information that you must hear immediately."

"Fine. Tell him to park his granite ass outside and we'll be down to speak with him later."

Gabriel shifted his gaze to Nefri, reaching to lift her hand to his lips. "My lady, I hope my humble establishment has been . . ."

"Yeah, yeah." Santiago wrapped an arm around Nefri's shoulder, firmly tugging her from Gabriel's light grasp. "Go away."

"Santiago," Nefri chided softly. She understood he was an alpha vampire who felt the need to flex his muscles when another alpha was near, but she wasn't a bone to be fought over. She had muscles of her own that could be flexed. "Thank you, Gabriel, for your most gracious hospitality."

Gabriel flashed Santiago a condescending smile. "Manners are a lost art among the children, I fear."

Santiago snorted, then deliberately slammed the door in Gabriel's face.

Nefri shook her head. Males. "Do you feel better?"

His arm tightened around her shoulder and without warning he was swooping down to kiss her with a fierce intensity. She stiffened in surprise, then, sensing his need, she melted against him. This wasn't about conquering her. Or even staking a claim.

It was an instinctive need to know she would willingly choose him above all others.

At last lifting his head, he regarded her with a brooding gaze. "Now I feel better."

She went on her tiptoes to nip at his chin. "We need to find out what information Levet has."

He grimaced. "I don't suppose I can convince you to let him wait a few hours?"

She gave a shake of her head, that strange sense of urgency returning with a vengeance. "I don't think we can afford to wait."

His eyes darkened, as if he shared her sudden unease. "Oh . . . hell."

Chapter 23

Styx's lair in Chicago

To Sally the bedroom she'd been given looked like something out of a glossy magazine.

As big as her mother's cottage, it was decorated in shades of sea foam green and silver. A massive fireplace consumed one wall with another wall lined with arched windows that overlooked a distant lake. The floor was covered by a Parisian carpet and the ceiling was covered with a painting of angels dancing among the clouds.

In the center of the room was a canopy bed with a pale green comforter that was perfectly matched to the chaise lounge set beside the windows. There was also a hand-carved armoire and a mirrored dressing table.

Clearly the gig of being the King of Vampires paid well, she wryly acknowledged, trying her best not to be intimidated by her surroundings.

It was bad enough that Roke had made her feel like the biggest loser to ever walk the earth.

"I couldn't possibly have been trapped with a worse mate if I tried. . . ."

Cold-blooded snake.

She wasn't going to be overawed by a mere house.

Thankfully while she was indulging in a hot bubble bath someone (she was betting on Styx's lovely mate, Darcy) had made sure she had clean clothing. She chose a pair of black spandex pants that she matched with a white muscle shirt.

It was the perfect outfit for the hours of meditation she would need while her spell continued to simmer in the kitchen.

Or at least, that had been the plan.

She'd barely pulled on the clothes and run a brush through her damp hair when the silence was destroyed by a sudden knock. She stiffened, already knowing who was on the other side of the heavy walnut door.

She could actually *feel* Roke. As if there was a physical connection between them.

Standing in the center of the room, she wrapped her arms around her waist. It would be futile to try and pretend she was asleep. Roke was a vampire. He could no doubt hear the sudden increase of her heartbeat and the rapid rasp of her breath.

Besides, he'd already proven he didn't give a crap about her or her feelings. Even if she was sleeping, he wouldn't hesitate to wake her up.

While she dithered, there was another impatient bang on the door, and Roke's voice sliced through the air. "Open the door, Sally. I need to speak with you."

Comforting her wounded pride with the lovely image of turning the creep into a slimy toad, she yanked open the door to glare at the unwelcome intruder. "Why?" she asked in sweetly sick tones. "Did you have a few more insults you wanted to share?"

"No. I did—" His words broke off as his gaze took in her skimpy top and the clinging pants. The pale eyes darkened to smoke, his features sharpening with a hunger she didn't need their bond to sense.

His lengthening fangs would have been the first clue.

Sally blushed, feeling ridiculously exposed beneath that searing gaze. Stupid considering she'd worn far less in public.

"You did what?" she prompted, clinging to the door and trying not to do her own share of staring. The arrogant vamp was well aware he was indecently gorgeous. He didn't need her drooling to stroke his ego.

He muttered something too low for her to catch before he was retreating behind his facade of stoic self-control.

"I did some research on the warehouse," he finished, his voice smooth.

Sally eagerly latched on to the distraction. Anything not to have to deal with the renegade excitement that fluttered in the pit of her stomach.

"What warehouse?"

"The one where the book was hidden."

She frowned, not sure where this was going. "Why?"

He shrugged. "I don't like mysteries."

Sally paused, knowing he wasn't being fully honest. There was some other reason for his sudden interest in the warehouse. Still, the sooner this conversation was over, the sooner he would leave. Why press for an answer he didn't want to give?

"What does this have to do with me?"

"Let me in, Sally."

"Fine."

With exaggerated reluctance she stepped back, allowing him to enter the bedroom and close the door behind him. Moving past her, he glanced around the room, his gaze lingering on the large bed.

"You're comfortable?" he abruptly demanded, acting almost awkward as he turned to study her heated cheeks. "You like the room?"

Something dangerous tugged at her heart. Something she

was quite ready to disguise behind a surge of annoyance. "Don't try to be polite, Roke," she muttered. "It doesn't suit you."

His lips tightened. "Do you want an apology?"

"Just say what you have to say and get out."

There was a tense silence, as if he were battling against some inner demon. Then with a shrug, he flipped open a manila folder he'd been holding in his hand.

"The warehouse was previously owned by Lacombe Industries," he said, his voice carefully neutral. "Do you recognize the name?"

She frowned. "The cosmetic company?"

"No." He studied the file. "They were listed as an import-export firm."

"Never heard of them." She stepped toward him without thought, her bare feet barely making a sound on the expensive carpet. "Why?"

"Spike worked his magic on the computer and traced ownership of the company to a"—he flipped through a number of pages—"Anya Dubkova."

She gave a loud snort. "A vampire named Spike? Is that a joke?"

Roke shrugged. "He doesn't seem to find it particularly funny, but the rest of us do."

She rolled her eyes. "Leeches."

Ignoring her brief interruption, he tapped a finger against the file. "Is the name Anya familiar?"

"Why should it be?"

"She was a powerful witch who was the head of the local coven."

"Oh." She felt a stab of relief. The last thing she wanted was to deal with the black magic. There was always a backlash. Not that she was going to admit her reluctance. She'd learned a long time ago never to reveal a vulnerability. "Good."

He lifted his brows. "Good?"

"If you can get the witch who cast the spell it's much easier for her to remove it than for me to smash my way past it."

He grimaced. "She's not going to be removing any spells."

Of course not. She swallowed a sigh. "Why not?"

"She and her entire coven were slaughtered almost thirty years ago."

Without warning he pulled out a glossy black and white photo that he shoved under her nose.

She blinked, plucking the photo from his fingers so she could focus on the image. Immediately she wished she hadn't.

Her stomach revolted as she took in the sight of the bloody female bodies that were spread across a cement floor. The warehouse? It was impossible to know, and it didn't really matter. Not with the gruesome tumble of corpses that had clearly been savaged.

She wasn't an innocent.

She'd been raised by a black witch and then eventually wound up in the service of the Dark Lord. She'd witnessed things that still gave her nightmares.

But this . . .

"Oh my god," she breathed.

"The massacre caused a panic at the time, according to the newspapers," Roke said. "Of course, the local police didn't realize the twelve women were witches. They assumed that a serial killer had collected them together and then murdered them in one bloody spree."

Sally shook her head. "No serial killer could have done"—she shuddered, refusing to glance any closer at the mutilated bodies—"this. Not to a coven of witches."

"What could?"

She shoved the picture back into his hand. "If they were caught off guard, then any number of powerful demons could have killed them."

She deliberately didn't use the word "vampire," but his

jaw tightened as he shoved the photo back into the file and pulled out a newspaper clipping.

"Here's a picture of Anya Dubkova before her death." He waited for her to take the clipping and study the picture of a middle-aged woman with silver hair pulled into a neat bun and a slender body attired in a business suit. She looked like a banker. "You've never seen her?" he prompted.

Sally lifted her gaze to regard him with a flare of impatience. "Do you know every vampire?"

"No."

"Then why would you . . ." She sucked in a sharp breath, startled by the realization that this man could still manage to wound her. You'd think she'd have developed a thicker skin. "Oh, I see. You assume that because she owned the warehouse where the book was hidden by black magic the witches must have been evil." She wrapped her arms around her waist. "And since I'm evil we must naturally be BFFs."

His eyes darkened at her accusation, but his expression remained unreadable. "I'm merely seeking information," he pointed out. "And there aren't so many covens that it would be a huge leap to think you might have crossed paths."

She allowed the clipping to flutter to the floor, turning to pace toward the windows. "I avoided witches after my powers became more obvious. I couldn't risk them suspecting I had demon blood." She studied the night sky speckled with stars. "If they didn't kill me they would certainly have turned me over to my mother."

Roke made a low sound and she felt an elusive emotion surge through their bond. It was gone before she could pin it down.

"How can we find out more about this coven?" he asked, his voice as cool and steady as ever.

With an effort, she forced herself to turn and meet his pale, guarded gaze. "I doubt that we can." She hesitated. She'd been taught from the cradle never to speak of the coven's private business. It wasn't a simple matter to overcome a lifetime of conditioning. "Witches are by nature secretive and they would have made sure that their private records were protected by a nullifying spell."

"What's that?"

"A spell that would be activated by their death," she reluctantly explained. "When they died their records, letters, and any personal information would have been destroyed."

He frowned, seemingly bothered by her words. "Except the book."

Oh. He was right. A book that was so dangerous it had to be hidden by black magic was precisely the sort of thing the witches would have made certain was destroyed rather than allowing it to fall into the hands of their enemies.

"Yes," she said with a slow nod.

"Why?"

A good question. Perhaps even a dangerous question.

She chewed her bottom lip, unaware of Roke's covert fascination with the unconscious habit.

"We won't know until I break the spell guarding it," she at last announced.

With a speed that was too swift for her to track, he was standing only inches away, his hands grasping her face so he could scowl down at her.

"No."

"No?" She told herself it was surprise at his abrupt approach that made her heart thunder in her chest and not the cool touch of his hands against her face. "What do you mean 'no'?"

"You're not going near that book until we find out more about what killed the coven," he growled. "And why."

She stilled. "You think the two are connected?"

"We've already determined that I don't believe in coincidences."

"Then surely it's all the more important that we find out what's in the book?"

"No." The pale eyes shimmered silver in the muted light, a hint of fang showing. "I don't care if I have to lock you back in the dungeon. You're not returning to that warehouse."

Summerset House

Santiago led Nefri down the back steps of the club, already sensing the vampires filling the public rooms. The word of Nefri's arrival had clearly spread like wildfire and every demon in the area was rushing to catch a glimpse of her.

Thankfully Gabriel had foreseen the impending crowd and had moved Levet to a secluded room beneath the garages with two armed guards outside to make sure of their privacy.

Perhaps a bit of overkill, but Gabriel was notorious for his detailed attention to his guests' comfort, predicting their every need. Just as Santiago was renowned for providing his guests with every wicked pleasure they could desire.

Using a hidden tunnel to travel from the house to the garage, they took the staircase down to what once had been a human bomb shelter.

The small square of cement was hardly designed for comfort, but Santiago fully approved of the fact it was secure, with no opportunity for their conversation to be overheard.

Not only because they needed to discuss the next step in their hunt for Gaius, but because he didn't need his fellow vampires seeing him in the company of the stunted gargoyle who was impatiently pacing the floor when they entered the room.

"Ah, at last," the creature muttered, his tail twitching as he came to an abrupt halt. "I have been waiting forever."

Santiago rolled his eyes, well aware that it had been less than a half an hour since Gabriel informed them that Levet had arrived at the club. Nefri, however, was swiftly moving forward to pat the tip of his wing.

"Forgive us, Levet."

The ugly little face lit with a sudden smile. "How can I stay angry? You are forgiven, *ma belle*."

Santiago noticed there was no mention of forgiveness for him.

"Thank you." Nefri smiled. "Did you have a reunion with Yannah?"

Levet heaved a tragic sigh. "*Non*. She was . . . unavailable."

"Ah." Nefri gave the delicate wing another pat. "Just be patient."

"Fah. I have been oh-so patient, but for what?" Levet spread his arms. "Heartache."

Santiago took an impatient step forward. He'd been forced to let the ridiculous creature trail along, but he drew the line at discussing the gargoyle's love life. "You told Gabriel you had some vital information that couldn't wait," he said in sharp tones.

Expecting the usual raspberry or a rude finger gesture, Santiago found himself frowning when the gargoyle instead gave a somber nod of his head.

"*Oui.*"

Okay. This couldn't be good.

"What is it?"

"Shay contacted me." Levet tapped a claw to his temple, indicating his ability to speak mind to mind with the Chicago clan chief's mate. "She said that Viper was unable to reach you."

With a muffled curse, Santiago reached into the pocket of his jeans to pull out his cell phone, not at all surprised to discover the battery had been drained.

Sex with Nefri was not only the most explosive pleasure he'd ever experienced, but it tended to create havoc with electronics. Oh, and created the most dazzling displays of color.

"*Dios,*" he muttered, aggravated by his dangerous lapse.

He should have checked his phone the minute he climbed out of bed. "What's happened?"

"There was a disturbance at your club."

He frowned. That was why Viper was trying to contact him? It didn't make sense. "There's always a disturbance at the club. Tonya can handle it."

"Actually . . ." Levet's wings drooped, a disturbing expression of sympathy on his ugly face.

Santiago shoved the phone back into his pocket, his muscles rigid with a sudden tension. "What?"

"She's been kidnapped."

He heard Nefri's soft exclamation of shock, but his focus never wavered from the small demon. "Tell me."

"One of your waiters called Viper and said that a vampire simply appeared out of thin air in the middle of your club."

He hissed. Only two vampires could appear out of thin air. And he'd been in the constant presence of one of them.

Which left . . .

"Gaius," he growled. *"Mierda."*

Levet nodded. *"Oui.* He appeared and grabbed Tonya. Then"—he gave a helpless lift of his hands—"poof. They were both gone."

Just for a second his savage burst of fury threatened to cloud his mind. Tonya in the hands of that demented freak? Perhaps even now chained to a wall while he tormented her?

The cement walls shuddered and the fluorescent lights shattered before Nefri laid a restraining hand on his shoulder.

"Santiago," she murmured softly.

Leashing his powers with an effort, he met her sympathetic gaze. "Why?" he rasped.

She continued to rub his arm in a soothing motion. Trying to tame the rabid beast?

"Why Tonya?" she asked.

"Sí." His fury remained, but Nefri's touch gave him the calm necessary to consider the situation with a much needed

clarity. Tonya needed a swift rescue, not her employer ranting and raving. "It makes no sense. Why would he take such a risk to snatch an imp from my club?"

Nefri nodded, easily following his logic. If Gaius was going to risk being captured, why choose Tonya?

"Does she have any special talents?" Nefri asked.

Santiago shrugged. "She's related to Troy, the pain-in-the-ass Prince of Imps, so she's capable of creating hexes powerful enough to ensnare even demons and, of course, she can create portals along with the usual imp talents."

Levet waddled forward. "Does she know secrets?" He pointed a claw at Santiago. "Have you been—what do they say—cooking the books?"

Santiago glowered at the small demon. "What the hell are you talking about?"

Levet blinked. "We were guessing why she was kidnapped, were we not?"

"No, she doesn't have any secrets," Santiago snapped. "At least none she shared with me. She's an organized, highly effective assistant who has the beauty of a siren and the soul of an accountant."

"You trust her?" Nefri carefully inquired.

"Absolutely," he growled without hesitation, well aware of what she was implying. "Tonya would never betray me. I would stake my life on it." He gave a restless shrug. "Besides, if she was working with Gaius why would he reveal their connection now? There's no benefit."

She nodded, but her expression remained troubled. "How long have you known one another?"

"Several decades."

"And you're"—she searched for the word she wanted—"close?"

He sent her a startled glance. "What are you asking?"

"I'm not behaving as a jealous lover, Santiago," she gently assured him.

"Then what does it matter how long I've known Tonya? I trust her—" His words came to an abrupt halt as he met Nefri's steady gaze. *Dios.* There was one reason someone would go to the effort of kidnapping Tonya. "He's using her to send a message to me," he said in rough tones.

"That would be my guess."

"Now the question is—"

Nefri grimaced. "What's the message?"

Chapter 24

Nefri grimly maintained her composure. Right now Santiago needed her calm, cool logic. Inside, however, she was battling a rising tide of fear.

She didn't know why Gaius would have discovered a sudden interest in Santiago. Or more likely, the spirit that was controlling him.

But she did know that Santiago would do whatever was necessary to rescue the female imp. Including putting himself in danger.

And there wasn't a damned thing she could do to stop him.

"It could be that he discovered we're hunting him." Santiago spoke his thoughts out loud, his barely leased fury dropping the temperature in the tiny room to near zero. "He could be hoping to convince me to give up the search in exchange for Tonya."

"But?" she prompted, hearing the lack of conviction in his voice.

"But it's not Gaius's style." With a sharp movement he was pacing back and forth, his hand instinctively reaching to pull out the Roman dagger he kept tucked in his back pocket. "He can be a hammer when necessary, but he prefers to be subtle. He's a master of diversion."

Nefri grimaced. Gaius had certainly managed to deceive her. He'd hidden his true intentions behind his genuine grief to gain access to her clan beyond the Veil.

A knowledge that still burned like acid against her pride. But she wasn't going to allow his abuse of her trust to blind her to facts.

"Yes, if he is actually still in the position to be master," she pointed out. "It's quite possible he's no longer making the decisions."

Santiago sent her a grim frown. "That doesn't make me feel better."

She shrugged. "It wasn't supposed to."

He continued his pacing, his hands clenching and unclenching until he at last came to an abrupt halt directly in front of her. "Nefri."

"Yes?"

"Tonya is family."

She reached to place a hand on his arm, able to sense his distress at Tonya's capture. It was far more than just the anger of an employer. Or a friend.

It was deeper. More personal.

"You rescued her," she said softly.

He gave a low hiss of shock. "I'm beginning to suspect you truly can read minds."

"No, but I know you." Her fingers tightened on his arm. "Styx pulled you from the blood pits and Viper gave you a home. They taught you honor and discipline and that a leader cares for those who are vulnerable."

He slid the dagger back into his pocket, his eyes dark with painful memories. "It's not my story to tell, but she ended up on the wrong side of an argument with a tribe of trolls and was sold to a slaver."

Levet gave a violent flutter of his wings. "Evor?"

The two males shared a rare moment of understanding. *"Sí."*

The tiny gargoyle trembled. Nefri had heard rumors that Levet had been held captive by the brutal slaver, along with Viper's mate, Shay.

"A very bad man," Levet muttered.

"Very bad," Santiago agreed. "If Tonya hadn't been so strong she would never have survived." His low growl trickled from his throat. "Now she's being held against her will again. I can't leave her in the hands of Gaius."

"Of course not." Nefri studied his stubborn expression with open concern. "But, Santiago—"

"I know it's a trap," he interrupted her cautious words. "I have to go."

"Gaius will be waiting for you."

The dark eyes smoldered with a ruthless determination. "There's nothing I can do to prevent that."

The fear that she was trying so desperately to control threatened to explode as she glared at him in helpless frustration. "I'm not going to change your mind, am I?"

His touch was tender as he cupped her face in his hands, but he gave a firm shake of his head. "No."

"Very well." She met his gaze squarely, her centuries of experience allowing her to transform the fear into stark resolve. What made a clan chief a leader was their ability to control their emotions rather than be controlled by them. "There's no longer any need to try and sneak up on him."

Santiago's expression became guarded. "You have a plan?"

"Not really, but we might as well use my medallion to travel," she said. "It will save us time."

He was shaking his head before she even finished speaking. "I can't pinpoint his exact location."

"Then we'll travel north until you can."

"Nefri . . ."

She pressed her hand to his mouth, her eyes warning that she wasn't in the mood to listen to his endless list of reasons why she shouldn't join him.

"Don't even bother."

His fingers tightened on her face. "Dammit, Nefri, we've agreed this is a trap. It would be beyond stupid for both of us to—"

"Three of us," Levet abruptly intruded into the conversation.

Santiago's eyes widened in horror. "Oh, hell no."

"Yes, the three of us," Nefri said.

Dropping his hands, Santiago glared at her tranquil expression. "Is this some sort of punishment?"

"We're partners." She stepped forward to place her lips against the stubborn line of his jaw. "Which means we stand together. Always."

He stiffened, clearly torn between his instinctive need to protect her and the understanding that she was a powerful weapon that might very well make the difference between Tonya's rescue or her death at the hands of Gaius.

"I knew you were a dangerous female." Pressing a resigned kiss to her forehead, Santiago headed for the door. "I need to speak with Gabriel before we leave."

Gaius's lair in Wisconsin

With an appreciative eye Gaius studied the female imp chained to the wall of the cellar.

He'd never been a lover of the fey, but there was no denying her emerald green eyes and tumble of flame curls could make any man want to spread her legs. Who wouldn't want to indulge in those lush, delectable curves barely covered by the strapless silver gown?

And then there was the warm scent of her blood. It was . . . intoxicating.

His fangs ached as he was struck by a sharp hunger. It had taken a considerable amount of energy to use his medallion to travel to Santiago's demon club and return with the imp. He needed to feed.

Unfortunately, he hadn't brought the female to his lair for a snack. Or even to pleasure him.

He needed her if he was going to persuade Santiago to accept his offer of reconciliation. And to convince him to assist him in protecting Dara.

Which meant no tasting the hostage.

At least not until she'd served her purpose.

Strolling forward, he crouched down to meet her gaze, enjoying the scent of plums that was spiced with a combination of fear and fury.

"You really are remarkably beautiful," he murmured, his finger drifting over the dewy skin of her cheek. "It's no wonder Santiago kept you as a companion for so long."

She choked back a scream. "I'm his employee, not his companion."

"More than that." His finger shifted to linger on the pulse that hammered at the base of her throat. The moment he'd appeared in Santiago's club he'd been drawn to the female. "It's distant but I can sense his claim on you. He considers you a part of his clan."

She licked her lips, making a visible effort to calm her nerves. "You're mental. I'm just a member of his staff." She futilely tried to arch away from his touch. "So if you're expecting to use me to get to him, then you're wasting your time."

Clever imp.

She had easily realized she was the bait and hoped to trick him into believing she had no value.

"No, he will come for you," Gaius said with an unshakable confidence. "Santiago is at heart a savior."

Her lips thinned, but she didn't try to argue. "What do you want with him?" she instead demanded.

"Only for an opportunity to tell him how sorry I am."

Her eyes narrowed in disbelief. "You don't need me for that."

Gaius shrugged. "He's too angry to listen to me unless I can force him to hear what I have to say."

"Kidnapping me is only going to piss him off. It certainly won't put him in the mood to listen," she pointed out, shuddering as his fingers drifted to follow the line of her collarbone. "Or to forgive."

Gaius frowned, his fingers moving to squeeze her throat. What did the bitch know? Santiago was his son. That was a bond that couldn't be broken.

"He *will* listen," he snarled.

"Okay, okay. He'll listen," she croaked, sucking in a deep breath as his grip loosened. "But I'm telling you he'll be a lot more forgiving if you release me."

His fury eased as he was distracted by the softness of her skin beneath his fingers and the scent of plums teasing his nose.

"Clever and beautiful," he muttered, lowering his hand so he could cup the ripe temptation of her breast.

She made a sound of distress. "Don't."

Her reluctance only fueled his stab of lust. "Does my touch repulse you?"

She shuddered. "Yes."

"I can make you like it." His grip tightened until she gave a small cry of pain. "I can make you beg for it."

The emerald eyes flashed with hatred. "Not even in a million years," she spat out, her chin inching higher. "I have royal blood flowing through my veins. I can't be enthralled, vamp."

"Royalty," he sneered. The imp thought she was above him with her noble blood? He'd teach her just how worthless it was. "Such a proud imp."

He could hear the leap of her pulse as he allowed his powers to fill the cellar.

"Stop . . ." Her magnificent eyes dilated with an uncontrollable lust. "I . . ."

He chuckled, running his tongue up and down his sensitive fang.

Maybe a small taste wouldn't hurt.

"Yes, my beauty?"

A layer of sweat bloomed on her skin. "What are you doing to me?"

He tugged at the hardened tip of her breast. "Do you want me?"

"No." She squeezed her eyes shut even as her body trembled with need. "You're disgusting."

He chuckled with cruel amusement, ignoring his weakness as he deliberately altered his appearance. In the distance he could feel his approaching guests and he intended to reveal the full glory of his new powers.

"Perhaps this shape will tempt you," he murmured, giving her nipple a more painful tug. "Open your eyes, Tonya."

Reluctantly lifting her lashes, she gave a gasp of shock as she caught sight of his features, which were now an exact duplicate of Santiago.

"Shit," she breathed, but Gaius didn't miss the increase in her pulse or the sudden shallowness to her breathing.

Her arousal wasn't entirely due to the lust that pulsed through the air.

"Is this better?" He leaned down to savor the scent of her heated blood. "Are you in love with your employer?"

A low groan was wrenched from her throat as she arched toward him. "Please . . ."

"What do you want?" he urged.

"You," she whispered, the chains rattling as she tried to reach for him. "I want you."

He smiled at the sound of soft footsteps on the stairs.

"You want Santiago?" he cooed.

"Yes, please," she moaned, panting with the desire that ran rampant through her blood. "Please."

He allowed his fangs to scrape down the curve of her throat. "I told you I would make you beg."

"Bastard," a furious voice snapped from the doorway of the cellar. "Leave her alone."

Gaius pulled back, but his gaze never strayed from the beautiful imp. It was unfortunate, but Santiago had to be reminded of Gaius's superior position. Even among family the hierarchy had to be established.

"But she is so happy to be with you," he murmured, turning her eager face so Santiago could see her pleading expression. "She's wanted you for a very long time, haven't you, imp?"

Santiago took a step forward, his fury a tangible force that beat through the cellar. "She has no part in this. Just let her go."

"I'm not going to hurt her," Gaius assured his companion. "I only wanted your attention."

"You have it," he snarled.

Straightening, Gaius allowed his shape to return to normal, a smile of warm greeting curving his lips.

First the stick and then the carrot.

It had always been his preferred style of leadership.

"My son."

Santiago grimaced, his attention shifting to the imp who curled her shivering body into a small ball on the floor.

"Let me have Tonya."

"Not yet." Gaius stepped forward to block the imp from Santiago's line of vision. "First we talk."

"Then you'll release her?"

"Perhaps."

Gaius studied the vampire whom he'd claimed as his son so many centuries ago. There were few changes. A vampire didn't age. But there was a hardness to the lean features that hadn't been there before Dara's death and a icy lack of pleasure in their long overdue reunion.

Stifling his stab of disappointment, Gaius glanced over Santiago's shoulder. He could feel a tiny demon just outside the door. A . . . gargoyle? A meaningless pest. He was far more interested in the thundering pulse of Nefri's power. His brows lifted as he realized she was moving away from the lair, not closer.

"Where is your companion going?"

Santiago grimaced. "She had a small task to finish."

It took a second for Gaius to realize that his former chief wasn't alone as she moved through the woods that surrounded the house.

"Ah." His lips twisted. "The humans."

"Nefri is surprisingly squeamish for a clan chief. She insisted that they be released."

"A bother, but they can be replaced," he murmured.

"You never kept a herd before," Santiago accused him, displaying his aversion for keeping a group of humans or lesser demons caged like animals. "Why now?"

Gaius gave a restless shrug. This wasn't what he wanted to discuss. "I must feed."

"And the torture?" the younger vampire pressed. "Did you develop a taste for pain after you became a slave for the Dark Lord?"

Gaius flinched, deeply bothered by his son's icy condemnation. "No," he protested, taking a step forward. "It's not for me."

Santiago stilled. "Then who?"

"Dara."

Chapter 25

Santiago narrowed his gaze.

What the hell?

Had Gaius gone bat-shit crazy?

It would, of course, explain his sire's shockingly filthy appearance and the strange glitter in his dark eyes.

But Dara? *Cristo*.

"I don't understand," he at last managed to growl, shifting so he could catch a glimpse of Tonya as she shivered on the dirt floor.

She looked shaken, but unharmed. Not that the sight eased the fury that beat through his blood. Gaius was going to pay for every bruise on her delicate skin.

A demented joy twisted Gaius's bloodstained face, filling the air with a dangerous sense of euphoria. "Dara," the older vampire said in a reverent voice. "She's been returned to me."

Yeah. Bat-shit crazy.

Santiago might have felt pity for the pathetic bastard if he hadn't betrayed everyone who had ever trusted him. Oh, and was even now threatening to destroy the world.

As it was, all Santiago wanted to do was chop off his head and be done with the nasty business.

But not yet, a voice warned in the back of his mind.

Nefri had insisted they needed information. And for now, Gaius was the only one who could tell him what the hell was going on.

"Dara has returned from the grave?" he repeated, making sure he hadn't misunderstood.

"Yes."

"You know that's not possible." He searched Gaius's expression for some sign he was being controlled by another force. At the moment he couldn't sense anything but the vampire's seething madness. "You watched her burn."

Gaius pressed a hand to his unbeating heart. "It's a miracle."

"Vampires aren't capable of regenerating once they're dead. They don't even produce ghosts."

An abrupt anger tightened Gaius's gaunt face. "I was promised this. She is my reward for my faithful service."

Santiago hissed in pain. Dara was a lovely, astonishingly gentle female who had blessed them all with her unwavering love. She wasn't a damned reward.

"A reward from who?" he forced himself to ask.

"From the Dark Lord."

Santiago shook his head. He'd known that Gaius had betrayed them to the evil deity for the opportunity to be reunited with his dead mate. But he still didn't understand why.

"I know you were grieving, Gaius, but you've never been stupid," he managed to point out, his voice coated with ice, but his weapons still sheathed. Kudos to him. "You had to suspect that it was a scam to lure you into the Dark Lord's power."

The once decisive, always-in-command vampire blinked as if confused by the question. "I had no choice. I had to . . ."

"What?"

"I had to bring her back."

Santiago stiffened his spine, refusing to acknowledge the soul-deep loss that flickered through Gaius's eyes. The same loss that he'd felt when Dara was taken from them.

"No matter what the cost?"

"No matter what the cost." Gaius turned to pace across the floor, his gait oddly unsteady. "I had no choice."

"So you keep saying, but we both know that's a lie."

"You don't understand."

A prickle of desperation crawled through the air. Santiago frowned. It wasn't the pervasive violence that had choked the air in Louisiana or even the fear around the schoolhouse where they'd found poor Melinda. But it was without a doubt coming from Gaius.

A new talent like his shape-shifting? Or a warning that the strange spirit was working through him?

Instinctively he shifted closer to Tonya. If things went to hell he wanted to be near enough to make a grab for her.

"What's to understand?"

"It was my fault."

Santiago frowned. "We all feel guilty for Dara's death. If I had been there then—"

"No." Gaius abruptly turned to face him, his eyes burning with a bleak regret. "The attack was my fault."

Santiago halted the denial on the tip of his tongue. Maybe this was more than the typical survivor guilt.

Maybe there was a deeper reason for Gaius's madness.

"Why do you say that?"

Gaius turned his head, as if unable to meet Santiago's steady gaze. "I had decided that our clan had grown powerful enough to expand our territory." He gave a short, humorless laugh. "After all, why be content with Rome when I could rule the entire empire?"

Santiago lifted his brows in surprise. "An ambitious plan."

"Oh, I intended to begin small." He waved a dismissive hand. "A simple takeover of the neighboring clan."

"You never said anything about expansion," Santiago accused him, belatedly accepting that he had never truly known this man. "I thought I was your most trusted soldier."

Gaius turned back. "You were my son, not a soldier."

"But you didn't trust me with such vital information?"

A hint of impatience rippled over Gaius's face. "Only because I hoped to achieve my goals without involving you or any other clan member."

Santiago shook his head in disbelief. "You expected the clan chief to hand over his territory if you asked nicely?"

"I expected a quiet dagger in the back to avoid a messy war."

Santiago curled his lip. Assassination. The coward's choice.

"Et tu, Brute?" he mocked.

Gaius waved aside his scorn. "A bloodless . . ." He grimaced. "Well, an *almost* bloodless coup is always better than war."

"Who was to hold the dagger?"

"I approached the neighboring chief's general," Gaius admitted. "I had heard rumors the vampire lusted after the chief's mate. It was a simple matter to convince him that once his chief was dead he could have the mate in his bed. I gave him my weapon to perform the deed."

Santiago pulled the *pugio* from the pocket of his jeans and tossed it in the middle of the floor. The silver blade of the Roman dagger shimmered in the light from the bare bulb hanging from the ceiling.

"This weapon?"

Gaius frowned, as if trying to figure out how Santiago had gotten his hands on the dagger.

"Sí," he said in a clipped voice. "Even though I wasn't going to be the one striking the killing blow, I wanted the clan to know who was behind the plot so they would bow to me."

Not only a coward, but a delusional coward.

Idiot.

He rolled his eyes. "You trusted a vampire who would betray his own leader?"

"A mistake." A surge of fury slammed into Santiago with enough force to send him reeling backward before it abruptly shifted to a vast, grinding sorrow. "But at the time I was blinded by my own arrogance. I was so certain I was stronger and smarter than any other vampire. I felt invincible."

Santiago heard Tonya's soft sobs even as he battled against the urge to fall to his knees beneath the weight of the choking sadness.

"What went wrong?" he asked between gritted teeth.

"I'll never know for certain." Gaius scrubbed his hand over his face, his shoulders bowed with a weariness he could no longer disguise. "Perhaps the general lost his nerve and confessed his sins to his chief, or he was foolish enough to brag of his plans to a fellow clansman. But it was two nights later when we were attacked. Dara was burned, my clansmen slaughtered, and I found that"—he pointed toward the dagger lying on the floor—"stabbed into my pillow."

"And so you sold your soul to make up for your bungled attempt to become emperor?"

"Dara paid the cost of my conceit," Gaius said, a visible shudder wracking his thin body. "I would have sold my soul a thousand times over to bring her back."

Santiago furrowed his brow, assuming the seeds of his sire's madness must have been planted in that moment. "Even knowing it's a futile dream?"

"I will admit that I began to fear that I'd been taken for a fool. The Dark Lord"—he spit out the name of his former master—"proved to be a disappointment. Or so I thought."

"What do you mean?" Santiago pressed. Not because he gave a damn. Gaius had proven over and over he was unworthy of Santiago's forgiveness. But he needed to understand how the vampire could have become infected by the dangerous spirit.

"I awoke in the warehouse to discover that Dara was with me."

Santiago shook his head. He'd been in the warehouse

during the bloody battle with the Dark Lord. Even with all the chaos he would have known if Dara was near.

"You mean with you in spirit?"

"No . . . she's here," Gaius insisted. "In this house."

Okay, enough. The vampire was either trying to trick him or so Froot Loops that he was imagining his deceased mate had been returned from the dead.

"I searched the house before coming into the cellars," he said, his flat tones warning he wasn't in the mood to be jerked around. "There's no one here beyond the humans and Tonya."

Gaius hesitated, his eyes shifting toward the open door as he used his senses to search for his missing mate. "She must have . . ."

"What?"

The older vampire frowned in confusion before at last giving a shake of his head. "She must be hiding until we're certain that you can be trusted."

"Me?" Santiago glared at the man who'd caused so much pain. "I'm not the one who betrayed my people."

Gaius winced, holding out his hand in a silent plea. "There hasn't been a night that has passed that I haven't regretted leaving you behind, my son."

Using the legitimate excuse to shift away from the gesture of reconciliation, Santiago edged to the side. Still, Gaius remained poised between him and the silent Tonya. He needed to get closer.

"It's too late. . . ."

"But it isn't," Gaius harshly interrupted him. "Dara has been returned. We'll be together as a family again."

Santiago swallowed a growl of impatience. Obviously his sire's insanity went beyond just thinking his mate was hiding nearby if he thought Santiago would ever consider him a part of his family.

"And that's why you kidnapped Tonya?" he snapped.

Gaius glanced over his shoulder at the trembling imp. "In part."

"What's the other part?"

There was a long silence before Gaius turned back. Almost as if he was debating how much to confess.

"Dara is in danger," he at last said.

Santiago didn't bother to try and argue that Dara couldn't possibly be in danger. He could only hope that they were at last getting to the point of Tonya's kidnapping.

"In danger from what?"

"The Oracles."

Santiago froze. Did Gaius simply sense that he was being hunted by the Commission? Or did someone—or something—whisper in his ear that the powerful Oracles were a danger to his dead mate?

He carefully considered his words. "Why would they be a threat to Dara?"

"Because she's . . ."

"Gaius?"

"Because she's not supposed to be here," Gaius whispered in low tones, acting as if he feared his words might be overheard. "That's all I know."

Santiago studied the vampire's gaunt face and the shadows beneath his eyes. Despite the blood staining his face that spoke of a recent frenzied feeding, he appeared like a man who'd been starved for weeks, if not months.

There was more wrong with Gaius than his missing sanity.

"What do you want from me?"

He again held out his hand. "Your forgiveness."

Santiago deliberately folded his arms over his chest. Not even to gain information could he offer absolution.

"You didn't kidnap Tonya for my forgiveness," he pointed out, his frigid voice making Gaius drop his hand in defeat.

"You are my son," he muttered.

"If you were so anxious for a reunion you would have

contacted me when you first returned from behind the Veil," Santiago reminded his sire. "Now tell me what you truly want."

Gaius hunched a shoulder. "You will learn to believe me."

"Fine." Tired of the vampire's insistence on pretending he gave a damn about his one-time son, Santiago called his bluff. "You want my forgiveness, then release Tonya."

Predictably Gaius shook his head, his hands plucking at the cuff of his dark silk shirt. He didn't seem to notice the material was frayed and coated with dust. Yet another indication that the vampire was out of his mind.

"I can't. Not yet."

"Why?"

"We must . . ." Something moved in Gaius's dark eyes. Something immense and . . . aware. Like a great beast that was hidden in the shadows, just waiting to pounce. "There's a book."

Santiago's muscles tensed, a sharp fear jolting through him. *Mierda.*

He wasn't mistaken. There was something *inside* Gaius. Controlling him without the older vampire even being aware of the creature.

Was this the spirit that the Oracles were hunting? The supposed creator of vampires?

And if it was . . . what the hell was he supposed to do about it?

For the moment it obviously preferred to keep its presence hidden. And Santiago was happy to pretend he hadn't caught a glimpse of the terrifying creature.

At least until he could determine exactly what it wanted with him.

"What book?" he asked, giving up any rash idea of trying to simply grab Tonya and flee.

At the moment, he wasn't sure any of them were going to get out of the cellar alive.

Or sane.

"A spell book," Gaius said, a throb of frustration beginning to beat in the air. "It's being protected by black magic. We need to destroy it."

Santiago didn't have to pretend his confusion. This was why he was lured to Wisconsin? Because of a book?

"I have no immunity to black magic," he said with a frown. "Neither does Tonya."

There was another unnerving flicker of the spirit as Gaius tilted back his head, seeming to be spreading his powers far beyond the cramped cellar. "There's a witch," he said.

Santiago struggled against an instinctive urge to reach for his sword. *Cristo*. His skin was suddenly crawling with the promise of pain. Like he was standing in the eye of a hurricane, just waiting for disaster.

"There are a lot of witches," he pointed out. Carefully.

"Only one who can break the spell."

Santiago grimaced. Only one? So was that good news or bad?

Impossible to say.

"What does that have to do with me?"

"She's in the lair of the Anasso."

"The Anasso?" Santiago made a sound of disbelief. "Styx is protecting a witch?"

"Sally, Sally, Sally." Gaius slowly smiled, his eyes once again distant. "She thought she could double-cross me, stupid witch. But she's made it all so much easier."

Santiago lowered his brows, wondering if Gaius was referring to the witch who had once been his fellow servant of the Dark Lord.

She must have been desperate if she approached the King of Vampires.

"I still don't understand what you want from me."

Gaius studied him with growing impatience. "I want you to get her."

"From Styx's lair?"

"Sí."

Santiago paused, sending a covert glance toward Tonya, who had shifted as far as possible from Gaius, her arms wrapped around her drawn up knees.

A noose was tightening around his neck and he didn't have a damned clue how to escape.

"Why not you?"

Gaius's mocking smile was so familiar that it caught Santiago off guard. Who was in control? Gaius or the spirit?

Or was it perhaps a strange combination of the two?

"I'm not precisely beloved among vampires."

"Traitors are rarely beloved among any species," Santiago couldn't resist reminding him.

Gaius narrowed his gaze. "Soon you will understand."

Santiago hissed at the sudden promise of violence that brushed over him. "Is that a threat?"

"I would prefer not to use threats." Gaius reached down to pick up the forgotten dagger, his nonchalance not fooling Santiago for a minute. "All I need you to do is get the witch away from the Anasso's lair. A simple enough task."

Right. Sneaking into a lair with a higher grade security system than the Pentagon, not to mention a dozen of the most powerful demons on earth, to snatch a witch who was presumably hiding from the spirit. Yep. Simple as pie.

"Why don't you use your . . ." He shuddered, forced to recall the creepy sight of walking into the cellar to see himself bent over poor Tonya. "Talent to shape-shift and just become me?"

Gaius smoothly turned to throw the dagger at the doorjamb, proving that for all his fragile appearance he maintained his impressive strength as the blade sunk hilt deep into the wood.

"Styx is already aware of my talent," he snarled. "He would

realize the minute I appeared without your scent that it was me."

Santiago lowered his gaze to the gold amulet that hung around Gaius's neck. He could feel the noose tightening with every passing second.

He might not know why Gaius was so anxious to get his hands on this mysterious book, or why it had to be Sally the Witch to do the destroying, but he sure as hell knew it couldn't be for anything good.

Which meant he had to find a way to stop him.

"Then why not use your medallion?" he hedged. "That's how you captured Tonya, isn't it?"

The tightening of Gaius's lips proved the vampire had already tried to penetrate Styx's house. "The lair is protected by a spell that prevents portals from being created inside the house," he grudgingly admitted. "I need you."

With a regretful glance toward Tonya, Santiago squared his shoulders and spread his feet in preparation for battle.

"No."

Gaius frowned at the blunt refusal. "My son, don't be a fool."

"There's nothing foolish in loyalty. I will never betray my clan."

Gaius flinched, then the shame on his gaunt face was replaced by a cunning that sent a chill down Santiago's spine.

The creature was once again in control.

"So easy to say when there's no cost to that loyalty," he purred, lifting his hand as if pointing to something above them.

"What do you mean?"

"Let's see how deep your loyalty runs."

Santiago shifted backward, sensing a sudden flow of fury, although it seemed oddly muted. As if it was being funneled away from him.

Half expecting the ceiling to fall on his head, Santiago

instead heard the front door to the lair being wrenched off its hinges followed by the unmistakable blast of Nefri's power.

"What the hell?"

"Santiago!" Levet called out in warning, then there was a thud, as if he'd been tossed into the wall.

He had half a second to turn toward the door before Nefri was in the room, her hair floating around her exquisitely beautiful face and her eyes glowing with a mindless rage.

Her features had been sharpened, the alabaster skin so perfect it shimmered like the finest silk. And her slender body sculpted with the grace of an Amazon.

She was as nature intended.

An exotic symbol of pure female power.

Santiago stood in speechless wonderment. A mistake, as Nefri's fierce gaze shifted toward the female imp chained to the wall.

Tonya cried out in fear as Nefri flowed forward, her fangs fully extended and her hands curled into claws.

"Nefri." He was moving before he could consider the consequences, placing himself between Tonya and the feral vampire. "No."

Nefri slammed into him with enough force to send him flying into the wall, his teeth rattling from the impact. He grimly ignored his cracked ribs and ice that was beginning to form on his skin as Nefri's fury blazed over him with frigid force.

He couldn't stop her. He'd always known in a head to head battle her strength was greater.

But he could try to distract her from Tonya.

After that . . .

Hell, what did it matter? Chances were good he would be dead. He didn't really need a long-term plan.

With that cheerful thought at the forefront of his mind, he launched himself forward, wrapping his arms around Nefri as he struggled to contain her without causing her any injury. He felt her quiver, the sweet scent of jasmine filling his senses as if she were battling against the violence that thrummed through her veins.

But even as a tiny hope began to form, Nefri was wrapping her fingers around his throat and he was lifted off his feet. He grunted, refusing to reach for his weapons. He wouldn't harm her. No matter what the cost.

Instead, he gazed deep into her eyes, allowing her to see the love that was branded onto his very soul.

A love that he'd never spoken, but had offered in every touch of his hand, in every lingering kiss.

He could only pray that she'd been able to sense what he'd been too cowardly to say.

Assuming the creature in control of Gaius was intent on enjoying his slow, painful death, Santiago found himself abruptly dropped as Nefri released her grip.

Falling to his knees, he glanced up to discover that she was staring blankly at the far wall, clearly oblivious to her surroundings.

Then, Gaius stepped between them, staring down at Santiago with a cruel smile. "I will release her on the world, Santiago," he purred. "I will release her and the only way to halt her rampage will be to kill her. Are you prepared to sacrifice her for your oh-so-noble loyalty?"

Santiago's gaze shifted back to the female who had sacrificed so much to protect others, knowing what her choice would be. She would demand that once again she be the one to suffer.

"Damn you," he rasped, already knowing what his decision would be.

Gaius grimaced, seeming to briefly come to his senses. "We are all damned, my son."

Chapter 26

Styx's lair in Chicago

Roke had never been the most flamboyant of his brothers. Or the most gregarious.

He was, in fact, a taciturn vampire who was as willing to share his feelings as a rattlesnake.

Tonight, however, there was no doubt of his emotional state. As he paced the carpet of Styx's study, his moccasins made no sound, but the floor shuddered beneath his feet and the recently repaired chandelier swayed as his power sent tiny quakes through the air.

Leaning against the massive desk, Styx folded his arms over his chest, his expression one of exasperation. "Roke, I understand your precaution, but—"

"No," Roke interrupted, halting his pacing to glare at his king.

"What if the book is important?"

Still dressed in jeans, a T-shirt, and his leather jacket, Roke shoved a hand through his hair. He'd almost ignored Styx's text that demanded his presence in the study. Unfortunately, it was difficult to ignore a royal summons.

"Then it will still be important a month or even a century from now," he growled.

"But—"

"No."

Styx muttered his opinion of pigheaded vampires before he pointed an accusing finger toward Roke. "Has anyone told you that the art of negotiation consists of both sides being willing to compromise?"

"This isn't a negotiation." Roke allowed Styx to glimpse his unyielding resolve. "Sally isn't going anywhere near that warehouse until we discover why that coven was slaughtered. And who did it."

They matched each other glare for glare, both too alpha to back down.

Then, with a shake of his head, Styx straightened from the desk. "Dammit. I'll have Jagr do some research," he snapped, his eyes narrowing in warning. "You need to concentrate on tracing Sally's family tree. The sooner you break the mating bond, the better."

Roke clenched his jaw, caught off guard by the raw stab of fury at Styx's callous words.

Magical trickery or not, the bond felt as real as any other mating.

Not that he was about to admit as much. To anyone.

Instead he shoved his hands into the pockets of his jeans. "You mean I'm actually allowed to leave Chicago?"

A punishing hint of pain crawled over his skin. A promise of what was possible if he truly pissed off his king.

"You've never been a prisoner, Roke," Styx said, arrogantly discounting his refusal to allow Roke to return to Nevada. "But why would you need to leave?"

"It's not like I can hop on demon ancestry dot com," he pointed out dryly. "If I'm going to pin down Sally's father, then I'll need to retrace her mother's footsteps."

Styx scowled, but having already commanded Roke to

find a way to break the mating, he could hardly forbid him from taking the steps necessary to discover the source of Sally's demon blood.

"I don't want you going alone," he at last muttered.

"I'll have Sally with me," Roke said, pretending the thought of having the exquisite little witch far away from the constant surveillance of Styx and his guards didn't send a flare of treacherous heat through his blood.

Who would ever know if he decided to steal a taste of her peach sweetness?

Dammit, no. She was off limits, he grimly reminded himself. Whether they were being watched or not.

The towering Aztec gave a shake of his head. "Not good enough."

Roke made a sound of impatience. "You just said I wasn't a prisoner."

"That doesn't mean you're going to meddle among witches without protection."

"Styx . . ."

A shrill chirp interrupted Roke's protest and Styx offered a mocking grin as he reached for the cell phone on his desk and said, "Hold that thought."

Roke bared his fangs as Styx pressed the phone to his ear, but his seething frustration was forgotten as Styx hissed in shock, a blast of his frigid power nearly knocking Roke backward.

Shoving the phone into the front pocket of his leather pants, Styx was heading toward the door, a force of nature that could destroy everything and everyone in his path.

"Come with me," he commanded.

Roke swiftly followed his king out of the study and down the hallway. "What is it?"

"Spike said that Santiago just arrived."

Roke lifted a surprised brow. The last they'd heard, Santiago was hot on the trail of his former sire. "He has news?"

"I suspect it's more than that."

Styx's power was making the lights flicker and the price-less portraits tremble on the wall. Instinctively Roke reached to pull free the dagger he'd tucked into the sheath hidden in his knee-high moccasin.

Something was wrong.

"Why?"

"When Spike told Santiago I was in my study, Santiago said that he was here on an errand from an old friend from Rome," Styx explained.

Roke frowned. "Does that mean something to you?"

"Gaius."

Roke instantly understood Styx's concern. Was Santiago sending a warning or a threat?

In either case, they needed to be prepared for the worst.

"What do you want from me?"

The vampire pulled out the massive sword strapped to his back. "Find Jagr and tell him to start a search of the grounds."

They had reached the stairs when Roke grasped his companion's shoulder and pulled him to a halt. "Styx."

The Anasso sent him a frown of impatience. "What?"

"I know Santiago is a trusted brother, but Gaius is his sire," he reminded his king. In the heat of the moment it was too easy to overlook the obvious. "That's a bond not easily broken."

Styx's expression was as hard as granite. "I don't question Santiago's loyalty, but I'm not blind to the fact a vampire can be torn by a competing allegiance." He grimaced. "Either to Gaius, or to Tonya."

"The imp?"

"She's been a part of his family for a long time."

"Then you realize that you shouldn't face Santiago alone."

Styx grunted as he was neatly cornered by his own admission that Santiago might prove to be a danger. *"Cristo,"* he muttered. "You're a pain in the ass."

"I try."

Pulling out his cell phone, Roke hit Jagr's number and concisely revealed what was happening with Santiago's arrival and Styx's order to start a search of the grounds.

The Anasso gave a rueful shake of his head before turning to jog up the stairs. "This way."

Roke was swiftly at his side, baffled as he realized they were headed toward the private wing of the house. "The bedrooms? What could he . . ." With a startled hiss, he came to a halt on the landing.

"Roke?"

Roke ignored his impatient companion, his hand lifting to press to his unbeating heart.

There was a tight ball of . . . what? Fear? Anger? Pain?

Actually it felt like a strange combination of all three.

He rubbed the spot in the center of his chest, baffled by the unfamiliar sensation. The feelings were inside him, but they weren't his.

Insanity.

No, wait.

It wasn't insanity.

It was . . .

"Sally," he growled.

His muscles suddenly clenched, a fear that was all his own catapulting him into action.

He moved down the hallway with a fluid speed, absently sensing Styx keeping pace while his concentration was entirely focused on his connection to his mate.

"Talk to me, Roke," Styx commanded.

"Sally's in danger." He reached the door to her private rooms and threw it open. "Shit."

Even prepared, the empty room hit Roke like a blow to the gut. Charging over the threshold, he released his hunter instincts, discovering the scent of a male vampire combined with the rich smell of peaches.

His mind clouded with pure possessive anger.

A male had forced his way into Sally's room. He'd put his hands on her. And then, he had the balls to try and take her away.

Roke would see him in hell first.

Headed toward the open window, he was momentarily distracted by the faint scent of blood. Lowering himself to his knees, he discovered a small red stain on the carpet.

The ceiling cracked and the drywall crumbled as his fury went nuclear.

"Goddammit," he snarled. "I'll kill him."

Wise enough not to startle a vampire on the edge of murder, Styx cautiously hunkered down beside him, his voice soothing. "Roke, it's only a drop. She's not badly hurt."

"Yet."

Styx grimaced. "Why the hell would he take her?"

"I intend to find out," Roke muttered, shoving himself upright and through the window in one smooth motion.

Behind him Styx blistered the air with curses, but Roke never slowed as he hit the ground and followed the scent of peaches through the moonlight that spilled over the manicured parkland.

Reaching the back gate, he caught the smell of yet another male vampire. This one laced with an unmistakable rot of madness.

Gaius?

Not that he gave a shit.

The need to rescue Sally was thundering through his veins, leaving no room for logical thought or strategies.

But as he stepped through the open gate, he was forced to an enraged halt.

The trail ended.

Just like that.

There one step and gone the next.

He tilted back his head to roar with a savage frustration,

indifferent to the scamper of terrified wildlife that darted into the nearby woods.

The sound was still echoing through the trees when Jagr and two of his Ravens appeared from around the corner of the high fence.

"Where is he?" Roke demanded.

Looking every inch the Visigoth chief, Jagr clutched a sword in one hand and a pistol in the other. Not that either was as dangerous as the lethal fangs that were primed for maximum damage.

"I don't know." The ice blue gaze continued to scan the woods that provided privacy for Styx's lair from his distant neighbors. "I caught a glimpse of him going through the back gate, but before I could get here he'd disappeared."

"Sally?" he managed to rasp between clenched teeth.

Jagr dipped his head. "The witch was with him."

Styx stepped through the gate, studying the tracks that halted directly in front of them. "Gaius must have used his medallion," he said before turning his attention to Roke. "Can you sense Sally?"

Struggling against his primitive instincts that rebelled at wasting even a second, Roke forced himself to close his eyes and concentrate on his mating bond. It was there. Oddly . . . muffled. As if something was trying to mask her presence from him. But there was no mistaking his sense of her just a few miles north of them.

"It's muted, but she's not far," he said, opening his eyes to watch Jagr and Styx exchange a startled glance.

"Is the medallion limited in how far it can carry more than one person?" the large Visigoth asked.

Styx shook his head. "I don't think so."

"Then why—" Jagr bit off his words as there was an unmistakable shift in the air pressure before the scent of granite filled the air. "Shit."

The male vampires turned, their expressions varying from

resignation to outright disgust as Levet seemed to step from thin air, closely followed by Yannah.

Either unaware, or just indifferent, to his frigid reception, the tiny gargoyle gave a violent flutter of his wings, his tail standing at stiff attention.

"Mon dieu," he breathed, clearly frazzled. "I hate traveling that way."

With a superior smile that all females perfected before leaving the cradle, Yannah smoothed the sleeve of her long white robe. "Don't be such a baby."

"A baby?" Levet puffed out his chest, looking more like a bantam chicken than a fearsome gargoyle. "Why I—"

"Levet, is there a purpose for your unexpected visit?" Styx said as he sternly broke into the brewing squabble.

Levet immediately forgot his grievances and waddled toward the King of Vampires, his expression troubled. "Nefri."

There was a collective mutter of unease as Styx glared down at the gargoyle.

The mystique of Nefri was great enough that the mere thought that she was anything less than impervious to danger was . . . troublesome.

"What about her?" Styx demanded.

"When Gaius kidnapped Tonya she knew that Gaius was plotting to use Santiago."

Styx grimaced. "And she was right?"

"Oui." Levet hunched his shoulders, his ugly features scrunched in distress. "We traveled to Gaius's lair and Nefri asked me to stay hidden so I would know what was occurring. She wanted to make sure I could go for help in the event that things went . . ." He waved his hands as words failed him.

"To hell?" Styx offered.

The gargoyle nodded. "To hell."

Clever of Nefri to make certain they could be warned, Roke silently acknowledged, but his shattering need to return to his hunt for Sally made him growl deep in his throat. Only the thought that the gargoyle might have some necessary clue to his mate's rescue kept him from charging through the darkness alone.

As if sensing his burning frustration, Styx reached to place a hand on his shoulder even as his gaze remained trained on the tiny demon. "What does Gaius want with Santiago?"

Levet wrinkled his snout. "He pretended he desired a reconciliation, but all he truly desired was for Santiago to sneak into your lair for the witch."

"Sally?" Roke stepped forward, his fierce intensity making Levet take a hasty step backward and Yannah move to the gargoyle's side as if to offer her protection. "Why?"

"She's the only one who can destroy some spell around a book," he hurriedly admitted, his hands rising in a gesture of peace. "I do not know any more, I swear."

"Do you think it could be the same book?" Styx muttered in astonishment.

Roke wasn't listening.

He didn't believe in coincidences.

Which meant he knew exactly where to find his missing witch.

The warehouse.

The warehouse north of Chicago

Over the years Sally had devoted a ridiculous amount of energy to avoiding a gruesome death.

Ever since her sweet sixteenth birthday it didn't matter where she went or how quietly she tried to live, there was always someone or something that wanted her dead.

So she wasn't sure why she felt so betrayed to find herself being kidnapped by a strange vampire and taken to Gaius, who was clearly even more demented than the last time she'd caught sight of him.

Surely the only surprise should have been if she hadn't been betrayed?

Still, she found herself glaring at the handsome vampire with the beauty of a Spanish *conquistador* and the aloof, stunningly beautiful vampire who stood in the corner like a freaking ice princess. As if she could make them feel guilty.

Yeah, and she was destined to win the lottery.

With a shake of her head, she turned her attention to her surroundings, feeling a stab of confusion as she realized they were in the same warehouse where Roke had taken her.

What the hell?

Somehow she'd assumed when Gaius had used his medallion to take them away from Styx's lair they would end up more than a few miles from the dangerous Anasso.

But then again, maybe he wanted her close. Didn't the ancient generals stick the heads of their hostages on a pike as a warning to their enemies? Gaius would want her mutilated body close enough so it couldn't be missed.

Wrapping her arms around her body, she at last turned to confront the vampire who had so briefly been her commander.

She sucked in a sharp breath.

Holy crap.

She'd wished bad things on Gaius. She might even have said a prayer or two that the arrogant SOB wouldn't survive the battle with the Dark Lord. But allowing her stunned gaze to drift down his gaunt frame covered with clothes a zombie wouldn't be seen dead in (yeah, really bad pun) and his eyes glowing with a hectic light, she had to admit that he looked like he'd been through worse than even she had hoped for.

He looked . . . pathetic.

Of course, she wasn't stupid. Even pathetic and batty as hell, he was a lethal predator.

One who could kill her with one strike of his massive fangs.

Licking her dry lips, she considered a number of spells she could lob at the vampire, only to discard them. Most of them were ineffective against the walking dead. Besides, she needed to conserve her strength until her enemy was distracted.

That way she could potentially use her powers to escape.

She wasn't a go-down-in-a-blaze-of-glory kind of gal. She preferred a run-like-hell-and-live-to-fight-another-day philosophy.

Keeping that thought firmly in mind, she held herself perfectly still as Gaius prowled forward, slowly circling her as if he'd never seen her before.

"Hello, Gaius. Long time no see," she said as she at last broke the thick silence, as always her nerves making her babble like an idiot.

He came to a halt directly in front of her, his eyes glowing with an odd radiance. "Witch."

"I've told you a thousand times, it's Sally," she snapped before she could halt the impulsive words. "It's not that hard to remember."

The vampire shrugged. "Your name doesn't matter."

Sally sucked in a deep breath, ignoring the heavy scent of vampires that filled the musky air. Wasn't there some sort of saying about catching more flies with honey than vinegar?

"No, I don't suppose it does," she muttered, pinning a stiff smile to her lips. "Look, I'm sorry, okay? I shouldn't have gone to Styx, but I"—her smile widened as she was struck by inspiration—"I was worried about you."

The lean face remained devoid of expression, but the glow in his eyes flared with something that looked like hunger. "How very extraordinary that you should be acquainted with my host," he said.

"Host?" She wrapped her arms around her waist as a shiver shook her body. "I don't understand."

He acted as if he didn't hear her, the unnerving gaze sliding over her pale face. "Perhaps it was merely fate ensuring that you would be available when I needed you."

"You . . . need me?" With a frown she glanced toward the male vampire who was hovering near the motionless female, pretending he wasn't listening to the conversation although his tension was a palpable force in the air. He didn't behave like an eager accomplice, not even when he'd kidnapped her from her bedroom, but it could all be an act. For now she had to assume he was one of the enemy. At last she glanced back to Gaius. "You didn't bring me here to punish me?"

He tilted his head to the side in a distinctly un-Gaius-like motion. "Punish you?"

"For going to Styx."

A smile that was more terrifying than reassuring curled his lips. "You aren't here for punishment."

"No?"

"No."

She shifted beneath the glowing gaze, feeling as if he were rummaging around *inside* her.

Even worse, she was beginning to suspect that the glow in his eyes was more than just madness or the compulsion she'd first assumed. He looked . . . possessed. As if he had been taken over by another creature.

It was freaking creepy.

"Then why?"

Without warning, Gaius (or whoever the heck he was now) turned to point at the hole that Roke had punched into the wall. "Because of that."

Sally was briefly disoriented, as much from the sudden realization that she could actually sense Roke through their bond despite the distance (if she hadn't been neck deep in trouble she might have wondered what was causing his frantic desperation). As from the struggle to accept that

Gaius had some other reason for kidnapping her than mere retribution for tattling on him to Styx.

"The safe?" she asked in confusion; then she gave a sudden blink. "No. The book."

"Yes."

She hesitated, hoping her sluggish mind would catch up with the rapidly shifting situation. "You want me to break the spell?"

Gaius made a sound of disgust. As if she was unbearably stupid.

He'd get no argument from her.

"There's only one way to break the spell and destroy the book."

She frowned. "Only one?"

Gaius nodded. "You die."

The words were said with such indifference that it took a second for Sally to react.

"No." She took a stumbling step backward, wondering if this was some hideous nightmare. "No, I have the counter-spell brewing at Styx's lair."

Gaius waved a hand. "A worthless concoction."

She pressed a hand to her racing heart, trying desperately to hold back her panic. "How do you know?" she forced her-self to ask. "I can promise you that my brews are more potent than most."

"There is no counterspell because it's sorcery."

Sorcery? She shook her head.

There were all types of magic.

Spells conjured by witches and wizards, both white and black. Demon magic that called on their natural powers. And the gifts of magic that were bestowed to prophets and other individuals blessed by fate.

Or cursed.

But sorcery was supposed to be an ancient magic that

came from a place deeper than spells brewed in a cauldron or even the bloody altars.

It came from the very soul, devouring a piece of a witch's life force with every use.

"I've never . . ." She shook her head. "I thought it was an urban legend."

"No legend, although from what I've discovered of this world, the magic is not nearly as potent as it used to be," the creature that used to be Gaius murmured. "Still once the spell is cast it's unbreakable until the last witch is dead."

Her mouth went dry. He spoke with an unshakable confidence. Right or wrong, he truly believed the book was protected by sorcery.

And that her death was the only thing that could give him what he wanted.

"I didn't cast the spell," she managed to croak.

"Of course not." A hint of impatience twisted the gaunt features. "It was cast at the beginning of time. When witches were in the power of the Oracles."

"Witches in the power of the Oracles?" She made a sound of shock. She'd always been taught that witches had been created out of a human need to balance the growing power of demons and their Commission. "Are you kidding me?"

Gaius shrugged. "Before the great schism."

"The great . . ." She abruptly pressed her fingers to her throbbing temples. "Never mind. I still don't understand what this has to do with me."

"For the truly powerful witches soul-bindings can be transferred from mother to daughter." His glowing gaze flicked over her slender body, which felt far too exposed by the skimpy muscle shirt and stretchy pants. "An unbreakable chain."

She forgot how to breathe as she accepted the only logical conclusion to his explanation.

"So my mother . . ."

"She was one of the heirs."

A shrill, humorless laugh was wrung from her throat. She'd never been truly satisfied with her mother's claim that she'd chosen to have a daughter to ensure her power base. After all, there was no guarantee that Sally would be born with enough magical abilities to be more than a drain on her resources. It was far more practical to take on an apprentice who was old enough to display the level of her talent and yet young enough to be molded into a loyal acolyte.

Now she understood.

Her mother needed a blood heir to pass on her duty.

"No wonder she was so anxious to have a daughter," she muttered, wryly wondering when her mother had intended to tell her the truth.

Perhaps on that memorable sixteenth birthday?

What a grand irony that would be.

"Yes," Gaius agreed.

"How many heirs are there?"

Gaius turned toward the gaping hole in the wall, his hatred toward the book pulsing through the air. Sally shivered, taking the opportunity to sneak a quick peek at the two silent vampires standing across the room.

The female remained impervious to her surroundings, but the male met her glance with a small nod of his head toward the door.

She frowned. What the hell did that mean?

That she was supposed to make a run for it?

That there were more enemies hidden outside?

That . . .

Her desperate thoughts were interrupted as Gaius abruptly turned back toward her.

"They began with thirteen," he said as he answered her question. "The numbers varied over the centuries."

"You kept track of them?"

He smiled with a cruel pleasure. "Most of them were kind enough to remain together in the same coven, so when the

Dark Lord began to thin the barriers between dimensions I was able to nudge my children into getting rid of them."

She knew. The minute he spoke the words she knew that he meant the coven that she'd seen so gruesomely murdered in the photo.

And he spoke of the massacre as if they were mere bugs being squashed.

Blessed goddess.

Her hand shifted to press against her stomach, trying to stifle the churning nausea.

"They were slaughtered," she said in a raw voice.

The . . . Gaius-creature shook his head. "All but one."

She swallowed the lump in her throat. "My mother."

The strange glow in his eyes flared, but prepared for his anger, Sally was rattled when instead it was her own simmering anger and fear that was stoked higher.

As if Gaius was capable of draining the emotions from her.

"I couldn't have known she had left the coven," he complained. "But when the spell remained intact I realized there must be one left."

She quivered, trying to regain control of her emotions. Now, more than ever, she needed a clear mind.

"Two left," she absently corrected.

That horrifying smile returned. "No. Only one. Now."

Profound shock gripped her, crushing any grief she might have felt.

She simply couldn't accept a world without the woman who had given birth to her.

"You killed my mother?" she rasped.

"Gaius was kind enough to perform the deed on our way to his lair in Louisiana," the creature murmured, speaking of Gaius as if he were a separate being.

She shook her head.

Dead.

"I . . . I can't believe it."

Gaius dismissed her distress with a wave of his hand. "Once again I was to be disappointed, but I was growing stronger every day. So long as the book remained hidden it couldn't do any harm." Gaius reached over to trail an icy finger down her cheek, tracing the path of her unconscious tears. "But then it called you here."

With a shudder of revulsion she took a hasty step backward, forcing her fogged mind to concentrate on the danger standing directly in front of her.

She would work through her grief and regret for her mother if she managed to survive the night.

Something that was looking increasingly unlikely.

"Called me?" she shook her head. "No, I came because I wanted Gaius out of the house."

"If it hadn't been that, it would have drawn you here by some other means," he assured her. "It felt my presence. It would have done whatever was necessary to get into your hands."

She glanced toward the hole in the wall where she could feel the steady pulse of the black spell.

A spell that had caused the death of thirteen witches, including her mother. And was now her supposed legacy.

"Why?" She turned back to the creepy, glowing eyes. "What's in the book?"

"It doesn't matter," he countered, clearly unwilling to reveal the truth of the book. "Once you're dead the book will be destroyed once and for all."

Sally braced herself, muttering an attack spell beneath her breath. She didn't believe it would actually damage the vampire, or whatever the hell was controlling him, but it was all she had.

Then, even as she felt a massive power beginning to build in the room, Gaius was suddenly turning toward the door, his hiss of annoyance scraping over Sally's raw nerves.

"I warned you, Santiago," he growled, seeming to forget Sally. "Now Nefri will pay for your arrogance."

Chapter 27

Santiago didn't do helpless.

After he'd been pulled out of the Gladiator pits beneath Barcelona, he'd sworn that he'd never again be in a position where he was at the mercy of another.

A mistake, of course.

He should have known that the minute he'd made that bitter pledge, it would curse him. Life was nothing if not perverse, and what could be more destined to force him to face his worst nightmare than declaring it could never happen again?

Now he stood next to Nefri, his muscles quivering as he battled his urge to charge across the floor of the warehouse and rip off Gaius's head.

He told himself he was biding his time.

That was why he'd agreed to kidnap the witch despite his grand pronouncement he would never, ever betray his brothers. And why he was standing here like a damned mannequin while the bastard revealed the truth of his reason for traveling to the warehouse.

He'd left his clue with Styx on the off-chance that the Anasso would be able to track them. And then positioned himself so he would be able to grab Nefri and escape if the opportunity presented itself.

Tonya, after all, had been left behind in Wisconsin and by now should have been able to create a portal to take her back to his club. So all he had to worry about was the female standing like a statue beside him.

But, while he could pretend he had some sort of control over the situation, the moment Gaius glanced in their direction he knew it was an empty lie.

He'd become a helpless pawn who had not only used his connection to the Anasso to kidnap an innocent young female, but he'd led his brothers to this warehouse all because he was willing to sacrifice everything and everyone to protect Nefri.

And now . . .

Now he could sense Styx and at least four other vampires approaching the warehouse and Nefri's power beginning to swell in an awful tidal wave of looming destruction.

Rock, meet hard place, a voice mocked in the back of his mind.

For all his efforts he'd done nothing more than make matters worse.

So what the hell was he going to do now?

Styx and his vampires would be breaking through the door in less than a heartbeat. At the same time Gaius would send Nefri into a mindless bloodlust. The battle between the vampires would be epic and violent and lethal.

Which meant that he had less than a nano-second to choose between two very bad, very awful decisions.

He picked the very awful one.

And more importantly, the one that Gaius would never have prepared for.

Not giving himself time to think, he reached down to snatch a stray piece of rebar off the floor. Then, as Nefri trembled beneath the surge of bloodlust, he stepped behind her and with one smooth motion he slammed the bar against the back of her head to send her crumpling to the ground.

The blow was hard enough to knock her out, but not hard enough to cause permanent damage. Which meant he would only have a few minutes to come up with a better plan before she was awake and on the rampage.

Using the fury that boiled through him at being forced to hurt the female he loved, Santiago turned and charged Gaius. With a roar, he pinned the vampire to the wall by the simple process of shoving the rebar through his heart and into the brick wall. Then with a twist he bent the rebar so it would be damned painful for Gaius to pull his way free.

Without missing a beat, he'd raced to slam shut the steel door that was the only entrance into the room beyond the windows covered by thick boards. Then, grabbing the handle, he yanked it upward, feeling the lock twist until it was jammed.

Only then did he spin on his heel to return and glare at the creature who'd caused nothing but pain and misery since its arrival in this world.

Pinned against the wall, the . . . thing seemed impervious to the rebar that was stuck through his heart, his eyes glowing with a hectic light even as the sluggish blood dripped from the hole in his chest.

But Santiago didn't miss the grayish hue of his skin and the way his clothes hung on his limp frame, almost as if he were shrinking with every passing second.

"Brutal, yet efficient. You make me proud," Gaius taunted. "Unfortunately, it will do you no good."

"I'm not done," Santiago growled, reaching behind his back to pull the *pugio* from where he'd shoved it into his jeans pocket.

Gaius's face remained slack, but Santiago sensed his surprise at the sight of the ancient dagger with its lethal silver blade.

"You can kill this host, but I'll simply take another," he warned.

Santiago's lips stretched into a humorless smile as he pressed the tip of the dagger to the center of his chest. "I'm betting that you can't take control of me before I stick this in my heart."

Gaius hissed, the glowing eyes narrowing at Santiago's threat. "Harm yourself and I will simply use the witch."

"I doubt it. You need her dead." Santiago shrugged. "Not the best qualification for a host."

Gaius shifted his head to stare at the mutilated door, his frustration battering against Santiago's emotions. "Your fellow vampires are swiftly approaching. Once they realize the door is blocked they'll find another way in."

He clenched his teeth against the swell of irritation, savagely reminding himself he was being manipulated. "But soon enough?" he managed to rasp.

"Time is meaningless," the creature smoothly countered. "We have an eternity."

Santiago gave a slow shake of his head, his gaze lowering to where the flesh around the rebar remained a raw, bleeding wound. It should have been healing by now.

"I don't think so. You're starting to fray around the edges," he said. "The question is . . . why?"

The hesitation was so brief that it would have been easy to miss. "I need to feed."

Santiago gave another shake of his head. Vampires might take longer to heal when they needed to feed. And even begin to look skeletal if they'd been starved long enough.

But they didn't begin to decompose.

Besides, if this . . . thing needed to feed, why wasn't he feasting on the witch's tangible fear? Or even his own fury?

"No."

"No, I don't need to feed?"

Santiago narrowed his gaze. "It's more than that."

Without warning Sally took a step forward, her arms wrapped around her slender waist. "The book," she said.

Santiago jerked his head toward the gaping hole in the wall where Gaius and this witch seemed to be convinced a book was hidden.

"Of course." He grimaced. He should have suspected the book was the culprit from the minute he noticed Gaius's impression of a zombie. If the bastard was willing to risk everything to get his hands on it, then it was obviously his kryptonite. "It must be draining him."

Gaius didn't bother answering. Instead his attention shifted to the sound of footsteps outside the door.

"Go away," Santiago shouted as the steel door shuddered beneath the impact of Styx's size-sixteen boot. There was another shudder, before the cement above the door began to crack and buckle.

Roke.

It had to be.

There was no other vampire who had his particular effect on physical structures. The powerful vampire was a walking, talking (okay, not so much the talking) earthquake machine.

"Dammit, go away," he shouted again, sensing Gaius's seething anticipation.

"Santiago, what the hell is going on?" Styx called through the door, his own power making the lights flicker.

Another crack appeared along the side of the door, making Santiago curse at Roke's persistence.

He had to keep them out of the room. Gaius wouldn't dare take one of them as a host when it might mean he was trapped on the other side with no way to reach Sally or the book.

He glanced toward the witch, who was studying the crumbling wall with an odd expression.

"Do you have a phone?" he demanded.

She blinked, glancing down at her clinging outfit that clearly had no place to hide the clichéd thin dime let alone a phone. Thankfully she resisted the urge to point out the obvious, and instead caught him off-guard when she squared her shoulders and tilted her chin. "I can reach them."

He frowned. "A spell . . . oh shit." He blinked in shock as she turned her arm over to reveal the distinctive tattoo that crawled beneath the skin of her inner forearm. "Who?"

A blush touched her cheeks. "Roke."

Taciturn, I-am-an-island-so-don't-screw-with-me Roke mated with a witch?

Fairly certain the entire world had gone mad, Santiago gave a nod of his head. "Warn them to back off."

"I'll try." She rolled her eyes as yet another crack appeared. "They haven't listened to me yet."

Trusting that the witch could convince the vampires to halt their assault on the door, not to mention Roke's seeming determination to bring the roof down on their heads, Santiago turned back to Gaius.

He hid his stab of shock as he realized that Gaius was a shade paler and several pounds frailer. *Mierda*. Even his hair was beginning to fall out.

Like he was a dog with mange.

"What's in the book?" he rasped, resisting the urge to reach up and make sure his own hair wasn't beginning to shed.

Surely he would sense if the book was starting to make him rot?

With a slow, deliberate motion Gaius turned back to study him with his glowing gaze. "Do you know who I am?"

Santiago shrugged. "Don't know, don't care."

"There are some who claim I'm your god," the creature informed him with an arrogance that he'd clearly bestowed on his children. "Without me you would never have existed."

Santiago was sublimely unimpressed. "God or not, we've done just fine without you for the past few millennia," he mocked.

"Not without me—I've been sleeping," the creature corrected him. "But what if you destroy me?"

"Can a god be destroyed?" Santiago demanded with a lift of his brows.

There was a low hiss. "The Dark Lord proved it's possible."

Santiago made a sound of disgust. "He was never a true god."

"Maybe not to you."

"And neither are you."

There was a calculating pause as Gaius no doubt considered the best way to manipulate Santiago into destroying the witch. The fact he wasn't using his ability to provoke Santiago into a bloodlust spoke volumes about the power of the book.

"But I am your creator," he at last said, his voice the dry hiss of a viper. "Can you be certain that my end won't also be the end of all vampires?"

No. He couldn't be certain.

Which was precisely why he wasn't going to let himself consider the possibility.

For now he wasn't going to concentrate on anything beyond destroying this monster and getting Nefri safely back to his lair.

"Sally."

He could smell the female's terror, but with an admirable display of courage, she moved to stand at his side.

Maybe Roke hadn't completely lost his mind in choosing this female.

"What?"

He slid a questioning glance in her direction. "Can you get the book?"

She chewed her bottom lip. "I'm not sure."

"I told you, only her death can break the spell," Gaius snarled, the glow from his eyes filling the room with a malignant light. "If you're truly determined to get your hands on the book, then you'll have to kill her."

Santiago refused to allow his gaze to waver from the witch's youthful face. "Sally?"

She was shivering, but with a grim determination she

studied the hole in the wall, as if she were actually able to see the strands of magic woven around the opening.

"If it's sorcery, then it can't be broken by magic."

"Kill her, Santiago," Gaius commanded, weakly attempting to stir Santiago's fear. "She's a danger to Nefri."

Sally lifted her hand, her breath hissing between her teeth as she sent Santiago a startled glance.

"What is it?" he asked.

"When I was considering how to get the book, I assumed it was guarded by a spell."

"And now?"

"If it's sorcery, then it can't be broken, but it can be—"

"Don't listen to her," Gaius sharply interrupted her. "She's a witch, my son. Her very essence is a lie."

Santiago ignored the disruption. "Can be what?" he pressed.

"Manipulated."

"Listen to me, Santiago," Gaius tried again to twist Santiago's emotions. "She was created by the Oracles to destroy me." He lifted a feeble hand. "To destroy *us*."

If anyone had told Sally that one day she would play the role of hero (or was it heroine?) she would have laughed until she peed her pants.

All she wanted was to lay low and keep her head buried in the sand when bad things were happening.

Even her days as the conduit for the Dark Lord had been nothing more than a desperate attempt to survive. She certainly hadn't drunk the Kool-Aid, and the minute she had the opportunity she'd given up all ties to her former allies.

Now, however, laying low wasn't an option. Which meant that she had to somehow figure out a way to manipulate the sorcery spell while keeping the vampire that was pinned to the wall from sensing her considerable power.

She didn't doubt for a second that the nasty creature would do whatever was necessary to stop her if he realized she might actually be one of the few witches alive today capable of gaining command of the spell.

Not vanity, just the simple truth.

"You keep changing your story," she accused the creepy vampire even as she tentatively opened a small crack in her magical barriers. Barriers she'd created and kept wrapped around herself since she'd nearly been killed by her mother. Nothing like a near filicide to keep a girl on her toes. "First you said I was born from a long line of witches to protect the book and now you claim I was created by the Oracles to destroy vampires."

"The Oracles created the first witches, you stupid bitch," the creature growled.

Against her will she found her attention captured by his claim. Was it true? Had witches truly been created by the Oracles or was this man just a raving lunatic?

Allowing a part of her mind to concentrate on unraveling the complex weaves, she sent the vampire a puzzled glance. "Created to kill vampires?"

The glowing eyes were turned in her direction, but Sally didn't have a clue if he could actually see with them. Not that it mattered. If he was like any other vampire, then his senses would be acute enough to pinpoint a roach a mile away even if he was blind.

"To contain me and mute our powers." He spoke the words with the certainty of a true believer.

Right or wrong, he was convinced that witches had been created by the Oracles as some sort of weapon against vampires.

Sally frowned. "Why would they create an entire species to contain you?"

"They were jealous of my powers," he said without hesitation. "They wanted me dead, but they dared not kill a god.

The best they could do was lock me away with their pathetic magic."

She grimaced; Sally was beginning to suspect that she'd grossly overestimated her skills as she realized that the web of magic was more than one spell. It was as if sorcery had taken the incantation of the thirteen witches and used each one to layer the spells one on top of the other. So it wasn't thirteen times stronger, but thirteen to the thirteenth power.

On top of that, now that she'd actually opened her barriers she could *feel* her connection to the damned thing.

Maybe the creature was right.

Maybe she had been called by the book to travel to this location at this exact time.

Weirder things had happened.

"Not so pathetic," she muttered.

Easily sensing her dismay, Santiago took a step toward her. "Sally," he prompted.

"I'm not certain, but I think the sorcery is more than just a protective spell."

The handsome vampire frowned. Obviously he was like every other leech who preferred to pretend magic didn't exist rather than try to understand a power he couldn't battle against.

"You're going to have to be more specific."

"The sorcery is coming *from* the book," she said, her tone hesitant.

"Which means?"

She hesitated, unconsciously nibbling at her bottom lip. It was a definite case of the blind leading the blind since her knowledge of sorcery could fit in a thimble.

Still, she had to do *something*. She could sense Roke's straining impatience. They had about two minutes flat before he smashed his way through the brick walls.

"I might be able to use the book . . ."

"Nooooo."

The hair-raising shriek came completely out of the blue.

Stumbling backward, Sally turned to watch a strange, black mist float out of the mutilated vampire's body.

At her side Santiago cursed, pressing the Roman dagger against his chest until she could smell his flesh beginning to burn and a flow of blood stained his T-shirt.

"Stay back," he rasped.

The mist seemed to hesitate, as if it understood Santiago's threat. Then, with a movement too swift for her eyes to follow, it darted across the room.

With quicker reflexes, Santiago was lunging forward. But as fast as he was, he was a half step too slow as the mist disappeared into the female vampire who had regained consciousness while they were focused on the mysterious book.

Time seemed to stand still as the beautiful woman watched Santiago rushing toward her with such an intense sense of loss it was painful to witness. Then, as Santiago reached her, those dark eyes were filled with an unearthly glow and her slender hands wrapped around the gold medallion at her neck.

Santiago cried out, but he couldn't halt the inevitable.

He reached for her, but she was already gone.

Santiago roared, his fury exploding the overhead lights and coating the walls in a layer of frost.

Nefri.

That bastard had taken his female.

He was going to rip him apart and feed him to the jackals. No wait. That was too quick.

He was going to . . .

"Santiago," a harsh voice broke through his searing rage. "My son."

With a growl he whirled toward Gaius, who remained pinned to the wall. His former sire looked like death. Literally.

His gray skin sagged to reveal the sharp angles of his brittle bones. His dark eyes were sunken, although they'd lost the weird-ass glow, and only a few tenacious clumps of hair remained on his head.

"Don't call me that," Santiago hissed, flowing across the floor, intent on finishing off the vampire he'd once considered his father.

Gaius's gaze was pleading as Santiago halted directly in front of him. "Please, I need to tell you . . ."

"What?"

"I'm sorry."

Santiago made a sound of disgust. Did this vampire truly have the arrogance to believe that after all he'd done—the abandonment, the betrayals, the treachery—that he could ever gain Santiago's forgiveness?

But even as he lifted his hand to strike the killing blow, Santiago found himself hesitating.

Nefri had disappeared using her medallion. Which meant he couldn't track her. It could take hours, if not days to discover where she'd gone.

The creature had been inside Gaius for weeks. If anyone would know where it was headed, it would be this pathetic wreck.

A gut-wrenching pain nearly doubled him over and with a savage anger he slammed his fist into the wall next to Gaius's gaunt face.

"Where did he take her?"

Gaius flinched, but he refused to be distracted. "Please, Santiago, I thought Dara had been returned to me. It seemed so real."

Santiago pulled back his lips, exposing his fangs in a visible warning. "Tell me where he took her."

"But she was an illusion," Gaius continued, as if Santiago might actually care that he'd been fooled into believing Dara had been returned. Gaius was eager to blame everyone but himself for his weakness. "Nothing more than a figment of my imagination."

"I don't give a shit." Santiago wrapped his hands around Gaius's too-thin neck. Every second separated from Nefri was like pouring salt on a gaping wound. "Tell me where they went or I'll kill you."

"You should kill me." Gaius gave a shake of his head. "I no longer matter."

"Goddammit." With an effort, Santiago managed to keep himself from crushing the bastard's throat. So long as Gaius was wallowing in his bout of self-pity he would be useless. "What do you want from me?"

Gaius licked his rotting lips. "I need . . ."

"What?"

"I need your forgiveness."

"Fine," Santiago bit out, willing to say anything to get Gaius to help him track Nefri. "You're forgiven."

The dark eyes softened with a soul-deep gratitude. "Thank you, my son."

Santiago tightened his fingers on his sire's throat. "Now take me to Nefri."

"Yes." With a visible effort, Gaius lifted his hand to cover the medallion around his neck. "Hold on tight."

Santiago scowled. "Why?"

"The medallion," Gaius rasped. "It will take us to Nefri."

"Wait," he commanded, glancing toward the wide-eyed witch. "Tell Styx what happened here. . . ."

His words were lost as blackness surrounded him and they were being catapulted through a rift in space.

Mierda.

Chapter 28

It was a gross understatement to say that Roke's patience was strained. It was, in fact, hanging on by a very slender thread.

Which was why it was no surprise that it snapped the second he heard Santiago's roar.

It wasn't that he didn't believe Sally's soft whispers in his mind (her ability to reach him telepathically was astonishing since it was a rare talent that usually only manifested itself between pairs that had been intimately bonded for centuries).

He fully believed that the spirit was capable of taking command of a vampire. And he equally understood the logic of keeping the creature contained by shutting him off from available hosts.

But logic was no contest against the instincts of a newly mated vampire, and the need to get to Sally was a force that wasn't going to be denied.

No matter what the consequences.

He stepped forward, ignoring Styx's grim presence. Jagr had taken the Ravens to circle the warehouse, making sure nothing could escape, and Levet had thankfully remained at the lair with his odd demon friend. But it wouldn't have mattered if they'd all stood between him and his goal.

He was getting to Sally.

Now!

He swung his arm, hitting the brick wall with enough force to make the entire building shudder.

"Dammit, Roke," Styx growled. "You said that Sally warned us not to enter."

"To hell with that," he muttered. "I'm done waiting."

"But . . ." Styx reached to grasp his wrist before he could widen the crack he'd just created in the wall. "You're going to bring the entire building down on our head."

Roke yanked his arm free, his fangs throbbing and his temper threatening to explode. "I don't care what I have to do. I'm getting into that room." His eyes narrowed. "Got it?"

"Yeah, yeah, I got it," Styx muttered. "Stand back."

Lifting his leg, Styx used his Sasquatch-size boot to kick the center of the door. Steel screeched in protest, but with two more kicks the stubborn door at last twisted off the frame, and before Styx could open his mouth to protest, Roke was leaping through the wreckage.

He had a brief glimpse of Santiago holding on to a vampire, or at least he thought it was a vampire—the pathetic male looked more like a rotting zombie. Then, just as he began to move across the floor, the two vampires simply disappeared.

Ignoring the bizarre vanishing act, Roke's attention honed in on the tiny female who stood near the safe hidden behind the crumbling wall.

The tightness in his chest eased at being able to see her and catch the sweet scent of peaches. But the driving fury at the knowledge she'd been stolen from him, snatched from beneath his very nose, had him storming forward, not halting until he'd wrapped his arms around her slender body.

"Are you hurt?"

"No, I'm fine," she said, but her voice quavered and her body shivered with the terror she'd been forced to endure.

"I swear, I'll kill that bastard," he snarled.

Her hand lifted to his chest. "Roke."

He gave a low growl as he sensed she was about to pull away, burying his face in the curve of her neck.

"Don't move."

"What are you doing?"

Like he knew? He was running on a primitive impulse and gut need.

"Just . . ." His hands ran a compulsive path down the curve of her back. "Give me a minute."

Styx cautiously moved to stand at their side, leaving enough space not to set off Roke's possessive fury. No doubt he sensed that Roke was on a hair trigger. Or maybe it was his bared fangs that gave it away.

"Tell me what happened," he said to Sally.

She gave another shiver and Roke tightened his arms around her, his head lifting to watch his Anasso with a feral warning.

"That creature—"

"Gaius?" Styx asked.

Sally nodded. "Yes, although it wasn't really him. He was being controlled by something inside him."

Styx glanced toward the safe just visible through the jagged hole in the wall. "He brought you here to get the book?"

"Yes."

"Why?"

"It can harm him."

Roke glanced down at her in surprise. "A book?"

She grimaced. "That or the magic in the book."

Styx matched her grimace, shifting uneasily. Roke sympathized with his king. Any vampire would rather fight an entire tribe of trolls bare-handed than deal with magic.

"Why you?" Styx abruptly asked.

Sally blinked. "Me?"

"Why did he go to the trouble of kidnapping you if all he

needed was a witch?" The towering warrior clarified. "He had to know it would alert us to his presence here."

She hesitated, sending a covert glance toward Roke before she returned her attention to the Anasso.

"Because the spell is bound to my soul," she at last revealed.

"Shit," Roke snarled, a sharp fear spearing through him. He might be clueless when it came to magic, but he knew that having Sally's soul bound to a spell was a very bad thing.

Dammit, why had he ever brought her to this warehouse? He should've had the sense to return her to Styx's lair the second he realized he was susceptible to her magic.

Now . . . He swallowed a curse.

No. As eager as he might be to blame himself, he knew fate well enough to realize that if it intended Sally to be reunited with the book, there was nothing he could do to stop the inevitable.

But that didn't make him any happier.

His dark thoughts were interrupted as Styx stepped toward the hole in the wall, his brows drawn together. "Sorcery?"

"Yes. I'm the last surviving heir." She bit her bottom lip, the scent of her lingering terror making Roke twitch with the need to rip the spirit into painful pieces. Several painful pieces. "If he can kill me, then he can destroy the book."

"No one's killing you," Roke snapped.

She flashed him a weak smile. "That was my hope."

Their gazes locked. His filled with a bleak promise of protection; hers filled with a rueful regret.

"Why can this book hurt the spirit?" Styx intruded into their silent exchange.

Sally shrugged. "I won't know until I manage to unravel the threads of sorcery protecting it."

Roke went rigid. "No."

"Roke." She firmly pulled out of his arms, her chin set to a militant angle. "We have to find out what's in that book."

His hands clenched as he brutally squashed the need to jerk her back into the safety of his arms. Instead he turned his head to glare at his king. "And if this is a trick?"

Styx arched a dark brow. "What kind of trick?"

"Maybe the damned spirit pretended the book could harm him just so we would do everything in our powers to destroy the magic that guards it."

"No." Sally gave a shake of her head, her nose wrinkling. "There was no doubt it was being affected by its proximity to the book. It was rotting from the inside out."

Roke folded his arms over his chest, his stance warning he was a male about to dig in his heels. "All the more reason to leave it alone until we know more about it."

"Under any other circumstances I would agree with you, *amigo*," Styx said, a hint of compassion on his face. "But in this case, neither of us is in a position to make a reasoned decision." He nodded toward Sally. "Only our expert can decide what's best."

She widened her eyes in faux shock. "You mean I'm allowed to have my very own opinion? Amazing."

"Sally . . ." Roke began.

"I have to do this," the stubborn witch interrupted him before he could even state his case.

He scowled. "Why?"

She lifted her hands in seething frustration. "Because there's a creature out there who claims to be the god of vampires and is convinced that his survival depends on my death. I'd rather get him instead of waiting around for him to get me."

"A good offense is truly the best defense, Roke," Styx said in tones that were clearly intended to be soothing.

Roke, however, was in no mood to be soothed. He was mad as hell at a fate that would force him into an unwanted mating (with a witch, for god's sake) and then once his most possessive instincts were fully committed, threaten to take her away.

"And if it was Darcy?" he accused him.

Styx rolled his eyes. "By now you should know that my mate charges into danger with nerve-shattering regularity."

Roke couldn't argue. The tiny pure-blooded Were was as irrationally stubborn and uncontrollable as Sally.

As if to rub salt in a very tender wound, Sally narrowed her eyes, the scent of peaches filling the air. "This is my decision, no one else's."

"Dammit." He squashed a wry laugh as he met her warning glare. He'd been so smugly certain he would be able to choose a submissive, easily trainable mate who would always understand that the duties of his clan came first. What he had instead . . . His heart gave a dangerous twist, something far more potent than a forced mating tingling through his blood. "What are you going to do?" he roughly demanded.

She turned to pace toward the gap in the wall, her hand stroking at the edges of the hole, as if testing the invisible spell.

"Sorcery is similar to magic," she said slowly, averting her face as if she could hide her uncertainty behind the satin curtain of autumn hair. "But the spells aren't connected to a specific incantation or brew or sacrifice."

"It's connected to you," he said in flat tones.

"Yes."

He took a step forward, his hands still clenched. "Which means?"

"That I should be able to peel back the layers of magic like an onion."

"*Should* be able to?"

She turned to meet his smoldering glare. "What do you want me to say? I've never tried to break through sorcery before." She gave a restless lift of her shoulder. "To be honest, I didn't even believe it truly existed." Sally then proceeded to tell Roke and Styx the rest of what had occurred in the warehouse before they had broken in as Santiago had asked her to.

"God almighty," he growled, his jaw clenched so tight his teeth threatened to shatter. "You're going to be the death of me."

Without warning her expression hardened, her hands landing on her hips. "No. That's one thing I won't be," she informed him. "I need everyone to leave before I start—"

He was standing in front of her, wrapping his fingers around her upper arms in an unbreakable grip before she could even blink.

"Forget it."

"Don't be so stubborn, Roke," she muttered, pretending she wasn't unnerved by his inhuman speed. "If the book could hurt the spirit, then there's a good chance it can hurt all vampires."

"Santiago looked unharmed before he disappeared," he reminded her. Not that he would have left even if Santiago had matched his decomposing companion.

At least not without this female.

Her lips thinned in annoyance. "I can't concentrate with you breathing down my neck."

"I don't breathe."

"But—"

"No."

"You might as well give it up," Styx drawled as he moved to stand beside them. "I recognize that expression. You'd have better luck arguing with that brick wall."

Her lips parted to continue the quarrel, then catching the determination etched onto Roke's face, she heaved a resigned sigh. "Fine," she grudgingly conceded. "But don't bitch at me when things go to hell."

His hand lifted to tuck her hair behind her ear, his touch gentle. "Then we'll go there together."

* * *

Beyond the Veil

Nefri had never been truly defenseless.

She'd been used, abused, vulnerable, and on occasion, so out of control she'd become no less lethal than a nuclear bomb.

But she'd always had her powers. Which meant she'd never truly known the terror of being at the absolute mercy of another creature.

Now she blinked as she glanced around the empty marble building with fluted columns, and a domed roof that was painted to resemble the blue skies no vampire had ever seen. Below her feet was a delicate mosaic and in the center of the building was a fountain that was surrounded by marble nymphs dancing in the spray of water.

It was a place of meditation, which meant that no one would enter once they sensed her presence. Thank the gods. But she couldn't hope that the spirit who had taken command of her body would be content to remain secluded.

Already she could feel her emotions being agitated by the creature, although she sensed he was still weakened. She had to get away from her people.

Or, if worst came to worst, she would have to end her life.

A small price to pay for the salvation of her clan.

Right. All very noble and completely worthless, she dryly concluded, as long as the spirit was in control of her body.

For the moment her only hope was that she could find a way to regain command. Or that Santiago would be able . . .

No.

The last thing she wanted was Santiago to be in danger.

If she tried to reach out for help it would be the Oracles. They were, after all, the ones who'd started this whole mess.

Trying to clear her mind enough to reach out mentally to Siljar, she was abruptly distracted as a vampire stepped in the room.

He was a short, bullishly built male with a bluntly carved

face and silver hair that was pulled into a tight queue at his neck. Oddly, he was dressed in a velvet tunic and leggings that had been the fashion centuries ago, with a heavy war hammer clenched in one hand.

Holy hell.

She would have stumbled backward in shock if she'd been in control of her legs. As it was, she was forced to stand in frozen horror as her former master strolled to a halt directly before her.

"Ah, my blessed daughter." Theo's voice rumbled through the thick silence, his pale brown eyes shimmering with the same insatiable greed she remembered with acute revulsion. "At long last."

"No," she hissed. "You're not real."

He sneered with pleasure at her swelling fear. "Did you miss me, my beautiful Amazon?"

Miss him?

She'd put him in his grave.

How else was she ever to halt the devastation he was forcing her to wreak on innocents?

So many killings . . .

"You're dead," she managed to grit.

"Dead, but not forgotten."

She felt her fear being shifted to fury, the emotion swelling through the air and spilling out of the building. Soon the intense passions would be infecting her people and the spirit would be able to feast to his cruel heart's content.

That's why it had created this vision of her former sire.

It had rooted around in her mind until it had managed to locate the one memory capable of producing the most intense reaction.

"No, I won't let you use me." Grimly she struggled to leash her anger, already sensing the bewildered reaction of her people. "Not again."

"But you're such a loyal soldier," he mocked, looking so

real that Nefri could almost sympathize with Gaius's belief that his mate had been returned to him. "So eager to please me that you were willing to destroy an entire clan."

"No."

"Now, now, Nefri," he chided. "Don't you remember?"

Against her will the memory of the brutal battle that had killed over two dozen vampires and their human servants seared through her mind, leaving behind an aching sadness laced with a crippling guilt.

"I remember," she whispered.

Theo laughed, relishing her pain. "Do you hear their screams when you close your eyes?"

Still locked in her paralysis, she could only tremble as the spirit ruthlessly played her emotions like they were a musical instrument.

"Yes."

"Do you taste their blood?" he pressed.

"It's over," she rasped.

"No, it's still there. The monster inside you just waiting to be released."

And that was it.

Her greatest fear.

The reason she had traveled beyond the Veil and devoted herself to creating a place of utter peace.

A Garden of Eden.

Only I am the serpent, a voice whispered in the back of her mind. *The devil just waiting to destroy paradise*.

"Stop," she cried.

"Aren't you tired of denying your emotions?" Theo asked, his tone lowering to become a hypnotic murmur. "Of being less than who you are?"

She desperately tried to block out the insidious voice, hearing the distant sounds of fights beginning to break out among her clan.

Violence where there had never been any before.

"I won't listen to you."

"I was so proud of you," her dead master purred. "A beautiful, lethal weapon who could make the world shudder in fear."

"No."

"But what have you become?" he persisted. "A shallow husk of yourself. A female who is forced to cower behind this Veil as if you're ashamed of your greatness."

Her muscles trembled as she tried to fight against the spirit holding her captive.

She had to get free long enough to find a weapon. She knew beyond a doubt once the spirit had fed enough to regain its strength it would send her on a bloodbath that would destroy her people.

She was going to die before she allowed that to happen.

Caught in the strange, motionless battle, Nefri almost missed the familiar scent that floated on the breeze.

"Santiago?" she whispered in confusion.

The vision of Theo briefly wavered, becoming a black mist, as Nefri concentrated on the sense of Santiago approaching the building. Then, with a sharp movement the illusion was coalescing and shifting to block her vision.

"Bastard," her sire growled. "Send him away."

"Never."

The pale brown eyes hardened with an ugly anger. "He's like all the others, can't you see that? He only wants to use you."

Just a few days ago the cruel taunt would have hit its mark. She'd been manipulated and abused too many times not to harbor a suspicion that anyone trying to get too close wanted something from her.

Now, however, she didn't hesitate. "You're wrong," she said with an unmistakable confidence.

"Why else would he be with you?" Theo demanded. "If he truly cared he would have listened when you insisted you preferred to be left alone."

A soft warmth flowed through her heart, replacing the

anger and pain and fear that had been coursing from her and pulsing through the air to infect her people.

"He cares about me."

"He only wants your power," Theo snarled. "With you he can take command of his own clan. Perhaps even challenge the Anasso."

"Nefri." Santiago's voice cut through the vision's filthy lies, steadying her.

"Kill him," Theo commanded even as he began to fade beneath the reality of Santiago's presence. "Kill him before he can destroy you."

Santiago stepped into the building, half dragging a sadly decomposing Gaius beneath one arm.

He walked cautiously forward, his dark gaze studying her with a fierce intensity. "Are you okay?"

"Stay back," she commanded, wishing he had never appeared despite the fact his mere arrival had given her strength.

She couldn't bear it if the spirit forced her to hurt him.

He held her gaze as he continued his slow pace forward. "I can't do that."

She trembled. "Please."

"Trust me, my love."

"I'm"—she could feel the spirit inside her trying to cloud her mind—"not in control."

"Then give me the control," Santiago urged, his beautiful face softened with an expression of love so pure it muted any attempt by the spirit to stir her anger.

Not that the spirit was about to give up without a fight.

Unable to claim her mind, it instead tightened her muscles, clearly preparing to attack.

"Santiago." Her eyes held a growing panic. "I can't."

"Yes, you can. You know I will always be here for you. I will never fail you." He held out one arm in welcome even as he clutched the seemingly unconscious Gaius in the other. "Trust me."

What was he doing?

Did he think she could actually fight off the spirit?

She might be powerful, but she wasn't Wonder Woman.

A cry was wrenched from her throat as her body was suddenly hurtling forward, her fangs fully extended. It was the only warning Santiago had, but it should have been plenty to give him the opportunity to dodge her attack.

Instead, he stood with an unwavering determination, barely flinching when she rammed into him with the force of a cement truck.

Her fangs sank in his neck as he wrapped an arm around her waist, his voice barely audible over the terror that pounded through her.

"Now, Gaius."

Chapter 29

Sally had never actually tried to walk around with an elephant on her back. It wasn't the sort of thing that even a witch did on a regular basis. But after the past few minutes she was pretty sure she now knew what it would feel like.

Kneeling in front of the safe, which had been fully exposed by the simple process of Styx and Roke bashing through the remaining bricks, she felt sweat trickling down her face and her muscles trembling in protest.

She'd used magic from the day she'd left her cradle. Maybe even before then.

She'd perfected the fine art of casting until she could perform them with flawless precision; she could brew potions that were so potent they sold for twice the usual price. And she could sense a spell from a remarkable distance.

But while she was highly proficient in the usual arts, she'd never actually tried to manipulate magic.

It was . . . exhausting.

Both mentally and physically.

Each layer of magic had to be carefully unraveled from the complex web, but it wasn't like they disappeared. She had to maintain her hold on each thread while continuing to loosen the others.

And all the while, she knew one wrong tug could create an explosion that would destroy even vampires.

Gritting her teeth, she tried to ignore her rapidly fading strength. Just a little more and . . . a moan was wrenched from her throat as she felt herself beginning to sway.

Crap, crap, crap.

She raised her hands to keep from falling on her face, but she'd barely moved an inch when strong arms wrapped around her and the sensation of cool, euphoric power pulsed through her weary body.

Roke.

He was using their connection to give her the strength she needed.

The debilitating fatigue faded from her mind and she tilted back her head to offer a grateful smile. "Thank you."

His lean, compelling face remained hard with disapproval even as he gently brushed a strand of hair from her pale cheek. "Sally, you can't keep going like this," he said gruffly.

"I'm close."

"I don't care." His voice was strained, as if he were barely preventing himself from physically hauling her away from the warehouse. "You're going to burn yourself out."

"I can't stop now."

The dark eyes smoldered with frustration. "You can at least rest."

"No. If I let go . . ."

"What?"

She wrinkled her nose. "Let's just say bad things will happen."

His arm abruptly tightened around her shoulders, his expression resolute. "How many times do I have to tell you? Nothing is going to happen to you," he swore softly.

A treacherous warmth threatened to melt her heart as he regarded her with an unwavering devotion. Her very own hero who would slay her endless parade of dragons.

Then she was grimly squashing the stupid thought.

His devotion wasn't real. It was nothing more than a symptom of the mating she'd forced on him.

It would disappear the moment they managed to break the bond.

And she would be an idiot to let herself believe for a second that beneath the sham of their mating Roke considered her anything but the enemy.

And that if they managed to survive the night, she would soon be alone, with no one to depend on but herself.

Again.

"Considering the fact I've had a bounty on my head since I was sixteen, there's a good possibility that it's going to be a daily lecture," she muttered wryly. "Or at least until—"

"Not now," he broke in, to her reminder this was only temporary.

"What can we do to help?" Styx demanded, keeping guard near the door.

"I don't think anyone can help," she admitted, her concentration returning to the numerous threads that she struggled to keep from slipping her magical grasp. "I have to do this on my own."

"But not alone," Roke whispered in her ear, tugging her until her back was pressed against the solid muscles of his chest. "Lean against me."

Her heart did that terrible melting thing again, but she focused her energy on the remaining weave that protected the book.

Even with Roke's added strength she was soon soaked in perspiration, her knees aching from being pressed against the hard floor, and her mind pounding with a headache that wasn't going to be cured by a couple of extra-strength aspirin.

Then, she slowly peeled away the last weave to reveal the book that the sorcery had been protecting.

A book that wasn't a book.

"Blessed goddess," she breathed in shock.

Roke stiffened. "What's wrong?"

"I removed the last layer of magic."

Styx was at their side before she could even blink. Damn vampire speed.

"And?" he rasped.

She instinctively pressed into Roke's comforting hold. It wasn't that he was any less intimidating than the King of Vampires. But he was at least . . . familiar.

"I'm not sure."

Styx warily glanced inside the top of the safe that had been ripped off by Roke.

"Can you sense the book?"

She shuddered. "Oh yes."

Roke shifted so he could study her troubled expression. "Is it magic?"

"No, it's a . . ." She bit her bottom lip, struggling to find the words to explain the darkness that threatened to suck them all into oblivion. "A void."

Styx turned to stab her with a piercing gaze. "A void?"

"Like a black hole that sucks away everything around it."

If she hadn't been so weary she would have laughed as Styx jumped away from the safe as if he'd been poked by a cattle prod.

"Are we in danger?" he growled.

She used her magic to probe the strange void, baffled by the sense that it was pulling in . . . something, but unable to determine exactly what that "something" was.

"Not immediate danger," she said slowly, grimacing at her companions' matching expressions of aggravation. "Hey, that's all I can promise."

Roke absently smoothed a comforting hand down her back. She swallowed a rueful sigh. He was obnoxious and arrogant and bossy beyond bearing, but someday he truly was going to make some female a wonderful mate.

"So how was this book able to hurt the spirit?" he asked.

Hmmm. How to explain what she was sensing to two vampires who made a habit of pretending magic didn't exist.

"It's not really a book," she at last admitted.

Predictably Roke frowned in suspicion. He understood a book. Even one that might hold magical spells. "It's not?"

She lifted her hands, searching for the right words. "It has the physical appearance of a book, but it's only a focal point for the power."

Roke frowned, but not bothering to try and question what a focal point might be, he honed in on the most important detail of her revelation. "That doesn't explain why it affects the spirit."

Styx paced toward the door and back, clearly lost in his own thoughts. "Santiago said that the creature feeds on emotion," he abruptly stated.

"So a void . . ." Roke's eyes widened. "Of course. It would starve him."

It took a minute for Sally to follow their line of logic, then she gave a sound of shock.

The void was absorbing emotions.

A perfect weapon to battle the creature.

Whether or not it was created to perform some other purpose was impossible for her to say.

"Can the book, or whatever the hell it is, be moved?" Styx asked, his warrior mind already considering the best way to use their unexpected advantage.

She shrugged. "In theory."

Styx nodded. "So now the question is, how do we track a spirit that can seemingly jump from body to body?"

It was Sally's turn to be struck by a sudden fear. Not for herself. But for Roke, who would insist on being a part of the hunt for the spirit.

"Santiago knows this is the only thing that can hurt the

creature," she hurriedly pointed out. "He'll do everything in his power to return him to this warehouse."

Styx looked far from pleased by her sensible suggestion. Like all vampires he had the patience of a human five-year-old.

Or maybe the need to leap willy-nilly into danger was a male thing.

"So we wait?" he growled.

She shrugged. "What else can we do?"

Without warning, Roke was straightening, dragging her upright so he could wrap her in his arms. "I know what you're going to do," he said in tones that made the hair on her nape stand upright.

"What's that?"

"You've done your part." He held her gaze, his expression ruthless. "It's time for you to return to your rooms."

"I agree," Styx abruptly nipped her urge to argue in the bud. "It's . . ."

There was no warning.

At least none that Sally could detect.

It was simply as if an invisible doorway opened and an entwined trio of vampires tumbled into the room.

"Too late," she croaked.

Santiago had endured torture on an epic scale.

In the Gladiator pits mere survival meant enduring pain that would kill a lesser demon.

But even prepared, he couldn't prevent his grunt of agony as Nefri's fangs sank into his throat and her claws dug deep grooves into his back.

Cristo.

He'd known she was lethal, but even without using her innate powers she was a formidable enemy. He would have only minutes before she tired of her game and ended him.

Time enough?

He was about to find out.

Keeping a death grip on the rapidly dying Gaius, as well as maintaining his hold on Nefri, he braced himself for their abrupt return to the warehouse.

He would never, ever get used to traveling through space like a damned Jinn.

His feet had barely hit the floor when he sensed Styx rushing forward.

"Santiago."

"Wait." He dropped Gaius so he could hold out a warning hand. "She's being controlled by the spirit."

"Good," the Anasso growled. "I've been waiting for the bastard."

On cue Nefri ripped her fangs from his throat, whirling to face the towering vampire.

"So. At last I meet the great Anasso," Nefri mocked, her power beginning to fill the air. "The King of All Vampires."

Styx moved backward, drawing Nefri away. Santiago sank to the floor, the blood dripping from his wounds as his flesh slowly knit back together.

"An empty title," Styx said, his voice taunting. "Almost as empty as that of god."

An eerie laugh fell from Nefri's lips. "Shall I demonstrate how wrong you are?"

Styx braced himself for the coming attack. "Roke, don't let her get past the door," he commanded. "And Santiago . . ."

"I'll guard the windows."

Santiago began to rise to his feet when Gaius grabbed his hand.

"My son . . . wait."

Santiago hid a grimace, knowing his former sire had only minutes left. "What do you want?"

Shaking from the effort, he grabbed the medallion and

with the last of his strength, he broke the chain that held it around his neck. "Here."

Santiago flinched from the medallion that had been tainted by the Dark Lord. The small piece of metal had caused untold misery. "Keep it," he growled.

"No . . ." Gaius grimaced, his rotting face a gruesome mockery of the handsome, vital vampire he'd been just weeks ago. "You must destroy it."

He was right.

Even if the Dark Lord was dead and they managed to destroy the spirit that was their latest threat, the medallion symbolized evil.

It couldn't be allowed to remain in the world.

Santiago reluctantly took the medallion. "I'll make sure it's destroyed."

"Thank you. I—"

"Don't," Santiago interrupted. He would never be able to fully forgive this man for his betrayals. Not when he'd nearly destroyed the world with his selfish needs. But a part of him now at least understood what would drive a man to such extremes. "I will remember my sire as the man who took me into his lair and gave me a home," he said in a low voice. "The man who taught me the meaning of family."

"Son . . . my son . . ." A shattered moan of relief hissed past Gaius's lips before the light died from his eyes and he was allowed to escape the slow, painful decay.

Rising to his feet as Gaius turned to ash, Santiago slipped the medallion into his pocket, determined to honor his sire's last request.

Then he turned just in time to witness Nefri sending a blast of power toward Styx.

The very air sizzled before the power smacked into Styx with enough force to send him flying into the far wall. The entire building shook from the impact, broken plaster cascading down on their heads.

"You truly can't think you can beat me," Nefri said in genuine incredulity. "I created you."

Styx pulled himself from the rubble, dusting the clinging bits of cement from his leather pants. "What makes you think I need to beat you?"

"Why else would Santiago so cleverly force me back here?" With a sharp thrust of her hand, Nefri's power again sent Styx crashing into the wall.

Santiago cursed, knowing that the violent collision with the wall had to be cracking bones and puncturing inner organs. The Anasso, however, refused to betray the slightest hint of vulnerability as he surged upright, allowing his own powers to knock Nefri backward.

"Because we have a gift for you," Styx drawled. "We've removed the protective spells around the book."

"No." Nefri hissed, her body growing rigid as the spirit belatedly realized the danger. "I won't be trapped. Not again."

Styx smiled. "Not your choice."

"Fool."

With a screech that nearly busted Santiago's eardrum, Nefri launched herself toward Styx, her power exploding through the room to send them tumbling to the floor.

Fighting against pulses of frigid energy that threatened to crush him, Santiago forced himself back to his feet. Step by painful step he inched forward, his heart clenched with fear as Styx struggled to hold off the vampire lost in her bloodlust.

Nefri went for his neck, her fangs instead sinking into the Anasso's forearm, which he raised to block her. His other hand shot out, gripping her lower face as he prepared to crush her jaws.

"Styx," Santiago called. "Don't hurt her."

The king turned his head to regard him with a furious disbelief. "Are you kidding me?"

"If you damage Nefri the creature will simply take control of you, then we'll never stop it," he warned.

Nefri's power was off the charts.

Styx, however, had gained a connection to thousands of vampires who called him their Anasso. If the spirit's infection could be transferred through his bond to his people . . . *mierda*.

Perhaps following his line of reasoning, Styx strained to contain the rabid vampire trying to chew her way through his arm, shifting his attention to Roke and the witch, who were kneeling next to the safe.

"Sally," he commanded.

"Yeah, yeah. I'm coming."

The pretty witch wrinkled her nose as she rose to her feet, reaching into the safe to pull out a book.

Or at least, he thought it was a book.

There was a hazy, insubstantial quality to it, as if it weren't entirely solid.

Typical.

Was anything what it seemed to be anymore?

Carefully she walked forward, an anxious Roke hovering next to her.

It was only as the witch neared Nefri that Santiago realized the fierce power that had been pulsing through the room had abruptly diminished.

Was Nefri so consumed by her bloodlust that the spirit had lost control of her?

Or was the approaching book draining its powers?

He had his answer when Nefri abruptly turned, her mouth bloody and her eyes glowing.

"No," she snarled, headed straight for the witch.

With a roar, Roke was shoving Sally behind him and meeting Nefri's charge.

"Dammit," Styx muttered, diving forward to grab Nefri with his one good arm. His other was a mangled mess. "Santiago, help me."

Santiago instantly moved to wrap his arms around Nefri,

realizing it was going to be impossible to convince Roke not to do his best to kill Nefri.

The male vampire's mate was in danger.

There was nothing he wouldn't do to protect her.

Just as there was nothing he wouldn't do to protect Nefri.

Trapping her arms against her slender body while Styx looped his arm around her waist, they pulled her away from the infuriated Roke.

It was a struggle, but the fact that they'd managed to contain Nefri at all was yet another sign that the spirit's resources were being rapidly drained.

"Sally, finish this," Styx commanded between clenched teeth.

The witch tried to step past her bristling mate only to be halted when he grabbed her arm and growled low in his throat.

"Roke," she murmured, her expression pleading. "You have to let me go."

He bared his fangs, any sanity lost beneath the primitive instinct to protect his mate. "No."

"We have to end this now," she said softly.

"She's right," a female voice said as a jolt of electric energy penetrated, and then smothered, the power surging from the vampires.

No one had to turn to know who had so unexpectedly crashed the party.

Siljar was the only one who could make such a spectacular entrance and overwhelm even the most dominant vampires.

Slowly the tiny demon moved to stand at Sally's side, her black almond eyes unblinking and her heart-shaped face somber. Wearing her traditional white robe and her silver hair pulled into a braid, she had the regal bearing of a queen.

"Let her go, vampire," she commanded.

"Shit."

With a glare that should have made the Oracle spontaneously combust, Roke grudgingly released his hold on the witch. Even lost in primordial instincts, a demon understood there was no fighting one of the Commission.

"I'll be fine." Lifting her hand, Sally gently touched his cheek before turning back to Nefri with a bleak resolution.

As expected, Nefri went wild as the witch moved forward.

Styx cursed, grunting as one of Nefri's arms came free so she could rake her claws down his face.

"Dammit, Santiago, hold on to her."

Santiago's knee shattered beneath the impact of Nefri's kick, and a rib cracked from the swinging elbow.

"I'm trying," he muttered, regaining control of her arms only to have her jerk her head backward to bust Styx's nose.

"Try harder," the king gritted, spitting out a mouthful of blood.

Together they slowly halted her struggles, her screams of frustration becoming whimpers of fear as Sally pressed the book against her stomach.

"If I die, she dies," the spirit warned, the glowing gaze turning toward Santiago. "Do you hear me, Santiago? This host will die just as Gaius did."

Siljar stepped forward. "Don't listen."

Yeah, easy for her to say.

Already he could begin to detect the damage being done to her exquisite face. Not that he gave a shit what she looked like. His love for Nefri wasn't about flesh and bone. But the fear that she would be destroyed along with the spirit threatened to tip him over the edge.

"You have a minute to do what you have to do," he hissed. "After that . . . I make no promises."

Siljar rolled her eyes, muttering something about leeches beneath her breath. Then she shifted her attention to Sally.

"I will need your assistance, witch."

Sally grimaced, her face drenched in sweat and her slender body trembling as she continued to hold the strange book against Nefri. "I don't know anything about sorcery," she said, her voice strained.

"I will start the weave; I just need you to help hold the threads."

It all sounded like gibberish to Santiago, but Sally gave a hesitant nod. "Okay."

Siljar closed her eyes and held out her tiny hands. "Let's begin."

Santiago was vaguely aware of Roke moving to support Sally's swaying body and Styx's hiss of pain as Nefri gave him another head butt, but his sole focus was on the woman wrapped in his arms.

He felt her shudder, her skin turning ashen as the witch and Oracle performed their mystical voodoo.

"Don't leave me, Nefri," he husked. "Don't you dare leave me again."

The glow began to fade from her eyes and for a horrified moment, Santiago thought he was truly losing her.

No.

He tightened his arms, silently *willing* her to survive.

At first he could feel nothing. As if she'd already slipped away from him. Then, as he stubbornly refused to concede defeat, he felt a . . . spark. The tiniest awareness of the female he adored beyond all bearing.

A relief so vast it threatened to send him to his knees flooded through him, and ignoring the crowd watching their every move, he gently cupped her face.

"Hey there, beautiful."

Her brows drew together as she struggled to focus on his face. "Santiago."

"I'm here."

She gave a slow, painful nod. "I need . . ."

"Yes, my love?"

"I need you to promise me."

He leaned closer despite Styx's growl of warning, trying to catch her soft words. "Promise you what?"

"Promise me you won't let the spirit control me again."

"Siljar is here with the witch," he tried to soothe, knowing that losing control of her body and power was her worst nightmare come true. "They're going to get rid of it."

She lifted her hand to weakly clutch at his arm. "If it gets loose again, I want you to swear you'll kill me before allowing it to use me."

A part of him wanted to offer comfort.

To say whatever was necessary to ease her fears.

But, a larger part understood he couldn't lie.

Not to a woman he intended to spend the rest of eternity with.

"No."

Her dark eyes filled with a fear that sent a stab of agony through his heart.

"Santiago, I couldn't bear it," she pleaded, her face still ashen and drawn with weariness. "You know I couldn't."

"And I can't bear to lose you," he said with a blunt honesty. He'd intended to save his proclamation of love until a more appropriate time. Like when the current life or death situation was over. Perhaps at a location that could be considered at least a little romantic. And at the very least, he'd intended for them to be alone. Now, he accepted that the time or place was meaningless. If the past few months had taught him nothing else, it was that there was no promise of tomorrow. He wasn't wasting another second without telling this woman what she meant to him. "You are my very reason for living."

The dark eyes softened with a love that he could tangibly feel flowing between them even as her expression remained set in stubborn lines. "But . . ."

"No." He brushed his lips over the chilled skin of her cheek to the corner of her mouth. "Ask me to be your mate.

Ask me to stand at your side for the rest of eternity. Ask me to love and honor and respect you," he husked. "But don't ask me to sacrifice you. I can't."

"There will be no further sacrifices required," Siljar said in a weary voice. "At least not today."

Santiago glanced up to discover Roke carrying an unconscious Sally toward the door and Siljar leaning against a pile of rubble. He frowned as he realized the book had disappeared.

"Where's the spirit?"

Siljar grimaced, her devastating power for once muted. "It has been sent to the Commission. There are those qualified to keep it imprisoned."

Chapter 30

Nefri regained her balance, although she allowed Santiago to keep a protective arm around her shoulders. She already sensed that there wasn't a power on this earth that could force him to release his hold on her.

Besides, she liked the solid weight. It reminded her that after endless centuries of being alone, she now had a companion she not only trusted, but who filled her heart with a joy she'd never dreamed was possible.

This man.

This glorious, irreverent, sexy vampire she loved without condition.

The man she intended to claim as her mate.

At least once she could be absolutely certain the danger was over.

"Why didn't you destroy it?" she demanded of the Oracle, belatedly noticing that the tiny demon looked as drained as Nefri felt.

"Because none of us could be certain what would happen if we did."

Styx stepped forward, his arm still healing from her savage attack and his face bloody. "Cryptic as ever, Siljar," he accused her.

"Not cryptic. The simple truth," Siljar answered, one of the few demons in the world not terrified of the King of Vampires. "The creature is dangerous, but it did spawn vampires as well as other species of demons." She shrugged. "To destroy it might very well damage its offspring in ways we can't predict."

Nefri gave a grudging nod. Life and death were a far more delicate balance than most people realized.

"So it's in that . . ." She struggled to remember through the haze that had clouded her mind. Hadn't the witch been pressing something against her? Something that had driven the spirit from her body? Ah, yes. "Book?"

"It's trapped in a vacuum between time and space," the Oracle said. "So long as it's properly monitored it won't be allowed to escape."

"Shouldn't you have thought of that before sending Nefri's clan into danger?" Santiago asked, as always living on the edge.

Thankfully, Siljar didn't appear offended. Instead she gave a lift of her brows. "Nefri's clan?"

Santiago tightened his arm around her. "*Our* clan."

Siljar smiled in satisfaction. Not the most reassuring sight considering the razor sharp teeth. "The sorcery created by the witches was enough to hold it prisoner for centuries."

Santiago lifted a brow. "So you had no nefarious purpose in allowing Nefri to lead her people beyond the Veil?"

"She came to me with a request for a place of peace."

"And?" Santiago pressed, ignoring Nefri's frown. He wasn't fooled for a moment by the Oracles display of innocence.

The tiny demon gave a dismissive wave of her hand. "And we hoped that having her people living beyond the Veil would give us an early warning if the spirit did start to waken."

Before Santiago could say something even more stupid than usual, Nefri smoothly cut him off. "But the spirit never disturbed my clan," she pointed out. "At least, not that we ever noticed."

The dark eyes suddenly held a deep, unfathomable wisdom. "Unfortunately, we didn't realize how thin the walls between dimensions had become. The spirit was able to remain hidden while manipulating a handful of vampires into killing the witches, and then slipping past the Veil using Gaius's medallion."

Styx snorted at the understatement. Nefri didn't blame him. The thinning of barriers had been more than unfortunate. It had been a breath from the apocalyptic.

"Oh yeah, and while the spirit was sneaking around, we were all nearly killed by the Dark Lord," he said dryly. "You remember that, don't you?"

"Of course." Siljar squared her shoulders, smoothing her hands down the robe that was once again a pristine white. "The Commission was concentrating on trying to locate several missing prisoners that escaped through the weakened dimensions while you put an end to the threat."

"Several?" Nefri muttered as the two males hissed in shock. "Do you mean—"

"Do you have the medallion?" Siljar interrupted, holding out an imperious hand.

Santiago hesitated, clearly consumed by a need to demand a further explanation of the missing prisoners.

Such as whether they'd been captured or were lurking in the shadows to cause yet another catastrophe.

Thankfully, her sharp elbow to his ribs helped him recall the dangers of antagonizing a member of the Commission.

With a grimace he dug into his pocket and pulled out the medallion. Nefri lightly touched his arm, knowing he would be suffering from the loss of his sire.

No matter what Gaius had done, they'd shared a connection that could never be truly broken.

"Here," he muttered gruffly.

"I'll take it." Siljar reached up to snatch it from his hand.

Santiago frowned. "It needs to be destroyed."

"It will be taken care of," Siljar promised, and with a wave of her hand, the medallion disappeared.

Whether it was hidden in the folds of her robe, or something more mysterious, was impossible to know.

Santiago wasn't satisfied. "Taken care of? Does that mean destroyed?"

Siljar offered her unnerving smile. "I must go." She paused to bid Nefri a low bow. "Nefri. We are in your debt."

Straightening, the tiny demon disappeared, leaving behind three vampires who were struggling to accept that they had actually survived.

"Someday . . ." Styx growled.

"Not now, Styx," Santiago said in soft but startlingly commanding tones.

"But . . ." Styx turned to glare at Santiago, then seeming to catch some unspoken message, he slowly smiled. "Right. I'll leave you to it."

They watched in silence as the massive vampire left the ruined room in a less dramatic fashion than Siljar. Still, it wasn't until they could sense the Anasso jogging away from the warehouse that Santiago grasped Nefri's shoulders and gently turned her to meet his somber gaze.

His lips parted, but Nefri had been waiting from the moment she'd been released from control of the spirit to offer her apology.

Not that an "I'm sorry" actually made up for trying to kill your lover, she wryly admitted.

"Santiago," she began, only to be outmaneuvered when Santiago placed his hand over her mouth.

"It's over."

She grasped his wrist to tug his hand away. "But I need to say I'm—"

"No."

She arched a brow at his arrogant tone. "No?"

"From this point forward, the past is done," he said, his eyes dark with a plea that tugged at her heart. "The only thing that matters is the future. Our future."

She hesitated, desperately wanting to accept his offer.

How many years had she wasted with guilt and regret?

How long had she denied her emotions out of fear?

"You think that's possible?"

His smile held an edge of sadness that spoke of his own loss. "We've both spent too long being haunted by events that neither of us could control." He cupped her face in his hands, his touch tender. "I want a fresh start. Don't we deserve it?"

She didn't know if they deserved it.

Her past wasn't entirely blameless. And the gods knew that Santiago was not an innocent.

But, deserving or not, her heart urged her to snatch at the happiness with both hands.

Well, after she'd tormented Santiago just a bit. He'd certainly done his share of tormenting over the past weeks.

"I'm not entirely certain," she murmured.

His brows drew together, his struggle against his instinct to toss her over his shoulder and demand capitulation etched on his beautiful face.

Their combined arrogance and demand for control would make life together a delicious battle.

"Why?" he at last rasped.

She offered a faux pout. "You hit me on the head."

"Ah." His frustration melted to wry amusement. "Yes, I know."

"That's it?" she demanded. "'Yes, I know'?"

He reached to curl her hand into a fist, pressing his lips to her knuckles. "You can hit me on the head if you want."

She trembled, heat exploding through her veins to sear away the lingering chill from the spirit.

"As hard as your head is, it would probably break my hand," she teased, moving forward to press against his lean body.

"True." He smiled with a wicked promise that made her toes curl in anticipation. "Which means you might as well mate with me instead."

"That doesn't make any sense at all."

"It makes perfect sense to me." He wrapped his arms around her, studying her upturned face with a possessive satisfaction. "You and I make perfect sense to me. Be my mate."

Her heart soared, but there was one last hurdle they had to confront.

"What about my clan?" she reminded him softly. She'd already prepared to step down from being chief. Her people would always have her loyalty, but nothing was more important than Santiago. "Eventually I'll be able to turn the leadership over to another. But for now—"

"I'm not asking you to choose between me and your clan, Nefri," he interrupted her, frowning as if he was baffled she would even suggest the idea.

"But your life is here."

Without warning he leaned down to kiss her with a blatant claim of ownership.

One she met with her own claim.

"My life is with you," he said against her lips.

And that's why she'd bonded with this vampire out of all the thousands and thousands of men she'd known over the centuries, she silently acknowledged, feeling as sappy as any overhormonal teenage girl.

He was arrogant and stubborn and possessive to the point of insanity, but he never tried to make her feel like she should apologize for her power.

He made her feel . . . proud.

Of herself. Of him. Of the partnership they were creating together.

"You could accept living beyond the Veil?" she pressed, needing him to be sure.

"Of course." The wicked smile widened, giving a flash of

fang. "I intend to open a fight club with a few fairies who know how to enjoy an orgy. . . ."

"Santiago," she growled.

He chuckled, brushing his lips over her forehead. "How many times do I have to tell you that you make it too easy?"

"Actually I intend to make it very hard," she warned. "Maybe if I keep you busy enough I can keep you out of trouble."

With one smooth motion he scooped her off her feet, cradling her tight against his chest as he headed for the door.

"But you like trouble," he reminded her, his expression promising all sorts of sinful havoc.

She looped her arms around his neck, the emotions she'd denied for so long flowing freely through her like the finest champagne.

"Actually, I *love* trouble."

Santiago stood with Viper in the corner of Styx's formal salon.

It had been three nights since they'd managed to . . . to what? He grimaced. He couldn't claim they'd defeated the spirit. But at least it was contained and now in the hands of the Commission.

Since then he'd devoted his time to keeping Nefri tucked in his arms. Not only because his insatiable hunger for her was a constant ache, but because he was determined to make certain she was completely recovered before returning to her duties.

Unfortunately, Nefri had decided she couldn't possibly be mated anywhere but in her private lair beyond the Veil.

So while he was fiercely happy to have her in his bed, he was growing restless to complete their mating.

Only when they'd shared their blood and bonded on the most primitive level would he be satisfied.

Tonight . . .

A tingle of anticipation raced through him as he watched Nefri move through the crowd that Styx had invited to send them off to the Veil.

He would have refused Styx's offer of a party if he hadn't known that powerful vampires from around the world had flocked to the Anasso's home in the hopes of meeting the mysterious Nefri.

And if he were being perfectly honest, he enjoyed watching the guests fluttering around her in obvious awe.

She looked like the perfect ice queen dressed in a silver robe that brushed the floor and her hair falling in a river of ebony satin down her back.

Aloof and untouchable.

Until he had her alone.

Ready heat swirled through him, making him shift in discomfort.

How much longer did he have to play nice?

He'd shared his beautiful mate long enough.

He was ready to get her alone.

And naked.

Definitely naked.

Perhaps sensing he needed a distraction before he went "caveman" and simply hauled her off, Viper moved to stand at his side.

"Are you sure about this?" his former clan chief asked, looking like a Regency dandy in his ivory velvet coat trimmed in gold thread complete with knee breeches. His long silver hair was pulled back with a matching velvet ribbon and his midnight black eyes held a lazy amusement that didn't entirely disguise his lethal power. "Living with a clan chief isn't easy."

"Never more sure," Santiago answered without hesitation, a smile of utter contentment curving his lips. "And she's a very special clan chief."

"You got me there," Viper admitted. "Still . . ."

"What?"

"You're leaving me in the lurch here."

Santiago laughed at his companion's petulant tone. "Why, Viper, I didn't know you cared."

Viper snorted. "You're a pain in the ass, but you're one of the best managers I've ever had. Who the hell is going to replace you at the club?"

"Tonya."

Viper hesitated, considering Santiago's recommendation with a frown. "She has the brains," he slowly conceded. "But she's distinctly lacking the brawn."

Santiago shrugged. He didn't doubt for a minute that the shrewd imp could easily fill his shoes. And he owed her one. Not only for what had happened with Gaius, but because of the fact he'd failed to realize she'd hoped for more than a mere employer-employee relationship.

"You have plenty of brawn," Santiago pointed out. "What you need is someone competent, creative, trustworthy, and capable of remaining calm when everything is going to hell." He folded his arms over his chest. "And it doesn't hurt that she's beautiful enough to make grown demons beg for a smile."

"I suppose I can give her a chance," Viper conceded.

"Good." He slapped his friend on the back. "Of course, you'll need to keep an eye on her."

"Why?"

"Because there are several other club owners who have tried to lure her away over the years," he said. "And without my charming presence to keep her loyal . . ."

Viper was moving toward the nearest door before Santiago could even finish.

Santiago chuckled, then sensing the approach of his soon-to-be mate, he turned to wrap an arm around her slender waist, tugging her close to his side.

Mine.

She readily leaned against him, a serene smile on her exquisite face.

"Why was Viper scowling?"

"Business."

She gave an absent nod, clearly something on her mind. "Santiago . . ."

"No, I'm not going to miss the club," he interrupted her, stealing a swift kiss. Just because he could. "And before you start worrying about my brothers, I intend to return and visit if and when I find myself missing them." He gazed deep into her eyes, allowing her to see the love that consumed him. "When I'm not busy with my new family."

A smile brighter than the sun spread across her face, her hand reaching to grab his fingers in a tight grip. "Are you ready?"

"For you?" He held her tight as the world began to melt away. "Always."

Roke drained his glass of blood as he watched Santiago and Nefri disappear from view.

About fucking time.

Styx had commanded that he attend the stupid party, despite his foul mood.

His duty was now officially done.

Setting aside his glass, Roke was on the point of slipping through a side door when the cool wash of power warned him of his Anasso's approach.

"Roke," Styx drawled. "Surely you're not going to run away so soon?"

Forced to halt, Roke scowled at his king, who was wearing a white silk shirt and black dress pants that didn't make him any more civilized than usual.

Not that Roke had any room to judge fashion. He was

wearing his customary jeans, leather jacket, and knee-high moccasins.

"I told you I didn't want to come."

Styx smiled, lifting his glass to sip the expensive cognac. "You tell me a lot of things."

"And you never listen."

"Well, you'll be pleased to know that as soon as Sally is feeling up to traveling you're free to go in search of her father."

Roke's scowl deepened.

Pleased?

Of course he should be pleased.

He should be dancing with joy.

He'd been straining at the leash to leave this damned lair so he could track down Sally's father. How else could he break the mating?

But strangely, he'd devoted the past three days to ignoring Sally's pleas to be released so she could begin the hunt, telling himself she was too weak to risk leaving.

He'd also assured himself that his hesitation had nothing to do with his growing bond with the female and everything to do with the agony of watching her lie as still as death after her battle with the spirit.

Twelve hours, sixteen minutes, and thirty seconds.

That was how long she'd been unconscious. He'd counted every tick of the clock as he stood guard by her bed. He wasn't going through that again.

Period.

"Why now?" he growled.

Styx shrugged. "I think we can safely assume that you've fulfilled your part in Cassie's vision."

"No shit," he muttered before giving a shake of his head. "I can't leave yet. Sally is still weak."

"She seemed fine earlier this evening," Styx said, his

expression suspiciously bland. "In fact, she came to me to ask for permission to go."

Roke's muscles clenched. Sally had gone to Styx behind his back?

She was *his* mate.

Any discussion of when they would leave and where they would go would be between the two of them.

"She's a female who too often thinks on impulse rather than reason," he said stiffly.

Styx narrowed his eyes. "All the more reason to get on with finding a way to break the mating."

Roke barely swallowed his growl. "I won't drag a barely conscious female around the countryside without even a clue to where we should start."

"Very well," Styx unexpectedly conceded, his smile worrisome. "Then perhaps you want to return to your clan? Sally is welcome to stay here."

"Don't even . . ." Roke forgot how to speak as his connection to Sally was abruptly stretched. Just like that. One minute she'd been upstairs and the next she was halfway across the country. "Shit."

Shoving his way through the crowd, Roke hit the hallway at a dead run.

"What's wrong?" Styx demanded, easily keeping pace as Roke headed up the stairs.

"Sally."

"Is she hurt?"

"She's gone."

"Gone?" Styx's power rattled the paintings on the wall. "Impossible."

Roke turned down the hall leading to Sally's private rooms. "I know when my mate has disappeared."

"She could never have gotten past the guards," Styx growled, tossing aside the unfortunate vampire who stepped out of his room to see what was going on.

"She's a witch," Roke reminded him, torn between anger and concern. There was nothing in their bond to indicate she was afraid or hurt. Which meant that she'd probably plotted this abrupt departure. Still, that didn't mean she wasn't in danger. Dammit. He should have locked her in the dungeons. "A very powerful witch."

"The house has been hexed to prevent magic," Styx argued, clearly disturbed by the thought that anyone could slip past his defenses.

"She did not use magic," an aggravatingly familiar voice said as the tiny gargoyle stepped out of Sally's room.

"Levet, now isn't the time," Roke snarled, needing to locate Sally's trail so he could begin the hunt.

"You will desire to hear what I have to say," Levet insisted. "I know where Sally is."

Roke halted, reaching down to grasp the gargoyle by the horn. He lifted him until they were eye to eye. "Where?"

The fairy wings fluttered in protest, but the gargoyle was smart enough not to press Roke's temper.

"I do not know the precise location."

The floor rumbled beneath their feet. "Levet, unless you want to become a wall ornament, you'll tell me exactly what you know." A hall table tumbled sideways, smashing the priceless vase into a thousand pieces. "Now!"

"She asked Yannah to help her escape," Levet said, his voice several octaves higher than usual.

"Escape?" Roke's brows snapped together. "She was a guest, not a prisoner."

"Maybe she did not recognize the distinction."

Roke dropped the beast, disliking the guilt that sliced through his heart.

He'd only been trying to protect her.

Hadn't he?

Thrusting aside the worthless questions, he forced himself

to swallow his pride. He could feel Sally, but she was too distant to pinpoint her direction.

"Can you follow them?" he forced himself to ask the gargoyle.

"Sally? Sadly no." Levet wrinkled his tiny snout. "But Yannah. *Oui*. I can follow."

"Good. We'll take my bike."

Styx reached out to grab his arm. "Roke."

"What?" he snapped, not bothering to hide his impatience. Every minute apart was another minute that Sally could be hurt.

"Be careful. And call if you need me."

Call? Not a chance in hell.

Once he got his hands on his missing mate they were heading directly for his clan in Nevada.

"I can handle my mate," he said dryly.

Styx's sharp laugh echoed through the hall. "Ah, the most common mistake made by every male of every species." He pressed his hands together, doing his best Master Po from *Kung Fu*. "You'll learn, young grasshopper. You'll learn."

Roke rolled his eyes, heading down the hall. "Let's go, gargoyle."

Please turn the page for

LEVET,

a bonus novella from Alexandra Ivy!

Chapter 1

Midnight in Paris

Walking through the dark shadows beneath the Eiffel Tower, Levet avoided the human tourists who strolled along the sidewalk to admire the carnival atmosphere that spilled through the streets despite the late hour.

Something inside of him seemed to bloom as he savored the sights and sounds that he'd been denied for so long.

He loved Paris.

It was the city of his birth.

The city where he'd first spread his wings and soared toward the night sky. The city where he'd first lost his heart to a naughty imp who'd lured him beyond the few cottages that were all that made up the early town and taught him how to please a woman.

And the city where his greatest enemies resided.

Enemies who also happened to be his family.

His sense of homecoming vanished like a bubble being popped.

Being different wasn't admired among the gargoyles. And, when it had been determined he was never going to grow beyond his miniscule three-foot stature and that his wings were going to remain as delicate as a dew fairy's that shimmered in hues of blue and crimson and gold, he was tossed away like a piece of rubbish.

No. He scrunched his ugly gray face into a grimace, his long tail twitching at the unwelcomed memories.

He'd been more than tossed away. He'd been banished. Shunned by his own people.

With an effort, he squashed the painful recollections and reminded himself he was no longer that frightened *enfant*.

Far from it.

Just a few weeks ago he'd stood up to the baddest of the bad.

He, Levet the Gargoyle, hero of all ages, had defeated the Dark Lord and his hordes of minions.

Cue swelling music.

Okay, there had perhaps been a few vampires and Weres who also helped destroy the bastard. And Abby had been there, the current Goddess of Light. Oh, and a Sylvermyst or two. And curs . . .

But he'd been the one who had struck the killing blow.

Right before the Dark Lord had skewered him with a lightning bolt that had burned straight through his chest and into his heart. If it hadn't been for Yannah's swift action he would even now be nothing more than toast.

Extra-crispy toast.

He heaved a rueful sigh, not quite as grateful as he should be.

The pretty, flighty, lethally dangerous female demon was enough to make any poor man's head spin.

For weeks she'd led him on a merry dance, appearing and then disappearing. Kissing him one minute and slugging him on the chin the next.

It had been . . . exasperating. But also thrilling.

What male did not love the *danse de l'amour*?

But after she'd rescued him from the cellar of the warehouse where he'd halted the looming apocalypse, she'd taken him to her cozy little home.

In hell.

Literally.

Fire. Brimstone. Ghouls.

And a full-blood Jinn as a next-door neighbor.

Not the most comfortable place for a gargoyle who was never so happy as when he was soaring across a star-spangled sky.

And then there was Yannah.

The female made him natty.

Or was it nutty?

Whatever.

She had gone from a charming, elusive tease to a female who was determined to smother him with her fussing and fretting. *Sacrebleu*. His wounds had fully healed. Well, unless you counted the bit of charred skin in the center of his chest. It was annoying to be coddled like he was a helpless *bébé*.

At last he'd had enough.

He needed space to breathe.

And more than that, he had a few ghosts to lay to rest.

Speaking of ghosts . . .

Halting just beyond the Eiffel Tower, Levet muttered a curse as he caught the scent of moldy granite. He'd known it wouldn't take long for the whispers of his arrival to reach the ears of his brethren.

No one gossiped worse than a clutch of gargoyles.

Still, he'd hoped that he could at least reach his mother's lair before being attacked.

Landing with enough force to send tiny quakes through the street, the two gargoyles (one male and the other female) spread a spell of illusion to hide them from the passing mortals.

Levet grimaced. The two were everything that Levet was not.

Towering over six feet with leathery wings that they tucked close to their massive bodies, they were creatures who would cause nightmares even among the demon world.

Their gray skin was the texture of an elephant hide and absorbed the moonlight. They had stunted horns that could smash through steel and long tusks that could pierce through armor. It was, however, their brutal features that truly reflected their savage natures.

Cold, ruthless, viciously unforgiving.

"Well, well," the female drawled, her gray eyes holding a cruel amusement that sent a chill down Levet's spine. "If it isn't my prodigal brother."

At a glance it would be impossible to guess that the three gargoyles were related. Claudine was his elder sister while Ian was a first cousin.

Of course, it wasn't just their appearances that were different, Levet consoled himself. His relatives were nasty-tempered monsters who terrorized lesser demons with spiteful glee.

Oh, and their sense of humor was nonexistent. Which meant that Levet couldn't resist tweaking their ugly snouts.

"Fred. Wilma," he murmured. "Where's Dino?"

Having come from the shallow end of the gene pool, the male demon furrowed his heavy brow in confusion.

"*Non*. You are mistaken. My name is Ian, not Fred."

"He knows your name, *imbecile*," Claudine hissed, slapping her companion on the back of the head. "As usual he believes himself to be amusing." She turned back to glare at Levet. "What are you doing in Paris?"

"I heard that Marcel Marceau was reviving his mime act." Levet flashed an innocent smile. "I didn't want to miss opening night."

Ian blinked. "But isn't he dead?"

"Shut up." Claudine gave Ian another slap, her gaze never

wavering from Levet. "You know you're not allowed in the city. The Guild kicked you out and Mother shunned you."

"Ah, dearest *Maman*, how is the loathsome old bat?" Levet drawled, folding his arms over his chest. If he was going to be squashed like a bug, he wasn't going to give Claudine the satisfaction of seeing his fear. "Still eating children for breakfast?"

"She has actually been plagued with ennui since she had her latest lover put to death." Claudine's smile was a cold threat. "Perhaps watching her deformed son being used for target practice will bolster her spirits."

Levet didn't doubt it would. His mother had a peculiar love for violence.

"Or perhaps I could chop you into tiny pieces and spread you around the city, *chère sœur*. Then *Maman* could spend the next century trying to put you together again."

"Such a large mouth for such a tiny creature," Claudine growled, pointing a claw in his direction. "It's time someone taught you a lesson in manners."

"Ah." Levet batted his eyes. "If only I had a euro for every time I heard that threat."

The female gargoyle growled like a rabid Were. Not at all attractive for a gargoyle.

And she wondered why she couldn't find a mate?

"Ian, get him."

Levet lifted his hands as Ian took a lumbering step forward. "Stay back."

Ian scowled. "Or what?"

"Or I will turn you into a newt."

The male gargoyle stumbled to a halt.

"Ian, did you hear me?" Claudine snapped.

"But—"

"What?"

"I do not want to be turned into a newt." He used a claw to scratch between his horns. "Wait . . . what is a newt?"

"*Mon dieu*. I am surrounded by morons," Claudine muttered. "He can't turn you into a newt, you fool, but I can cut off your head and have it mounted on Notre Dame."

"No need to be rude," Ian muttered.

"*Oui*, no need to be rude, Claudine," Levet mocked.

"Ian, get him and cut out his tongue."

Ian took another grudging step forward only to halt again when a flaming arrow flew directly between his horns.

"What was that?" the male gargoyle demanded, casting a swift glance down at his huge body as if he was afraid he'd been transformed into the mysterious newt.

Levet didn't have a clue, but he was never slow to take advantage of a situation. It was the only way for a three-foot demon to survive in a world where "only the good died young."

"You didn't think I would come to Paris alone?" he warned. "I have dozens of allies waiting to rush to my rescue."

"Grab him," Claudine demanded, abruptly ducking as an arrow threatened to skewer her thick skull. *"Merde."*

"You capture him." Ian launched himself into the air. "I am going home."

With a muttered curse, Claudine was swiftly following her cousin. Both were bullies, and like all bullies they had a large streak of cowardice.

"You won't escape without punishment, Levet," she shouted over her shoulder, her leathery wings barely visible against the night sky. "That much I swear."

Flipping her off, Levet turned to scan the nearby bushes.

"Who is there?"

There was a rustle of leaves before a slender, golden-haired female stepped into view.

Levet gave a low whistle of appreciation.

Sacrebleu. All nymphs were beautiful, but this one was drop-dead gorgeous.

Blessed with a silken curtain of golden hair she had wide blue eyes that were framed by thick, black lashes and set in a perfect oval of a face. Her lush, mouthwatering curves were delectably revealed by her skinny jeans and the scooped top that gave more than a hint of her full breasts.

"I'm Valla," she said, holding the bow at her side, the remaining arrows strapped to her back.

"Ah." Levet performed a deep bow. "I am deeply thankful for your timely diversion, *ma belle*."

Her lips twisted as she turned her head to reveal the side of her face that had been hidden by shadows. Levet gave a soft hiss at the sight of her skin that had been savagely marred by thick, disfiguring scars.

The sort of scars that came from a deep burn. Or a magical spell.

"Not *belle*," she corrected in flat tones. "As you can see I have become the beast, not the beauty."

"Do not say that," he protested, his tender heart squeezing in pity.

"Why not? It's true enough." Glancing toward the sky, she began walking toward the Parc du Champ de Mars. "Let's get out of here before your friends decide to return."

With a brisk waddle, Levet caught up with the retreating nymph.

"I am of the opinion that beauty truly is skin-deep and that what is beneath the surface is what is important," he informed her.

She shot him a wry smile. "Yeah, and size doesn't matter, right?"

"Touché," he conceded with a grimace. He, better than anyone, understood the heavy price of being "different." "You sound American."

They moved into the surrounding neighborhoods, by-passing the various hotels and shops.

"I lived there most of my life," she said. "Until—"

"Until?"

"I was captured by slavers."

"Oh." Levet shuddered. He had his own tragic past with the ruthless bastards. "I hate slavers."

"Yeah." The nymph turned onto a residential street, her profile outlined by the streetlamps. "I'm not so fond of them myself."

"They damaged your face?" he asked.

"I was determined to escape." She gave a lift of her shoulder. "Even if it meant I was permanently damaged by forcing my way through the magical barriers."

Levet was struck by a niggling memory.

Something about a nymph being held hostage by slavers . . .

Ah . . . *oui*.

He remembered.

"Valla. The nymph," he breathed in triumph, following his companion down a narrow alley and into an inner courtyard with a marble fountain surrounded by a pretty rose garden. "Jaelyn has been searching everywhere for you."

"The Hunter?" She glanced over her shoulder in surprise. "Why?"

Jaelyn was a rare vampire who'd been trained as a Hunter. During one of her missions to discover who had the balls to kidnap vampires, she'd been locked in the cells of a slaver, along with this nymph. She'd never forgiven herself for leaving the pretty young female behind.

"She has been tormented by the knowledge that she failed you in the slaver cells," he told Valla. "She needed to know your fate."

"Oh." Valla halted at what appeared to be a brick wall. "You know, I never resented her for leaving me there, but I did blame her for refusing my plea to kill me," the nymph admitted with blunt honesty, giving a wave of her slender hand to part the illusion so they could step through a door into a small, but elegant apartment.

"I, for one, am very pleased she ignored your plea," a male voice murmured as a tall, handsome vampire attired in a Gucci suit and handmade Italian leather shoes rose from a wing chair that was set near the marble fireplace.

Unreasonably handsome, even by vampire standards, the male had dark hair slicked from his pale, lean face and a wide brow. His nose was carved with bold, arrogant lines and his dark eyes glowed with a smothering power.

"Elijah," Valla murmured in obvious pleasure.

Moving to stand at her side, the vampire studied Levet in obvious warning.

"Who is this?"

"I am Levet." Levet performed a small bow, his wings spread to display their shimmering colors. "At your service."

Rising, he met the vampire's hard stare. "I've heard of you," Elijah said, his voice accusing.

Levet blinked at the odd words. "But of course you have heard of me. Who has not?" he demanded. "I am a warrior of great renown."

The male thinned his lips. "What are you doing in Paris?"

Levet tilted his chin, refusing to acknowledge that he'd been thoroughly routed only minutes after arriving in town. It was a temporary setback.

"I am here on a spiritual journey."

The vampire arched a dark brow. "Then you won't be staying?"

"Elijah." Valla flashed a frown at her male companion before turning her attention to Levet. "Don't listen to him. He has a delusional theory he owns the streets of Paris."

The vampire's icy power flowed through the room. Like a deluge of water that could drown the unwary.

"It's no delusion," he said. Not arrogance. Just absolute

confidence that he was master of his domain. "They do belong to me."

"You are the clan chief?" Levet asked, even though he knew the answer.

"I am."

"What happened to Pierre?" Levet referred to the clan chief that had ruled Paris when he'd been just a youngster.

Elijah flashed his massive fangs. "Let's just say that he decided to retire."

"Really? I didn't know clan chiefs could retire."

"It wasn't voluntary."

Levet's tail twitched. *"Mon dieu."*

The vampire took a threatening step forward. "Precisely."

"Stop trying to frighten my guest," Valla chided.

"Oui." Levet tilted his chin. "Stop trying to frighten her guest."

The cold, dark eyes narrowed. "Be careful, little demon. The gargoyles aren't your greatest danger in Paris."

Valla rolled her eyes. "Come with me, Levet, and I'll make you some tea."

Chapter 2

Valla hid a smile as she led the tiny gargoyle down the hall to the kitchen that had recently been remodeled with pretty white cabinets and stainless steel appliances.

As much as she might love Elijah, it was always fun to poke a few holes in his massive arrogance and at the same time reestablish the boundaries that he continually tried to smash through.

Besides, she found that she enjoyed Levet's companionship.

She didn't feel threatened by his light flirtations. A rare and wonderful sensation after she'd been brutalized while held captive by the slavers. In fact, he was the only male beyond Elijah she'd ever invited into her home.

"This is your apartment?" Levet asked as he took a seat at the dining table and watched her put the kettle on to boil.

She pulled two cups from the cabinet and grabbed a plate of cookies.

"Elijah is kind enough to allow me to stay here."

"No." The rich male voice stroked over her like the finest satin. It didn't matter how many years she'd known Elijah, his voice always made her shiver. Well . . . her and every other woman in Paris, she wryly acknowledged. "Elijah grudgingly allows you to stay here because you've refused the number of other homes I've offered you," he continued, as he prowled across the floor to gently tuck a curl behind her ear.

It was an ongoing fight.

Elijah insisted that she belonged in his lair near the Champs-Élysées.

Valla refused to give up her independence. It was bad enough he'd emphatically demanded that she live in one of his numerous properties.

"I won't take advantage of your generosity."

His hand cupped her cheek, his gaze smoldering with a frustration that filled the air with a sharp chill.

"Valla."

The touch of his lean fingers against her face sent an ache of long-suppressed hunger shivering through her body. Only this delectable, sexy, aggravatingly stubborn vampire could stir the desires she'd thought dead forever.

"There's no need for you to stay, Elijah," she murmured in husky tones. "I know you must be busy."

His brows furrowed, his eyes darkening as he easily sensed her reaction to his touch.

"You think I'll leave you alone with a strange demon?"

"The choice isn't yours," she reminded him. Gently.

"Dammit, Valla."

She heaved a sigh. It would be so easy to give in to his demands.

She would be protected, cosseted, her every need and desire fulfilled.

Just like a favorite pet.

"We've been through this before," she reminded him, an edge of steel in her voice. "You're my friend, not my keeper. If you can't distinguish between the two, then I'll have to leave Paris."

With a growl, he swooped his head down and kissed her.

Just like that.

Caught off-guard, her lips parted in helpless need, her entire world tilting on its axis. Elijah had always treated her like a fragile doll. Not a flesh-and-blood woman.

Now she quivered beneath the blazing pleasure that exploded through her nervous body.

"This is what I want," he rasped against her lips, his fingers stroking down the tender curve of her neck before he kissed her again.

This time she was prepared for the combustible heat that stole her breath away and made her stomach clench with a surge of excitement.

Oh . . . yes.

Her lashes fluttered downward as the desire flowed through her, as heady and intoxicating as the finest French champagne.

"Elijah—" she breathed, not certain what she needed, but knowing only he could satisfy the restless ache that burned deep inside her.

Then, the shrill whistle of the pot had her pulling back with a confused blush.

Still seated at the table, Levet awkwardly cleared his throat.

"Maybe I should leave?"

"Yes," Elijah agreed, his dark gaze smoldering with a dangerous hunger.

"No," she hastily countered, acutely aware that if she had been alone with Elijah she would have already ripped off his Gucci suit and had her wicked way with him. Not the best way to convince the crazily possessive man that she wanted to maintain her independence. She held the dark gaze. "Please, Elijah."

His jaw tightened, but clearly sensing now was not the time to press her, he gave a grudging nod of his head.

"I'll make sure you weren't followed. But I'll return." He sent Levet a warning glare. "Soon."

Valla busied herself making the tea as Elijah turned to leave the apartment, taking with him the frosty disapproval and pulsing power.

She breathed a faint sigh of relief, carrying the tray to the table and taking a seat.

"A little on the possessive side, is he?" the tiny gargoyle asked.

She shrugged, sipping the tea with an odd sense of disorientation.

Something had changed.

She just wasn't sure what.

"He feels responsible for me," she murmured absently.

Levet snorted, reaching for a cookie. "Responsibility isn't the only thing he feels."

Heat stained her cheeks. "Maybe not. He is a male, after all, but—"

"But what?"

Her fingers lifted to trace the scars that marred her cheek.

"After I escaped from the slavers I just wanted to crawl away somewhere and hide." She shivered at the painful memories. "I don't even remember how I made my way to France, but I was floating down the Seine on a rapidly sinking boat when Elijah found me and took me to his lair."

"Ah." His wings fluttered. "Your knight in shining armor."

"Something like that."

"And that's a bad thing?"

She hesitated, trying to put her nagging concern into words.

"Not bad," she at last said. "He's like most clan chiefs."

"Arrogant pain in the *derrière?*"

She gave a sudden laugh. The small demon really was a charming companion.

"I was going to say that he's obsessed with protecting the people he considers it his duty."

"Including you?"

"Elijah sees me as a damsel in distress, not a flesh-and-blood woman." She grimaced. "I don't want to be rescued."

The gray eyes held an unspoken sympathy. "What do you want?"

"What every woman wants." She glanced toward the window overlooking the rose garden drenched in silver moonlight. "To be loved."

Chapter 3

Elijah made a sweep of the dark streets, pausing long enough to warn his lieutenants that the gargoyles were looking for trouble before heading back toward Valla's apartment.

He smiled wryly as his feet followed the familiar route.

If he had any pride, he'd be heading back to his own lair. There were, after all, hundreds of beautiful women who would be eager to indulge his every desire. Hell. He could stop on the nearest street corner and within minutes there would be a dozen females hoping to capture his attention.

But the pride that had once led him to battle the corrupt chief to take command of Paris had been lost the moment he'd discovered a half-dead nymph floating down the Seine.

Even now he could remember the shock of recognition as he'd carried her in his arms to his lair, her golden hair flowing over his arm and her stunning blue eyes dazed. He'd known that he'd been waiting for this woman from the moment he'd awoken as a vampire.

She was his destined mate.

Unfortunately, the aggravating female hadn't been prepared to accept her inevitable fate. And who could blame her?

She'd spent months being raped and tortured by animals before she'd managed to escape. And even then she'd nearly died. If it hadn't been for his healers she would be in her grave.

Was it any wonder she needed to keep the world at a safe distance?

Including him.

So he bided his time, taking what Valla would offer and all the while leashing his hunger by a very thin thread.

A thread that had nearly snapped tonight, he remembered with a stab of white-hot excitement.

The taste of her lips had been even sweeter than he'd fantasized.

As ripe as strawberries with a hint of honey.

And her response . . .

Merde. Her desire had been every bit as eager as his.

If they'd been alone, he'd have taken her against the cabinets.

Instead he was walking the streets, still hard and aching with no immediate hope of relief.

His foul mood wasn't improved as he entered the shadowed courtyard to discover the small gargoyle standing beside the fountain.

"What are you doing out here?" he demanded.

The creature gave a flap of his fairy wings. "Trying to help you."

Elijah arched a brow. He was the most feared predator in France, perhaps in all of Europe. Even Victor, the clan chief of England, approached him with care.

"You imagine you can help me?"

"I may be small, but my powers are mighty."

Elijah couldn't resist. "So mighty that you're hiding in a nymph's apartment?"

Levet shrugged aside the insult, his polished tail playfully stirring the water that pooled at the base of the fountain.

"As you can imagine, I'm not a favorite among my people."

He shrugged. "But soon enough I will be reinstated into the Gargoyle Guild."

"Hmm." It couldn't be too soon for Elijah. Not that he was jealous of the gargoyle, he hurriedly assured himself. Of course he wasn't. Not even if Valla had shared her all-too-rare smile with the tiny demon. A smile she never shared with anyone but him. "And how do you propose to help me?"

"Beyond being a formidable warrior, I am also a favorite among females."

Elijah rolled his eyes. "What you are is delusional."

"Mock if you wish, but I can tell you that you have been a fool not to tell Valla how you feel."

Elijah stiffened in shock. Every demon in Paris might know that he was panting after the elusive, beautiful nymph like a werewolf in heat, but not a damned one of them would have the balls to mention it.

Certainly not to his face.

"That is none of your business," he said between clenched fangs.

"No, but I believe that Valla has earned a chance to be happy."

His brows jerked together. "I have every intention of making her happy."

Levet gave a lift of his hands. "Not unless you convince her that you don't consider her a burden."

"A burden?" Elijah cast a brief glance toward the nearby door to Valla's apartment, making sure she couldn't overhear the bizarre conversation. "What the *diable* are you talking about?"

"She fears that you consider her to be just another responsibility that you must bear."

Responsibility?

He'd all but gone on his knees to beg for a place in her life. Hadn't he?

With a strange lack of his usual grace, he walked toward

a window that offered a glimpse of Valla straightening the pillows on her froufrou couch.

As always he was struck by the stunning beauty of her golden hair that haloed her delicate features and the wide, guileless blue eyes. And that lush body . . . *mon dieu*, he'd spent endless hours imagining the feel of those curves beneath him.

But at the same time he couldn't deny a fierce urge to protect her.

She was so fragile. So exquisitely vulnerable.

Had she mistaken his instinctive need to keep his mate from any possible harm with a sense of duty?

"That's—" He gave a frustrated shake of his head. "How can she be so foolish?"

The gargoyle joined him near the window. "Have you given her reason to think she means more?"

Of course not, he wryly conceded. He was a male. He didn't talk about his feelings. She was simply supposed to know what was in his heart.

"I need to speak with her," he muttered, sending his companion a warning frown. "Alone."

"Naturellement."

Chapter 4

Waiting until the vampire had disappeared into the apartment, Levet squared his shoulders and marched out of the courtyard.

Bien. No more Monsieur Nice Guy.

He'd been caught off-guard by his sister and cousin.

Now that he was fully prepared, he wouldn't be halted from his goal.

He had his courage firmly intact.

Oh, and he'd managed to "borrow" a disguise amulet he'd seen laying on Valla's counter when she'd been busy making tea.

The tiny bit of gold was now hung around his neck by a leather string and would make him invisible to all but the most powerful witches.

This time, no one would sense he was coming.

Puffing out his chest, and spreading his wings, Levet took to the air, soaring over the city as he headed toward the Latin Quarter.

It was . . . stunning.

Even after he'd traveled around the world and seen some of the most spectacular sights to be found, there was nothing quite so beautiful as Paris at night.

At last reaching his destination, Levet carefully landed on the shadowed street, studying the Gothic church that was situated only a few blocks from the Seine.

Constructed in the sixth century on the site where a hermit had lived and prayed, the Church of Saint-Séverin was built in the shape of a long, narrow hall. It had a tower, along with ornately topped pillars and pointed, Romanesque arches for windows and doors.

Tourists came to admire the Gothic architecture and to stroll through the gardens, or even to enjoy the Greek restaurant just down the street. But the *pièce de résistance* was the gargoyles who had stood guard for centuries.

During the daylight hours all gargoyles turned to stone. Unlike Levet, however, most were capable of altering their shape which meant that even the largest demon could shrink down to fit on the side of a building. What better place to hide from the humans than in plain sight?

At night they came out to play.

And pillage and plunder and create all-around mayhem among the demon world.

Usually they left the humans alone. . . .

Usually.

Realizing that he was delaying the inevitable, Levet squared his shoulders and headed into the church. He didn't pause to admire the peaceful beauty of the nave, instead he headed directly toward the bay door that opened into the garden that had once been a graveyard.

He was here with a purpose. Why the purpose had suddenly become so important . . .

He gave a sharp shake of his head.

Bah, that was a question for later.

Bypassing the long galleries that had been reconstructed to their medieval glory, he headed toward the very back of the garden. At last reaching the spot he was searching for, he sucked in a deep, steadying breath.

Only when he was mentally prepared did he step through the illusion that hid the ancient stone building.

Levet grimaced. Home, sweet home.

Waddling up the stairs that led to the door, he felt a familiar sense of bleak yearning tug at his heart, swiftly followed by a bitter sense of betrayal.

There were no happy memories to ease his return. No sense of comfort.

His childhood had been a miserable fight for survival among his brutal siblings. Oh, and the last time he'd seen his mother, she'd tried to kill him.

Hardly the ingredients for a happy family reunion.

Reaching the door, he wasn't surprised to find it unlocked. What demon would be stupid enough to enter the lair of the doyenne of the gargoyle nest?

He stepped into the large room with a lofted, cathedral ceiling and plenty of room for a gargoyle to spread her wings. The floors were made of hardwood and deeply gouged by his mother's five-inch claws. And high above were wide windows that offered a view of the night sky.

The rest of the interior was something out of an *Arabian Nights* nightmare.

Crimson painted walls, gold and black silk pillows piled in the middle of the floor with a large *hookah* set beside them.

Levet had never been sure if his mother's fantasy was to be the sheikh or the harem girl.

And not knowing was the only thing that kept him out of therapy.

"So it's true," a female voice boomed through the air, the floor shuddering beneath the weight of the approaching gargoyle. "The prodigal son returns."

Levet froze. He would not run. He would not run. He would not run.

Reaching up, he tugged off the amulet that had obviously

been deactivated by the spells of protection that surrounded the lair.

His mother was nothing if not thorough.

And cruel.

Excessively, spectacularly cruel.

The thought whispered through his mind as his gaze skimmed up the stout legs that were heavily muscled and covered by a reptilian gray skin. A long, surprisingly thin tail curled around the feet tipped with claws. His gaze lifted to his dear old *maman's* hefty body, which had grown even wider since Levet had last seen her, with wide leathery wings that spread in a ten-foot span from her back. Up ever higher, Berthe's face was a perfect example of gargoyle beauty.

A short, thick snout. Small gray eyes that peered at the world from beneath a heavy brow. Two fangs that were big enough to be called tusks curved from her upper gums to reach her pointed chin. And on top of her broad head she had two sharp horns that were polished to gleam in the candle-light.

Levet forced a stiff smile to his lips. "*Bonsoir, Maman.* You are looking . . ." He allowed his gaze to shift back down to her wide girth. "Well fed."

Berthe shrugged. Unlike most females, gargoyles had no issues with weight.

Their philosophy was the bigger the better.

"Gregor proved to be a disappointment so I had him basted in a lovely rosemary and garlic sauce and roasted over an open fire," she said with a light French accent. "He was far more satisfying as dinner than he ever was as a lover."

"Charming." Levet ignored his mother's jaundiced glare at his pretty, fairy wings. "Did you eat my father as well?"

"Do not be disgusting," the female growled. "I am not a cannibal."

Levet kept his expression guarded. Gargoyles were like most demons. They were willing to take lovers from many different species, although they usually chose a gargoyle when they were in heat.

Halflings weren't unheard of, but they were rare.

The fact that his mother had always refused to name his father had made Levet assume his parentage was yet another source of shame to the family.

"So my father was a gargoyle?"

Berthe snorted, thankfully unaware of how much the information meant to her son.

If she knew it could be a weapon to hurt him with, she wouldn't hesitate to use it.

"What sort of question is that?"

"A rather obvious one, I would think." Levet spread his stunted arms. "Just look at me."

Berthe narrowed her eyes to beady slits. "Your father was a fearsome warrior who sired many sons who brought him nothing but pride."

Levet's tail twitched. He didn't know if he was pleased or disappointed by the information.

He was demon enough to take pride in the thought that his father was admired among gargoyles. Bloodlines were always important.

But for centuries he'd blamed his lack of gargoyleness on his father.

Now who was he supposed to hold responsible?

"So what happened to me?" he demanded.

Berthe curled her snout in blatant disdain. "A freak of nature."

Levet grimly pretended her words didn't cut. "Or perhaps your bloodlines are not as pure as you thought?"

A hint of smoke drifted from a flared nostril. Berthe was one of the rare gargoyles who could breathe fire. Which, of course, explained her position as doyenne.

"More likely a curse from the gods," she countered, hate glinting her gray eyes. A hate that had been more destructive to Levet as a child than any of the vicious beatings. "I was warned to have your head removed the minute you were born." She gave a flap of her enormous wings, nearly sending Levet tumbling backward. "Unfortunately I was too tender-hearted to follow the wise advice."

Levet gave a snort, refusing to acknowledge the age-old sense of betrayal.

"Tenderhearted?"

"Oui." Berthe moved to settle her bulk on the satin pillows, her wings draped over the floor and her tail swishing around her feet. She portrayed the image of languid indifference, but Levet wasn't fooled. She might look like a lumbering brute, but she could move with the speed of a striking viper. "I allowed you to survive with the hope that you would overcome your disfigurements and grow into a prince worthy of standing at my side. You should be grateful."

Grateful.

The word echoed through Levet, abruptly altering the pain he'd sworn he'd never feel again to a rush of fury.

"Grateful for what? I spent my childhood being brutalized by my siblings."

His mother shrugged. "Did you expect to be coddled like a human baby?"

He ignored her taunt. "And when I at last left the nursery I became the target of every gargoyle who thought it was amusing to toss me into the fighting pits and see how many demons could beat the heebie-jeebies out of me before I passed out," he hissed.

Berthe furrowed her brow in confusion. "The . . ." She made a sound of impatience. "Oh, la la. It is bejesus, you ridiculous pest."

Levet waved off her sharp words. "You did nothing to protect me."

"Only the strong survive in our world."

Levet planted his fists on his hips. "Is that your excuse for trying to kill me when I hit puberty?"

She trailed a claw over a scarlet pillow, her expression devoid of regret.

"It was obvious you were permanently deformed. It was my duty to rid the nest of such a blatant weakness. Every doyenne understands the necessity of pruning the deadwood from the family tree."

Enough.

He hadn't come here to resolve his childhood trauma. He might be immortal, but not even an eternity would be enough time to work through his mommy issues.

It was time to get down to business.

"So what if I was to prove that I am more than deadwood?" he challenged her. "That I am a prince in the truest sense of the word?"

"Impossible."

Having expected scorn, Levet wasn't prepared for the sudden unease that rippled over his mother's ugly features. As if she was afraid of what he might say.

And he most certainly wasn't prepared for the lethal flames that she burped in his direction.

"Sacrebleu," he cried, diving behind his mother's favorite Moroccan chest. She would never fry the camel leather inset with enough precious gems to rival the crown jewels. "What are you doing?"

She was on her feet, her tail quivering with an unreasonable fury.

"Finishing what I began when you were young."

Levet hunkered behind the chest.

Merde. This could be going better.

It was time to pull out his only weapon.

"I demand a tribunal," he said in shaky tones.

A tribunal was the gargoyle equivalent of *People's Court*. Or a pirate's parlay.

"Denied." Another belch of fire, nearly singeing the tips of his stunted horns.

Levet tucked his wings tight against his shivering body. Had he once said that vampires were the most unreasonable creatures to walk the earth?

He clearly owed Viper and Styx and all the rest of the bloodsuckers an apology.

Not that they would ever hear it from his lips.

He did have his pride.

Even if it was a little scorched.

"You cannot deny me," he said, as the fire died. "I am a pure-blooded gargoyle despite my . . . deformities."

"I shunned you."

Levet was prepared.

"Ah, but I am a prince." He peeked around the corner, meeting his mother's infuriated glare. "Those of royal blood can demand a hearing regardless of their sentence."

Berthe was forced to hesitate.

Gargoyles might be savages in many ways, but the Guild was ruled by a strict code of laws.

There was a long silence as his mother ground her teeth, smoke still curling from her nostril. Then, her eyes narrowed with a cunning satisfaction.

"The elders are not in Paris. There can be no tribunal without them."

Levet made a sound of disgust. How many demons had stood shoulder to shoulder to battle the Dark Lord while the gargoyles had been MIA?

"You mean the cowards are still in hiding?"

Berthe stomped a massive foot, making the entire building shake.

"They don't answer to you."

"Bon." Cautiously Levet moved from behind the chest. He didn't want to become a charred briquette, but then again he was tired of cowering. He was now a bona fide hero.

Wasn't he? Straightening his spine, he tilted his chin to meet his mother's glare. "Then you will stand as judge."

There was a low hiss as his mother snapped her wings to their full width. An impressive sight meant to intimidate.

"This is a trick."

"No trick," Levet denied. "You are doyenne. It is within your powers to pass judgment."

"I did," she growled. "You were banished."

"I was banished without a fair hearing."

"Because you fled like a spineless Guttar demon."

Levet waved his hands at the absurd accusation. "You were trying to kill me."

His mother curled back her lips to fully expose her tusks. "And now I shall finish what I began."

"Non."

Without giving himself time to think, Levet held up his hands and released a blast of magic.

It wasn't that he didn't trust his skill . . . *non*. That was not true.

He *did* doubt his skill.

For all his bluster, he could never be certain what his magic would do.

One day it might be nothing more than an embarrassing fizzle.

The next it would explode out of him with the force of a nuclear blast.

Tonight, however, it did exactly what he desired.

Shimmering strands of magic flew from the tips of his claws, slamming into his mother with enough force to pin her to the wall.

It was . . . a miracle.

Clearly as astonished as Levet that his spell was working, Berthe struggled against the delicate filaments that were holding her captive.

"What have you done?" she screeched.

Levet took a bouncing step forward, regarding the spiderweb of magic with a smile.

"I tried to tell you that I have grown into a warrior with batty skills. Hmm . . . or is it mad skills?"

The powerful gargoyle tried to breathe fire, only to discover the bonds holding her also suppressed her magic.

Yeah. Go, Levet.

"Release me," Berthe snarled.

"Not until you've given me my hearing."

The gray eyes smoldered with the promise of death. "You will pay for this."

"Really?" Levet breathed an exaggerated sigh, feeling all cocky with his mother incapacitated. Hey, who knew how long it would last? He had to take pleasure where he could find it. "Gargoyles are tediously repetitive in their threats. You really should consider hiring a vampire to write you new material. They are the experts in terrifying their enemies."

"You would, of course, admire your new masters," Berthe spit out. "To think my own son has become the flunky of the leeches. It's enough to break a mother's heart."

"A flunky? I am servant to no demon." Levet puffed out his chest. "Indeed, I am revered as a legend of heroic proportions."

"Your proportions are an embarrassment," his mother mocked. "Just as you have always been."

He strutted forward, refusing to acknowledge the words hit a perpetually tender nerve.

He was no longer the old Levet who allowed himself to be judged by the size of his body. He was a giant among demons, regardless of his height.

He lifted his hands. "We shall see."

"What are you doing?" Unease twisted her ugly features. "Stay back."

"Frightened of your pathetic, spineless son, *Maman?*"

"I am weary of this game."

He gave a flutter of his wings, proud when they captured the light to glitter with brilliant shimmers of crimson and gold.

"Then put an end to it."

She pressed against the wall, her eyes wide as Levet halted directly in front of her.

Why?

Was she truly afraid of his dubious magic?

That seemed . . . unlikely.

It had to be something else.

But what?

His churning thoughts were brought to a sharp end as his mother glared down from her towering height.

"Stop this, Levet."

He froze, his stomach knotting in pain. *"Mon dieu."*

"What?"

"That is the first time I ever heard my name on your lips."

She belched, attempting to hide her concern behind the more familiar disdain.

"You aren't going to snivel, are you? I would rather you kill me than be forced to listen to you blubber."

Levet shook his head, thinking of the vampire clan that had adopted the Dark Lord's offspring without hesitation. They had fought to the death to protect the babies and would do so again.

And the gods knew that Salvatore, the King of Weres, was foaming at the mouth with excitement as the delivery day for his litter drew ever nearer.

Of course, Kiviet demons ate all but the strongest of their offspring at birth, so it could always be worse.

"Tell me, *Maman*, do you love any of your children?"

"Love is for weaklings," she sneered. "Or humans."

It was precisely what Levet had expected. And yet . . .

He swallowed a resigned sigh.

"Then why procreate at all?"

"To strengthen my power base."

He studied the creature who'd given birth to him for a long minute. For the first time he wasn't overwhelmed by her ginormous power. Or cringing beneath the crushing disapproval of his lack of mass.

She was still huge. Still scary. And still filled with hatred toward him.

But seeing her clearly, she appeared . . . diminished.

"You know, I thought I hated you," he said slowly. "Now I realize that I pity you."

His mother gave a genuine huff, as if outraged by his words. "I am the doyenne of this nest," she hissed. "The most feared gargoyle in all of Europe."

"Non." Levet gave a shake of his head. "You are a lonely, bitter old woman who has nothing but an empty title and the delusion that it makes you important."

Fury flared through her eyes before the cunning expression made a return. "If you care nothing for me then why are you here?"

"Chasing shadows, it would seem."

"Then release me."

Levet rolled his eyes. "Nice try."

"I will give you a ten-minute head start before I track you down and kill you."

"Tempting, but . . . I think not."

"Very well." Her lips stretched into a tight line. Was that supposed to be a smile? *Sacrebleu.* "I'll give you an hour."

Levet considered. Really and truly considered. Perhaps for the first time in his long life.

What did he want?

Clearly he would never earn his mother's approval. Or repair the wounds of the past. Or find . . . what did the humans call it? Closure.

But he could have something that had been stolen from him.

"I want what is rightfully mine," he stated in clear, dignified tones.

The gray eyes narrowed. "An empty title?"

"Of course not," Levet said in confusion. Only females were allowed to inherit the place of doyenne. "Claudine is your heir."

"But you could be a prince."

Once, he would have given anything to reclaim his royal title. Now he gave a shrug of indifference.

"Not if I'm dead."

Berthe silently weighed her options, her crafty brain searching for a way to convince him to release her from his spell without actually having to offer something of value in return.

"We could perhaps negotiate a truce," she grudgingly conceded.

Levet folded his arms over his chest. "The only thing I desire to have is my place restored among the Guild."

Berthe made a choked sound, genuinely shocked by his demand.

"Don't be an idiot. They would never accept you."

"They will once you add my name to the Wall."

The Wall of Memories was hidden beneath the sewers of Paris. Who had built it or why it was located in the sewers had been lost in the mists of time, but a gargoyle's name magically appeared there when they were born, officially giving them their place in the Guild. The same magic wiped out their names when they died.

Or, like him, were stripped of their place within the Guild.

It was rare, but a doyenne or elder could return a name to the Wall.

"Never," she rasped.

Levet squared his shoulders. "Oh, make no mistake. You will personally inscribe the letters."

"You cannot compel me to write your name," his mother blustered. "It must be done willingly."

"I am aware of how it works."

She pressed against the wall, her expression wary as Levet raised his hands.

"Then how do you intend to force me to return you to the Guild?"

Levet squashed the unworthy sense of pleasure at having power over his mother.

This was not supposed to be revenge.

It was justice.

"Allow me to show you," he murmured, sending his memories of his battle with the Dark Lord directly into her brain.

Her claws dug into the floor, her skin fading to a sickly shade of ash.

"Sacrebleu."

Chapter 5

Valla had finished washing the tea plates and was wiping down the counter when she noticed the elegant Waterford crystal dish was empty.

"Oh, damn," she breathed just as a prickle of awareness feathered over her skin.

How was it possible that the icy brush of Elijah's power could send a rush of searing heat through her?

It was like explaining how photons could be in two places at the same time. A mystery.

"Valla." With a speed that continued to astonish her, Elijah was standing at her side, his presence a sexy, tangible force that wrapped around her. "What is it?"

She fiercely tried to control the leap of her heart and the quiver of excitement that clenched her stomach. A vampire could sense arousal at a hundred paces.

"Where is Levet?"

Elijah tilted back his head, allowing his senses to flow through the neighborhood.

"He's gone."

"And so is my amulet."

A frown marred the strikingly beautiful face. "You lost it, or it was stolen?"

"Not stolen . . . borrowed," she corrected him. "Or at least that's my guess."

The vampire wasn't impressed; his dark eyes filled with fury.

"If the gargoyle is a thief, I'll track him down. I promise he won't be returning."

She swallowed a sigh. A part of her would always appreciate Elijah's fierce desire to protect her. But she was tired of waiting for him to see her as a grown woman who was more than capable of taking care of herself.

She'd been doing it for a very long time.

"I want him to return."

"Que?" the vampire demanded with obvious impatience. "He already stole your amulet—who knows what he might steal next?"

"I don't care about the amulet." She chewed her bottom lip. "I'm concerned about Levet's reason for taking it."

Elijah shrugged. "He could pawn it for a small fortune. Lesser demons often use thievery to support themselves."

"Stop being such a snob," she chided, absently twirling a golden curl around her finger. It was a habit she'd acquired when she was just a young girl, still innocently believing that she would find her Prince Charming and settle down to raise a dozen little blue-eyed nymphs. The habit was the only thing left of that silly, idealistic little girl. "Levet came to Paris for a purpose. I have a feeling that he hoped the amulet would assist him in his goal."

He gently reached to tug the curl from her finger and smoothed it behind her ear.

"If you don't care about the amulet being stolen, then why are you troubled?"

"I'm worried that Levet will be hurt," she murmured, resisting the urge to stroke her cheek against his hand. Like a cat demanding to be petted. "When I found him near the tower he was being attacked by two large gargoyles who clearly didn't like him."

The temperature dropped until Valla would swear she could see her breath.

"Mère de dieu," Elijah growled, his fingers cupping her chin in a grip that forced her to meet his dark glare. "You weren't stupid enough to interfere, were you?"

Her muscles clenched, her eyes slowly narrowing. There might have even been a bit of steam escaping from her ears.

"Stupid?"

He missed the edge of danger in her voice. The clan chief might be a cunning, lethal predator who ruled most of France with a brutal force, but he was still a man.

Clueless.

"Valla, pure-blood gargoyles are not only one of the most dangerous demons to walk the earth, but they're ruthless, amoral, and happy to slaughter the innocent."

"I'm not a complete idiot, Elijah," she said, pronouncing the words with a slow, deliberate enunciation. "I know that gargoyles are dangerous."

His jaw knotted, as if battling against the urge to toss her over his shoulder and haul her to the protection of his lair.

Predictable.

He wasn't going to be happy until he had her locked away so he wouldn't have to worry about her.

"Then why would you put yourself at risk?"

"I saw a creature in need so I did what I thought was necessary." She met his burning gaze without flinching. "Besides, I was never at risk. I fired a few arrows from the bushes."

"You think a bush would have protected you from gargoyles?"

She knocked away his hand, annoyed that even when she was furious with this vampire she still longed for his touch.

"This conversation is over."

"Valla . . ."

"No." She pointed a finger into his obscenely handsome face. "I'm not a child that needs to be told what I can or can't do."

The chill remained, but it was no longer edged with anger.

Instead, a far more dangerous emotion swirled through the air as he studied her with an unwavering focus that made her heart slam against her ribs.

"Believe me, I have never mistaken you for a child."

Her lips parted to point out the numerous occasions he'd tried to coddle her, but the words went unspoken as he grasped her face in a firm grip and kissed her.

Or more precisely, he devoured her.

Her hands lifted to grasp his forearms as his tongue slipped between her lips, tangling with hers as he maneuvered her until her backside pressed against the counter.

He tasted of raw male power and opulent sensuality. A taste that was swiftly becoming her addiction.

A groan was torn from her throat as his thickening arousal pressed against her lower stomach, his fangs fully extended. Heat pooled in the pit of her stomach, spreading through her body.

Oh . . . crap, she was melting.

And it was the most wondrous thing she'd ever felt.

Easing his kiss, Elijah stroked his lips over her flushed cheek and then down the length of her neck, finding a sensitive hollow just below her collarbone.

Lightning zigzagged through her, setting her blood on fire with a need she'd never even dreamed possible.

When she was young she'd thought passion was a sweet, giddy emotion. She'd certainly felt it often enough among the nymph males who were renowned for their beauty. Then, she'd been captured by the slavers, and desire had become dark and ugly and terrifying.

Something to be avoided at all cost.

But now . . .

Now this vampire was revealing that physical need could be thrilling and consuming and so intense that she was shaking from the power of the sensations pulsing through her.

"Elijah," she croaked.

"Hmm."

"What are you doing?"

He chuckled, his hands skimming down her back before slipping beneath her shirt to tease the tense muscles of her stomach.

"Proving I do not see you as a child."

"But . . ." She forgot how to speak as his hands skimmed up to cup her bare breasts. Nymphs never needed to wear bras. "Oh."

He pressed his lips directly to her ear. "Do you like that?"

Like?

Her breath left her in a rush as his fingers teased the tips of her nipples to stiff peaks. Her toes curled in her shoes and her fingernails dug through the expensive silk of his shirt.

Dear god. It was nothing short of paradise.

"I can't think," she breathed.

"*Bon.*" His lips nuzzled up her throat and along the line of her jaw. "Just feel, *mon ange.*"

That was the problem. She was feeling too much.

The exquisite brush of his fingers over her sensitive breasts. The tantalizing press of his erection against her lower stomach. The silken glide of his tongue over her lips.

It was overwhelming.

She shivered. "This is madness."

"The most delicious madness," he murmured, kissing a path toward the side of her face she always kept turned.

Immediately she was jerked out of her sensual haze, a sharp-edged panic making her shove her hands against his chest.

"Don't."

Elijah stilled, seemingly caught off-guard by her reaction. Then slowly he lifted his head.

"Valla, look at me," he commanded softly.

"I can't."

"Do you trust me?"

It was a ridiculous question.

They both knew that he was the one and only person in the entire world that she trusted.

Still, she knew that her answer was important.

"Yes."

"Then look at me," he urged.

It took a long minute to gather her courage. Then, with a frustrated sigh, she tilted back her head to discover him regarding her with a somber expression.

"Happy?"

His hands shifted to stroke her neck lightly. It was a gesture of reassurance from a vampire.

"Tell me what you see."

"Fishing for compliments?" she tried to tease.

"I want you to look into my eyes."

"Why?"

"Because I want you to see what I see."

She found herself peering into the dark, velvety depths of his eyes. Not because he commanded it. She no longer took orders from anyone. Especially not from an arrogant, sexy, overly possessive vampire.

But because she truly needed to know what he saw when he looked at her.

A pathetic victim in need of his constant care?

A scarred nymph he pitied?

Or Valla. A woman who he desired?

"What do you see?" she whispered.

"A strong, beautiful survivor," he said, his voice low and hypnotic. Not vampire-mind-control hypnotic. Just deeply compelling. "A woman who could so easily have broken, but instead fought to reclaim her life." He paused, his gaze deliberately moving to study the silvery scars. "I admire you more than you will ever know."

Her hand instinctively lifted to touch her ruined face. "These . . ." He captured her hand, pulling her fingers to his lips. "Are a testament to your courage."

She shuddered, unconsciously pressing closer to Elijah's hard body.

"I hate them."

"Because they mar your face?"

She shook her head. "Because they remind me . . ."

"Valla?" he gently prompted when her words faded.

"Of the men who hurt me."

"But they didn't cause these scars." Before she could stop him, Elijah bent his head to trace the raised ridges with his mouth. "They came from your escape," he murmured against her sensitive skin. "They're a badge of honor, *mon ange*. Wear them with pride."

She held herself rigid, but she didn't pull away. Odd. She'd never allowed anyone to touch her face.

"Easy for you to say," she muttered, more for something to say than to chastise him.

His reaction was . . . epic.

"Easy?" The icy power returned, this time shattering her crystal bowl as he yanked his head back to reveal a lethal power glowing in the dark eyes. His features seemed sharper, as if the ivory skin had been pulled tighter over his elegant bones and his fangs shimmered with a dazzling white. This wasn't the charming Elijah who could kiss a woman into bone-melting surrender. This was the vampire who'd claimed Paris from a clan chief who'd ruled this territory for over a thousand years. "Do you think that I haven't been tormented by the knowledge of what you endured?" he rasped, a vase on the table exploding. "Do you think I wouldn't give everything I possess to turn back the clock and protect you from the nightmare?"

She licked her dry lips. "Elijah."

"Do you think I haven't had every one of those bastards tracked down and eliminated?"

She blinked at the stark confession. What did she do with that?

A better woman would no doubt be horrified.

She knew Elijah well enough to realize that his means of elimination would be a slow, appallingly painful death.

But the knowledge that the bastards that had tortured her for so long were dead . . . and that they'd suffered . . . well, she didn't feel at all horrified.

She felt liberated.

"You did that for me?" she asked, her voice hoarse.

"Those I could find." A grim smile touched his lips. "I discovered that Viper, the clan chief of Chicago, had most of them wiped out after he found his mate at one of the auctions. I had to be content with only a handful of trolls and a half-breed ogre."

She managed a faint smile at the edge of annoyance in his voice. He wasn't pleased his thirst for revenge had been cheated by a fellow clan chief.

"I don't know what to say," she said so softly only a vampire could have caught the words.

He leaned down until they were nose to nose, his power losing its icy edge to stroke over her skin in a soft caress.

"Say that you are as happy as I am that you survived," he murmured.

"Of course I'm happy."

"Then rejoice in the evidence of your escape." He pressed his lips to her scars. "I do."

Elijah had had the best intentions when he'd come into the apartment.

He'd planned to corner Valla and convince her that he

didn't have a savior complex or whatever other lame excuse she'd invented to keep a barrier between them.

Then he was going to reveal what he'd known from the moment he'd scooped her out of the Seine.

She was his mate.

And he would spend the rest of eternity, if necessary, convincing her that they belonged together.

But he'd been distracted by her concern for the pesky gargoyle. And more delectably distracted when he'd been goaded into kissing her.

Now he was determined to prove that the scars that marked her face only added to her beauty.

And if words couldn't do it, then he was willing to use more direct methods.

Like a return to the delectable kissing . . .

That seemed a good place to start.

Pressing his lips against the jagged patch of skin that had been ruined by a spell meant to kill her, he savored the heat and tantalizing scent that had haunted his dreams for far too long.

She stiffened, but didn't pull away, her breathing shallow as he continued to caress the physical proof of her survival. He took his time, trailing his lips over the delicate shell of her ear before returning to her cheek.

It wasn't until her rigid muscles slowly began to loosen that he allowed his exploration to expand to include the line of her stubborn jaw and the enticing length of her neck. He shuddered, his hands slipping beneath her shirt to cup the lush abundance of her breasts.

Mère de dieu, he loved the feel of her softness in his hands.

He was going to love the feel of her breasts in his mouth even more, he decided, tugging the top higher as he dipped his head down to capture the tip of her nipple between his teeth, taking care not to break the fragile skin with his fangs.

He might be ready and eager to complete their mating, but

he wasn't going to risk creating a bond she wasn't prepared to accept.

She'd had too many things forced on her over the years.

Wrapping his arms around her slender waist as she shivered in pleasure, Elijah teased her tender nipple with his tongue. They groaned in unison.

The taste of her was succulent. As sweet as fresh peaches. And her scent . . .

His cock threatened to explode as her arousal spiced the air.

He wanted to strip off her clothes and take her against the counter.

Or maybe he would lay her across the dining table and feast on her for the next century.

Of course, she might prefer the comfort of her bed, he silently acknowledged as he turned his head to capture her other nipple between his lips.

A soft mattress. Moonlight spilling over her luscious body as he settled between her legs and thrust deep inside her. A locked door to keep out unwelcome intruders.

Oui. The bedroom was swiftly becoming the preferable option.

Lifting his head, he claimed her lips in a kiss that was slow and deep, demanding everything she had to offer. At the same time his fingers threaded in the satin softness of her golden hair.

There was no hurry, he reminded his aching erection. This wasn't sex.

It was making love in the finest sense.

Her hands drifted up to clutch his shoulders, as if her knees had suddenly gone weak. But even as he was congratulating himself on her sweet capitulation, she was pulling back to suck in an unsteady breath.

"Wait."

With a low growl, he pulled her back so he could bury his face in the curve of her neck.

"I have waited too long, *mon ange*."

She shivered, but despite her obvious arousal she didn't melt beneath his irresistible touch.

Stubborn female.

"I'm worried about Levet."

"Don't be." He lightly ran his fang along the low neckline of her top, chuckling as she gave a strangled groan. "He can take care of himself."

"You don't know that."

"I know that no one interferes in Guild business." He licked the racing pulse just below her jaw. "Not unless they want to end up dead."

Her hands pressed against his chest. "You're not scared of the gargoyles, are you?"

"A challenge, *mon ange?*"

"A simple question."

He reluctantly lifted his head to study her flushed face with a resigned amusement.

She wasn't going to let this go.

Which meant there was no comfortable mattress or lush female curves in his immediate future.

Not until he'd convinced her to forget Levet.

Something he sensed was going to be easier said than done.

"Paris belongs to me, but I have no desire to start an unnecessary turf war with the gargoyles," he explained in gentle tones, his gaze absorbing the spectacular beauty of her passion-flushed face surrounded by a mane of golden curls. It was the soft blue eyes, however, that pierced his unbeating heart. She'd been to hell and back, but there was an innate purity in her that could never be diminished. Was it any wonder his jaded soul was so fascinated? "Enough blood was shed when I became clan chief."

She blinked in surprise. He rarely shared his world as clan chief. Why burden her with the darker side of his position?

"You mean when you battled to take the place of the former leader?"

"*Oui*, and then for the next several decades after claiming Paris."

She paled. "Decades?"

He grimaced. During those dark days he'd often wondered if he would survive from one night to the next.

"It's traditional for each demon species to try and kill the new leader of vampires."

"Why?"

"In part because they enjoy any excuse to try and kill a vampire, but more importantly to make sure a chief is strong enough to keep control of his territory," he explained. "A weak chief is an invitation for constant upheaval, not only among his clan, but from outside threats. Peace comes from strength."

"And now?"

He arched a brow, belatedly sensing the tension that hummed through her body.

"Now?"

"Are you safe?"

"A clan chief is always a target," he admitted, unable to resist outlining her lips with the tip of his finger. "Either from an ambitious vampire who wants to challenge me for my position, or from any number of demons who I've pissed off over the centuries."

"Not hard to believe," she muttered, although the words didn't disguise the concern that darkened her eyes.

"Most are convinced the world would be greatly improved if they could remove my head from my body."

With a gasp, she pressed her hand against his lips, her expression troubled.

"Don't say that."

A fierce satisfaction cascaded through his body at her plea. Gently, he pried her fingers from his lips.

"Careful, Valla," he teased. "Or I might think you care."

"Of course I care," she said without hesitation. "I don't want you hurt."

He pressed a kiss to her palm, his thumb stroking her inner wrist.

"Then you at last understand why I'm so anxious to protect you."

She thinned her lips as he neatly turned the tables on her. "Maybe. But—"

Hmm. Perhaps he hadn't turned any tables. Neatly or otherwise.

"I don't think I'm going to like this."

She pulled her hand free to touch his face, the light caress sending jagged bolts of arousal through his body.

He could count the number of times she'd ever purposefully touched him. And never with such a lingering intimacy.

"It terrifies me to know your position makes you a constant target," she whispered.

He held her worried gaze. "It's my duty."

"Yes," she agreed with a nod. "And while I hate the thought that you're in danger, I would never try to stand in your way."

The direct hit came without warning, leaving Elijah gaping at her in bemusement.

Hoisted by his own petard, he wryly acknowledged, recalling how often he'd tried to prevent her from even leaving her apartment without him at her side.

At the time, he'd thought he was revealing just how much he cared for her. Now . . .

"Is that what you think I'm trying to do?"

Her fingers drifted to brush over his lips, her expression somber.

"A partner should make you stronger, not weaker."

She was right. Of course she was.

As much as he might hate to admit it, his rabid need to

protect her was more about his constant knowledge of how close she had come to dying before they'd ever met, than keeping her happy.

Selfish even by his standards.

"Oh . . . *merde*," he growled in resignation.

She eyed him warily as he stepped back to tug her shirt into place, his entire body screaming in frustration at the realization he wasn't going to get relief any time soon.

"Elijah?"

He grabbed her hand, pulling her toward the door. "Let's go find that annoying gargoyle."

Chapter 6

Levet quivered as he continued to project his memories into his mother's unwilling mind, dangerously close to exhaustion.

Sacrebleu. How much longer could he hold the spell?

The fear had barely had time to form when Berthe gave a low groan, her eyes wrenching open to stab him with a malevolent glare.

"Enough."

Levet halted the memories, but retained control of the magical web that held his mother captive.

She wasn't looking nearly as impressed as he'd hoped.

"You have seen what I did?" he demanded.

"Oui."

"And you acknowledge that I faced my enemy with courage?"

She pulled back her lips to emphasize her massive tusks. "I will admit you did not flee like a coward."

Levet narrowed his eyes. "Perhaps we should begin again."

"Non," Berthe rasped, the heat of her fury filling the air. "You behaved with . . . courage."

Levet scowled. He had stood before the most evil creature ever to have been created and refused to yield.

How many demons could claim such a feat?

None. That was how many.

He grimaced. *Non.* That wasn't entirely true. There had been others. But no gargoyles, he hastily reassured himself.

He alone had represented his species.

Which made him excessively special.

"Why is it so hard for you to admit?" he snapped.

Berthe glowered at him, her heavy brow furrowed. "I don't want you back in the Guild."

Levet blinked. Well, that was . . . blunt.

"Why? Do you imagine I will somehow contaminate your precious nest?" He curled his snout in disdain. "I can assure you I have no intention of returning to the bosom of my dysfunctional family."

She made a sound of shock, as if she couldn't imagine a creature not longing to be a part of her nest.

"Then why do you insist on being returned to the Guild?"

Levet smiled. When he'd traveled to Paris he hadn't truly known what was driving him.

Now he understood with perfect clarity.

"It's my right," he said with simple honesty. "Now tell me why you're so reluctant to put my name on the Wall."

Berthe clenched her jaw, clearly loath to confess the truth. Then, perhaps sensing that Levet was stubborn enough to keep her trapped until she shared, she gave a low curse.

"Because you make me . . . less."

"Less what?"

She turned her head, as if unwilling to meet Levet's puzzled gaze.

"While you are shunned you are forgotten by my people. But with your name returned to the Wall it will be remembered that you are my son. I will be ridiculed for producing a—"

"A what?" he prompted, his curiosity overcoming his self-preservation.

A common occurrence.

"A freak," she said with a shudder.

He flinched, feeling like he'd been slapped.

But why?

His mother had devoted his entire childhood to pointing out his numerous flaws. Until he'd nearly allowed her to convince him that he was deformed.

No more.

"I do not make you less, *Maman* dearest. You were born without a soul," he informed her, his voice clear and perfectly steady. "And I thank the gods that I am different from you. My life has mattered. Truly mattered. You will never be able to say the same."

Berthe blinked, almost as if his words had struck a nerve. But even as he leaned forward to savor the brief victory, she had twisted her ugly features into a scowl.

"Release me," she commanded.

"You will give me what I demand?"

A low growl vibrated the air. *"Oui,"* she at last managed to spit out.

"Cross your heart and hope to die?"

"Levet."

Levet grimaced. He had no choice but to trust her word. One more second and he would collapse. Far better to allow her to think he'd released her out of the goodness of his heart.

"Bien. Let's go," he said, dropping his hands as the threads of magic unraveled and then disappeared with an audible hiss. He had barely managed to suck in a weary breath when his mother was surging away from the wall, grasping his wing between her claws. *"Mon dieu,"* he squeaked, as she gave a mighty push with her legs, sending them crashing through the ceiling. "Slow down."

"Tais-toi," Berthe snarled, spreading her wings to soar across Paris at an impressive speed.

Dangling at an awkward angle, Levet heaved a resigned sigh.

When was he going to be treated like a hero?

It was all very annoying.

Within a few minutes, they landed at an isolated tributary that dumped into the Seine. There was a long-forgotten entrance to the sewers hidden by a powerful illusion, which Berthe stomped through, not even bothering to glance in Levet's direction.

Blowing a raspberry at her retreating back, Levet slowly followed in her wake. A task made easy by the cramped size of the tunnel that had been chiseled deep in the ground.

Taking full pleasure in watching his mother smack her head into the ceiling as she wrenched her large body through the doorway that protected the inner sanctum, Levet waddled in behind her.

The cavern was large, but empty beside a number of torches that spread a soft glow over the gray stone and the lone desk just a few feet from the door.

"Doyenne." Rising from his seat behind the desk, a gargoyle several inches shorter than Berthe and built on far more slender lines, hurried forward.

Levet skipped out of the way as Emery performed a bow, deliberately ignoring Levet's presence.

Ah . . . the pleasure of being shunned.

Not that Levet wanted to be acknowledged by the fussy bureaucrat who always acted like he had a stick stuck up his *derrière*.

"Emery." She waited until the Protector of the Wall straightened, her expression impatient. "I have an official pronouncement."

The gargoyle blinked, his wings fluttering in sudden agitation.

"But . . . the elders."

Berthe grabbed her companion by the horn, dragging him until they were snout to snout.

"Do you question my right to rule this nest?"

"*Non*, Doyenne," the peon said anxiously.

"Then stand aside."

Emery hastily scrambled back to his desk, his leathery wings pressed tightly against his body as he tried to make himself as small as possible.

Levet knew the feeling.

His mother was an expert at making a man wilt.

With a suitably dramatic motion, Berthe turned to face the far side of the room. She gave a wave of her hand, causing the torches to flare higher so the smooth wall was revealed.

Levet felt a tingle of ancient power rush over him, in awe, as always, at the sight of the ancient artifact.

An object of magic, the Wall of Memories defied all laws of physics to soar through the ceiling into an endless darkness. Not that Levet glanced up. Infinity always made him dizzy.

The names etched into the stone shimmered in the light, pulsing as if in time to each individual heartbeat.

Berthe waved her hand and the names shifted, as if she'd turned the page. Another wave, another page.

Silence filled the cavern as Berthe continued to search through the names, at last squeezing her hand shut to freeze the Wall.

Then, stepping forward, she pointed her claw at an empty space on the stone.

"I, Doyenne of the Ascaric nest, do hereby un-shun Levet, son of Berthe, to the Guild of Gargoyles. From this night forward he is to be accepted within the Guild with full rights and voting privileges."

There was a faint gasp of disbelief from Emery, but Levet's attention was focused on the Wall as an unseen power skimmed over the stone, leaving behind his name etched in elegant script.

His chest swelled as pride filled his heart to overflowing.

He might be stunted. His magic might be . . . unpredictable.

And he might need a *Dr. Phil* intervention when it came to Yannah driving him batty, but he had done the impossible.

He was once again a full-fledged, card-carrying (okay, there wasn't actually a card) member of the Gargoyle Guild.

Life was good.

Valla allowed Elijah to escort her back toward her apartment with conflicted emotions.

On the one hand, she was disappointed they'd been unable to find Levet. As good as Elijah might be at tracking, he couldn't fly, and while they'd hit most of the usual hangouts for gargoyles, they hadn't managed to catch Levet's scent.

She was desperately worried for the tiny gargoyle.

On the other hand she was breathlessly giddy with the transformation in Elijah.

She didn't know how or why, but for the first time he truly seemed to see her as a woman, not a victim. And not just in a physical sense, although his determined seduction had been spectacularly wonderful.

He'd actually listened to her when she'd complained he treated her as a child. And even gone against every instinct he possessed to allow her to enter the seedier parts of the city in an attempt to find Levet.

Oh, she wasn't an idiot.

She knew he could never share the intensity of her feelings. He might genuinely desire her, but she would be nothing more than a passing distraction who would be swiftly forgotten when his attention was caught by a new lover, or by his true mate.

She ignored the pain that knifed through her heart.

She'd waited a long, long time for Elijah to even acknowledge her as a woman.

Why shouldn't she enjoy the ride for as long as it lasted?

They'd reached the boulevard that ran past her apartment, when Elijah grasped her elbow to pull her to a halt.

"Valla."

She tilted back her head to study his pale, perfect face.

"What is it?"

He paused, as if considering his words. "It's growing late."

Valla frowned. She didn't have the superior senses of a vampire, but she could tell time.

"There's still a couple of hours before dawn."

"True, but—"

Hmm. Something weird was going on. But what?

"Elijah, is something wrong?"

He stepped forward, gently cupping her face in his hands as he allowed her to glimpse the hunger burning like an inferno in his eyes.

"If I return to your apartment it's going to be more than a couple of hours before I'm prepared to leave."

A raw, primitive excitement rushed through her. "Oh."

"Oui." His thumb absently stroked the rough skin of her cheek, his gaze trained on her lips. "Oh."

Valla didn't hesitate. Somewhere down the road her heart was bound to be broken, but if she'd learned nothing else it was to grasp happiness when it was offered.

"The apartment is built to protect a vampire," she said, her voice husky. "You would be safe."

He shuddered, his fangs glinting in the streetlight. "You understand what I'm saying?"

A shy blush stained her cheeks. "You want to become my lover."

His hands tightened on her face, his expression stark as if he was gripped by a powerful emotion.

"Much more than your lover, *mon ange* . . ." he began, only to halt as he tilted back his head and tested the air. *"Merde."*

"Danger?" she breathed, her gaze searching the shadows for an intruder.

"I smell gargoyle," he muttered.

"Levet?" She pulled free of his grasp, heaving a sigh of relief. "Where?"

Far less enthused, Elijah jerked his head toward the narrow alley that led between the buildings.

"He just landed in the courtyard."

Ignoring Elijah's grumblings, Valla turned to hurry through the alley.

"Thank god."

Landing in the center of the courtyard, Levet was startled when he caught Valla's scent coming from the street rather than her apartment.

A momentary fear clutched his heart at the thought that the vulnerable young nymph had been out on the dangerous streets alone before the frigid pulse of power assured him that she was far from alone.

Entering the courtyard, the pretty female rushed to his side, her smile as brilliant as the lights that lined the Champs-Elysées.

"There you are," she breathed. "I've been worried."

"Forgive me, *ma belle*," Levet said with genuine regret. He truly had not intended to upset his newest friend. "I had a long overdue appointment with my mother."

"Are you okay?"

He smiled, his wings fluttering with pleasure. "I am perfect."

"That's a matter of opinion," Elijah muttered as he moved to stand beside Valla, his arm wrapping around her waist with an obvious intimacy.

Ah. That was a new development.

Levet blew a raspberry in the vampire's direction. "Not even you can spoil my mood, leech."

Valla bent down so she could study his pleased expression, her hair shimmering like the purest gold in the moonlight.

"What happened?"

"I have been officially returned to the Gargoyle Guild," he announced in grand tones.

She blinked. "And that's a . . . good thing?"

"But of course."

"Then I'm happy for you."

She leaned forward to place a gentle kiss on top of his head, her lips barely brushing between his horns before Elijah was determinedly pulling her back to his side.

"If you have managed to complete your business, then perhaps you should be on your way," the vampire growled, clearly jealous.

As well he should be, Levet smugly acknowledged.

He was a babe-magnetron.

Or was it magnet?

Whatever.

"Really, Elijah," Valla chided softly.

"*Oui*, really, Elijah," Levet echoed, his hands planted on his hips.

Elijah's fiercely handsome features revealed he was at the end of his patience, but before he could react, there was the unmistakable sound of flapping wings coming from above.

Levet abruptly glanced upward, his tail twitching. "Uh-oh."

"What?"

"Fee-fi-fo-fum, I smell the stench of gargoyle scum," Levet muttered.

There was the distinct aroma of moldy granite before Claudine and Ian descended from the rooftops to land in the center of the garden, crushing the marble fountain beneath their feet.

"Mon dieu," the vampire snapped, glaring at the two gargoyles that filled the courtyard with their gray, massive bodies.

"Elijah," Valla gasped. "Do something."

"I can't believe this." With a shake of his head, Elijah stepped forward. "Stop there, gargoyles."

Levet allowed the bristling vampire to distract his unwelcome relatives.

Being a hero didn't mean he had to be stupid.

And he was still weak from his encounter with his mother.

Besides, Tweedle Dee and Tweedle Dum clearly needed to be taught a lesson in manners. And Elijah was just the vampire to teach them not to drop in unannounced.

Too thick-skulled to be aware of the danger she was in, Claudine stepped forward, her massive form consuming a large amount of the courtyard despite having her wings folded back.

"Clan chief." Her voice echoed off the buildings. "We have no fight with you."

Elijah folded his arms over his chest. "Then turn around and walk away."

Claudine scowled. There weren't many demons willing to stand up to a fully grown gargoyle.

"We've come for my brother."

Elijah cast a bored glance in Levet's direction. "He doesn't seem interested in yet another family reunion."

"Oui," Levet agreed, waving his hands in a shooing gesture as he sternly reminded himself that he was no longer afraid of the evil creatures who'd tormented him his entire childhood. "So, go away."

A hint of vapor curled from Claudine's nostril. She didn't have the fire of her mother, but she could belch a foul cloud of smoke.

"I don't know how you had your name returned to the

Wall, but I warn you, I won't be satisfied until you are once again shunned," she growled.

"So you seek to revoke Mother's direct proclamation?" Levet mocked. "Perhaps you've even decided it's time to challenge her to become the doyenne?"

Ian took a hasty step away from Claudine. As if afraid of being contaminated.

A legitimate fear.

Berthe would destroy anyone who even hinted at mutiny.

Claudine shook her massive head. "Mother would never have revoked your banishment."

"I assure you that she did."

The gray eyes narrowed with suspicion. "How?"

Levet gave another shooing wave. "Go ask her."

"I'm asking you."

Levet rolled his eyes. He'd known word of his return to the Guild wouldn't make his family happy, but he was in no mood for yet another *répugnant* confrontation.

"I simply revealed my part in saving the world from utter destruction. How could she not include such a hero in the Guild?"

"Liar." Claudine stomped her foot, making the ground quake. "You are a pathetic weakling that offers nothing but shame."

Levet heaved a resigned sigh. "As I said, go ask her yourself."

"Non." A dangerous expression twisted his sister's ugly face. She didn't like being thwarted. Especially not by her deformed, height-challenged younger brother. "You might have deceived Mother into returning you to the Guild, but I intend to make sure it's a short stay."

He spread his wings, resisting the urge to take yet another step closer to the vampire.

He was a hero. . . . Hear him roar.

"You don't have the power to shun me."

Claudine pulled back her lips to expose her tusks in a visible threat.

"Perhaps not, but I have the power to kill you."

Levet blinked in shock. It was against Gargoyle law to kill another gargoyle unless they were banished.

Or unless a formal challenge had been issued. And really, who wanted to deal with the paperwork?

"I'm a member of the Guild," he reminded his whack-a-doodle of a relative.

"Not for long."

Raising her hands, which had claws long enough to skewer Levet, Claudine stepped forward, reluctantly followed by her partner in crime, Ian.

Levet squared his shoulders, summoning the last of his fading power.

"Merde," Elijah snapped, clearly at the end of his patience. "I told you to stay back."

"This is Guild business, vampire," Ian growled. "You don't want to interfere."

"What I want is to be left alone with the woman I love," Elijah informed them, a smile curving his lips at Valla's gasp of shock. "And if that means killing you to accomplish that goal, then that's what I'll do."

"Love?" Valla squeaked, her hands pressed over her heart. "Did you say you love me?"

Elijah turned to wrap the bemused nymph in his arms even as the two gargoyles took another step forward.

"Ummm . . . maybe we could discuss this later?" Levet murmured, delighted that the foolish vampire had at last confessed his feelings, but wishing he'd chosen a more suit-able time and place.

For all his newfound confidence, he was fairly certain he couldn't defeat two full-grown gargoyles at the same time.

Even Batman had a sidekick.

Indifferent to the danger, Elijah studied Valla's upturned face with open adoration.

"Of course I love you, you stubborn female," he said in husky tones. "What do you think I've been trying to tell you for the past six hours?"

She blushed. "I thought you wanted me to become your mistress."

He shook his head. "Not my mistress. My mate."

"Mate?" Her blue eyes widened with shock. "Are you sure?"

"Why else would I find the most ridiculous reasons to show up on your doorstep? Why would I all but ignore my duties to spend time with you? Why would I hire twenty different chefs until I found one who baked your favorite raspberry tarts just like you wanted them?"

"Oh." She blinked, her shaky hands lifting to touch his face. As if she had to make certain he was real. "You made me think that you were just worried about me."

"I'm worried about me," he growled. "I can't live without you."

"Oh, Elijah," she breathed, tilting back her head as he claimed her lips in a kiss of sheer joy.

Levet tugged on the vampire's pants as Claudine raised her massive foot, clearly aiming at his head.

"*Oui.* This is all very touching," he said. "But we are about to be squashed like bugs."

Lifting his head, Elijah pointed a hand at the female gargoyle.

"Don't even think about it."

Claudine reluctantly lowered her foot, but the ground shook as her power filled the air.

"Give me the gargoyle, vampire, or pay the price."

A nearby bench crumbled into a pile of marble dust as Claudine released a trickle of her magic. Elijah frowned.

"You're starting to annoy me."

Ian puffed out his chest. "Then give us the gargoyle."

The vampire tucked his golden-haired companion behind him as the temperature dropped by several degrees.

Elijah was clearly done playing.

"No."

"Why?" Claudine snapped. "He can't mean anything to you."

"He made me realize how blind I've been." Elijah smiled. Not the most comforting sight considering his massive fangs that gleamed with a snowy white in the moonlight. "That's enough for me."

"Fine." Claudine lifted her hand. "Then you will feel my wrath."

"Sacrebleu." Levet's wings twitched in annoyance. "What a breeze hard you are."

The beady gray gaze jerked in his direction. "Breeze hard?" the female rasped.

Valla cleared her throat, still hidden behind Elijah. A wise choice. One tiny mark on her white satin skin and the vampire would go nuclear.

"I believe he means blowhard," she explained.

"How dare you," Claudine screeched. "I will turn you into—"

"Oh, shut up." Levet lifted his hands to send a bolt of magic directly at the bane of his existence, astonished that it didn't sputter and die.

He was, after all, weary to the bone.

There was the sound of sizzling; then Claudine gave a cry of pain as she went sailing backward, taking out two benches and a lamppost before hitting the building behind her.

"Nice shot," Elijah murmured, flowing forward to block Ian's massive fist heading in Levet's direction.

"Merci," Levet thanked his companion, shuddering as Elijah squeezed hard enough to crush the bones in Ian's hand.

"Non . . . please," Ian panted, his tiny eyes bulging with

pain as a layer of ice began to crawl over his scaly skin, turning it from gray to blue.

"Are you done playing?" Elijah murmured softly.

"Oui."

Elijah dropped the gargoyle's hand. "Then get your companion and get out of here."

Edging backward to keep his gaze on the lethal clan chief, Ian grabbed Claudine's arm and yanked her to her feet.

The female gargoyle gave a groggy shake of her head, her hand pressed over her injured chest as she glared at Levet.

"This isn't over, brother," she hissed.

Elijah stepped forward, his power lashing through the air with enough force to make the large gargoyles shiver in pain.

"Not only is it over, I warn you that if you dare to harm Levet while he is in my territory I will make certain that the entire Guild is punished," he said, his voice sending a hidden dew fairy fleeing in fear. "Do I make myself clear?"

"But . . ."

"Oui," Ian interrupted Claudine's whining, tugging her to the center of the garden. "It is very clear."

"Bon. Now leave," Elijah commanded.

With a flap of their leathery wings, the two large demons were in the air and disappearing among the tiled rooftops.

Levet smiled. It had been years since he'd been forced to leave this city he so dearly loved.

Now he realized he'd allowed fear to keep him away. Not fear of his family, although that's what he'd always told himself, but fear of his own inadequacies.

He wouldn't allow them to keep him away again.

Realizing that Elijah had returned Valla to his arms and was studying her with blatant lust, Levet hid a smile.

"I believe that is my cue to leave as well," he murmured.

The two separated so Elijah could give a regal bow of his head.

"I am in your debt, gargoyle."

Levet gave a lift of his hands. "All in a day's work for a knight in shining armor."

Valla stepped forward, the lingering wounds in her blue eyes replaced by a sparkle of hope.

"I hope you find who you're searching for," she said softly.

"Sometimes a man simply has to enjoy the chase," he murmured, offering a low bow. *"Au revoir."*

With a smile, Levet spread his wings and flew toward the stars.